CHANGING TRACKS
The Dominion Falls Series 1

Sarah Cass

Historical Romance
Romantic Suspense
Historical Western Romance

A Divine Roses Ink Book
Historical Romance
Romantic Suspense
Historical Western Romance

PUBLISHER
Divine Roses Ink
http://www.divinerosesink.com

Other Books in
The Dominion Falls Series

Independent Brake
Derailed
Dark Territory
Green Light
Runaway Train
Home Signal
Red Zone

Coming Soon in
The Dominion Falls Series

Dust Raiser
Blizzard Lights
Dead Man's Switch
Bird Cage
A Highball Arrangement
Douse the Glim
Blood
Grave Digger
Bad Order

Books by Sarah Cass

The Tribe Series
The Tribe
The Wolf
The Chief
The Raven
The Lake Point Series
Santa, Maybe
Deep-Fried Sweethearts
Stalled Independence
Witch Way
A Thorough Thanksgiving
Eve's New Year
Heartstrings & Hockey Pucks
Luck of the Cowgirl
Stars, Stripes & Motorbikes
Free Falling
Love for Hire
Haunted Hearts
Stand Alone Novels
Masked Hearts
Leap

Dedication

As this hit the shelves, it is officially my
ten-year publishing anniversary (2/8/23).

So this one is for all the readers.
The ones who have found me, and stuck
around to see what else I write.

You've helped make this journey so much fun,
and you've pushed me to do more,
different, and better.

Thank you!

Table of Contents

Study the past if you would divine the future.
-Confucious

Drip, drip, drip—from a tangle of muscle and bone the drops of scarlet fell in slow motion to stain the thin, white layer of snow. Bile rose in her throat, threatening to spill over when a finger twitched on the hand lying in the middle of the tracks.

Her eyes remained glued to the sight. If she dared to raise her eyes she'd see him—the rest of him. Murmurs around her sank into her awareness. Whispers of shock, protest, and accusation. They said she pushed him.

In an instant, time sped forward to return to its chaotic pace.

With a gulp she lifted her eyes to see the mangled mass of man left over. His blank stare ripped her heart out through her gut. A cold sweat broke on her forehead and she unleashed a terrified scream.

Wrenched deep from her soul, pulling on seven years of horror, suffering, anger, regret, and intense fear—a scream unlike one she'd ever heard. She wanted them to worry, to fear, to take her away and hide her from the continuing evil. They could kill her and it would be less painful than her never-ending torment.

The murder had been her undoing and she welcomed the end, letting her screams echo until her voice grew hoarse—not ceasing even then. Not until the sharp sting of a syringe plunged into her arm hit her did silence come.

Awake in the asylum she had a moment of clarity, realizing her fatal mistake.

The truth would come far too late to save the life she'd tried to save.

The answers meant to ease souls would never have a final conclusion.

Insanity.

Medication clouded her thoughts, dragged her into darkness.

She had something to do.

The memories slipped away the more medicine she received.

Terror.

HE was there. HE had not let her be. How had HE found her? HE had come to save her, but HE was no savior.

Clouds wrapped around the memories, the person she was faded into the false bliss of medicine. She welcomed it, welcomed the escape from HIM.

Until the morning one memory rose, and she heard the voices from the train station again. "She pushed him." "She *killed* him."

They would see her hanged, or see her die in this place. She couldn't die. She had to…

What *was* it she had to do again?

For weeks she tried to push through the hazy fog that shrouded her memory and rational thought, to latch onto anything. She floundered, lost in the sea of what she was supposed to do, trying to appear normal—to accept the 'family' that came to visit but felt so wrong, so not like her true family.

HE was still there. Though she could not remember all, she knew not to trust HIM; but dared try to use HIM for her escape. Her recuperation would speed her trial, and she had to escape before that happened.

HE took her away, out of the asylum in the middle of the night. They raced off on horses, hopping a train to head west.

There she tried to rid herself of HIM. Her memory faltered, but she knew HE was to blame. Her faculties were still not complete and HE got the upper hand with little effort.

Then she was falling, a strange clang like a bell rang through her body before she tumbled over and over.

The clear blue sky grew dark in her vision; black seeped in around the edges. A cool rush at the back of her head was the first clue, followed by thick dampness sliding along her hand.

Blood.

"Oh," she whispered.

Her blood.

Then HE was there, filling her vision before all went dark.

For if in any manner we can stimulate this instinct, new passages are opened for us into nature, the mind flows into and through things hardest and highest, and the metamorphosis is possible.
-Ralph Waldo Emerson

"I'll take one card." Cole Mitchell's smooth voice surged under the din of his crowded saloon. The enthusiastic determination of the brunette whore on his lap didn't mess with his focus, at least not that he let anyone know. That's how he always kept things. He maintained control, distance, always. No one got close beyond the physical.

Two of the four men opposing him folded their cards on the spot. Cole only chuckled, not wavering when Daisy's hand slipped down to tease him through his trousers.

Shouts on the other side of the saloon drew the attention of the other players, but Cole didn't move an inch. Once in a game nothing could distract him, not even any of his whores, so a brewing fight near the bar didn't worry him in the least.

He sat back to give the two miners a chance to fold or meet his large bet. He loved this part. Years had honed his poker face and he knew they'd never find any tells.

Their hesitation lingered, so he shifted Daisy to a more gratuitous position. His wink drew a short laugh from her. He added another chip to the pot and signaled to his business partner behind the bar.

Graham Cooke's perpetual bored stare cast onto the fight before he shrugged and poured a drink for the man in front of him. The burly man only played the part of bored and useless most of the time. If you were in a fight, Graham and his brute strength were what you wanted at your back. A vicious smirk wiped the boredom away moments before he fired his pistol in the air.

With that the fight ended. Stillness fell over the bar for all of two seconds before the usual din trickled like a stream bursting through a dam until it blew into full volume. Satisfied the moment had passed, Cole turned his attention back to the game.

He laid out his cards to show his straight flush, another winning hand. He nudged Daisy to collect his winnings and pushed his cards to the dealer, Cuddy. "Another round. Give these men another chance to win their earnings back."

Graham's voice rang out over the din, "Hammy. That wasn't an open invitation."

Amid his own laughter, Hammy kept trying to pry the gun from his holster. The scruffy old man's drunken state made his fingers clumsy, but eventually he'd succeed at freeing the weapon.

Cole tensed and gripped Daisy's wrist to stop her teasing.

Daisy's attentions ceased. "You want me to distract Hammy again, Cole?"

"Like you do best." He smacked her on the ass, shifting in his seat to hide the hard-on she'd left behind. Once settled, he focused on his fresh hand. A full house. After tossing in his ante, he checked to make sure Daisy had managed to distract Hammy enough.

The old man blushed and fumbled, but still managed to free the gun from his holster. Graham grabbed for the weapon to pull it out of reach of the boozed man.

"No. That's mine," Hammy slurred. His hand clenched tighter around the weapon, yanking it to his chest. Those drunken fingers were too close to the trigger for Cole's liking.

His cards spilled to the floor and he moved across the room with speed and precision. Cole grabbed the gun just as it fired toward the ceiling. The saloon fell silent again. "Hammy."

A crash and a yell from the door drew the attention of every soul. Cole ignored the swinging doors in favor of the pile of bloody fabric on the floor. As he wrenched the gun from Hammy's hand, someone else called for Graham who ran over to the body.

"It looks dead." This from his oldest whore, Iris, who had a habit of pointing out the obvious.

Graham peeled away blood soaked hair stuck to the woman's face. He held his fingers in front of her nose, not once touching the bloody creature. "Yup. She's dead."

"I didn't shoot her," Hammy protested. "I didn't kill no one."

"Shut up, Hammy." Cole knew the weapon had fired toward the ceiling. He was more concerned about the matter of a possible dead body on his saloon floor. That sort of thing tended to clear out the joint earlier than he liked.

Cole walked over to the body and knelt beside her to see for himself. Blood and dirt caked her hair until he couldn't tell what color it was. Bruises spotted her face, blood crusted at the corner of her lip.

The clothes that covered her form were ragged, coated with dirt and blood, but had once been refined. There wasn't an inch of her that wasn't encrusted in some form of mire, blood, or muck. Just where had she come from? From what he could see of her features, he'd never seen her before in his life.

Unbidden, his hand reached out to touch the bruised flesh of her neck. A weak throb pulsed against his fingers. He held his breath, unable to believe it was real in her state. Then another weak pulse hit his fingers. His eyes narrowed. "Graham, you idiot. Daisy!"

"What the hell are you talking about? She's dead." Graham's eyes flashed. His fists clenched, ever ready for a fight. "I got plenty of dead to be burying. I ain't lying."

"She's about dead, but she ain't yet. Daisy, get your ass over here."

"Keep your shirt on." Daisy knelt across from him. Her fingers brushed his aside to press into the woman's neck. The silence in the bar grew deafening. She bent to press her ear to the woman's chest. "She's alive."

The declaration stirred the saloon back to life. Customers cleared everything off the bar. Daisy rushed into the whores' room without another word. Cole shoved Graham aside and slipped his arms under the woman's back and knees.

Bracing his legs, he lifted her with great care. A quiet groan filtered under the din around them. Her bloodied and bruised features stirred.

Then her eyes opened.

Despite her near-dead state her gaze locked onto his. Eyes blue as the lake drew him in. A strength shone out of them that contrasted with the state of her body.

For one heart-stopping moment the world stilled around him.

In that moment something indiscernible changed. Deep in his soul he felt something break free. An emotion he thought he'd killed years ago—compassion.

The strength he'd seen soon gave way to a sea of confusion and fear in a way that made him want to comfort her. Worse, he wanted that comfort to be genuine.

"I got ya." A moment of relief passed through him when her eyes fell shut. When she gripped his shirt again he did his best to ignore her.

She opened her mouth, but another groan escaped and then a sound he recognized all too well thanks to the bevy of drunks that crossed his door every night. His nose wrinkled as his shirt soaked through with her vomit and her head fell back.

Any concern he felt flew away. He set her on the bar without further ceremony. While Daisy pulled instruments from her doctor bag, he glared at her. "She threw up on me."

A smile played on the corners of her lips. "So I see."

Hammy shouted again, "I didn't shoot her."

"Shut up, Hammy," Cole snarled. "Daisy, get her taken care of and off my damn bar. I'm going to change."

Daisy went so far as to salute him. "Yes, sir." The second her attention turned to the woman, she began to bark orders of her own to those around her.

Cole stormed toward the back of the saloon to tear up stairs. As he circled around the balcony toward his room at the front, he couldn't help but glance a few more times down toward the bar and the woman on it. Grumbling under his breath, he rushed the last few paces to his room and slammed the door.

The wet shirt clung to his body. "Damn woman."

He peeled off the shirt and threw it aside. Thankfully he'd filled his water pitcher earlier that night. He poured it into the basin and grabbed the sponge in a tight grip to plunge it into the water. Anger over his flash of concern for the woman fueled every movement until he'd cleaned the offense of her stomach off his chest.

If Graham or anyone caught on, he'd never hear the end of it. He leaned on the dresser, his head lowered. He took a bracing breath to shove back the lingering emotions.

To erase the feel of her, he rubbed his arms until they were almost burning with heat. He grabbed a shirt and the lone bottle of whiskey off his barren shelves. The liquid fire burned down his throat, but failed to touch the emotions he'd rather it burned away.

"Cole." Daisy's voice interrupted his internal struggle.

Twitching his lips, he studied his empty room. *"What?"*

"You don't want me in, so you'd best come here, I'm not talking to this wall."

He walked a few paces so he could see around the wall he'd installed to keep anyone from seeing in his room. "Speak or leave."

Daisy's brow creased as she stood at his door. She tried to wipe blood off her hands with a towel. "She's got more injuries than her head. It's bad. I need to operate. Graham said I could use his place."

He'd seen the woman, broken and near dead. They wanted to move her? Daisy had to be insane. "Is it safe to move her that far?"

"It's not safe to move her—period. I don't know where she came from, but she's lucky to be alive at all." Pursing her lips, Daisy stomped her foot.

He walked away, knowing she wouldn't dare stick one toe over the threshold. Sure enough, when he turned, still barely in sight of the door she stood there, red as a beet, her toe tapping the line he enforced.

"The less we move her, the better."

"Just get her in a room and off my bar. I got a business to run."

"I'm going to need help. Graham's been drinking too much again."

"Then find help."

She took a step forward, one dangerous step into his domain. "Cole."

He narrowed his eyes. "Get out."

"Fine. I'll have Hammy get Martha."

"You keep that uptight biddy out of my saloon."

"Then stop dilly dallying and get downstairs to help me. It's you, Martha, or she dies. Simple as that."

He stalked across the room to shove her back from his door. The stubborn lift of her chin almost made him slam it. He had a split second to decide. The woman could still die, but if she had any chance at all. "I'll be down in two shakes."

"You'd better be."

He slammed the door, annoyed by the brash confidence Daisy adopted whenever she got to play doctor.

Last thing he wanted to do was help on this surgery. The idea of it brought to life feelings he wanted no part of. In the brief minute he'd held her broken body she'd felt right—and brought to life feelings he preferred to leave buried deep.

"She's just a woman." He stormed downstairs toward the room the crowd gathered around. Shoving his way through, he shut the door in their faces and rolled up his sleeves.

"Wash your hands."

"I know what to do. Don't forget who owns who." Cole met Daisy's challenging glare with one of his own. "Don't forget your *patient*."

"You are so damn testy." She cut away the woman's clothes. "What has gotten into you?"

"Nothing. Just work."

"Yes, *sir*."

The leaves of memory seem to make a mournful rustling in the dark.
—Henry Wadsworth Longfellow

"Co-ole." A familiar young voice echoed into the quiet saloon.

Graham stepped outside and blocked the door with his bulk. "Get outta here, kid."

Cole snorted at Isaac's protest. Graham's decree had no impact on the boy. The bundle of childish energy barreled under the doors and Cole got to his feet.

Isaac squeaked when Graham tried to grab him, weaving and darting under the tables. Through the yells and protests of the handful of customers, he scampered across the saloon.

The sight of Graham chasing the kid around the place got Cole laughing enough to wipe out any annoyance he might have felt. When the child made to dart past him, Cole reached out to grab the straps of his overalls. With Isaac's legs still running, Cole lifted him off the ground to eye level.

Isaac froze with his arms and legs spread wide. With a big grin, he pointed at Cole. "Wow, you're tall."

"What d'ya want, kid?" Cole didn't stop chuckling, despite the presence of a kid that was supposed to be annoying. Everyone assumed he hated kids, but damned if

Isaac wasn't amusing. The only reason Isaac's mom, Cora, tolerated Cole—he had a tendency to make her kids laugh.

"Daisy said to tell ya 'bout the lady. Miss Martha said to leave you alone, but I camed anyway." Isaac grinned. "Daisy made it a secret and smiled real purty."

Cole smirked. "You're seven."

"She's still purty."

His laugh boomed through the saloon and he dropped his arm, still holding the child off the ground all the way to the door. "What are you supposed to tell me, kid?"

"My name is Isaac." Unlike his brother, Isaac avoided propriety when he could. A quality Cole admired.

"I know." Didn't mean he'd use it.

"She said the lady is up and eating and I should tell you that."

"She did, did she?" Outside, Cole still didn't release Isaac. With a firm grip on the wriggling child's overalls, he carried him across the street to the boarding house. Isaac's giggles and cheers at every step bolstered Cole's amusement further. Pounding on the door, he gave Isaac a brief smirk before straightening out his face when the door opened.

"What do you want?" Martha frowned in disapproval. Her graying hair and the lines on her features made her look years older than he knew her to be. "Don't you have a bottle of whiskey to finish?"

"Well, I would, but I found this under my table." He lifted Isaac again, much to the boy's delight. "Thought I'd return it to Cora."

"Put him down! He'll get hurt if he falls."

"Do I look like I'm about to drop him?" Cole shook the boy, eliciting another high-pitched giggle. "Don't sound like he's complaining."

"Put him down."

"Fine." Cole lowered his arm to release the boy. He fought back his grin when Isaac disappeared into the boarding house. When Martha started to close the door, Cole clamped his hand on it. "Heard she's awake."

"What's it to you?"

"She owes me a shirt."

"Cole Mitchell, you're a terrible man. That poor woman has been through enough. Just leave her alone."

The door slammed in his face and Cole snorted. Like Martha could tell him what to do? He turned his gaze toward the balcony. He knew from previous reports, and the activity he'd seen from his room at the saloon, that the stranger was recuperating in the room up front.

It would be easy to climb up onto the porch railing and pull himself onto the balcony. Or to round the building to take the stairs to get to the balcony.

But why would he? Throughout the week he'd checked on the woman that had done nothing but drop dead—or close to it—in his saloon. Not even he knew why he'd bothered.

It had to be curiosity. Pure and simple.

After all, he'd spent years not caring about anything. One woman couldn't change that. The only way to end his interest would be to see her awake and weak. Helpless—just like every other woman. Yes, that's why he hopped onto the railing, and up onto the balcony.

Then he hovered outside her door. There would be no need to go inside once he saw her as she was expected to be, fragile.

The woman that sat on the bed didn't look one bit like the creature he'd plucked off the floor of his saloon. She'd cleaned up good.

There was nothing weak or helpless about her. Not from his vantage point. Despite being declared dead a week ago, she sat tall, cheeks flush with color. She spoke to whomever was in the room with her.

Her gaze landed right on Cole where he stood outside the door. Rather than crying out in alarm or surprise, one delicate brow lifted. He could swear a smile tugged up one corner of her appealing, plump pink lips. Instead of acknowledging him or letting the others know he stood there, she went back to sipping her soup.

Why wouldn't she tell them he stood there? He couldn't see anyone else in the room, and they couldn't see him. Only the stranger could see him through the partially open door.

Damn her for showing signs of proving him wrong. He needed to know more.

Still, he didn't move. She'd falter. He waited for the weakness to show. All he got was a wince when she set her soup on the bedside table.

She threw the covers off her legs. Without shame, every inch of limb to her ankles and toes showed, not common by any woman that claimed to be 'proper'. "It's blazing hot," she grumbled through Martha's gasped protest.

"It's indecent."

After another glance right at him, she only smiled at Martha. He'd been around enough lies in his life to know fake pleasantry when he saw it, and she oozed it when she smiled at Martha. "It's just us girls here."

"And Isaac," Martha half shrieked. The muslin got thrown back over the stranger's legs. "It's just not proper."

"Apparently, I prefer comfortable to proper." Her annoyance made him chuckle.

Why she still hadn't seen fit to tell anyone he stood there, he couldn't say. The smile that curved her delectable lips professed her amusement.

He stepped closer, enough to see more of the room. Still, only Martha came into view next to the woman's bed.

"It don't matter none." Cora didn't try to hide her laughter. "I'm taking Isaac home. I got a bunch of miners to feed in a few hours. Eat up. I'll bring you more soup tomorrow, until Daisy says you can eat real food."

"Thank you." For a moment her voice faltered, a hint of weakness revealed as her skin paled. Shaking, her hands brushed along her curly golden hair. Now free of blood and mire, it simmered in the sunlight streaming into the room. Soft tendrils that escaped the loose bun she wore fluttered around her face at her harrumphed protest to Martha tossing the sheet back across her legs.

Why in hell did he care?

The clamor of Isaac racing down the stairs lasted for two seconds before she tossed the sheet aside again. "Thank heavens."

"Miss, please."

Miss? Miss what? Why didn't they say her name?

Again. Why did he care?

"It's hot. I don't care who sees my ankles. Isn't my recovery supposed to be about making me comfortable?" The fragility disappeared. The venom in her tone seemed directed at Martha, whose wounded features showed she hadn't missed that fact. "I may not know who the hell I am, but I do know that right now I don't care about what you think is proper."

"Easy," Daisy's voice finally piped up from somewhere in the room. Where in the hell had she been? "No yelling. You can sit however you want, just try to stay calm. Eat some more soup. You need your nourishment."

"Look, Mrs. *Starbird*." Funny, she said the Indian name with the same disdain as half the people in town. Apparently she didn't care none for Indians or the white women that married them. "I appreciate you allowing me to stay here while I was unconscious."

"It was the only decent thing to do." Martha sounded shocked anyone would think she'd do less. Piety was her specialty, after all.

"Of course it was. But if you don't care for how I act now that I'm awake and in moderate control of my faculties, I'll try to find somewhere else to stay."

"You could stay at the saloon." The words were out of Cole's mouth before he could stop them. He took two steps inside the door, creating a stir of activity in his wake. It was official: he was insane.

The stranger didn't take notice of the sudden flurry around her. Muslin got thrown back over her legs. Martha huffed and fretted, her face red and thin lips pursed. "What are you doing?"

Daisy maintained calm, but moved in a protective stance in front of the woman. Protective of her patient or her own standing—he couldn't be bothered to care which. "Where did you come from, Cole?"

"Outside. Martha wouldn't let me in, so I came a different way." Cole didn't bother to hide his smirk. "Came to let the dead woman know she owes me a shirt."

Her eyes narrowed, Daisy shook her head. "If you'd just wait—"

"Who are you?" Her soft voice drifted from the bed, careless of her interruption of Daisy. Quiet, but demanding attention. Her deep blue eyes sparkled with barely concealed amusement. "Or rather, why would you barge so brazenly into a room full of women?"

From where he now stood he could see her pale skin, the sunken eyes, all the faint signs of weakness she worked hard to hide. Her spunk covered most of it more effectively than any of his whores' powders could have done. He nodded a greeting. "Name's Cole. You threw up on me so you owe me a shirt. How 'bout you? Who are you?"

"I—well, I'm not certain." Not even a hint of a smile.

"You ain't sure?" Cole chuckled. His grin grew when a smile flickered across her features. Even beat up, she could still find amusement in her situation? He had to admit he liked that.

"She can't remember anything." Daisy folded her arms across her chest. Her attempt to take a stand wouldn't work with him. Never had.

"I told you to stay out," Martha huffed. The battle over the sheets still raged. Every few seconds she tried to cover the woman. The covers were always tossed off a second later. For a moment she gave up to glare at him. "I told you she's been through enough."

"She don't remember what she's been through." Cole laughed. "So what's it matter?"

A sharp bark of laughter from the bed interrupted Martha's protest. Despite flashes of pain flickering across her face, the woman kept laughing. Her hand pressed against her stomach and a gentle shrug lifted her shoulders. "What? He has a point."

With one strong push of his hand he moved Daisy aside and sat in the chair next to the bed. "Don't remember, huh?"

"You'll remember in time," Martha soothed, spreading the sheet up to the woman's chest. "You haven't been awake more than a couple of days."

"Couple of days? Is that right?" Cole sought out Daisy where she hovered nearby.

Daisy raised her chin in defiance. It didn't last long, as she quelled under his dark look. He'd ordered regular updates when he'd let her come over to stay with her patient instead of remaining the saloon to work. She wasn't earning him any money, in fact she was costing him, the least she should do was follow orders.

The sheets were pushed down with an exasperated sigh. A harsh groan emerged from the woman on the bed. "Would you leave?"

Martha gave Cole a pointed look as she pulled the sheets back into place. "You heard her."

"Not him—you." The woman shoved off the sheets again. She had only herself to blame that he noticed her slim ankles, the unbruised calf, and the creamy milk color of her thighs. The simple chemise she wore didn't cover nearly enough to let him ignore it.

"Excuse me? But this is—"

"Your boarding house. I know. You're a *wonderful* person for letting me stay here." Her tone of derision brought his focus back to her. She pursed her lips at him and he knew his wandering attentions hadn't gone unnoticed.

Cole grinned and shrugged. He didn't care if she knew. Shame for anything he did wasn't all too common.

"But as I said earlier." Once her attention diverted back to Martha, his went right back to her bare legs. "I will find somewhere else to stay if I must. For now I—"

"Martha, you're annoying." He was a man of few words, while it was clear she was a woman of plenty.

"You're an eloquent bastard, aren't you?" The woman smirked, maybe just a bit annoyed at being interrupted. "You can't be polite?"

"She won't leave if you're nice about it." Cole leaned back. "You talk too much."

This time she perused his form, and he let her take her time. The more her gaze traveled, the more his skin tingled and his trousers tightened. By the time she finished, her mouth formed a slight O. "Thank you for your opinion." For a split second exhaustion appeared. It dragged on her features until he swore she would faint.

Martha didn't take notice. "Well, I never! Spoken to like this in my own—"

The woman's hand clenched the muslin under it and life flew back to her features. "If my desire to have as much quiet as possible bothers you, that's too bad. Soon as possible, I will leave this place. Until then, please let me be."

Martha huffed, but with no other argument she stormed from the room. The minute she did, the stranger's head dropped, the energy draining from her body. It happened so fast, his heart stopped. Worry crept back through the cracks in his armor.

Daisy shoved him aside before he could react, checking over the woman. "Damn it, Cole. Why did you have to do that?"

"What in hell did I do? I just came over."

"You have to make everything so volatile. She's only been up for two days. She can't handle this kind of stress." She moved around the other side of the bed. "Help me."

That would mean touching her again. So very tempting, but so very risky.

"Cole. She'll fall of the bed. Move her."

This time he did move, his hand slipping along the woman's thigh before hooking under it. Damn, it was as smooth as it looked. This could get dangerous. She could be dangerous.

"Now that she's up, maybe it's time for me to get back to work," Daisy finally spoke, still fussing with the bandage on the woman's stomach.

"No."

"I'd like to get back to—"

"No." He wouldn't get back in her bed, not for a while. Work—well, it could wait until this stranger got out of the woods. "I don't care what you'd like."

"Cole." The hand that tucked in the stranger's sheets now reached for his. Pleading green eyes bored into his. "I'm going stir crazy. She's out of the worst. At least let me have some fun."

"Playing doctor is fun for you, remember?" He threw her hand aside, unable to stop himself from sitting on the edge of the bed rather than returning to the chair. Before she'd become his favorite whore, Daisy had been a doctor, the only one in town. Her skills were coveted in a doctorless town, that's what had always made him keep her as his favorite. At the moment he no longer cared. "Leave it at that or you'll be sorry."

A soft groan interrupted Daisy's reply. Before he knew what happened, Cole hit the floor. Flailing limbs accompanied the scream emerging from the woman before he managed to grab her hands. Terror erased any of her earlier moments of laughter, a nightmare filling her blue eyes with tears.

He practically had to sit on her to get her to stop. "Hey. Stop hitting me."

Terror stretched her mouth open for another scream. He cut short the shriek with his hand and her body stilled in response. After a minute she blinked, her focus returning to him. Clarity cleared away the tears as she blinked again. Her fingers wrapped around his wrist and she nipped his palm. When his hand pulled away, her brow rose. "Please get up. I won't scream again."

"Promise?"

"Cole." Daisy dropped into her chair with a growl.

After he released her, he stayed close. The soft touch of her hand and warm nip of her teeth still burned against his flesh. "What was that?"

"I don't know. A nightmare, I think." Her eyes fluttered close a moment, her fingers squeezed and released the bedding. Without thinking about it, he set his hand on hers to still it. "It's a hazy fog. All I remember is terror."

"Well, that sounds pleasant," he muttered under his breath. She shifted beneath him. He changed his hold on her arm to help her sit. "Sure you should sit up? Did you hurt yourself?"

"I don't like lying down. Helpless. I'm all right." Once upright again, the woman sighed. "My head."

"You fractured your skull. I'm sure it hurts," Daisy started.

"No. I mean, yes it does. That isn't what I mean." She stared at a picture on the wall. "It's filled with thoughts, but none of them feel like mine.'

"You just woke up a few days ago. I'm sure it will all return with time and healing."

The woman scoffed. "How can you be certain? You don't know what happened to me. I don't know what happened to me. How long have I been here?"

"Just over a week." Daisy shook her head. "We don't know where you came from. You fell into the saloon on a busy night—no one saw you come into town and no one knows you. You were a mess when you arrived."

"I still am." Her brow creased with pain when she shifted position. Bright eyes locked with his again. "Was it your saloon then?"

"What gave me away?" Cole tugged on his worn down vest. "Don't I look the part of a respectable man of business?"

Those tempting lips twitched again. A peek of pink tongue appeared and her lips tensed as though she was trying to hide laughter. After a moment the tension released and she dared to wink. "Of course. It was the smell of alcohol that clued me in."

"Sure it was."

"If Cole hadn't taken a look himself, you'd be in a pine box now," Daisy interrupted the line of conversation. Her entire body was as tense as he'd ever seen it.

Cole rolled his eyes. "Graham may be an undertaker, but he's clueless."

"'I was lost in reveries of death, and the idea of premature burial held continual possession of my brain'." The woman's eyes closed again, a tear slipped down her cheek.

His brow furrowed, Cole shook his head. The words were painfully dismal and morbid, but he hadn't the slightest idea what she meant by it.

"It sounds vaguely familiar." Daisy scratched her head.

"Edgar Allan Poe." The stranger opened her eyes. "Like I said—thoughts that are not my own. So many. Hugo, Goethe, Longfellow. How do I know their words and not my own? What has happened to me?"

Daisy set her hand on the woman's shoulder. "We'll find out. That means your brain is still strong—it's good. Perhaps you'll remember."

Cole felt a strange sinking of his own heart at the woman's disbelieving scoff. When her eyes tightened and the strength in them faded into shimmering hints of her fears, his own need to comfort her returned. He cleared his throat and clenched his fist at his side before he went to grab her hand again. He had to change the subject. "So we still don't know what to call you."

Her face relaxed and after a swipe at an errant tear, she shook her head. "I have no idea. From the moment I woke I've been trying to remember anything and I've come up blank. Only the words of others seem clear."

"Well, with word traveling around town fast we've been using 'Jane Doe'. At least then you aren't just 'that woman'." Daisy shrugged. "It's not the most creative name, but maybe it will do until we figure out who you are."

"Jane," she repeated. Nodding, she closed her eyes again. "Jane Doe will suffice."

Another tear escaped down her cheek. Cole got the strangest urge to wipe it away. "Sure we can't come up with something more creative?"

"Like what?" Jane found a smile. "What sort of name could you come up with?"

"I gave Daisy her name." Cole winked at Daisy's snort.

"Shall we stay in the realm of flowers? How dainty. Perhaps Lily or Rose?"

"Azalea." He chuckled.

Daisy frowned. "So we're going with Jane?"

"I don't know. Azalea is amusing." Jane rested her head back, her body relaxing with each breath. Her hand slipped from its protective stance on her belly to the bed. "But Jane…is fine."

Unable to resist touching her hand, he let his fingers close over hers. The simple touch, and the strength of her return squeeze, eased his concern. "I gotta get back to the saloon. Daisy'll stay here until you're doing better."

"Soon as I find a way to garner some funds, I'll repay you the shirt I owe you."

"You'd better. Wouldn't want a debt hanging over your head."

"Of course not. Goodbye. Cole." Her fingers gave his another small squeeze before going lax. The life faded from her features again. He loathed admitting the concern growing inside him.

"Jane. Welcome to Dominion Falls."

"Dominion Falls." She frowned deeper. "Good to know where I am, even if I don't know who I am."

"Seem to have a good idea who you are, or at least what you think," Cole objected. He stood. "Daisy. I expect you'll be staying here a while longer. Martha kicks her out, tell me. I'm sure there's somewhere else she can stay."

Daisy flew to her feet, following him to the balcony. "Cole."

"Get back to work." Cole turned. Her hands on immediately settled on his chest. He gripped her wrists. The touch that had once heated him up now only turned his stomach. "You always tell me how much you miss doctoring."

"Right now that ain't all I miss."

Over her head, he found Jane watching the exchange with interest. She was a curious one. Daisy's huff drew his attention back. "A few more days ain't gonna kill you. Then it's back to work—helping the rest of men in town with their ailments."

"And you? Or are you looking for a new favorite?"

"I ain't looking for nothing."

"You know, if you aren't pleased anymore, Guy has been rather persistent.'

"I know. I turned down his offer." Cole shoved her hands aside, but stepped closer. He leaned down to mutter in her ear. "You came to me willingly, practically begging. I own you. Don't you dare forget that."

"But if you don't want me…"

"Guy wants you for the same reason I do. To say he's got a doctor in house, keeping his whores clean and adding income. You can still serve your purpose without me having to touch you." The allure of the blond inside soured his desire to bed even his best whores.

"She's trouble."

"Don't know what you're talking about." He pulled back, looking over her shoulder. Jane had fallen asleep, her features relaxed without hints of the earlier nightmare. He spoke again to convince himself as much as Daisy, "She's nothing."

"Then why are you here?"

"She owes me a shirt."

*Begin at once to live, and count each
separate day as a separate life.
—Seneca*

"Anything else?" Rusty Piper, the editor for the town's newspaper, spoke into the silence.

Jane turned away from the sun she'd been soaking in. The man's curly red hair was a humorous nod to his name. The spectacles he wore should have helped to age him, but the smattering of freckles across his nose made him appear half his thirty years.

She knew he hoped for more, some flicker of memory to make this new article different than the first few. Unfortunately, no matter how many times she searched her own mind for anything to give him, to give anyone, she came up blank.

With a deep sigh she turned her head away again. "I wish I could have been more help. In all honesty, I'd give anything to have more information."

"That's what this article is for." Rusty leaned forward. His brow wrinkled in what she was certain was meant to be a reassuring note of concern. Like with almost everyone else though, it felt tainted with pity. "To try to find some information for you. I just wanted to make sure you didn't have any further thoughts you wanted to add."

"No." The gentle drifting of the clouds soothed her. She'd stuck simply to what few facts she had—unwilling to reveal to him the depth of emotion that threatened to overwhelm her. A deep breath caught the surge before it escaped again, and she pushed it as deep as possible. "I hope it's enough. You have no more information than you did before."

"Don't worry about that. Everyone's still curious enough—they won't care if the information is fresh." He stood and held out his hand. "Thank you for meeting with me."

Standing as well, she shook his hand. "Thank you Mr. Piper."

Once he had excused himself, she walked to the railing and took a deep breath. The bustling town had a now familiar mix of foul and pleasant smells. Over the past week she'd learned the lay of the town from her confinement. Daisy had been willing to talk about almost anything in the town, anything that didn't relate to the saloon.

She'd learned Dominion Falls had been founded almost twenty years prior by Martha's parents as a mining camp. With time it had grown into a semblance of a town, thanks to the careful manipulations of Benjamin Daugherty, the town founder. The mines still drew gold and now silver ore, and they'd become incorporated just six years ago after the first silver strike.

Beyond the history, something nagged at her. Something told her she should know this town. The name had been familiar from the first time she'd heard it, but why? No one knew her there; if they did she'd know by now.

Off to the west with the setting sun behind them, the mines still churned and would until dark. Down below the foothills sat Miner's Row, perpendicular to First Street where she currently lived. The first buildings had been built there, from the large mercantile and restaurant to the miner's supply shop and the barbershop.

A small church sat across from the mercantile on the corner between the two main streets in the town. A dozen buildings sat between there and her current location, each with another business thrilled at the prospect of the approaching length of train tracks connecting them to full civilization.

Several buildings down on another balcony stood Guy Forrester, owner of the one saloon that took the step to call itself a hotel. Casino tables, a higher class of whore, plus rooms you could rent without buying time with a companion.

According to Daisy, Guy wanted more power. He aimed to form a government and take over as mayor. The epitome of wealth and arrogance that was a man named Jackson Krenshaw seemed intent on helping him achieve that goal. Jackson had come to the camps as soon as he'd heard of the Daugherty's strike and made it his mission to become one of the wealthiest in town, succeeding with annoying aplomb.

For his part, he had higher aspirations than town government. He wanted Colorado to be a full-fledged state. Once that happened, he wanted to be governor, or perhaps senator. Anything to be above everyone else.

It seemed everyone in town itched for power in some way. While the town had been incorporated six years ago, it took the approaching tracks to really begin blossoming. Where street vendors had been the norm for years, buildings were sprouting up everywhere to accommodate stores over carts. The town had begun with two streets, and now there was a third road parallel to Miner's Row with several stores and a library she had an itch to get into. On either side of First Street were two dirt tracks doing their best to become streets, each with a few skeletons of buildings rising from the soil.

Below her the street buzzed with activity. As the sun set vendors shut down their carts. Women enticed the passing men into saloons. The town always kept moving, even in the middle of the night. Once dark came, the saloons saw all the action.

She heard the now-familiar voice of Graham Cooke, but avoided looking at the saloon across the street. Instead she let her gaze fall to the east. Cora said her husband Kelly had searched for her trail. He'd found one from the eastern mountain range.

He searched as far as the foothills and found no sign of a horse or wagon—nothing that showed where she'd come from before that or how she'd made it so far. The only clue she had—the east. Her heart clenched, her mind racing so fast the world spun beneath her.

Gripping the railing tight, she closed her eyes and took several deep breaths. She didn't understand how her mind could work so well in the now, only to fail every time she tried to search it for answers.

"Jane?"

Jane straightened at Martha's voice, exhaling the burgeoning emotions again. "Yes?"

"We were just going to have supper. Did you want to join us?"

Jane contemplated a moment. She wasn't hungry—but did she want company? While Martha wasn't her favorite person, she had started to relax in the past week. Probably because that intriguing man, Cole, hadn't come by to help annoy her again. Plus, Jane was too busy recovering and coping to be too antagonistic. Still, the woman felt obligated to tell Jane just how improper her behavior was at every turn.

At this point Jane was too busy figuring out how to live and whom she was to care about proper. Rather, she felt far more interested in the improper. Right down to the books she'd requested from the library.

Truth be told, she left the scandalous books out just to see Martha blush and attempt to hold her tongue every time she saw them. Jane knew it needled the woman to no end. It gave Jane a fair bit of amusement in her current inhibited life.

It was lonely. Perhaps she should go to dinner, even if it meant tolerating Martha. She was certain Cora would be there and Jane did enjoy Cora and her husband Kelly's company.

Jane produced as strong a smile as she felt capable. The moment before agreeing, she changed her mind. "I'm not hungry right now. I think I'm just going to enjoy the sunset and then get some sleep."

Martha nodded. "I'll have Arthur bring you some food after a while, in case you change your mind."

"Thank you. I appreciate it." Jane kept her smile until Martha left the balcony. She turned back toward the street with a sigh. Dropping her elbows to the railing, she rested her chin on her hands and pursed her lips.

Nothing. She still had no idea why Dominion Falls seemed familiar.

A shout and a cheer from below drew her attention back to the saloon. Graham leaned against his post, his short, stocky frame and bald head illuminated by lamplight. His chortling grated on her nerves despite the amusement she got at the way his belly shook from his laughter.

Daisy warned her that the chunky appearance of Graham was deceptive. Underneath the hints of excessive weight, the man was a bull; winning boxing matches whenever he had the chance. A bit of hidden strength that bore no evidence in the thick features seen from her perch.

The door to the saloon swung open and out stepped the man's polar opposite. Cole Mitchell was the antithesis of his partner. Tall and lean, he radiated strength and power. In his brief visit she'd detected a hint of wicked humor, contrary to Graham's crassness.

Unable to stop herself from admiring the man, she straightened to absorb every inch of his lanky frame, which towered over everyone in the vicinity. She bit her lip, enjoying the flash of muscular forearm he showed with his rolled up sleeves, right up to the long fingers rolling a cigar around before placing it in his mouth.

His brown hair lay unkempt, falling into his face. She knew for a fact his eyes were a captivating icy blue. Yes, she'd have to be dead not to admire the man. At least that's what her body kept telling her.

Right at the moment she felt her stare too blatant, his eyes turned toward her balcony. Unbidden, a smile curved her lips. His wink drew pleasing warmth to her cheeks, one she didn't bother to hide.

After a few moments, the staring contest broke by a lewd comment from Graham to a passing customer. With a pinch of regret, she turned her attention elsewhere.

Her gaze fell to the east again, and the smile faded as the haunted emptiness returned just as fast as it had left. A familiar pressure that often accompanied her attempts to remember left her chest heavy.

The pressure built until she gasped for air, backing away from the railing several steps. Her back hit the door to her room hard enough to rattle the panes.

Escape—getting away from the sameness of her room and out in the open air. Maybe then she could find something to help pick up the missing pieces. She needed answers that eluded her, as she remained stuck in the same room with the same people every day. A break in the monotony might help her breathe again.

She spun under a sudden desperation and rushed through her room. Once her door was open she stopped.

Downstairs she knew Martha and the Turners were enjoying a happy, hearty meal together. Too many people, none that she wished to face right then.

Once again she backed up until her back hit the railing. No one could see her like this, none of them. Panic crawled its way up her throat until it tightened in a squeak of exhaled air.

She dug her nails into the wood of the railing, staring at the closed door of her room before dragging her gaze back east to the distant mountains.

Air returned in a rush as she raced toward the stairs leading off the balcony. Careful to not race down them even though every instinct told her to run fast. She gathered her skirts and crept in bare feet down the stairs.

She pressed her hand to her sore ribs before moving to the corner of the house. With careful steps, she slipped between two closed vendor carts to cross the street. She darted between two buildings, then broke into a run to head out into the open fields beyond the town.

She ran as if her life depended on it for as long as she could. Wind rushed through her hair, drying her tears before they could slip down her cheeks.

In what seemed like no time she became breathless. She slowed to a stop, only to realize she'd made it quite a distance. Hundreds of yards, perhaps half a mile. The lights from the houses along main street were mere pinpricks in the darkness.

The dark of night crept ever closer. The mountains' black relief against the starry sky didn't answer her desperation. How could she have traversed from those mountains into town as wounded as they told her she'd been?

The distant light of the railroad camp to the northeast drew her attention before she turned back toward town slowly. What she saw now would have been what she saw when she came into town, but it stirred nothing. The glimmer of life she'd felt, the spark of hope faded as her mind remained blank.

Trembles ripped through her body as she stared at the town, and then the army camp to the south before turning back to where the mountains stood dark and silent. Her desperate internal pleas received no answer from the stony silence in the distance.

A sob wrenched from her gut and she fell to her knees, her hands hitting the dirt. In the safety of the cloak of night she released her tight hold on her emotions. Fear poured out in salty streaks as she sank back onto her ankles. She lifted her gaze to the heavens and cried, "Please, God. Please. Something. Anything would be better than this nothingness."

Falling forward again, the parched ground beneath her unforgiving even under the onslaught of tears. Her fingers dug into the harsh dirt. "Please. Help me. It's so empty…lonely…I'm afraid…help me find who I am…"

Cries filled the quiet of the night, stilling even the crickets as she unleashed the pent-up emotions of the week. Thoughts of returning before she could be missed disappeared in the river of tears. The weight of despair pushed her down until she lay on the ground, her forehead rested on her arm.

One last whimper escaped as she regained control of her emotions. She used the pool of her skirts to wipe at the tears and snot, wishing for a handkerchief to make herself presentable. A shout for Jane echoed through the night and her attempts to collect herself. She allowed one last sniffle before she pushed herself to her knees. "Just leave me alone."

Rather than the silence she expected, Cole spoke right behind her. "Best answer. They're gonna find you anyhow."

She about jumped out of her skin. "Cole." She got to her feet fast enough to make her ribs smart. Mortification that she'd been seen for who knew how long ripped at her guts. Still, when he handed her a handkerchief over her shoulder, she realized she didn't mind so much.

"Running away ain't the way to make them leave you alone." His voice lingered close. The heat of his breath on her ear sent a shiver down her spine and warmed away the last of the embarrassment. "They're do-gooders. You won't escape so easy."

"Who said I wanted to escape?"

"You're here, ain't ya?" His hand rested on her shoulder, easing the last tremor of tears.

How had he done that? Eased her with a touch? Known she was here? What did he want? She didn't care. For some strange reason, his presence was enough. "I don't want escape."

"Really?"

"I simply wanted to be left alone." Once she'd cleaned the offensive tears of her breakdown she shoved the handkerchief in her pocket.

"Near as I could tell you was." His low chuckle rumbled in her ear.

"Jane. Where are you?" Arthur's voice echoed a short distance away.

The young voice of Arthur gave her pause. Being found by Cole was acceptable; having a child find her was not. Not wanting to be found yet or for Cole's hand to leave her shoulder, she lowered her voice. "Not quite alone."

"I suppose not."

She leaned against him, grateful for the comforting arm that held her tight. "Why did you follow me?"

"Saw you sneaking across the street. There's Indians 'round here, ya know. Not safe to be out on your own."

"Not much feels safe." She'd whispered it under her breath, and was grateful that if he'd heard, he ignored it. Another approaching shout for Jane made her spin to bury her face into his chest as if she needed it to hide in the dark night.

"I thought seeing the town as I'd seen it—being away from everyone—something would help me remember."

"Didn't help none, did it?"

"No. Not a bit. I have nothing. I have nowhere."

Cole pulled her further into the night when Arthur's voice drew ever closer to where they stood. "The martyr Martha will let you stay long as you need. Makes her look good."

"Well, where else would I go? I have no family. No funds to sustain me in any fashion. I believe I'm rather stuck where I am. Whether I like it or not."

"Guess you need to find a job."

"If that's an offer, no."

"You ain't no whore. Never could be. Bet you'll figure something."

She shrugged. "At the moment, I'm wondering if I'll ever feel…normal."

"Normal ain't nothing but your way of thinking."

In that moment, with one phrase, she found a smile. The idea was so simple, yet so profound it warmed her panicked soul into a smidgeon of peace. "Thank you."

"Don't thank me. Got a reputation to maintain."

"I have none. I need to earn one, I suppose. Would you take me back to town? I'm tired and sore now."

"Sure you want a reputation this soon?" A low chuckle carried in his voice. One finger trailed along her arm. The heat of his body warmed away the last of her tears and made her want to melt into him.

She thought perhaps in his arms she'd find a quiet night's sleep, a deep rest that had eluded her since she'd come to life in that blasted boarding house. "'Reputation is an idle and most false imposition; oft got without merit and lost without deserving'." Jane couldn't stop her smile. For a moment she imagined she could see his brows furrow in the dark.

He grunted and squeezed her arm. "What?"

"Shakespeare. Damn words."

"You can say that again." His laughter got lost in another shout from town.

She took a shaky breath. "I'd rather choose my own reputation, not let them choose it for me. I think it's time I figured out how to live."

"Careful what you ask for." Cole's arm circled her waist and he scooped her into his arms. Her shriek only brought his laughter. "Don't you dare beat on me. I'll drop you in the dirt."

"Boor." His laughter shook her sore bones, but she didn't hit him. In truth, it was the last thing she had in mind. On the way back to town everyone approached with chastisement and concern. Her attempts to thank Cole were lost in the arms pulling her away from him.

He faded into the crowd long before she finished her apologies and got back to her room. Exhaling an annoyed breath, she poured water into the basin before carrying it out onto the balcony with her.

Ignoring the twinge in her ribs, she set the basin on the ground and sank into the rocker. A long sigh escaped as she set her filthy and scraped feet into the cold water. She was relieved to revel in the closest to quiet the town ever got.

For the first time in the entire week she'd been awake, a lamp lit the room across the street from hers. Curiosity pulled her forward, wondering at how this room at the end of the saloon's second floor remained so dark when the rooms on the rest of the floor got so much use.

Then Cole crossed the window, reappearing a moment later with a whiskey bottle in hand. One curtain pulled closed, but he stopped before drawing the other side.

She rose, the footbath no longer of interest. The way he leaned against the window frame, staring. He couldn't see her, could he? Her lamps were off, her candle doused. The lamps of the street didn't shine on her balcony.

Yet he stared right where she stood. Her heart quickened, fluttering into her throat before she tried to force it still. She didn't know this man. She didn't know herself. So why did his mere presence stir her to such excitement? It was a curious sensation.

One she wanted to know much more about. Soon. Very soon.

Some minds seem to almost create themselves, springing up under every disadvantage and working their solitary but irresistible way through a thousand obstacles.
—Washington Irving

"Well, why not?" Cora sounded petulant as a two-year-old denied candy. "You said you need a way to earn some money."

Jane couldn't help but laugh. "I'm merely uncertain. Your offer is kind. I will certainly consider it."

"Especially now that you have an account here." Cora pointed to Jane's full basket. "Plus you said you wanted something to occupy your time."

"She ain't gonna let up, not when she's got herself a point," Kelly offered with a bright grin. "Don't see how it could hurt."

It had been two weeks since she'd woke in Dominion Falls with nothing but a few nightmares. Jane set her basket on the counter. "I'm still gaining my footing. To be honest, I think there is something I'm more suited for."

"Of course." Cora squeezed her arm. "At least now the option is there. I won't be rescinding it if you ever need it.

Until then, Kelly and I aren't going to do anything with your account so long as you don't abuse it."

"I appreciate you allowing me to get a few items without any income. You have both been so generous." Jane had filled her basket with a few books, a bottle of simple perfume, and a brush. She grabbed the slimmest book from the lot. "I don't think I'm going right back to my room. Could I return to pick this up later?"

"No need." Kelly waved off her request. "Arthur will be home from school soon enough. I'm sure he won't mind bringing it by the boarding house."

Cora nodded in agreement. "Don't you worry none. Just be careful where you choose to relax and enjoy your day. The vultures are circling since Rusty's latest article."

Both Guy and Jackson kept trying to garner her attention for reasons far beyond her understanding. "I noticed. I'll be careful."

Jane stepped out of the building and took care down the steps as her body still ached if she moved too jarringly. She surveyed the bustling street quietly a moment with her book clutched to her chest.

After her excursion into the night the week before met with failure, she hadn't left her room. Her attempts at distraction failed as she'd given into the grief and fear—and the request that she let herself heal before she did anything of the sort again.

Now only little lingering physical aches remained, along with the large void in her own head. A void that she'd been disturbed to realize she'd become accustomed to.

The day before she'd decided to stop pitying herself, to accept that there was no way to learn the truth locked in a dismal little room without a thing to call her own—not even a life.

So she took up Kelly's offer of an account at the store. The books felt right, as had the pleasing scent of the perfume. Now she had things to call her own—she just needed to get herself back into life. With or without a past, she wanted to live.

Beyond that, she had one other idea she wanted to try. She wanted to follow her own trail. Somehow there had to be answers along it. Failing that, she had no idea what to do.

Sill contemplating how to acquire a horse and someone to accompany her, she barely heard the voice to the right.

"It's Jane, right?" He stood at least half a foot shorter than she, but built like a locomotive. The blood on his apron and meat on the cart let her know his occupation.

She caught his infectious smile. "Yes. That would be me."

"Good to meet ya. Call me Wills. Here." He shoved a small package of brown paper into her hands.

She turned it over. "What's this?"

"Jerky." He held up his hand when she tried to protest. "No charge this time. Read Rusty's article."

"Thank you. Wills, you said?"

With a face-splitting grin the man bowed so low his head disappeared behind the cart. He popped back up and winked. "Best not forget it."

She couldn't help but laugh. "I do believe you are poking fun at my situation, Wills. Should I be offended?"

"Nah. I gave you jerky."

Another laugh bubbled out. "Then I'll not be offended. Thank you."

"Jane." He tilted his head. Before she could say anything further, he barked out across the street a loud, booming advertisement of his wares.

Laughter carried through her soul as she tucked the small package into the purse she'd hung from her belt. The simple kindness reasserted the hope she'd given up on for a few days. Life might become full and exciting, even if she didn't remember. When several wagons headed toward her, she slipped onto the boardwalk opposite the Silver Saddle Casino and Hotel.

She considered heading out into the field beyond town to read in peace. Yes, that was what she should do, and all she needed. At least that's what she tried to tell herself. Her destination had nothing to do with her search for answers.

The internal argument flew from her head when someone bumped into her, causing her to stumble a step. Grunting, she gave the retreating back a frown. "Excuse me."

Another bump came within moments, but this time the person lingered. An intrusive hand groped her rear end, sparking a flare of fire.

She could handle being bumped into by one too rude to care. However, she'd be damned if she would allow herself to be groped without permission. Once the hand disappeared from her skirts, she reacted on instinct.

Turning fast, she kicked her leg out enough to trip the man. The way he hit the boards hard satisfied her to no end.

Unwilling to leave it there, she stepped on his hand before storming down the boardwalk. The shout behind her increased her pace. A glance over her shoulder revealed he'd taken chase, his face twisted in anger.

Then she hit a solid wall.

Cole gripped her arms, picked her up, and set her behind him. Jane couldn't even speak when Cole positioned himself between her and the approaching man. Graham stood by yawning—but through the yawn every muscle in his arms tensed. His posture straightened, fists clenched on his crossed arms.

"Problem, Mack?" The smooth timbre of Cole's voice sent a shiver down her spine.

"You saw what she did." Mack puffed his chest, not a hint of fear despite the way Cole towered over him.

"Saw what you did too. Seemed a fair trade to me."

The muscles in her cheeks twitched in an attempt to hide her smile.

"That little bitch—"

"Excuse me." Safety be damned, she would not stand to be called such a name. She stepped free of the relative safety behind Cole. "You ignorant brute. If you want to grope, find a whore and pay for it like any man with a brain. Or go home and poke your wife—if she'll let you."

"Trying to get yourself killed?" Cole gripped her arm. She tried to yank free to no avail, despite the fact no pain at all came from his hold. He hissed, "Shut that mouth of yours. Ya know how to do that?"

"Don't tell me what to do."

"If you know what's good for you—"

His body slammed into hers hard enough to send them both flying. Her back cracked against the hitching post, knocking the air clean from her lungs. Cole's arm jerked and he pulled away so violently her whole body wrenched sideways. She had to grab onto the hitching post to keep from dropping to the ground.

By the time she managed to catch her breath and steady herself, Cole and Mack circled each other. A drop of blood at the corner of Cole's mouth showed Mack had managed the first hit.

"Stop it." She didn't want an outright battle. Some instinct pushed her into action. She shoved off the hitching post and raced toward the two men, aiming for Cole.

Cole grunted when she barreled into him, his raised fist opening to grab her. They hit the wall hard. His arm slithered around her waist and spun them so she was against the wall. He cursed at a solid thump this back, his body jerking in reaction. "Damn woman."

"Mack. That's enough. Get whiskey and a woman that'll listen to you. This loon ain't worth your time." Graham laughed. Mack's protest dissolved into the noise from the saloon.

She tried to ignore the solid, strong chest her hands rested on. The air thinned until it seemed a rare commodity as opposed to the abundance she was used to. "Did he hit you hard?"

"Damn straight." His voice poured over her like warm molasses. His lips at their every movement entranced her. "Mack ain't no shirk."

"Sorry." It came out breathless, but she couldn't help it when his hard body pressed into hers. Every inch of her came alive. Heat coursed through her veins and along her flesh.

"No you ain't."

All she could do was smile. Protesting would only lead to him calling her a liar.

"You always stop fights like this? I sure ain't complaining if you do." The grip on her arms loosened, his fingers kneading. A half smile drew the corner of his mouth up and she got the strange urge to stand on tiptoe and nip at his lower lip.

Warmth tingled in every muscle; spreading in ways she knew ought to be considered indecent. Her breath hitched. "I, um…I wouldn't know."

"Guess you wouldn't. If you really don't remember, that is."

The words acted like a bucket of cold water. She shoved him away. "Well, Mr. Mitchell. I appreciate your attempt to protect me—or whatever the hell it was you were *actually* doing. However, I don't require any assistance from you. I can take care of myself."

"Mack ain't afraid to hit a woman, even if she ain't his to hit. Best not try to *take care of him* again or you'll end up where you was."

"What difference does it make to you?" She stepped around him, folding her arms across her chest. When she couldn't see his damn smirk the anger came easier.

"Not a bit."

"Then shut up." Damn it, she'd turned. He had her trapped in ice-blue pools of laughter. Once again her nerves lit with sensations far from anger. This man would be trouble. Divine, insatiable trouble.

His brow rose and a low chuckle carried toward her. Cole drew closer. For every step he took forward, she took one back, until she hit the hitching post. His hands rested on either side of her. "If I don't want to?"

Determination set in her jaw. His proximity stimulated nerves all over and he had yet to touch her. This would never do. She had to stop him. Why? She didn't know. She only knew that she must before things got out of hand. "That would be too bad."

"Why's that?"

"Because then I'd have to do this." Her knee rose in a swift motion right between his legs. His pained groan turned her frustration to amusement. When he stumbled back, she giggled and straightened her disheveled skirts. "Good day, Mr. Mitchell."

She made it across the street with some measure of disappointment she'd been unimpeded. Staring through the alley to the open fields where she'd thought to go read, she realized that she'd dropped her book in the scuffle.

Worse, after her fit saying she didn't need his assistance, she realized she did. If she wanted to follow her own trail, she couldn't do it alone. She didn't have the faintest idea where to begin such an endeavor.

Logic told her if she asked Kelly he'd help, but she felt bad enough over all he and Cora had already done for her. To ask him to leave his business for a full day to help her on what was certain to be a fool's mission seemed too much.

Cole.

Despite the encounter she'd walked away from, her stomach did a little flip. He intrigued and excited her, certainly. However, she also had an unusual sense she could trust him.

Ridiculous. Attracted as she was to Cole, she knew nothing about him. Instinct screamed at her to trust him, but how could she when she didn't even trust herself? Frustrated, she stomped her foot in the dirt in a childish manner.

The idea of asking Cole seeped through her brain like a cancer until it took over every thought. Warmth rushed through her, the memory of how it had felt pressed against him filling her mind and body.

With a bit of hesitation she turned around, not sure it would be smart to return. A familiar twinge struck her heart. "I'm alone. I can't afford to waste the chance."

Voltaire says we are rarely proud when we are alone. Yes, she had to admit pride was rather pointless at this juncture.

She took a deep, bracing breath before crossing the street once again. Cole still stood outside, now with company. Daisy draped around him in an unseemly fashion. Jane rolled her eyes at the display even as her stomach twisted.

Cole had seen her, no doubt. He lifted his cigar to his mouth and looked away. Biting back her emerging temper, she turned her attention to Daisy.

"Jane." Daisy leaned against Cole with a self-satisfied smile. She slipped her hand behind her. Cole's appreciative moan deepened her smile. "How are you feeling?"

"Much better." Jane somehow managed to keep her tone pleasant despite the urge to grit her teeth and the growing levels of bile in her esophagus. A guttural sound from Cole made her fists clench. She wanted to turn away from the scene and the unnatural jealousy it inspired in her, but she put all her effort into keeping decorum. "I do thank you for your estimable care while—"

"Estimable?" Cole's attention returned, a wicked smirk curving his lips.

"I apologize. I forgot you prefer to act like an uneducated ogre." Jane's temper railed against her attempts at calm. "*She done real good.* Is that more your level? Or is sex the only thing you understand?"

"For someone who ain't got a clue who she is, you sure got a high opinion of yourself."

"What I *have* is a grasp of the English language."

"Um, Cole. Jane." Daisy straightened. After a moment she tugged on Cole's vest. "Why don't we head inside? I think you've had enough conversating for today."

He was infuriating, maddening, and Jane couldn't tear her eyes from his or slow her ragged breathing. In what could be her dumbest move yet, she stepped forward. "Wait. I'm sorry."

That's all it took for him to flash his teeth and push Daisy away. He waggled his eyebrows, both stimulating and annoying her. "Really?"

"Yes. I was…" She hesitated. Her temper died easy enough once she thought he wouldn't hear her out. She squared her shoulders to face it dead on. "I actually had a favor to ask."

"You been yelling at me, sayin' you don't need my assistance, you hit me, and *now* you wanna ask a favor?"

His laughter fueled her desperation. She stepped close enough to touch his arm. "Please."

Daisy moved back to Cole's side to tug his arm. "Ain't a good time Jane. Maybe you should find someone else to ask."

Cole's intense stare made Jane squirm. He shrugged Daisy off his arm. "I'd like to hear what you gotta ask so bad."

Jane glanced at Daisy. "Would you mind?"

"Don't matter none if I did. He'd send me anyway." Daisy stormed into the saloon. The doors slammed open before swinging violently shut.

They swung back and forth a few more times before stilling. Jane stepped back from Cole's presence. He distracted her so thoroughly, she needed a moment. She took the advantage of someone crossing between them to gather her thoughts. With a sharp exhale she turned away to lean on the hitching post.

He leaned next to her. "It ain't gonna help ya to—"

"Please don't." Desperation laced through her tone. The moment she recognized it, she groaned in frustration. Burying her face in her hands she muttered, "I'm so tired of this."

"Of what?"

"Knowing nothing." Before he could interrupt she blazed forward. "Knowing no one. Not even myself."

"Seem to know enough to speak your mind."

"Does that bother you?"

"No." The absolute shock in his voice caught her attention, and delight.

She smirked. "Something wrong?"

"It should. I mean, you are a woman." He eyed her appreciatively. "And women should keep their mouths shut. They don't get opinions."

"Just because you own the women you bother to keep company with, meaning they must do as you say does not mean they lack opinions. All it truly means is you lack the fortitude to listen to them."

"If you're trying to curry favor, you ain't on the right path."

"You just said it doesn't bother you I speak my mind." She leaned closer. "Is it you don't care for my opinion? Or you don't like hearing the truth?"

Matching her stance, he eyed her from top to bottom and back again. A grin spread across his features. "You don't get intimidated easy. Good way to get yourself killed. Most men around here don't mind looking or touching, but they don't want a woman saying what she thinks."

"Thanks for the advice."

"That mean you won't take it?"

"I'll take it under advisement."

"So, no."

"May I ask my favor now?"

His brow rose. "You got me curious enough. Will I like it?"

"Perhaps. I'd like to ask you to help me follow my own trail."

"Kelly's the tracker."

"I'm asking you."

"Why? Unless you want something else too?"

"You're infuriating."

"You like that." He chuckled.

Puzzlement clouded her thoughts for a moment, and his continued laughter let her know it wasn't lost on him. Nodding, she set her hands on her hips. "I do."

"Why?"

"If I knew, I'd tell you, of that you can be sure. As for following my trail, I could ask Kelly, but I've leaned on his and Cora's generosity rather enough."

"So you thought you'd see if I had any?" He snorted. "I don't."

"No, but you're curious enough about me you'd say yes. I know very few people in this town and you're the only one that has given me the indication you'd be totally honest. Even if I didn't want to hear it."

"I have?"

"Why did you follow me last week? Was it only because of the Indian threat?"

The muscles of his jaw flexed and his hand tightened on the post. He diverted his gaze, giving a shrug. "Ya ran off the balcony real fast. Like someone was chasing you. Wanted to be sure you was all right."

"Were you trying to figure out if I've been lying about my amnesia?" She held her breath. This answer meant everything. She knew plenty of people had their doubts, and she wondered if his earlier comment was true doubt or him needling her. Somehow she knew she'd be able to trust whatever he said.

"No."

Her breath escaped, a rush of relief filling her as the air departed. "So will you help me?"

He studied her a long minute. "What's in it for me?"

"We'll take one horse. Two people. One horse. Plenty cozy, don't you think?"

"When do you wanna leave?"

Truth is always strange.
—Lord Byron

"So that's it?"

The medicine bag snapped shut. Daisy didn't even smile. "You're well enough to ride. Don't try to race or you're going to be sore."

Jane didn't know what to think. During her healing period Daisy had talked far more than she did now. The exam had been more cursory than polite, and if Jane had never met her before she'd have said she needed to work on her bedside manner. "Well, it's been good to see you again. Thank you for stopping by."

"Don't thank me. I was sent, remember?"

"Oh." Jane snorted. So that was the reason for the cold attitude. Jealousy and bitterness. "Now I understand why you've only touched on my health. Goodness Daisy, I think we talked more when I was unconscious. I'm sorry if you're insulted that Cole had you check on me. I'd think as a doctor you'd want to, but I've never been one, at least I don't think I have."

"I do as I'm ordered, my feelings aren't a factor. They never were, anyhow."

Jane had a myriad of comments to make on such a statement, but chose to bite her tongue. She tugged her corset strings tight as possible and tied them off. Upon completion of her task, she caught Daisy's glaring reflection in the mirror. "What?"

"Why did you ask Cole to take you today? Kelly's the tracker."

"Is Cole not capable of the task?"

"Sure he is. Kelly's better." Daisy scowled. "It ain't like you know him."

"I've only been allowed out and about for a few days. When I asked Cole to help he was one of only a couple of men I knew to be capable of performing such a feat. While I've begun to know more people the more I'm out and about, there aren't any I'd trust for this task."

"You don't know him. Plus, you asked after arguing with him."

"He needled me and I lost my temper." She pursed her lips, caught in a flux of emotions. Frustration and amusement both over the turn of the conversation; and sorrow over the wedge it had shoved between her and Daisy. Of course, there was also some confusion over Daisy's apparent jealousy. As a brothel owner, she suspected this wasn't the first time Cole's attentions had wandered, and it wasn't even like the pair of them were intimate. "Kelly's done too much for me. I had to start doing *something* on my own."

"So you chose *him* to *do*?"

Jane laughed. "Are you insinuating something?"

"I'm not blind."

"Of course not, but if you're making such an insinuation, I have to ask why. You are certainly not his wife. You're his property—by choice, mind you."

"Some pieces of land are more fruitful. They get more attention and more plantings. If you get my meaning."

"Your innuendo is not lost on me. You are his favored one?"

"For three years."

Jane studied her own reflection while she digested the revelation. "Three years? Is that how long you've been working for him?"

"You mean *owned* by him?" The venom in Daisy's tone wasn't lost on Jane, but she only nodded. Daisy frowned. "Yes."

The defeat that took over the single syllable in place of the fire of moments earlier made Jane cringe. "How did you come to be owned? You're intelligent. You're a doctor."

"Women can't be doctors."

Jane's heart sank further at the anger and moroseness in Daisy's tone. What could have made a woman so determined to be a doctor that she succeeded against the odds turn into this woman before her? "Oh. Then, how did you manage it? You are an educated doctor. If it has only been three years since you became a whore, how is it you've forgotten that?"

"It doesn't matter. It's what I am now. I made my choice. And I know that look Cole's got about him. You're a prize to be won. He got himself a doctoring whore, now he has a new goal."

"I'm not a prize to be won. I won't become a whore, no matter how desperate for funds I may be. Whatever his intentions, they aren't necessarily mine."

Daisy's eyes narrowed. "So you have no designs on Cole?"

Jane was not one to lie, so she answered as best she could in her state of confusion over the man. "I am not blind or dead. He is attractive, as I'm sure you know far better than I." The man lit a fire in her, but she didn't think she'd act on it. Not now.

"So you do want him."

"What I want is to find out who I am. I find Cole attractive, but I'm not looking for anything but my own self." If pressed further, she'd have to admit she wouldn't stop it if nature took its course, but she wouldn't look for any more trouble than she already had.

"Then tell him as much."

"Why? So he'll take you back to his bed?" Jane's suspicions were confirmed when Daisy's cheeks flushed. "I can no more control that man than you. I can't even control my own life or thoughts half the time. I'm too busy looking for myself to try to find a man. What I'm looking for are a few friends. He fits the bill."

"Friends?"

"Yes. Friends. He made me laugh when I was scared out of my gourd. He is annoyingly, refreshingly honest. He's not afraid to tell it like it is while most people are afraid to offend delicate sensibilities I don't actually possess. I like honesty."

"So you say. Yet you act like one who wants him in your bed."

Jane tied her purse to her belt. She was tired of the endless cycle of the conversation. It was time to move on. She grabbed the burlap bag of food from the floor. "I'm attracted to Cole, but I'm not going to jump right into bed with him. End of story."

"Good."

"Anything else?"

"I need to get back to work."

Jane didn't follow immediately. Cole didn't seem the type to keep a favorite so long—to keep ties to anyone long. She wondered if it had anything to do with the fact Daisy was a doctor. For that matter, she wondered if Daisy didn't realize it could be the reason and chose to ignore it.

She brushed aside the thoughts when she realized the time. Rather than be late, she rushed from the room. Somehow she managed to catch up with Daisy right as she stepped onto the saloon's porch. A whistle drew both their attention left. Jane turned, a grin sprouting soon as she saw the large horse Cole stood next to. "Isn't the white horse a bit of an oxymoron?"

"Can't you ever put that tongue in the stable?"

"You're taking Faro?" Daisy's frown deepened. "Why not Brag and Bluff?"

"Brag and Bluff?" Jane laughed. When Cole scowled, she sucked her lips between her teeth in an attempt to stop her mirth.

"Faro's the biggest one I got. Best for carrying two." Cole stopped glaring long enough to smirk and waggle his brows.

"Carrying two?" Daisy planted her fists on her hips. Her brow furrowed. "Really?"

"Get inside, Daisy. Artie's been waiting on you for fifteen minutes." When she protested, he pointed toward the saloon.

Jane drew closer to the man and his steed. His low rumble of laughter brought warmth to her cheeks. Just being in proximity to him made her doubt her own declaration of friendship. "You're making her jealous, you know."

"Whores ain't allowed to get jealous."

"And what did I tell you?"

"Are ya getting on or what?"

The saddle sat above her head, barely within arms' reach. Had she ever ridden a horse? The twinge in her gut made her wonder.

Warm air on her ear shocked her into a gasp. She couldn't stop the tingle that coursed through her when he muttered, "Problem?"

"It's just a rather…large…horse.'

"Thank you."

The heat in her cheeks intensified. Every moment around this man stimulated her. It wouldn't do to let him know in such a blatant fashion. Sucking in some air, she narrowed her eyes and shoved the bag of food at him. "I told you I'm not sure I've ridden a horse before."

Muttering under his breath, he tied the bag to the saddle before he stepped closer. "This woulda been easier if you'd put on trousers like I told ya to."

"That isn't why you wanted me in trousers. You want to get as close as possible. I'm certain, resourceful as you are, you'll manage just fine with me in a dress."

"I do like a challenge."

A hum of discontent escaped, but she turned her attention to the saddle. Much as she was loathed to admit it, he had a point. The layers of petticoats would be a hinderance with two of them, even though Faro was rather large.

"Need help?"

"Yes." She sighed, turning her back to him. "We need to get rid of these petticoats. Probably the overskirt should come off as well."

"Yes ma'am. Right away, ma'am."

She chuckled at the eagerness in his tone, and the way he slapped her hands away when she tried to open the button on the overskirt. Rather than argue, she simply grasped her waist band several inches from the opening on either side.

Several glances cut their way at the scene of Cole practically stripping her down in the street. Her body jerked as he tugged ties loose and popped buttons free.

Finally the motion stopped. She hopped a couple of times to let the skirts puddle at her feet. With another shimmy from her that drew a groan from the man behind her, she stepped over the pile of skirts.

"Was that necessary?"

"No, but it sure was fun." She turned to face him in order to fasten her skirt back in place. With the leer he wore she didn't dare trust him to do it himself.

The sensation of her layers being gone made her feel almost as though she wore nothing. Even heavy as her very full skirt was, with the layers missing she felt out of sorts.

"Well, I should see to returning those back to my room."

"No need. *Daisy.*"

Jane scoffed. "You ordered her inside to work, now you're ordering her outside?"

"You bet."

She pursed her lips at the idea he was playing the power card so heavily. It wasn't an attractive look on him.

He must have sensed it, because his toothy grin simmered into a near-scowl. "Would ya rather leave them here?"

"Of course not. I don't need random men coming to sniff my skirts because they can't even afford your nickel whores."

"Nickel?" He barked out a laugh, but stopped as another woman emerged. "Iris. Where's Daisy?"

"Servicin' Archie. Whatcha want?" The woman was rather seasoned for a whore, aged older than Cole by Jane's guess. Her glance Jane's way was almost contemptuous.

"Jane needs her petticoats taken back to her room. See to it, would ya?"

Iris' nose wrinkled, accentuating the stark lines on the sides of her mouth. "Really? I could be in there earning."

"It'll take ya two shakes. Longer you argue, longer it takes." Cole moved to Jane's side, jerking his head to the pile. "And stay outta her things. Ain't your business."

Iris actually saluted the man before bending to gather up the pile of cotton and muslin.

Jane covered a snort with a cough before turning back to the horse. "Reprobate."

"Proud of it, too. Now, we getting on or what?"

"Right. Into the saddle." Once again she eyed the saddle with a careful eye. It didn't seem too difficult, despite the height of the horse. If she moved just so, she could grab the pommel.

She lifted a foot into the stirrup, careful to arrange her skirt so it was mostly out of the way. After a small hop, found it not as difficult to get up as she'd imagined. Halfway up, she let out a yelp when his hand planted on her rump and pushed her the rest of the way.

He had the sly grin of a fox that had just landed in the henhouse. At her tsk, his brows rose in mock innocence. "What?"

"Did you enjoy that?"

"Not near enough."

"I imagine you'll find a way to make it up to yourself."

In a heartbeat, he swung into the saddle behind her. "You complaining? This was your idea. We could still get Brag and Bluff."

"How gentlemanly of you to offer." Jane's further retort was cut off when he lifted her skirts and pulled her rear tight against him. Her eyes widened in surprise, and she sat still for a brief moment. The simple action had caught every nerve in her body on fire. She rearranged her skirts to cover what he'd flashed to the world. It didn't escape her notice that every move and twitch she made had an effect on the bulge pressed against her backside.

His hands remained under the layers of fabric. Strong fingers gripped her hips. "Ain't ever been called a gentleman before."

"How surprising," The droll statement rolled off her tongue automatically. She allowed a smile in response to his laughter. "Since we're up here and ready to go, wasting more time seems rather pointless."

"Then give me the damn reins." His large hands emerged from her skirts and slipped down her arms. The gentle touch rubbed just enough to raise gooseflesh. She shivered when he closed his hands over hers before grabbing the reins ahead of her grasp.

A simple shift of her position in the saddle drew a noise akin to a growl from deep in his chest. Her own body still trembled from his suggestive touches, so it pleased her to feel his strong response to her own. With a satisfied sigh, she released her hold on the reins and leaned back against his chest.

"You're enjoying teasing me, ain't you?"

"No more than you are." Feeling his laughter rumble through his chest, she grinned. "Now that we've given everyone plenty to stare at and talk about, may we go?"

"You got it." He turned Faro to head east out of town.

They'd made it beyond the houses when a group in the distance caught Jane's attention. Her state of relaxation flew away when she realized they were Indians. "What in heaven's name?"

The group approached the army encampment to the south of town. Three soldiers on horseback surrounded a small group of Indians. A rope tied to each prisoner in a line before it hooked on the leader's saddle. He didn't move at a cruel pace, no pride or triumph brightened his somber features.

Jane's stomach twisted. "Who is that in the lead?"

"Major Webb. It's about time he got some Indians captured. He ain't been doing much good. He's been foolish counting on Starbird to handle things peaceful-like when the renegades ain't doing nothing peaceful."

"Those don't look like renegades."

"Nah. Don't matter. An Indian's an Indian, right?"

Only women and one old man were in the line of prisoners, but still Jane shuddered.

"Let's get going."

She nodded. When he set Faro to a good pace, she leaned against him again. The lull of the horse did little to relax her this time as they drew ever closer to the foothills.

By the time they reached the base of the hills an hour later her head spun in circles. Her heart pounded a furious pace. The familiar pressure on her chest returned with each step Faro took. Her nails dug into the leather of the pommel to redirect some of the tension.

"Kelly said he tracked you this far. Didn't go much farther. Ain't too safe with all the renegades and it's mountains for miles from here."

She felt a nudge and realized he wanted a response. All she could manage at first was a nod. She licked her lips. Her throat seemed dryer than the parched earth all of a sudden. "I'd like to go farther. We still have time, right?"

"Plenty. We came on horseback instead of by foot like Kelly did. We'll go until we gotta eat, then turn back."

After a whispered thank you she closed her eyes. In her efforts to will memories forward, she barely heard his comments about the fading trail. She opened her eyes again to focus on her surroundings. Time passed in the periphery. She continued to grip the pommel to stop the shaking that had taken root in her limbs.

"Trail's too faint to follow from up here." Cole dismounted and led Faro deeper into the trees, further up the hill. Once in a while he'd squeeze her leg. It wasn't until she actually turned her full attention to him that she realized it was out of concern.

She managed a semblance of a smile. "Sorry. I'm…"

"Get down. You weren't on no horse. Maybe it'll help."

"Good idea." His hands grasped her waist so she let him guide her down off the large horse. She straightened her skirts, scanning the unfamiliar terrain with some doubt. "Are you certain this is the way?"

"Whatever happened to ya, you were still bleedin'." He crouched, waiting for her to follow suit before pointing to a blood-spattered rock.

"Couldn't that be from an animal?"

He pointed to a nearby sapling with a cracked branch about the height of her shoulders. "Too big for most animals. Might have been a deer, but this is the same trail we've been following. I'm guessing it was you."

She turned her gaze to the cloudless sky, and once again took note of her dry mouth. "I suppose the lack of rain has been a blessing for me. This would all be gone, wouldn't it?"

"Probably." Cole helped her to her feet. He made sure they both sipped from the canteen before he pointed through the trees. "Trail ain't moved. You came due west. I ain't gonna be far behind. Take your time."

She didn't know what to say. He'd practically read her mind. Despite her need for his assistance, and gratefulness over his companionship, she'd hoped for some time alone. A bit breathless, she shook her head. "How did you—"

"Just figured if it were me, I'd wanna be alone. We ain't got much time 'til we need to eat. Guess I can let ya have it. I'm staying close just in case. Renegades and all."

"Thank you, Cole." At his nod, she turned away. With a deep breath to brace herself, she headed in the direction he'd indicated. Moving through the trees, her throat closed as the fear and confusion filled her again. Perhaps going it alone had been a bad idea. Without the distraction of conversation, reality became suffocating.

She pushed through, hoping against hope this blood specked trail would lead her to some answers. Her gaze passed through the trees, to the ground, and then back to eye level. She wasn't able to see the trail Cole said was clear, but she knew he'd tell her if she strayed from the correct path.

Her mind spun to find anything that sparked some recognition. Every step felt weighed down, every moment pulled her heart deeper into her chest. Half an hour later she sank to her knees. She dropped her head, her shoulders sagged, and she barely found the strength to draw her hands together to whisper a silent prayer.

Cole's hands closed around her arms. A burst of strength revived her slightly as he lifted her to her feet. "Up you go. Let's get some food."

"Just a little farther." She left the grip of his arms, but he caught her hand. Desperation pulled her forward several more steps, dragging him behind. "I feel like I'm so close."

"Do ya really?"

"No." She turned away from her progress at one small tug from him. Her shoulders dropped as he pulled her closer. One last glance over her shoulder caused her to look a second time. In the distance she thought she spotted something out of place. "Wait. What's that?"

"What's what? Jane. Wait."

She rushed toward the foreign object until it came into view. A large skeleton, parts skewed about the small break in the trees, a set of ribs still arched over the ground. Even though her brain made the connection, her voice squeaked. "What—what is that?"

His hands settled on her shoulder to pull her back against him. "It *was* a horse. Looks like it dropped a couple weeks back. Not much left of it now."

"A horse." Nausea twisted her stomach in knots. Cole moved around the carcass to grab a saddlebag half hidden under brush. His mouth moved, but she heard nothing. Her heart raced faster, and she closed her eyes.

Buzzing filled her ears. Images flickered behind her eyelids, shadowy and dark, horror lifting the hair on the back of her neck. Nothing clear, nothing solid, but the feelings threatened to overpower her. "I stole it."

Cole gripped her arm. "You stole the horse? Jane, that's a hanging offense."

"I had to," She whispered. Nothing made sense. The words escaped before she could process them. "I—he was after me. It was his. I took it. He was going to kill me."

"Who?"

"I don't know. I don't." The moment passed as quick as it had come. She sank to her knees, her body cold in the absence of the terror she'd felt. "I don't know. I only know he was going to kill me."

The saddlebag landed in front of her. A book skidded out of the otherwise empty pouch. He knelt beside her. "Are you sure?"

"He was going to kill me." Jane repeated the words, over and over and over again. Someone had wanted to kill her, wanted her dead. She said it again, and again.

A sharp sting to her cheek brought her back to reality. Her hand flew to the offended area. She turned to glare at Cole. "What the hell?"

"You weren't answering."

Horror chased away anger. Tears filled her eyes so fast she had to look at the ground. She wouldn't cry. No one could see her cry.

"Do you really remember?"

"Yes. No. It was so brief. More like a feeling. I just—I knew…" Her whole body shuddered.

He gripped her shoulders. "Jane."

"The horror. The certainty I was going to die. Being chased."

"Anything else?"

"Falling."

"What?"

"I don't know. I was pushed. Pushed from—something. I don't know. Everything is so confusing. Nothing makes sense. So many feelings, yet nothing is clear. He was going to—"

"Kill ya. I got it." He released her shoulders. "Least you got something."

"It's nothing." She flew to her feet. "Nothing at all."

"Sure it is. Ya know you didn't come from nowhere."

"Yes, I certainly do." When he stood, she narrowed her eyes at his towering form. She snarled, "And I know someone tried to kill me. Is that supposed to *comfort* me?"

"You didn't come out here for comfort. You came for answers."

"Shadowy memories of terror are *not* answers."

"Two hours ago you had nothing."

"What did I do? Why was someone chasing me?" She lost the battle against her own tears. They clouded her vision. The gentle brush of his thumb to her cheek wiped an escapee away. "Who was I?"

"Couldn't tell ya." His hands ran along her arms. "But what did you expect?"

"I expected—I wanted—I thought maybe if I—I don't know."

"You figured if you came out here, you'd remember and be whole?"

"Is there something wrong with hoping it would work that way?"

"If you're gonna let it crush you every time it don't work, yeah." He folded his arms across his chest. "If you really don't remember, what made ya think standing around here looking at a trail of blood would give you answers?"

She frowned when he turned his gaze south. What could be so distracting, she didn't know. Her stomach still twisted in knots. "The questions are what kill me. The constant, eternal questions. What's my real name? Was I married?"

"Jane. We gotta move."

"Do I have children? Did I even want them? If I did—why in heavens would I? Where am I—"

"Jane. We gotta move—*now*."

The pounding of hooves hit her ears, but she made no effort to move. "Did I have a family? Friends that would claim me? Or look for—"

She grunted when he grabbed her around the waist to run back toward Faro. When the hoof beats grew louder and closer, he threw her to the ground. They rolled until they were still, hidden under the cover of low-lying brush.

The second she opened her mouth to yell his hand clamped tight over it. He pressed his weight into her when she struggled. She squeaked and smacked his sides.

"Renegades," he growled in her ear.

The pounding of hooves grew louder still, vibrating along the ground. She lay frozen. Figures tore through the trees yards away, heading north. Hooves and shadows were all she saw, but the whoops and cries from the renegades made her heart pound in abject terror.

Yet she wanted nothing more than to run, to scream at God himself for the answers she couldn't find. The terror from the flicker of memories battled with the fear of the renegades until she could no longer breathe.

A trickle of moisture ran along her temples. Her muffled sobs poured into Cole's chest. Once they were accompanied by the sounds of the forest returning to life, she fought against him, beating him as hard as she could.

Cole took the first few hits with little more than a grunt. He rolled off her with a dark frown. The second his weight was gone, she screamed. He snatched her arm. "Are ya trying to get us killed?"

"Why shouldn't I? Since the first attempt was a failure, maybe I should try again."

"Are you some kind of idiot?"

"That's another excellent question. I'll add it to my never-ending list." Her tirade squeaked off when he gave her a hard shake. The jolt only raised her ire. The man had no clue. No one did. No one could know the empty, consuming terror. She gripped his forearms. "Try living without any knowledge of who you are and tell me not to hope for answers."

"Hope for all the damn answers you want, but trying to get yourself killed is just stupid. Now let's get out of here. Fast. Before you add scalping to your list of injuries."

She poured all of her anger into the glare she leveled at his back as he rose. After a moment she flew to her feet behind him. "What do you care?"

"I don't." He leveled a scowl over his shoulder.

She shoved him, wrapping her arms around herself. Rather than try to move closer, she strode several feet away through the forest. "You're a nice diversion from the emptiness. You can even make me laugh. But you can't tell me how to think, how to *feel*."

"Maybe I shoulda left you for the renegades."

"Maybe you should have. A scalping death has to be better than this never-ending pit of emptiness."

"You're plum crazy."

"I could be. No one knows for sure."

"So that's it?" His derisive snort filled the gap of silence left by her lack of answer. "You're just gonna give up. Good. I'll get you back to be town and be done with ya. Get back to *normal* life."

Normal? She had no idea what that meant. No reason to return to town. No one there could help her. "Don't bother."

"Excuse me?"

"I don't want your company any longer. Go back to town on your white horse and leave me be. I'll walk back, or maybe I'll move on."

"Stop acting like a no-account woman."

"I *am* a woman." Jane spun on him. "In case you hadn't noticed."

"Oh, I noticed. You're plenty woman. But you ain't ever acted like a weak, spineless thing since I met you. That ain't you."

"You don't know me well enough to make such a determination."

"Neither do you."

A frustrated scream didn't cover her anger, but it was all she had. She spun on her heel to head back to the spot where they'd found the horse carcass.

"Thought it could make ya laugh."

She chose to ignore him as she came upon the site again. The book caught her eye. She knelt down to pick it up. Her fingers slid along the worn leather. With a shaky breath, she turned it over. "Edgar Allan Poe."

"More memories?"

"'The ghastly Danger to which I was subjected haunted me day and night. In the former, the torture of meditation was excessive. In the latter, supreme. When the grim Darkness overspread the Earth, then, with every horror of thought, I shook—shook as the quivering plumes upon the hearse'."

"Jane."

The words refused to leave her mind, accompanied with a sense of terror and disgust that filled her by repeating them. They had to mean something. "No memories. Just Poe's words. Poe's dark, morbid thoughts."

"Let's get back. I'm done."

"With what?"

"Dealin' with you." Did the man want to drive her mad? Or just get her to stop crying? No matter which, he'd failed. He only managed to infuriate her again.

"Well excuse me." She pushed to her feet; the book still clutched in her hand. "I told you to go and I meant it. I'll take my chances with the Indians." Her body went numb the second the words left her mouth. Maybe she was insane.

He tossed her over his shoulder and headed back toward where they'd left Faro. Even though she beat and kicked to get free, he didn't budge from his path or drop her. "Stop acting like a fool. Get back on the damn horse."

"Put me down you stupid son of a—" A shriek curled out from her belly when she dropped toward the ground. She hit the earth hard enough to jar her teeth together. Her senses returned in time to realize she'd been dropped next to Faro with Cole glaring down at her.

"You wanna draw them renegades back with your shrieking, fine. I'll leave ya to them."

"Good. Be a heartless oaf. I don't care. Excuse me for wanting to know more than *anything* who I *am*."

"Just get on the horse or I'll put you on myself."

"Don't you dare." She stepped back. "You can't just shut me up and drag me back to town because my emotions disturb you. Just because you're afraid to feel anything at all doesn't mean everyone is."

He took a step toward her. "You're getting on my last nerve."

"Who cares? *This*? This is not about *you*. This is about me. I have nothing. Nothing at all but my emotions and I'm damn well going to feel them when I *need* to."

"I ain't dealing with a hysterical woman."

She slapped him hard. "Then leave."

He froze, his eyes growing dark as his scowl deepened. Grabbing her wrist, he dragged her, kicking and screaming, the few feet to the horse.

The moment he stopped pulling, she fought harder. Pounding her fists into his chest, his arms…she even got a few kicks to his shins.

Strong arms wrapped tight around her. Shock silenced her fury.

The moment she stilled, his hold changed. While he still had her pinned against him, his hand slipped up to press her head close against his chest. His other arm lowered to wrap around her waist, holding her in an unyielding, but gentle grasp.

A deep, wrenching sob ripped through her at the change and she collapsed against him. The hold she'd fought enveloped her, creating a sanctuary she hadn't expected. It didn't loosen. He didn't tell her to stop. She gripped his shirt as her tears dampened the material, relieved to have his safety and warmth to cling to.

Her tears slowed, but neither of them released their tight hold. She relaxed in the strong support his arms supplied. Her composure returned the longer he held her. After a few deep breaths she pulled back. The loss of his embrace created a palpable discomfort. "I'm ready to go back."

He remained silent until she managed to lift her gaze to his. "Good."

She stood quiet while he moved about, doing what, she didn't know. All the fight and anger had drained from her. Now she was simply tired and resigned. When he placed a biscuit in her hand, she nibbled on it as expected. By the time he untied Faro from the tree, she'd finished her biscuit and taken the obligatory drink from the canteen.

He hopped into the saddle and held out his hand. She glanced once more to the east before releasing a resigned sigh. With that, she took his hand and let him help her up behind him. Leaning into his back, she wrapped her arms tight around his waist.

Neither spoke the entire return ride to town. Not even their stomachs dared lament the pitiful lunch they'd eaten.

His fingers laced with hers in a gesture of silent comfort. Despite the help the simple support gave, she yanked her hand free the moment the town came into view. No matter how she felt, no one needed to know how much he'd helped her.

She straightened to judge the distance to the ground again. Rather than wait, she swung her leg around and hopped off the still-moving horse. While he danced nervously away, she ran ahead of Cole to the boarding house, relieved he didn't shout after her.

Cora rushed up before she'd made it past the saloon. "The railroad was attacked again. Army said they came from the south. We were worried they crossed your path."

"They did." Cole's voice carried down from Faro. "We heard them but got out of sight. I think they were too hurried to get to the railroad, didn't take notice. No one was hurt."

Jane cleared her throat. "I need to go lie down."

"Wait." Cora grabbed her arm. "Did it help? Did you remember?"

Exhaustion stalled her response. Her eyelids fluttered as if to keep away tears her dry eyes weren't going to bear. If she could get away without a reply, she would. "Not enough. It only made things worse. I really need to lie down. I have a headache. Excuse me."

"All right. I'll bring you supper later," Cora said. "We can talk then."

"No. I'm not hungry. Can we talk tomorrow, please?" Jane tried to force a smile, but knew it was far from reassuring. "I need to get some rest."

Jane raced to her room the second Cora agreed. Closing the door, she leaned against it to sink to the floor. Dark images drummed at the back of her eyelids. Terror kept her heart pounding, her fists clenched.

Unable to ease her racing head, she crawled to the bed and climbed in fully clothed. Unmoving, she lay there until dark fell. Not even the hands folded on her stomach twitched.

It took repeating Whitman's verses over and over to get her mind settled enough to think about sleep. In the middle of 'The Body Electric' she managed to doze off.

A thump and the flick of a match startled her. Her bedside lamp sparked to life, illuminating the shimmering lines of a whiskey bottle.

She sat, not entirely surprised to find Cole gazing down at her. Even in the weak lamplight she could see the intensity of his stare. Her heart stilled. For a moment she had to fight the urge to run into the warmth of his embrace. It simply wouldn't do. She had to fight it. "Cole…"

"I need a drink."

"Don't you always," she murmured.

"You need a drink. Might as well drink together."

A small laugh bubbled up and made an escape before she could stop it. "I need a drink?"

"Think you can handle it?"

"I wouldn't know."

"One way to find out." He poured whiskey into two glasses and handed her one. "Don't think. Just drink."

"My mind stops even less than my mouth does."

"How terrible for ya."

She hummed her agreement. The amber liquid caught the lamplight. After a deep breath, she lifted the glass to her lips. The whiskey burned down her throat to her belly, where it sent a warm wave through her. "It doesn't sicken me. I think I like it. Could I have more?"

"Sure. You play poker?"

"Cole."

"Don't remember, eh? At all?"

"No. Will I enjoy it as I do the whiskey?"

"Only one way to find out." He pulled cards out of his back pocket. While she righted herself and got out of the bed he sat at the table and shuffled. Once she'd joined him, he pulled something else out from behind him and slid it across the table.

She closed her hands over the worn leather of the book they'd found. "I forgot."

"I know."

Before she could second guess herself, she reached out to set her hand on his. She set aside her book to meet his eyes. "Thank you."

"I told ya. Don't mention it. Got a reputation to keep."

Her lips twitched before she gave up and let the laughter free. "You've already ruined it with me."

"Maybe you ain't the one I'm trying to fool."

Heat flooded her cheeks, the admittance pleasing her far more than she thought it would. "Good to know."

He tapped the cards on the table. "You better be a fast learner."

"And if I'm not?"

"Just don't cry again."

"Not even if I lose."

The true genius shudders at incompleteness-
and usually prefers silence to saying something
which is not everything it should be.
-Edgar Allen Poe

"I still don't get it." Martha's pacing near wore a hole in the floor.

Jane laughed. Martha's questioning drove her nuts. She ignored Martha in favor of Cora, who was adjusting her corset. "One more time. I've had to wear it loose because of the tape on my ribs. I want it tight."

Cora adjusted her hold on the laces. "All right. Ready?"

Martha threw up her hands. "Yesterday you two screamed at each other right outside the saloon. Like you were going to kill each other."

Jane exhaled with a nod. A squeak escaped when Cora yanked good and tight. She grabbed the laces to tie them around. The moment she caught her breath, she addressed Martha's rants. "We weren't screaming."

"Yes you were." Cora's voice danced with laughter. "I've never seen anyone draw a crowd like the two of you."

"Well, he is infuriating," Jane acknowledged with a grin. The argument the day before might have been trivial, but it had drawn quite the crowd. Something about him stimulated her from anger to pleasure and right back again. She didn't want it to end, at least not the pleasure part of it. He made her feel alive. Like a real honest-to-goodness person instead of a hollow form with no real soul of her own.

"Three days ago the two of you were quite cozy on that beast of a horse. My word, he practically stripped you down in the street for all to see."

"I asked him to assist me. We couldn't ride together in that saddle with all of my layers."

Martha's jaw dropped. Across the room, Cora's did the same.

While Jane waited for them to recover, she adjusted the lay of her skirt. It would do her no favors to show how she enjoyed the horror on Martha's features. After all, by all accounts Martha and her husband had been caught in some compromising positions before they were married.

"You asked him to undo your petticoats?"

"It was a two-person job."

Cora sighed. "I—oh, Jane. You're terrible."

Jane allowed her smile free at Martha's deep red blush. "No more terrible than spending the night in the mountains with your man before you were wed."

"I—we—*Jane*. That's neither here nor there. Cole lifted your skirts and showed your ankles to the world." Martha pegged the direction Jane's thoughts headed, whether she meant to or not. "Behavior like that, you've got the whole town talking. Thinking that perhaps—"

"What?" Jane turned to face Martha. "That I'm being seduced? What makes you think it isn't I doing the seducing?"

"Jane."

Jane grabbed her bodice to occupy herself with dressing rather than let free her burgeoning giggle. She enjoyed toying with Martha far more than she should. It was almost more unseemly than her behavior with Cole. "He's a friend."

Cora's brows rose high enough to be almost hidden in her lunatic fringe. She brushed at the layer of bangs and shook her head. "Friend? Is that all?"

"Yes. That's all. He's a friend. I don't understand why it is so scandalous to have a male friend. If there's some flirtation involved, what of it?" Jane set her fists on her waist. Over the previous few days things certainly had changed. While her past was no clearer, her present was becoming more like something she'd craved all along—life.

Martha sighed. "I think you're playing with fire. Cole is not someone to be trusted. Maybe you shouldn't—"

"Why not? I appreciate you are concerned. I more than appreciate the fact you are kind enough to continue to allow me to stay here. However, I do not appreciate you trying to put your own opinions one me. I understand you and Cole have no love lost because he hates Indians and you happen to me married to one."

"Jane," Cora admonished in a hushed tone.

"What? Am I wrong?" Far as Jane could tell, she was stating facts. "Starbird is an Indian, at least he was last time I checked. Even if he's spent his time acting the part of a white man for fifteen years. Either way, it's of no concern to me. I like Cole. I enjoy spending time in his company. End of story."

Cora folded her arms across her chest, her mouth already opening in protest. Jane chose to ignore her, picking up the books she intended to return to the library. She rushed out the door and downstairs to avoid further debate.

"Jane." Cora's quiet voice followed her. Several buildings away from the boarding house, Cora put her hand on Jane's arm. Pulling her to the side, she frowned. "Jane. I know you want to figure out who you are, but we should talk about Cole. Word is that he has some rather specific plans for you."

"Specific plans? Like what?" Jane stood tall, eyeing the woman she knew was only concerned for her. "That he wishes to make me a whore? It won't happen."

"Graham says he's got designs on taking you on as one of those soiled doves."

"Graham? You're serious, aren't you?" Jane pressed her fingers against her forehead, trying to keep back the growing headache. How anyone could believe that brute of a man was beyond her. Especially someone that had known him even longer than her. "Cora, I won't become a whore. I doubt Cole thinks I would become a whore. If he did tell Graham such a ridiculous thing, it was all bluster."

"Would you mind if I ask why? Why Cole?"

"Didn't Martha just ask a similar question?"

"Yes. I just don't think you say everything you're thinking around her."

"Probably because I don't." Jane chewed her lower lip and turned her gaze away. She wished she could confide in Cora. Several days ago she'd told Daisy she had no designs on Cole and at the time she'd been honest. Now things were different. "I don't understand why everyone is so fascinated by this?"

"For one, they're fascinated by you and your amnesia. Also, you hardly seem the type of woman to consort with a man like Cole. It garners attention."

"Honestly." Jane could have been annoyed by the gossip and attention, but she'd rather worry about more important things. She turned her attention toward the saloon and allowed a shrug. "I would be lying if I said I didn't find Cole quite attractive. The way things are, I live in a state of nothingness most of the time. Cole is…stimulating."

"Jane, you aren't actually making time with him?"

"Sex?" Jane grinned at Cora's blush, and the heads that turned their way from the simple word. She shook her head. "No, Cora. He hasn't even tried to kiss me, not that I'd stop him if he did. Part of me is very curious. I don't remember having sex, but it does sound quite interesting."

"Just what sort of books are you getting out of the library?"

"Ovid, Goethe, Whitman. They're fascinating."

Cora flushed again. "Why don't you consider finding something less provocative? You should be careful around Cole. We can't be sure he's not trying to abuse your situation."

"If he was going to abuse my situation, he would have. He's been in my room until almost three in the morning every night this week and has not made one move toward the bed."

Leaving Cora standing with her mouth agape, Jane flounced down the boardwalk with a triumphant grin. Within a minute she'd made it to the small newspaper office nestled in the cramped space between two much larger buildings. She stopped just in time to avoid barreling into the person leaving the office.

The warm laughter of the man grabbed her attention. She raised her gaze to find smiling, deep green eyes. She couldn't help but peruse the handsome features of the Major she'd seen from a distance only days before. He was younger than she'd first suspected. "Oh."

"Sorry about that, ma'am. I almost knocked you down." A hint of a southern accent filtered into the words, tickling another smile right out of her.

"No apologies necessary, Major Webb. I wasn't paying attention."

"Apparently neither of us was. But you have me at a disadvantage, ma'am. You seem to know who I am. May I have the honor of the same?"

"You could if I knew who I was." At the furrow of his brow, she laughed. She couldn't deny his attractiveness, or the bit of fun she could have. Cole had certainly played his own games, she wondered how he would react if she turned the game on him. "You may call me Jane. I'm afraid I don't recall my real name—or anything beyond when I woke in the boarding house several weeks ago."

"So you are the infamous Jane Doe?" A warm smile lit up the tired features of moments earlier. A strong, clean-shaven chin, soft and kind eyes. Both of which would be pleasant distractions from her incessant thoughts of Cole.

"That would be me." Jane nodded. "And I'm afraid I only knew who you are because you were pointed out to me. I do appreciate the in-person introduction."

"As do I, Jane." He tipped his head, touching his cap before moving to leave. "Good afternoon."

"Good afternoon." She took a step toward the newspaper office.

"Jane."

She smiled; glad he'd stopped her. "Yes, Major?"

"Perhaps you'd accompany me to lunch at Turners?"

Jane pondered what the simple matter of lunch with the Major would to do the gossip over her personal life. There would most certainly be renewed vigor of the salacious whispers. Handsome though he might be, the Major couldn't compete with Cole. He hadn't the personality to match. Not that this would stop anyone, including Cole, from wondering. It could be rather good sport. "It would suit me fine, Major. I have several errands to run first. Shall we meet there at one?"

"I would be delighted."

"I'll see you then." After a wave, she slipped into the newspaper office. The moment the scent of ink and paper hit her, the task she'd set out to complete took over her focus. She approached the counter fast. "Rusty."

Rusty looked up from his task at the press, a smile flickering across his features. "It's good to see you, Jane."

"And you. Forgive my rush to task, but I must ask how many papers you have sent my article to."

"Oh." He wiped at the ink on his hands. For a moment his gaze flickered over her shoulder, his brow creased. The moment passed and he headed to his desk. "Let me see. I've sent it to most of the papers in the area. Denver, Pueblo, Manitou, and Colorado Springs. Then we've gone so far as Salt Lake and San Francisco to the west—"

"Stop sending it out, please." Her desperation returned once she realized how far her story had spread. After the nightmare of horror she'd felt when following her trail, she was now almost afraid to find out who she was—most especially by the person that wished her dead. "I'd like to stop searching for now."

"Well, why would you want to?" From behind her came an unexpected, and most unpleasant voice. One she'd heard on several occasions, and done her best to avoid—Guy Forrester.

She frowned at Rusty, but immediately felt guilty as an embarrassed blush blazed across his freckled face. It wasn't his fault. She should have seen Guy sitting by the window. If she hadn't been so singled minded, maybe she would have. She wrinkled her nose, but pushed forward a smile out of all the politeness she could muster, and turned around. "Mr. Forrester. I didn't realize you were here skulking about."

"I'm hardly skulking." Guy folded his paper. He rose from his seat. After he'd tucked the paper under his arm, he held out his hand. "I always come in to get Rusty's first printing. I must say I'm pleased to see you. You're a difficult woman to get a hold of. Well, for most of the men in town."

"No one gets a *hold of* me that I don't wish for, Mr. Forrester." Jane turned back to Rusty. "Would you please stop circulating the story?"

"If you really want, but why, Miss Jane?" Rusty's brows knit together. "Don't you want to know what happened to you?"

"Yes, Jane. Don't you want to know?"

She sucked her lips between her teeth, not willing to spill her private fears to the man leering at her. Instead, she took Rusty's arm and dragged him toward the back of the office. She glared at Guy until he had the mind to pretend he wasn't eavesdropping. With a frustrated sigh she lowered her voice. "Rusty. What did I look like when I arrived here? I had to have been put into that state by someone's hand. Someone had to have—"

"I see," Rusty muttered with wide eyes.

"I'm afraid before I figure out who I am, the wrong person could find me."

"It's too late to pull the articles and notices already printed, I'm afraid. However, I will cease to forward them."

"Thank you." Jane hugged him tight. "I'll let you get back to your printing. Excuse me."

"Jane." Guy took her arm with a smooth gesture when she tried to pass. He slipped her hand into his arm and held it there with his own. Though she tried to pull free, his grasp was far firmer than it appeared to the naked eye. "Walk with me."

"I'd really rather not."

"Guy, leave her alone," Rusty protested.

"What was that?" Guy narrowed his eyes back toward Rusty. He smirked when Rusty backed down and cowered by the printer. "Just a short walk, get to know each other a bit."

"Why would I want to do such a thing, Mr. Forrester?"

"Call me Guy."

"No. I don't believe I will." She rolled her eyes when his response was a laugh. Her mouth tensed and she tried unsuccessfully to withdraw her arm from his grasp. He pulled her alongside him out of the office. "Release me."

"You don't even know what I want to talk to you about. Please grant me the opportunity to entice you with my thoughts."

"I sincerely doubt you could."

"Shouldn't everyone be afforded the opportunity? I assure you it will be most beneficial."

"I asked you to release me. I will not be manhandled. If you really wish to speak to me, you wouldn't resort to manipulating a situation to your advantage. You would allow me to reject you and then entice me with your supposed benefits."

He eyed her. "I have tried that method. You continue to reject me. I have an idea that very well could—"

"I said release me."

A gravelly voice marred by a slight slur interrupted Guy's tirade. "The lady said let go."

Jane twisted to peek over her shoulder. The older man behind her had an air of familiarity, though she couldn't place him. Her brow furrowed as she studied his scruffy appearance, but she couldn't help but return the shy smile he gave her.

"Hammy," Guy snapped. "This is none of your concern."

"It ain't right to hold a lady when she asked to be let go." Hammy drew his chin up and managed to look proud and strong.

Jane tried to tug her hand free. She gave Hammy a wink. "Thank you. Is it really Hammy?"

"Name's Gilbert Hamm. Everyone calls me Hammy." He looked down with a shuffle of his feet. "Come on, Guy. She don't want no help from you."

"You think she wants the help of a drunk that thought he'd shot her dead?" Guy grinned at Hammy's embarrassed mumbling. "Go back to Cole's saloon with the rest of the riff-raff. Jane's obviously above you all."

"I'm not obviously anything," Jane protested. "And I'll ask you one more time to release me or you will never gain a proper audience."

Keeping a hold on her hand, Guy removed it from his arm and kissed the back. He winked. "I do look forward to obtaining a *proper* audience then."

"When I deem I am ready." She yanked her hand away. Her nose wrinkled as she wiped it on her skirt. "Mr. Hamm. Thank you for your assistance."

"Aww, ain't no big deal, Miss Jane."

She leaned in to kiss the older man on the cheek. "It was to me." After one final glare at Guy, she turned to head to the library. This time when her mind raced, it was with the confusion of the present instead of the unknown past.

There are times when fear is good.
–Aeschylus

"Well, I must apologize."

Jane took Webb's offered arm with a smile. "I can't imagine why. I had a delightful lunch."

"I'm afraid I dominated the conversation."

"Nonsense. It was a refreshing change. I rather enjoyed it." Throughout lunch they'd received snooping glances, although Jane was certain Daisy had gleaned the most enjoyment. Jane sighed and gestured around the room. "They are all far too busy talking about me. I enjoy the chance to talk to someone else. I don't remember much interesting about myself to contribute to lively conversation."

"But there are far more appetizing conversations than my past."

"You mean the war? It wasn't unappetizing. You kept decorum and I must say, I'm surprised you're such a gentleman after witnessing such horrors."

"Everyone witnesses horrors at one point or another." Webb held open the door. "How we deal with them is what's important."

"You still struggle, though. That's why you're here, isn't it? Why you tried to work things out through Starbird? You'd rather do things peacefully."

"I suppose that's true. Although sometimes I'm not sure there is such a thing as a peaceful end to the Indian issue."

"Is it true you haven't heard from Starbird in weeks?" His silence spoke volumes. The frustrated crease on his brow made her smile. "Just say you aren't at liberty to discuss. That frown ages you ten years. You do take your job to heart."

"Too much. I don't agree with the cruelty most men practice on the Indians."

"Why not?"

"I don't agree with cruelty to any human."

"Hence, why you defected to the North. I understand, but I've heard tell these Indians are savages and have done just as bad and worse to white men."

He looked down at her. "Have you met one?"

"No. Well, I met Starbird once, but I was still in too much pain to pay him any mind. I do admit he made me uncomfortable."

"Then let's try another route. Would you call all men cruel?"

"No. I wouldn't even call most men cruel. They like to pretend they are, but they aren't. All men can be reduced to size with a vice or two." She chuckled. "I see. Some Indians may be savages, but that does not mean they all are. I must give you credit, Major."

"How so?"

"I believe you are the first soul to have presented me an argument for the Indians that I would consider. It is logical and fair, as opposed to an appeal of the heart."

"Glad I could be of service. But please, Major is a bit too proper."

"Then what shall I call you?"

"My name is Marshall."

She giggled, covering her mouth immediately in an attempt to hide the sound. Her cheeks grew warm at her automatic reaction. "Sorry. I shouldn't laugh at your name."

"If you'd let me finish I would have told you," he chuckled, "that I don't care for the name either. Most of my friends call me Al."

"Al is better." She laced her arm with his again. "I think I can say that without giggling."

"Glad to hear it."

"Major Webb." A soldier raced up to them, his horse dancing at the sudden stop.

Nodding to Al, she smiled. "Go. Duty Calls. Thank you for lunch."

He tipped his hat, muttering a quick goodbye before heading over to the soldier. With a sigh, she resumed her path down the street. She'd enjoyed her lunch with the major, but her thoughts still drifted to Cole.

She berated herself for thinking about Cole. Why worry about any man? There were far more important things to focus on. Her missing years, for example. Still, nothing had proved as enjoyable as Cole.

Every night he climbed her balcony to her room. They talked, they drank, and talked some more. He tried to teach her poker, which she was terrible at. She hadn't a clue why he directed attention at her, much less why it pleased her so much. He had plenty of women, a saloon full of them at his beck and call. All she had was—nothing. Not even a memory.

With Al part of the equation now, she wondered just how much more chaos he would add. For a moment she considered taking Martha's advice and focusing on her past. Perhaps it would be best if she didn't worry about building a life until figured out who she was.

"No," she whispered to herself. "I can't hide away. I have to live, make what mistakes I will or I'll never figure this out."

She clapped her hand over her mouth. If people didn't already think her half-crazed, they'd certainly think so if they saw her talking to herself.

Straightening her shoulders, she resumed her path down the street. Cole glared at her from three buildings away. She allowed a feeling of triumph that her innocent lunch might have inspired his current state of discontent. As she approached, she slowed, hands clasped behind her back.

She held his gaze steady. Carefully she schooled her features, allowing no sign of her inner amusement. Only a single brow raised until she'd passed. The sound of his bootsteps right behind caused a crack in her armor, so a chuckle slipped free. Stopping short, she grunted when he bumped into her. "Cole?"

"Have a good lunch?"

"Actually, I did. Cora made a lovely meal today. Baked trout with—"

"Ain't talking about the food."

She pivoted and sighed. "You mean the company? First of all, Major Webb was perfectly polite. Second, what concern is it of yours? We're just having fun, aren't we? Friends. Nice and easy. After all, you have plenty of entertainment."

"But soldier boy?"

"That's what you're concerned about?"

"He's boring."

"Maybe he is, maybe he isn't. Only way for me to figure out is to get to know him. Just as I'm getting to know you. Besides…"

He jumped when her body leaned into his. A curse slipped from between his lips. It excited her the way a simple movement could affect this man.

"It wouldn't be right to ask for an exclusive…friendship. And you hardly seem the type for anything more."

"I ain't."

"Good. Because I don't think I am either."

"Really?"

She grinned at his sudden, wicked smile. "Really. I must say that I've begun to learn about myself, Mr. Mitchell. Not in the sense of who I might have been, but rather who I am now."

"So what are you learning?"

"I find that—"

Gunfire echoed through the town. Close behind came whoops and yells. Cole pulled his gun from its holster. "Get inside, Jane, quick."

Unable to comply, she found her feet stuck to the boards, her gaze stuck on the group of men racing through town. Their exposed dark skin, the paint that covered their faces and parts of their bodies dominated her vision. Her heart pounded like the drums of the charging savages, beating in her ears. Her mind screamed at her to move, to get away.

"Jane."

Cole and Graham's shouts and gunfire filled her head.

Someone shoved her through the saloon doors. The rapid thump of the swinging doors slowed to a stop. She leaned against the narrow strip of wall between the door and the window. Her frozen body came to life with a series of shivers.

The window shattered.

A bullet whistled past less than a foot away. She shrieked. Her hand clutched her chest. Her corset thwarted every attempt at a deep, steeling breath.

The room darkened. Her breath came in short spurts. Sweat broke across her flesh, chilling her to the bone.

She stared through the shattered glass where the last Indian had raced past, unable to focus on anything else. Terror burned through every muscle, through her very veins from a place she didn't recognize, a place so deep she could focus on nothing else.

"Jane." Cole's voice stirred her away from the iron grip of horror. There was an amusing mixture of frustration and concern in his tone, but she couldn't move her lips into a smile. She couldn't move at all. A strange trembling took over her whole person. Her hands shook; her breath trembled in its vain attempts for air.

"What the hell is wrong with her? Don't she know how to move?" Graham's snarl melted into the other voices in the room.

A hand touched her arm. She had to even out her breath somehow. Nothing she tried worked. With wide eyes, she looked up at Cole. She grabbed his arm so hard he flinched.

"Damn it, Jane."

"Can't…"

Graham walked into the narrow field of her tunneling vision. "What's your problem?"

"Breathe…"

"What?" Graham barked near her ear.

"She can't breathe, you idiot. Jane, open your corset." Cole's grimace grew fuzzy.

Her fingers wouldn't function to undo the hooks of her bodice. The world spun.

"Oh for cryin' out loud." Cole grabbed her bodice. Buttons clattered along the floor. With little effort, he popped open the busks of the corset. "What a useless piece of clothing."

The minute the corset released its hold, her lungs expanded with a deep breath of air before everything went dark. The last thing she heard was the simultaneous cursing of Cole and Graham.

Cover that bosom.
I must not see it.
Souls are wounded by such things,
and they arouse wicked thoughts.
—Moliere

A muffled din woke her. Shelves of liquor and glasses towered above her toward the ceiling. With a deep breath she noticed the shifting of her corset, the stays were loose around her ribs. After another deep breath, she turned her head.

Cole sat a few feet away on a crate. His elbows leaned on his knees. The man's powerful gaze didn't shift from her for one moment. He rested his chin on his hands, his brow pursed until she turned more toward him. Then his eyes lit with a fire, his gaze wandering from her face toward her chest.

Heat prickled along her flesh under his absolute intensity. Unsure what to say or do, she simply spoke with a most ineloquent, "Well."

"You panicked. Daisy says you're fine. Just needed air. Here."

She sat to take the glass he handed her. "Thank you. I'm sorry. I heard you tell me to move, and I tried. Truthfully, I did. I just couldn't seem to manage to get my feet to move."

"I'll remember that next time."

"Next time?"

"Once the damn Indians start attacking the town, they ain't gonna stop."

"Wonderful." Moisture lingered on her brow, and she lifted a hand to wipe it away. As she did, once again his gaze lowered to her chest. Warmth coursed through her, and she hurried to take a sip of water to try to quell the heat before it took over her body.

"Martha's preaching it's 'cause the army took prisoners that weren't renegades." The mundane talk meant nothing. He inched closer. Closer still.

"Of course she is." Jane managed to breathe. The air in the room thinned, no longer giving her what she needed to breathe and live. The nearer he came, the more the heat spread, tingling along her chest until her breasts ached under his scorching stare. She set down the glass to grasp her corset. "I should probably—"

"No." His hand closed over hers. "Don't."

"Cole…" Her breath hitched when his finger extended to brush along the lacey border of her chemise. Skin pebbled under the gentle, yet insistent touch. The ache in her chest slid lower, between her legs. A shiver ran down her spine, and she now understood more of what the words of her favorite poem *Pent-up Aching Rivers* meant. Still, propriety begged her to offer some measure of protest to such pleasure. "Why not?"

"Do you really want me to stop?"

God, no. Not for anything. She'd begun to realize that nothing she'd read could come close to describing the pleasure possible. She wanted this. She most definitely wanted him.

Her hand relaxed. She let it fall aside, giving him free rein to do as he wished. The delicate fabric of her chemise crumbled under his touch, the calluses on his fingertips caught in the delicate threads. His fingers ran along the curving swell of her breast, a teasing, light touch that set her burning nerves aflame.

Unbidden, her back arched. Too far. He was too far away. She wanted him closer, though she still wasn't sure why.

Like he'd read her mind, he slipped off the crate to kneel in front of her. His lips hovered close to hers. He moved his entire hand between fabric and flesh.

No longer teasing, his fingers kneaded along her skin. A shockwave of pleasure jolted through her when he pinched her taut nipple. She didn't even try to stop her whimper. Her body trembled in anticipation. She wanted more.

She wanted to feel him again, but had to order her lax body to cooperate. When her hands moved, they landed on his strong chest. She slipped them along the fabric to his shoulders. A tremble ran through the man. Could her simple touch have brought him pleasure?

Their breath mingled. A hint of whiskey, the lingering whisper of cigar smoke she'd tied to him since their first meeting. She wanted nothing more than for him to show her what a good kiss was. The thought made her fingers clench in anticipation so hard her nails dug into his shoulders. His low moan rumbled through her.

They were centimeters apart now, but he still hadn't made that connection. She fought the urge to whimper.

"Cole." The whisper of his name appeared to jolt through him, sparking him to move again. Her whole body tingled in anticipation, she closed her eyes moments before their lips met.

"Cole." Daisy's voice doused the passion back to a slow burn.

They jumped apart, though Cole lingered close, his fists clenched on either side of her.

Disappointment. Frustration. Damn Daisy for interrupting. Jane's body still tingled, longing for his touch. She flew to her feet when the door swung open, venting her frustration on the corset that now refused to close.

"Cole."

"What's the problem?" His tone dropped with annoyance to rival her own. Cole glared at Daisy as he rose to his feet, hands still clenched beside him. "There a fire?"

"No. It's the Army."

Cole snarled. "What about them?"

Daisy's gaze flickered between the two of them, her frown settled deep in her brow. "They're here asking about you seeing Lewis in that lot."

"What?" Jane gasped. All attempts to put her corset back together abandoned. "What do you mean you saw Starbird?"

"He was with the renegades." Cole ran his fingers through his hair. His back to Daisy, he rested his hand on his hips. He glanced at Jane. "It was his war paint. The bastard defected to the other side."

Jane's fingers twitched. Of all the things she'd imagined as the reasons for Starbird's disappearance, this had been the one she'd feared the most. "That's why he's gone missing?"

"Martha's saying it ain't him." Daisy shrugged. "But the Army wants to ask. What you saw and all."

"Yeah, yeah. Got it." Cole moved closer to Jane again. "Jane…"

Pleasant heat rose to her cheeks again. She so wanted Cole to ignore the Army in favor of remaining with her. Improper or not. "Should I thank you again?"

"Sure wouldn't mind a proper apology." His wicked smirk never wavered.

"Cole. The Army." Daisy's nostrils flared, her foot actually stomped as she faced off with him. Her hands on her hips, a tiny huff crossed her lips.

His gaze darted to Daisy. "Yeah. I got that. Talk to ya later, Jane."

"I'm quite certain you will." Turning her attention back to her corset, Jane struggled for several more minutes before managing to get it closed. By the time she did, Cole was gone, but much to her chagrin Daisy was not. Last thing she wanted to deal with right then was Daisy's jealousy. "What?"

"Just friends."

"I wasn't lying when I said that."

"And now?"

"If you must know, my curiosity has increased. The interest seems mutual and I'm not going to discourage it." Jane shrugged. "I'd like to enjoy myself, no matter whose company I'm in."

"He's going to use you up, just like he does everyone."

"And yet you still want him for yourself. Are you 'used up'?" Jane frowned. "Daisy, I don't care who Cole makes time with. Given the type of man he is, if and when I decide I want to take him in my bed, I won't expect anything more."

"He don't just keep me around 'cause I got medical training." Daisy straightened. Her words didn't carry the force of conviction. "There's a lot more to it."

"Then why worry about me?"

"Because you're gonna cause him trouble. He likes things simple."

The art of life lies in taking pleasures as they pass, and the keenest pleasures are not always intellectual, nor are they always moral.
—Aristippus

"What are you looking at?" Graham sneered over his coffee cup.

"You." Cole laughed. For the past fifteen minutes Graham had missed all attempts at conversation as he'd ogled the tiny woman at the nearby counter of the combination restaurant and general store. "Watching the wash girl."

"Don't know what you're talking about." Graham drank from his mug, which had to be full of cold coffee by now. The man made a real effort to stare at the table.

"You been watching her since she got in here. Come to think of it, you watch her every time she comes in for our wash, too. Ya sweet on her? She's a tiny slip, you're a full-on beast."

The Chinese girl peeked their way for the briefest moment. Cole and Graham sat in the half of the general store dedicated to Cora's restaurant. The girl, though Cole guessed she was more woman than girl, was exchanging Cora's clean table linens for dirties. Cole liked the table they sat in because it gave them prime chance to see all the happenings in the store. That's how Graham had spotted her entrance.

"You're crazy." Graham finished his coffee, slamming his cup down. "I got a girl."

"Don't stop you from dipping into the talent pool at our place." Cole loved finding Graham's weaknesses and this could prove to be a gold mine. Eyeing the Chinese girl was too good to ignore. "Becky know you got your eye on Chinatown?"

"Shut up, Cole." Graham's engagement to Becky wasn't anything but a sham. A way to get hold of her dowry. Everyone knew it, too.

Cole chuckled. "Why? If you're just stepping out, it's one thing. Ya do that all the time. You ain't getting moony over her, are ya?"

"You got no room to talk. What do you like about the mindless woman?"

"She ain't mindless, just don't have a memory. Oh, your girl's leavin'."

"She's not my girl."

"What's stopping you from seein' if she could support the weight of a bear like you? She's always so quiet, that's how you like 'em."

"Thought that's how you like 'em too."

Determined not to let Graham turn tables, Cole only laughed and took a long drag of his cigar. He blew the smoke out in a careful breath to leave rings in the air, his grin grew. "Oh, I get it now. That's why you're so worried 'bout how clean our sheets are. It ain't about good business. It's about getting more glimpses of her."

"Shut up." Graham got to his feet. "I'm gonna go get the rest of the bodies set for burial. They're not going to put themselves in pine boxes."

"What's her name anyway?"

"Linh," Graham said before he could stop himself. "Damn it, Cole."

Cole dropped his head back and let his laughter boom through the restaurant. "Sucker."

"Bastard."

Still laughing, Cole finished off his own coffee as Graham left. After a few minutes he tossed some money on the table and stood to leave. On the porch he paused to survey the bustling street for possible business.

Instead of business, he noticed a familiar figure in the distance. Her blond hair shimmered in the sunshine, and her bright green dress stood out in a sea of browns, reds, and filth. He leaned on the porch post to enjoy the view.

His lips twitched as Jane made her way through the bustling street, ever closer to where he stood. He knew what everyone with a penchant for gossip suggested. Unseemly acts. Between he and Jane. Many of which he certainly wouldn't mind enjoying with her. Yes, he'd relish making the rumors true.

Unlike most women, she didn't mind the gossip. None of it seemed to embarrass her as it would most others. He knew she reveled in making everyone guess, too. If he were frank, he had to admit he didn't know what drew him to her.

She was smart, but brains had never impressed him before. She cleaned up damn good, that was for sure. He was drawn to the sway of her hips. Even more to the curve of her lips that greeted every soul in her path.

Somehow she fit into the town like she'd always been there, even with the more rough and tumble men. With a no-nonsense attitude, she knocked them all down if they pushed too hard. The Indian attack had been enough to freeze her up, but nothing else seemed to faze her.

He let himself consider Daisy. For three years she'd been in his favor. She had smarts, and her looks weren't too shabby either. Her skills as a doc had always won over any issues he'd had. He no longer cared as much about keeping her happy to keep a doctor in the house. She was under contract, and she liked doctoring. He didn't need to keep her happy.

Once Jane had arrived, he'd all but lost all interest in Daisy, or any of his whores for that matter.

It bothered him. He figured it had to be the chase. Once she gave in, he'd be done with her as he had with more than his share of women. Yeah, that was it…the chase.

His musings were distracted by Graham standing in the door of his office talking to none other than the Chinese girl, Linh. Laughter bubbled, emerging loud enough to catch Graham's attention. Cole could only shake his head at the ugly gesture he received in return.

"Something amusing?" Jane slipped past him, no hint of a smile.

"Maybe."

Jane picked through the apples on display. "I see. Well, please continue to enjoy your amusement."

He cursed his body's instant reaction when she leaned over the bin. The simple action accentuated every tempting curve. The corset she wore pinched her waist tight. A bustle helped fill out her curves, but he knew the ass underneath was firm and round. Unable to stop himself, he walked over.

He leaned against the fruit bin, enjoying the generous amount of skin revealed by her low neckline. It had been a few days since he'd risked touching the soft flesh. He longed to do it again, to see if her reaction was as severe. Her enthusiastic response had been everything he'd imagined it would be, which made stopping near impossible.

After a few minutes of his staring, she warranted him a glance. "Yes?"

"What?"

"If you're looking for something else amusing, you won't find it here. I'm running a few errands before I head back home. No more, no less."

"Don't mean ya can't amuse me." He grinned at the playful smile she offered. Somehow he forced his hands to remain still. She leaned over close to him. The moment the soft scent of her perfume touched his nose, he inhaled instinctively; oranges and jasmine. Nicer than he let his girls wear and far more intoxicating.

Wisps of hair swirled up in his exhale, trembling down to land on the edge of her throat. He licked his lips, wanting to feel how soft that spot was. To nip, to suck, to—just how would she respond to his attentions in that sensitive bit of flesh? Before he could stop it, his hand moved to brush the hair aside. He had to force himself to retreat and covered the movement with an unneeded scratch to his side.

She set down the orange she'd been inspecting. "Well, I'm afraid I have a list of things to do today. And you know what? I could search all day and *amusing Cole Mitchell* would not be found there."

Saucy. What a challenge she could be. He doubted she could be tamed, and he wasn't sure he wanted her meek. Hell, he'd love to try anyway.

He moved behind her, planted one hand on either side of her. The fire that had been lit just by seeing her blazed higher. He had to touch her.

With controlled eagerness, he leaned closer. He fought off a groan as her curves molded against him until he was pressed flush along her back. Her body stilled so completely, he wondered if she could feel his heartbeat. Her skin was smooth and fresh, like she wasted the water to bathe every day.

A faint sheen to her skin betrayed the heat of the day, but he wanted to know it came from her reaction to him. He blew a short breath against her ear, grinning as her body twitched in sudden tension. Her fingers gripped the orange she'd been looking over. He leaned as close as possible to her ear. "You sure about that?"

She couldn't hide the tremble that ran through her entire body, he was too close to miss it. Silence lingered as her breath grew raspy. Clearing her throat didn't stop the husky whisper of her voice once she found it. "Yes. I'm certain."

He chuckled low and deep. This time when he spoke, he made sure his lips brushed along her ear. "What a shame."

The smallest squeak slipped from her lips. Her knuckles whitened around her basket.

"I was looking to keep amused today."

A long, shaky breath slid from between her tense lips. Her eyelids fluttered before closing as she took another slow breath. "You have plenty to keep you amused at your saloon, don't you?"

Then she did him in.

He had no one to blame but himself, either. He'd been the one to make sure he pinned her tight. His enjoyment over the way she fit against him left him ill-prepared for her retaliation. Yet here she was, the plump curve of her rear rubbing against him as she tried to move.

If she was looking for escape, he wasn't about to grant it. The thought of pinning her down and taking her in front of the whole town wasn't out of the question. The way she kept rubbing against him made it a definite possibility. Never had a woman made him ache like this with just a twitch of her ass.

Without realizing it, his own thoughts distracted him enough to relax. She took the opportunity to turn within the cramped space he'd granted her. She didn't try to escape. No, if anything, she now leaned into him.

Her hips pressed into his, her stomach curved into him with enough pressure he was sure he could feel the stays of her corset. While her hands sought purchase on the fruit display behind her, her breasts strained dangerously above the line of her bodice. Once she'd found claim with her hands, the soft swells pressed into his chest.

It was all he could do not to lean down and bite them.

Somehow his triumph became hers, and she knew it, too. The proof spread across those plump, pink lips in a smirk he knew all too well. "Far more willing women at that."

He licked his lips as he pondered assaulting hers. "You saying you ain't willing?"

Breathless, she could barely form the words. Her chest swelled and retreated with each bold attempt for air. The strain could be heard in every syllable. "Does it really matter to you?"

The words drew his attention back to her eyes. Did it matter? It sure did. If he got her, he wanted her willing, begging, but willing. He could tell she was, but he wanted her to admit it. He wanted to hear her say it.

Closing in on her lips, he nodded. Just a whisper away he stopped, and heard the unmistakable hitch of her breath when he did. "It matters."

"Jane Doe." The smug voice of Jackson Krenshaw shoved its way between them sure as a bucket of cold water could have. "I have been trying to get a moment with you for days."

The moment flew away, clear in the way her gaze hardened and her lips thinned. Cole cursed under his breath. The tension washed from Jane's body quicker than it had from his. Yet the woman made no move to squirm away from him.

Even though the bastard had walked up without any acknowledgment of the position they'd been in, without a whisper of apology, Jane managed to smile. It was only the grace of her smile that relaxed Cole enough to back up one little step.

On any given day the sight of Jackson would annoy Cole. On this particular day, at this particular moment, he had even less tolerance than normal. The man stood on thin ice. Cracked, thin as paper ice.

"You may call me Miss Doe." She kept a tone beyond polite, but distant. No hint of the usual sparkle or humor. At least none of the humor Cole knew so well. "As to getting a moment with me, I couldn't imagine what purpose you would have. What exactly is it you believe you can gain from me? I have no wealth, no status. I am under the impression that those are the sort of things you covet most."

"And I thought you were above listening to rumors and gossip." Jackson cut Cole a glare. "Then again, I thought you were above a great deal more than you seem to be."

Cole's fists clenched. He'd like nothing more than to beat the smug smile right off the bastard's face. A shift in Jane's stance stopped him from making a move. She pressed back into him, blocking his motion with her body. Of all the distractions worthy of stopping him, this one would work— at least for a moment.

Biggest problem being he now couldn't see her face. Without that advantage he couldn't gauge her real feelings against the pleasant tone she used. "Touché, Mr. Krenshaw."

Touché? What the hell did it mean?

"Rumors aside, why don't you tell me what you really want? I would enjoy being done with this foolish pretext." Jane took a step forward. The cool air she left behind didn't douse Cole's growing temper.

"Please, call me Jackson." Jackson took her hand, his smarmy lips pressed to the back of it. By rights, that was Cole's hand to kiss. Every inch of Jane's flesh was—wait. What in blazes was he thinking?

"Or you could call him Nancy." Cole stepped close to Jane again. Despite his attempts to stop it, the desire to claim her kept growing. He sure didn't want the likes of Jackson getting his greasy hands on her. "We all do."

She elbowed him in the ribs even as a soft chuckle reached his ears. She directed her soft murmur at him. "Be nice. You don't have enough wealth to truly insult him. He thinks you're beneath him."

"He thinks I'm beneath you." Cole chuckled. Jackson's face darkened to a shade of purple at their conversation, but Cole wasn't about to stop. It was far too much fun watching the snob squirm, and knowing Jane was at least responsive to the game, and him. "Not that I wouldn't mind being beneath you."

Her head turned just enough for him to spot the smile tugging on her lips. The pleasant flush to her cheeks spread down her neck. Then his glimpse of her reaction was gone as she turned her full attention back to Jackson. "Please be quick. I have things to do today."

"I've read Rusty's articles about your plight. I must say I've been rather moved by your situation." Despite his words, there was no sign of concern on the man's features. He looked more like a hunter stalking his prey.

"Obviously it hasn't moved you too far, for you're standing right in front of me." Jane wiped her hand on her skirt the moment Jackson released it. "I asked you to please be quick."

"Of course. I know you have little to call your own. You fell into this town with nothing. No home, no money, no means, not even a name." Jackson smiled, giving the air of a snake ready to strike. "I have a proposal that could ease some, if not all, of those ailments."

That got Cole's attention. What was the bastard planning? Jane had to know that Jackson was devious. In a heartbeat he fixed it so she no longer stood in front of him. In fact, he pushed her behind him. "Just what are you after, Jack?"

"I'm not after anything." Jackson shifted position for a more straight-on view of Jane. "I merely wish to help this fine young woman make a good start in our town."

Jane gripped Cole's arm, but he brushed her hand aside to jab his finger into Jackson's chest. "She don't want, or need, your kind of help."

Jackson smirked. "Now-now Cole. She hasn't even heard my proposal."

"She don't need to. You're up to no good. She's got brain enough to see that." Cole took a step forward. When Jane tried to slip around him, he easily maneuvered her back behind him. She needed to let him take the intimidation route, she wouldn't be able to scare the slime.

"If she's got a brain, let her decide. I'm certain she'd find my offer intriguing. It would certainly help her get her footing in this town."

Cole's shoulders tensed, his fists clenched tight. After another step toward Jackson, he snarled, "I told you. She ain't interested."

"Oh, really? You don't even know what my proposition is. Neither does she. Don't worry. You don't have to wrap your little brain around it, Cole. Let me handle things. You are beneath her. I've heard how intelligent she is. You couldn't hold a candle to her."

"I ain't beneath her yet. That'll come and so will she." Cole grinned at the twist of disgust on Jackson's face. The only detriment to his current amusement was the sudden stop in Jane's fight to get around him.

"You have no class, Cole Mitchell. What do you think you're going to do for her? Offer her a position in your saloon? Let her entertain the basest rank of humans that patronize your business? Maybe you'll let her become your special girl like Daisy?"

Cole's lip curled. He took a step closer. The insinuation he'd make a tough, strong, independent woman like Jane a whore was enough to make him raise his fists. "You saying I would make her a whore? Jane ain't no whore."

"Oh, so maybe you'd dare to keep her all to yourself?" Jackson stepped closer. "You think she's better than a whore—but not better than being the private whore of someone like you? You can offer her *nothing*."

"Cole, stop." Before Cole could punch the idiot, Jane shoved him hard. Somehow she'd forced her way between them and had one hand on either of their chests to hold them apart. "Stop."

Not that Jackson needed to be held back. He straightened his jacket like Cole had actually had the pleasure of beating on him.

For Cole it was only the fingers on his chest keeping him from acting on that desire. When it turned into both her hands flat against his chest, his fist dropped. The fact she wanted him to stop—it shouldn't have mattered, but it did.

"Miss Doe, I must apologize for his brutish and crass behavior."

"Don't you apologize for me." Cole raised his fist again, but Jane didn't move. Even when he bumped into her, she held her ground.

"If you would like to hear my offer, please stop by my office here in town tomorrow. Rest of the week I'll be out at my claim and wouldn't dare suggest you come to such a rough place. You are too much of a lady for that lot of men."

Cole didn't dare look down at Jane. No, he'd keep his eye on the toad in front of him. Sneaky, tricky, manipulating bastard.

"Perhaps, Mr. Krenshaw."

Shock ripped through him, dropping his fist back to his side. Jane's lips curved into a damned appealing smirk. Cole narrowed his eyes. She'd wanted his attention, that was all. She wouldn't actually go see him, would she?

"Glad to hear it. I promise you won't be disappointed." Jackson drew her away. Once again he pressed his lips to the back of her hand.

Cole grabbed her arm the second Jackson vacated the porch. He spun her toward him. "What in blazes are ya—"

His head whipped to the side, a harsh sting coursed through his cheek from the pure force she'd put into the slap. "I'm not interested in being the middle of a pissing contest over territory. I am *not* your property. Don't you *ever* presume to speak for me again, Cole Mitchell."

Glowering, he rubbed his cheek, unwilling to admit how much the blow stung. He set his jaw. No woman was daring enough to lay a hand on him, and he didn't like that she thought she could. All his former amusement had disappeared in her outburst. "Crazy bitch."

"Oh, please. You are such a presumptuous brute. I could have handled Mr. Krenshaw all on my little lonesome. I don't need to be protected from *you*. I certainly don't need to be protected from the likes of him."

"Look, Jane. I can—"

"Stop. I don't care." She fumed. The deep breaths she took in her anger made her chest strain against its restraint.

It served to distract Cole from the strength of his anger, and remind him of the other emotion he thrived on. Lust.

"I won't be spoken for by anyone. Most certainly not by you. At this point I don't even wish to see you." She snatched her basket, not removing her glare from him for a second. Then without another word, she stormed off down the street.

By rights he should be furious by her slap, and public dressing down, but he could only chuckle and shake his head. That was it. The fire. She may have been beat down and she may have even given into the grief, but she hadn't given up.

That's what made her different than so many other women. There was not one thing to pity about her.

The flounce of her bustle disappeared into the crowd, and he hopped down the steps to follow. His grin faded into a determined line. This time he wouldn't be interrupted. This time he would have his taste.

He got to the boarding house and stormed up the stairs. Inside her room a tantrum raged full bore. He couldn't help but grin when her books slammed down on the table, rattling the vase on top of it.

The moment she spotted him, he moved. It took four steps to get to her and another two until they slammed into the balcony door. Nothing short of a bullet to his brain would stop him from finally getting his kiss.

His hand slipped along the curve of her neck, caressing the flesh before yanking her closer. Claiming her, he plunged his tongue inside at her gasp. With practiced care sand skill, he searched the depths of her mouth.

She didn't tense beneath him, didn't fight or say no, thank whatever God still listened to him. Soft lips yielded to the pressure of his and her hands laced into his hair. Her moan coursed right through him to his toes. One arm wrapped around her waist to pull her pliant body flush against his.

He nibbled her smooth, supple lips. He reveled in the fact she tasted as sweet as she smelled. Within moments her tongue met his and they clashed together, fighting for dominance before he gave in and let her test the waters. Once she'd had her taste, their lips danced together as if they'd always known each other.

She shuddered against him, her low moan mingled into the kiss. Her body hung limp in his arms. She was all his and he enjoyed knowing it. His fingers buried in her hair, knocking pins free as his tongue kneaded hers until he'd drawn another moan from her.

He pulled back, letting out a mischievous chuckle. He brushed his thumb along her swollen lips, his eyebrow rising when she arched toward him. With no effort, he could take this further and she'd be oh-so-willing. The idea was tempting, but he didn't act on it. "Don't worry. I ain't gonna speak for you again. Not now that I know how to shut ya up."

Her body stilled and her eyes widened. Despite a good fight, a grin escaped after her gasp. "You egotistical, cocksure, presumptuous brute. Go on. Get out of here. Next time you wish to enter my domicile, knock."

Not fighting her playful shove, he let her push him from the room. Next time it would be at her invitation, he had no doubt. He winked as he leaned on the doorframe. "Ain't much fun if I knock first."

She slammed the door in his face.

Laughing, he lifted his hand and rapped on the door. Her spirit made this fun. More than a challenge, a game. One he would gladly play knowing where it would end.

"Go away, Cole."

"It ain't next time yet?" The girlish giggle that filtered from the room made him need to cover his mouth to hide his own laughter.

"No, Cole. It most certainly isn't."

"Shame."

"Goodbye, Cole."

*Let the devil catch you by a single hair,
and you are his forever.
-Gotthold Ephraim Lessing*

San Francisco

Clara lived.

But how?

When he'd last seen her riding off on the horse he'd stolen, she'd been on the brink of death. He cursed himself for not being diligent. He should have followed to make sure the task had been completed.

He dropped his gaze back to the article in the paper.

We found her near death. A miracle brought her back to life, but robbed her of her memory. If you are missing someone dear to you matching her description, you'll find her in Dominion Falls.

How she'd survived all the way to that wretched town, he had no idea. Their lack of knowledge over her origins were a blessing in disguise. There was one former denizen of the town that would know her origins.

It also proved her claims of amnesia could not be true. The fool. Such a simple game. She was smarter than that. He'd trained her better.

Now he'd have to defer from his current course. He had to finish the job. The one he'd started on that train.

She'd been compliant the whole ride. The change in her from the drugs made him wonder how long it would be until she'd be useful again, or if she ever would. As he studied her, her eyes lifted to him.

Desperation, the sweet sting of fear, made him smile.

"Who are you?"

"I have no name. Don't you remember?"

"No," she sobbed. "Who are you?"

"I have no name. But where we are going, you can call me Johnny."

"Who am I?"

"What did the doctor's tell you?"

"They said I was...someone else. They were wrong. It wasn't right. I don't remember...why don't I remember?"

He leaned forward. "Asylums do wondrous things to some, horrors to others. It appears you are bearing a horror. I'm sure it will fade with time."

"I shouldn't be here. Someone...someone is..."

"Looking for you? Of course they are. You're wanted for murder, my dear."

"No." A sob wrenched from deep in her belly, the wail filling the luggage car. Shaking her head, she tried to push herself to her feet. "I didn't...I couldn't kill..."

"Are you certain? You wanted him dead."

"Who? No. No, I wouldn't. Why are you doing this? Are you going to hurt me?"

"I saved you from the asylum."

"You are no savior."

"No. I'm not."

She flew at him, shrieking like a banshee.

She managed to dig her nails into his cheek before he backhanded her. When she stumbled, he grabbed her arm and threw her across the car.

Climbing over the bags she knocked over, he picked her up by her arm. "Don't worry. We'll make sure you find a new life. We do it often enough. Or if you want out…"

"If out means away from you, yes I do."

"Good." He didn't hesitate a second longer in dispensing her just punishment.

She fought back at every hit, every cut from his blade. With surprising ferocity for one so lost she managed to dodge some of his blows, while managing to make a few of her own.

Her cries filled the air as he got the upper hand. He had to let her suffer for all her failures. When the fight had gone from her and she lay in a pile of fabric, he slowed.

Her cornflower gaze fell on him, damp with tears. Bruised and bloodied arms raised in a pitiful display of protection. Her voice trembled in a weak whisper. "Please. Don't hurt me."

For a moment it was Constance, for a moment. Bloodied, broken, clinging to the lifeless child. Begging forgiveness. Not from him, but from God.

"Please. Who are you?"

He jolted back to the disgustingly weak vision before him. Dragging her by her hair to the end of the car, he slid open the door. He held her over the edge as tracks raced past below them. "Still want out? Or do you want to know the secret you've forgotten? You'll never find it this way."

Then she managed to startle him. Despite her wounds, she fought. In the end her efforts were in vain because in fighting off her attack, he shoved her off the train. She landed on the tracks and tumbled away.

Using as much care as he could, he leaped from the train. An injured wrist had been his reward, as had finding her still alive—staring at the sky.

He'd wasted precious time stealing a horse. By the time he'd gotten her deep into the mountains where her body wasn't likely to be found, it had been dark.

While he'd set up camp, it had started to rain. That's what woke her, he was sure of it now. She'd been awake when he'd gone to take his constitutional. Taking his horse, she'd disappeared into the dark.

He didn't bother to track her. The way her head had been split open, and the injuries he'd seen fit to deal had left her close to death. She wouldn't survive for long.

But she did. Clara lived.

He didn't believe the amnesia story one bit. Why else would she choose Dominion Falls? He wondered what possible gain she hoped for choosing that town. Did she hope someone would recognize her?

Not likely.

Perhaps she hoped her husband would return to where he'd once lived. That he could save her from her fate. Or that she could return to him what she stole from him.

Too late. She should have abandoned hope long ago. Now he knew she lived. He would see it through to its end this time. Its slow, torturous end.

Then she'd know. She'd watch everything she tried to protect destroyed right before her eyes. Yes, he'd finish what he started, and she'd regret her mistakes.

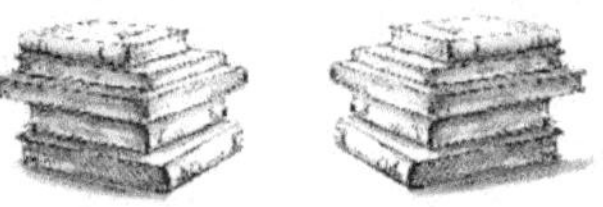

If you are out of trouble,
watch for danger.
-Sophocles

Dominion Falls

"I do think this will allow you to use all of your considerable skills, Miss Doe. I have heard so much about your way with people, what could be better?" Guy smiled way too bright. Triumphant. Annoying, but far less annoying than Jackson insinuating himself into the meeting.

"I'd like a chance to fully review this contract first. In case you slipped up on any grammar." Jane snatched the contract from his hands. "After all, we wouldn't want a simple mistake in grammar to somehow lead me to becoming a highly unwilling whore now, would we?"

"I would never make such a mistake, my dear."

"Do not call me that. I'm not your *dear*. Miss Doe will work fine." Jane pursed her lips. Simply being called 'my dear' sent shivers down her spine for reasons she couldn't explain.

"Once you sign it, you will have a job…and this." The pouch Guy dropped onto the desk hit with a heavy thump. "Your loan of three hundred dollars. As specified, you'll pay back over time with interest, of course."

"I believe we specified 1.8% not 2.3." Jane flipped to the next page. As she read, her frown deepened. "And this conflict of interest clause? Do you truly believe you can dictate who I make time with? Because if you do, this will never work. Strike it."

Guy turned such a bright shade of red; Jane both found it comical and worrisome. Jackson couldn't keep his laughter silent behind the angry hotel owner. Guy pursed his lips. "I can't have you giving the services I pay you for freely to Cole."

"What I am doing with Cole has nothing to do with you, this hotel, or his saloon. That is simply pleasure, friendship, and quite frankly, none of your business." Jane sighed and read further, ignoring whatever blubbering he kept on with. "This breach of contract clause? You gave yourself an out, but I don't have the same privilege."

"Well, you are a woman."

"And a fair bit more intelligent than you if you thought I'd let any of this slip. Including this paragraph about repaying my loan with *other* services should my hotel management not increase your business? There is no way on earth I will ever be a whore, not for you, not for anyone. I am my own woman, and belong to no man." She shoved the paper back across the desk. "Fix it."

"At least not a paid whore," Jackson murmured.

"Why exactly are you here, Mr. Krenshaw? If it's to insult me, you are doing a stellar job. If it's to prove you are an ass, you're doing even better." She rose. "Guy, I expect you to fix every point of contention on that contract. Only then will I sign it."

"Wait a moment." Jackson set a hand on her arm. The simple motion made her cringe in disgust. "I have a proposal."

"You already made your proposal. Two weeks ago. I found your offer offensive and obtrusive. A marriage of convenience. Yours, not mine. No thank you." Jane tugged her arm free of his slimy grasp. "Good day."

"This is different." Jackson held out the chair she'd just vacated. "Please."

His pleasant demeanor didn't fool her for a second, but she still sat. After all, curiosity ran too rampant through her soul to not hear him out. "Please be quick."

"I'm certain, clever as you are, you're aware of the aspirations I have for this town, not to mention this territory." Jackson perched on the edge of Guy's desk. His smug smile had returned. "Guy has similar ambitions, if smaller in scale."

Jane bit down on her cheeks. It took a lot of effort to keep back the biting words similar to those she'd spewed at the man just two weeks ago. Then he'd dared to suggest marriage, on the premise of securing her station in the town. This time it seemed his aspirations were quite different. Once she could control her tongue, she forced a smile. "Of course. You want power. Pure and simple. Government for the town. Statehood for the territory. And a shiny throne for you to rule over all."

This time Guy was the one who couldn't control his laughter.

Jackson's smug smirk twitched, a clear struggle to maintain his pleasant demeanor. "That isn't quite what I mean."

"Of course not. I apologize." She folded her hands in her lap, blinking expectantly. "Please, do go on."

"With my plans I could, in fact, attain a position by helping all you described to happen. Of course, I'm not the only one, but I'm certain my plans will see fruition." Jackson's face softened, almost euphoric at the mention of the power he wanted. "Steps are already being taken toward statehood, after all. This town needs a government so its leaders can be at the front of that movement."

"I still do not understand what this has to do with me." Jane fought the urge to fidget her way right out of the room.

"I'm sure your quick mind hasn't missed the questions I've been asking you." Guy managed to get a word in with Jackson lost in the bliss of imagined power. "All politically minded, all related to this town."

Of course she'd noticed, she'd have to be a fool not to. She wouldn't acknowledge it yet. First she wanted them to admit what they wanted.

"You've got a good head for politics. It's also clear how much this town has embraced you despite your scandalous reputation." Guy smirked. "We'd like to benefit from your knowledge and…people skills."

"I want more money." Jane didn't consider greed one of her vices. In fact, her current salary would be more than generous for the simple life she'd managed to establish, even with her admiration of fine clothes. Still, these men understood money first, people second. Plus, she'd never help either of them without something in return for the trouble of dealing with them.

"You're already receiving thirty dollars a week." Guy straightened, his eyes narrowed. "That's an incredibly generous salary, all things considered."

"If you expect me to help the likes of you two become more palatable to the people of this town, I expect to be paid more. That job alone is worth three hundred a month, just to put up with Jackson." Jane pursed her lips and gave Jackson a cold look. "Although, I certainly cannot make promises that I'll succeed. Some things are beyond help."

"I'll cover another twenty dollars a week. If you succeed." Jackson had emerged from his reverie more cocksure than ever. "So long as you succeed."

"No. No stipulations, and the money comes from Guy. If you pay him and then he pays me, fine. My contract is with Guy alone. Not the Silver Saddle, and not with you. I'm not certain I could ever help you." Jane kept her smile pleasant as possible. "Even miners know a snake when they see one."

Guy leaned back, his hands folded across his stomach. He studied her in complete silence. Jackson's sputtering attempt at a guffaw didn't faze him. "Ten more a week. If you do well, I'll raise it. I can only promise ten for now. Dr. Stone just arrived today and I have to pay his salary as well."

Jane stood. "Put that in the contract. We'll set a two-month review on the raise?"

"That's acceptable." Guy rose and shook her hand. "Give me a few hours to have this fixed. We'll meet at say three o'clock?"

For a moment Jane thought Guy might be likable under his attitude. Perhaps working as a manager at his hotel wouldn't be so horrible, after all. No, she had to be fooling herself. At least it was a job so she could pay her own way for a change. She shook his hand without a smile. "Three o'clock. Good day, gentlemen."

Before Jackson could add anything else, she darted from the room. She'd made sure her contract was with Guy alone for a reason. He seemed far more the reasonable one of the two. Of course, that's probably why Jackson had not shown up until today.

She wouldn't allow Jackson to use Guy as a tool to get to her. Her ties would remain solely to Guy. Not to a hotel Jackson could buy and if Guy reneged, she would have her out.

"Where ya going?" Cole's voice broke through her thoughts.

"I have an appointment." Just the sound of his voice made her lips tingle in anticipation. Since that first kiss, she'd had the pleasure of several more knee-wobbling kisses. She had to admit she'd enjoyed them even more than she'd imagined. It made her wonder just how much she'd enjoy furthering their relationship.

A nudge to her ribs startled her from her thoughts. Shaking her head, she turned her attention back to Cole. "I'm sorry, what?"

The warm rush of a blush flooded her cheeks at his knowing grin. He squeezed her elbow. "I said I thought you already came from a meetin'."

"I did, but I have plans to meet with Major Webb for lunch."

"Didn't know that."

"Too bad." The frustration creasing his features pleased her. At least allowing the kisses hadn't lessened his attentions as of yet. Shrugging, she turned her gaze back to the front as they continued down the middle of the street.

"Any particular reason you're leading him on?"

"What makes you think I'm leading him on?" She struggled to keep her lips from turning into a smile. His consternation, and perhaps jealousy, kept her giddier than she should've been.

"Well you are. Aren't ya?" Cole pulled her to the side of the road as a wagon approached.

"Major Webb is fully aware of what I expect out of our relationship. I have no secrets." She tilted her head to meet his gaze straight on. "Are you still jealous/"

"You bedded him yet?"

"No." Hands on her hips, she lifted her chin in defiance. "I haven't even been to bed with you and you are in my room at all sorts of inappropriate hours."

"And you're at the army camp at inappropriate hours too."

"So you are jealous. Good to know."

He narrowed his eyes; his fists clenched so tight the muscles of his arms showed through his sleeves. A harrumph redirected her attention back to his frowning lips. "Wonder if you've always been this difficult."

"Long as I can remember." The laughter she'd held back escaped, and brightened when Cole joined her within moments. She stepped closer. "Rest assured that I don't know Al quite as well as I do you."

"So the pansy ain't kissed ya yet?"

Jane's laughter faded and she pursed her lips. "Must you always be such a brute?"

"Looks that way."

"Why?"

"Told ya."

"You have a reputation to maintain. Right." She tugged the edge of her bodice straight and turned away.

"Jane." The full length of him pressed into her back, his hands grasping her elbows in a firm but gentle hold. "I don't know how."

"How to what?" She remained still during his silence to give him time to come up with anything. Part of her hoped he'd admit his weakness, the rest of her feared he'd retaliate with a sarcastic answer. No answer came, which comforted her fear enough for her to relax back against him. She set her hand on his. "I noticed."

"Whores are all I know."

"Somehow I doubt that, but I'll accept it for now." She tried to step out of his embrace, but he held her firm. "Yes?"

"You're complicating things." His voice held a gruff note. "I'm used to simple."

Jane laughed. It only took a gentle tug to pull herself free and spin around. "I thought you enjoyed a challenge."

"I thought I did too." Cole's lips drew into a wicked grin. "You and your damn words are making me think I could do without."

"You'd be rather bored, and you know it." She laced her arm through his. "Now let's go before you make me late."

"Maybe I was hoping you'd skip lunch."

"Sorry to dash your hopes." She nodded as greetings came their way, responding back to them all with a smile.

After she'd stopped long enough to inquire after one of the passing miner's children, she grinned up at Cole's furrowed brow. "What?"

"How do you know Miller?"

"I talk to people, Cole. Have you ever tried it?"

"Not much." He winked at her laugh. "There anyone in town you don't know?"

"I'm not certain. I believe there are a few that never leave their homes that I haven't had a chance to meet. Why?"

"No reason."

She shrugged, slowing their pace. Not for the first time in recent weeks, she felt drawn to the gun vendor. Despite her lateness for lunch, she moved close to the cart to peruse Zeb's wares.

Cole followed. "What is it?"

"Just looking." She moved closer to examine a particular weapon on display.

"Cole. Looking for a new weapon?"

"No. Perfectly happy with my Walker." Cole patted his side arm. He nodded to Jane. "She's the one looking, Zeb."

"Oh, little lady. You got good taste, but that Remington ain't right for a lady to have." Zeb leaned on the cart. "Too powerful. You'd never be able to handle it."

Jane snapped her head up to glare at the presumptuous man. "Why on earth would you say that, Zebediah? What do you presume I would be able to handle?"

"These here." Zeb pulled out a tray and set it on top of the cart. "The Derringer is perfect for a little lady like you."

"They're puny." Jane scanned the miniscule guns in disgust before turning her gaze back to the Remington.

"Made for a lady's delicate hands." Zeb pushed the tray forward. "If ya want a weapon, it's your best bet. Easy to handle and still kills well enough."

"If you're at point blank range," she muttered. "No thank you, Zeb."

Cole shook his head. "He's right, Jane. An 1858 ain't easy to handle."

"Says the man with a Walker Colt hanging from his hip." Jane rolled her eyes and turned away, heading down the street again.

"So ya like my gun?"

Stopping short, she gasped when he bumped into her. She smirked at the wicked thought crossed her mind. Not one to let propriety stop her, she voiced the wickedness. "How would I know? I've never touched it."

His laughter followed her all the way up the steps to Turner's. Lunch with Al was brief, but proved amusing. He spoke of his childhood in South Carolina, and the sort of pranks he and his cousins played. Once the meal had concluded, he kissed the back of her hand and asked her for a walk later that evening.

After she'd agreed, she started down the familiar path to the library. Halfway down the street she hesitated. The hair on the back of her neck stood on end. The sensation that someone followed her stirred her belly into nervous jumping so quick she spun around. No one stood out, but a shiver ran down her spine nonetheless.

She shook off the sensation and finished her journey to the library. Inside she chose some books, then left to get back to the boarding house.

She hadn't made it two steps when someone barreled into her. A twinge shot through her wrist when she hit the ground. Her books scattered amidst a nearby thump and male grunt. Clearly she wasn't the only one caught off guard.

Sitting up, she rubbed her aching wrist. "Sorry. I wasn't watching where I was going."

The cowboy pushed his hat back. "Ain't a problem. I wasn't watching neither."

"Still. I am sorry."

"You're the one cradling your wrist. Need to get to the doc?" He helped her to her feet, studying her with an intense gaze. His cold smile didn't reach his brown eyes at all. Long stringy brown hair settled around his shoulders under a large Stetson. The smile he offered felt off to the smell and filth covering him, for his teeth weren't rotted like one would expect.

"No. I just landed hard, and I still say it was my own fault." Every muscle in her body tensed. She wanted to run, but didn't know why. No man she'd met made her feel so uneasy. Not until him. Rather than keep facing the eerie feeling, she bent to gather her scattered books.

"Ain't no one's fault but fate." He tipped his hat. "At least let me buy ya a cup of coffee for your trouble."

His eyes were piercing. The weight of his stare accused her of something. What, she didn't know. A stirring of fear settled in the pit of her stomach.

She felt compelled to say yes, as if saying no would cause trouble.

A nod formed before she could force out the smile that eventually followed. The smile seemed as necessary as going with him. "I think I can handle that. But if you buy me coffee, I should buy you one. After all, it was half my fault."

He laughed. "Sounds fair."

"By the way, my name is Jane…and you are?"

"Just call me Johnny."

Farewell happy fields where joy forever dwells:
Hail horors, hail.
—John Milton

"I don't believe you."

Johnny's laughter filled her stunned silence. Throughout the conversation he'd been too pleasant, too quick with a smile. Like he was trying to placate her into liking him, into trusting him. "Why not?"

"The stories you tell, they are too fantastical. Too much so to be true," she finally said.

"Haven't you heard that truth is always strange?"

"Of course. Lord Byron said 'For truth is always strange; stranger than fiction'." The anger that creased his brow at her citation didn't help Jane's mood. That anger kept appearing between his too-quick laughter and smiles; burgeoning up like an air bubble in a muddy hot spring. The longer she sat there, the more uneasy she became.

"Exactly. And my stories ain't more unbelievable than yours. Forgetting everything but how to function? Don't seem possible."

"I wish it was a lie." The familiar churning of disquiet welled within her. She ran her finger along the rim of her metal cup as she tried to push it back. With a deep breath, she took another sip of coffee, once again finding his eyes piercing through her. Anger hardened his features, but in the blink of an eye he smiled with a warmth that almost erased her fear. Almost.

"Why would you wish that?"

"Because none of this is easy. Having nothing. No sense of self. Not knowing if you have friends or family that miss you. Being surrounded by strangers."

"Some people might prefer to live that way."

"Intentionally? Well, why on earth would they?"

"No ties holding them back. Some of the more devious might see it as a way to get away with things they wouldn't otherwise."

Her mouth went dry when he leaned toward her and she struggled to make sense of his logic. "It makes no sense to me."

His hand shot out to grasp hers tight, pulling it closer. Dark eye leveled at hers. "Ain't everyone led a privileged life. Some wanna escape. Some prefer to be unknown. Free. Able to do as they please without repercussion. Don't you think?"

In a flash he grinned again, releasing her hand. She pulled it back to rub the feeling away. "If that's true, then they're fools. Having had memories and a life ripped forcibly from me, I can't imagine entering such a state willingly. Now I must go."

"Now-now, my dear. Ain't I allowed to disagree?" The intensity of his stare burned along her skin, making her shudder inwardly.

Shifting uncomfortably, she edged her chair backward as he leaned closer. Her unease grew with every moment. "Disagreement aside, I really must—"

"Jane," Jackson interrupted. When he spotted Johnny at the table, he stopped. "My apologies. I didn't know someone was with you."

She had never been so relieved to hear Jackson's voice. She flew to her feet and smiled so bright Jackson's eyes widened with surprise. "Mr. Krenshaw. No apology necessary. What did you need?"

"I just wanted to tell you Guy's waiting for you. Said he finished up the changes early." Jackson extended his hand. "Shall I walk you there?"

"No. I can walk myself. Thank you, Mr. Krenshaw. Good day." She couldn't manage a nod to the stranger. Pressure settled down hard on her heart, threatening to burst her chest wide open.

The man was a stranger, but every instinct told her to run, and run fast. So she did, bursting from the general store and racing toward the Silver Saddle. Could she have known him once? Before she forgot everything? If so, why didn't he say anything? Could he be the one who'd tried to kill her?

"Jane?" Guy interrupted her dark thoughts, and a tight grip on her arm pulled her back to reality. How had she gotten to his office so quick? "Are you all right?"

"Yes. I'm sorry. You finished the contracts?"

"Of course. I wanted to speak with you about something."

"Can it wait?" Jane forced her hands still, gripping the contract tight. If he hadn't fixed the issues, she couldn't tell. Her mind struggled to form a coherent thought. "I just want to sign this and get back home. We can discuss particulars tomorrow."

"As you wish."

Jane signed the papers and grabbed the pouch Guy handed her. Without another word, she darted from his office. She had to get away. She had to hide. There was nowhere to go but her room, so she clamored up the steps of the boarding house. She slammed the door and locked it tight, not wishing to be disturbed for anything. Certainly not by the cowboy.

She gripped the back of a chair to still her shaking hands. Why had the man made her so uneasy? With the exception of the renegades, no man had made her feel such discomfort. Certainly no man had caused such a terrified reaction. Not even Jackson and Guy—they simply annoyed her to no end.

This man. This Johnny. His behavior unsettled her more than the town idiot who walked around all day carrying a rotten orange like it was a baby. She didn't know what to make of it, but she didn't like it. Taking a deep breath she told herself she could handle it, push through it like she always did. She simply needed a few minutes to collect herself.

Cole had left a bottle of whiskey behind on her table. She rushed toward it and downed a glass as fast as possible. Nerves left her wanting to pace, but she slipped out onto the balcony hoping some fresh air would ease her soul.

With a deep breath, she tried to will away her churning stomach. She couldn't shake the sensation that something was terribly wrong and if she thought hard enough she'd know precisely what it was. A trickle of moisture slid along her cheek and she swiped at the senseless tear in anger.

She turned her gaze toward the saloon in hopes of spotting Cole; perhaps he could help, or at least distract her. Instead her heart twisted to find Johnny staring right at her from the saloon porch. She lost control of her limbs. They stumbled back without her order. Spinning, she raced into her room and slammed the door, locking it as well.

She tried to explain away the terror that filled her, but logic gave her nothing. No reason for a stranger to illicit such a base reaction. None of it made sense.

At that moment nothing made sense.

The pressure on her chest grew, pounding up into her head. Sleep wouldn't come easy, if at all. Too many questions, too many fears.

I have, indeed, no abhorrence of danger,
except in its absolute effect-
in terror.
-Edgar Allen Poe

Sleep evaded her.

All night Jane had lain awake. She'd turned away Al when he'd arrived for their walk. In the middle of the night she'd even ignored Cole's tapping on her door.

Her reward for such a denial had been the sight of him draped over Daisy like a wet blanket. It was immature and if she'd been of sound mind she might have gone over and said so.

Instead, she'd run like a scared child when Johnny had stepped from the shadows.

The panic still had no logical justification, but struck deep in her heart. Without any further regard to Cole she'd run all the way to the Silver Saddle.

Now she only wanted to eat, but had to start her first day of work. The lack of sleep and lack of eating left her grouchy and intolerant of Guy. She was able to partly pull it together enough to be civil to the other employees and customers, but by lunch she was starved.

She didn't cook or enjoy taking meals with Martha, which left only the tavern and Cora's to get a decent meal. Her stomach growled so loud she could deny it no longer. She could only hope the strange cowboy wouldn't be there to distract her from her food.

"Afternoon, Lady Jane."

"Mr. Hamm." She never could stop her smile at the man's voice. Jane couldn't help but like the dear old man. Despite his propensity for drinking, he'd been nothing but kind to her.

Once upon a time he'd been a miner, but now did most of the carpentry around town. Not that he'd ever been good at mining, but he shone at carpentry. He grinned his gap-toothed grin. "Cora's got chicken and dumplings today. Hope you're hungry."

"Starved, Mr. Hamm. Starved." Jane gave his shoulder a squeeze, hopping up the stairs far more relaxed. At least for all of ten seconds.

A long, loud series of yips and whoops froze her in place. She recognized the Indian yells from the last attack in no time.

Run. She should run. Just a few feet into Turner's. She shouldn't look toward the sound.

A crack sounded so close her ears popped. Sharp needles of pain buried into her cheek. The wood porch post beside her had splintered at the impact of a bullet. The bullet had come close. Way too close. Time to run.

Run now.

Why wouldn't her feet listen?

The stream of horses pouring over the rise thinned, but the red men were now just feet away. She couldn't not see them. Or make the image of cold eyes, black streaks, and a bright red star fade from her sight.

Her feet ignored her commands. They refused to carry her away from the screams of her friends as they ducked for cover, or away from the overwhelming scent of gunpowder. Even as the gun barrel swung toward her and time itself slowed, her feet wouldn't move.

"Jane." Kelly's shout burst through the loud buzz of fear in her own mind.

It got her feet moving. She turned toward the store, made it one step. Fire ripped through her ribs and arm. A second impact took her the rest of the way to the porch. This one was a human, the weight of a full grown man pushed her flat to the porch, yelling for her to stay down.

An instant after they hit the porch, Kelly's weight disappeared. His shout was just another echo into the cacophony around her.

The rising shriek never escaped. A second crack of gunfire sent another shockwave of terror through her. A third brought Kelly's weight back on top of her. A warm, wet tickle ran along the back of her neck, her arm.

Blood trickled into her vision, dripping from her arm onto the porch. The unmistakable scream of Cora let her know whose blood. Kelly's.

A sob wrenched up from deep within, making the almost forgotten pain burst forth from her ribs. With a gasp, she tried to move, but the weight of Kelly was too much. She'd gone from being unable to move out of terror to being pinned by the weight of her own foolish fear.

The heat of her wounds increased until her whole body trembled. Yells and screams echoed around her, Cora's loud cries were accompanied by Graham's surprisingly kind words of support and concern.

A touch to her back let her know they weren't ignoring her. Not that it mattered. She knew Kelly was dead.

Someone poked her wound. Her whole body jerked in response. A scream wrenched out from her gut.

"Easy, Janey." Graham pulled at the fabric around the wounds, not stopping when she shrieked and cried. "You got a lot of buckshot in here. Want me to get that fancy new doc Guy brought in?"

"No." She tried to move through the pain and push herself onto her good arm. Pain slowed her movements and the trembling wouldn't stop. Her voice shook, but she had to keep moving. She was alive. She couldn't waste that. "Daisy."

"Lady Jane." Hammy's voice bullied over the cacophony. "You dead?"

She couldn't help her weak laughter. "No."

"I'll get Cole for ya."

"No, Ham—"

"He's already gone. Moves fast for an old drunk." Graham chuckled. "Leastwise this time I know you aren't dead. Gotta check the other wounded. We'll send a wagon for you to get back to the saloon."

Jane nodded, unwilling to let anyone know how weak she was. The world spun, growing fuzzy in front of her eyes. Somehow she'd gotten herself to a sitting position and now regretted it rather thoroughly. When she passed out she could end up falling right down the steps.

"Jane."

Cole's smooth voice broke through the comedic mental image of her own eventual topple down the stairs. She grinned when she turned toward him, and tried to blink through the black haze filling her vision. "Cole...I need...Daisy..."

"Aw, hell Jane. You froze again, didn't you?"

"No. Yes. I moved—guns fast, me slow." Her body drooped without her permission. Cole's curse hit her ears as his strong hand caught her under her back. She whimpered. "It's my fault. I didn't move. Kelly tried to help me. He tried. All my fault."

"Wagon's on its way, Jane."

"He tried to help stupid, scared me," she whispered. Bloody hands shook in her lap. "So sorry. I'm so sorry."

"Jane," his subdued tone cut under the continuing shouts around them. Somehow the silky timbre calmed her internal panic. "It ain't your fault. The damn Indians did this."

"He had a star."

"What?"

The smile she wore didn't fit. Why couldn't she stop smiling? "The Indian...he had a star. Right...there." Her finger poked into his cheek, leaving a stain of blood behind.

His frown deepened. "Ya sure, Jane?"

"Yup. I was frozen, remember? He had a star—red star. Red..."

"Jane."

"The cowboy's scary."

"Jane." His hand brushed gently across her cheek. "Keep talking."

"So tired."

"Jane."

Her head dropped back and her eyes fluttered closed. A shudder ran through her body as she gave into the pain.

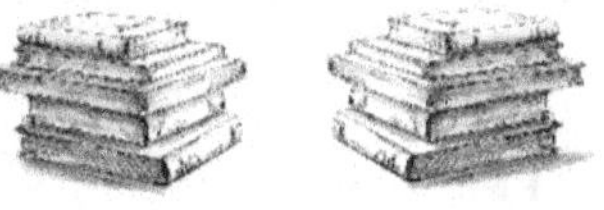

Spirit has fifty times the strength and staying-power of brawn and muscle.
—Mark Twain

Cole kept tight hold of Jane's hand as the wagon came to an abrupt stop in front of the saloon. Worry held his focus so strongly that he only had a passing thought of how his concern might seem to others.

He'd already seen Jane close to death once, he didn't care to see it again. Her features seemed so pale with the streaks of blood across her cheeks.

Whether it was her blood or Kelly's, he had no idea. Panic stirred him into motion. He gathered her close in his arms, leaping down from the wagon.

Jane groaned at the impact, sending a flood of relief through him. She wasn't dead yet.

He rushed into the saloon to find chaos everywhere. Wounded were being brought in, laid across tables, in the downstairs rooms.

Daisy barked orders to those helping. She spotted Cole and strode toward him, calling out more orders with every step. "Set her down."

Cole dropped Jane's rump on the table, keeping her pressed to his chest while Daisy examined her. "She got shot."

"Buckshot. A fair good deal of it. She'll have to wait."

He all but snarled at her. "What?"

"There are people with more grievous injuries that need surgery. They come first." She glanced toward the door. "You can remove the buckshot. You've done it before."

"Give me some of that sleeping stuff."

Her features twisted in a grimace before she met his gaze. "I'm running low. Supply wagon is weeks late because of the raids. I gotta save it for the surgeries."

"Ya want me to put her through that pain?"

"Sorry. Get the supplies off the table. I need to tend to Miller, excuse me."

Cole's gaze followed her path through the saloon to the man she'd mentioned. Miller had a good chunk out of his cheek. With a sigh, Cole turned his attention back to Jane. He hefted her back in his arms, calling for the barber, Lucky.

Lucky glanced up from his stitching. "What?"

"You gotta get the buckshot outta her."

"He's helping me with surgery, him and Graham. Do it yourself." Daisy breezed past him to the table laden with tools. She grabbed several quickly and dropped them on top of Jane where she hung in his arms. "Could use your help when you're done with her, too."

Cole glared at her, but she'd already turned away to bark more orders. With no other choice, he scanned the bustling bar. Most of the wounded were downstairs, he assumed the worst were in the rooms across from the bar for surgery.

He adjusted his hold on Jane before heading for the stairs. He took her to the room beside his, gingerly setting her on the bed. She groaned again as he set her on her back.

"Sorry. Gotta get this stuff off ya first." He gathered the stack of muslin, tweezers, scalpel, a perfume bottle that held whatever Daisy used to make stuff clean, and another tool with a brutally sharp point on the end.

Jane offered him no reply, but her eyes fluttered open.

"Hey. We gotta get the buckshot outta you. It ain't gonna feel good."

For the briefest moment the familiar spark of fire lit her eyes as her lip quirked. "It won't?"

"I got no chloroform. Daisy's near-out, and wagon's been delayed because of the raids."

Her eyes widened, a hint of worry making them shimmer.

"I'll get ya some whiskey to help." Without thinking about it, he kissed her temple on his way to his feet. In his room he grabbed all three bottles on his shelf. He didn't figure Jane was the only one that would need a drink after this.

He carried them back to the room she lay in to find her already passed back out. Once he'd set aside the whiskey, he pulled her to sit so he could strip her down.

Easy as ever he got her stripped down to her corset, but there he got stuck. Though he popped the busk open easy enough, his fingers shook with each small whimper of pain from her. With her corset laced so tight he couldn't release the knot for nothing. Finally he used the knife in his boot to cut her free.

She gasped, her eyes flying open when the fabric tugged away from her flesh.

"Can ya lift your arms?"

Her skin paled, but she offered a weak nod. Slowly her arms raised, her features drawn. Somehow she kept silent, releasing a shaky breath as she lowered them the second her chemise was off.

Cole helped her lie down on her stomach. Her face turned toward him, streaks of blood from Kelly still stained across her pale cheek. "Want some whiskey?"

She shook her head weakly. "Just do it."

"Let me do one before ya say that." He moved her arm up and took the step to wrap her fingers around the bar of the footboard. "Hold on."

She didn't argue a lick, her fingers tightening around the bar with all the strength he imagined she could muster. He sprayed the starburst of a wound with the spray Daisy had given him.

Right at the dark center of the wound several small balls sat near the surface. He plucked at them with the pointed tool. Jane flinched but didn't cry out while they came loose.

He got to a deeply embedded ball and hesitated. A glance told him she watched him carefully. Despite the pain streaking her face, leaving her ashen, her eyes were sharp as ever.

All he could do was mutter a quick sorry before he tried to pry the small ball free from her flesh. Her whole body reacted this time, and the ball slipped away when she contracted away from him.

Every inch of him wanted to walk away right then, let someone else deal with this. He couldn't watch her like this.

Still, he remained, knowing she'd hate any other but Daisy to manage it. With clenched teeth, he prepared for another go. "I didn't get it."

Her hand clamped over his wrist before he could make contact. "Jane. We gotta get it out or you'll get infected."

"I know. Give me a moment, and something to bite on. They don't need my screams downstairs."

Cole couldn't stop his double take at her words. He met her gaze quietly. Pain etched across her features, but she still had a stubborn resolve. "Whiskey?"

"Yes." She let him help her sit. While she chugged the bottle of whiskey he'd handed her, he slipped off his weapons.

He slid the belt free of the holsters and set aside the guns. She took the belt he handed her in one hand, continuing to suck on the bottle of whiskey. On a normal day he'd tell her to slow down, but for once he wished she'd make herself numb with the drink.

The bottle nearly empty, she wiped her mouth. Once again she accepted his help to get back to lying on her stomach. The belt ready for her to bite on near her mouth. "I believe I'm ready."

"You gotta try to not move."

"I'll try. You be fast as you can."

"I'll do my best." Once she had slipped the belt between her teeth and taken hold of the bed, Cole turned his attention back to the wound.

Quick as he could he worked, digging ball after ball out of first her side, and then the small smattering that had met her arm. She passed out from the pain within a few minutes, only to jerk awake occasionally when he really had to dig. At those points her features would twist in horrible grimaces of pain.

Not once did she scream, and he couldn't deny how impressed he was by that. Especially with the torture he had to be inflicting on her.

When he finally finished, he wrapped her careful as possible so as to not wake her. He knelt beside her, brushing some curls off her temple. Her breathing was shallow, and she didn't stir at his touch.

He pressed another kiss to her temple before taking the time to redress her in the chemise. After he'd wrapped her in the blanket from the bed, he picked her up. He'd take her to her own bed to recover, visit as soon as he could.

Only problem is he needed someone to keep an eye on her and monitor her healing. Daisy would be busy, and therefore so would the saloon.

On his way across the floor, the perfect solution came upon him. One man was nuts enough about Jane to make certain she did well, but wouldn't do a thing to harm her or touch her. "Hammy! Follow me."

"You bet." The old man hopped into step behind him without one question.

"I need you to do me a favor, Hammy." Cole kicked open Martha's front door without ceremony, heading for the stairs. "Really, the favor is for Jane."

"Anything for the lady, Cole. Ya know that."

"I do. That's why I'm asking you."

A mixture of admiration and pity is one of
the surest recipes for affection.
–Arthur Helps

Unbelievable.

Three days ago Jane had been peppered with buckshot. After the messy job he'd done ridding her of it, Jane had to be in a lot of pain.

But there she stood, hovering at the edge of the large crowd gathered in the cemetery. She kept away from the mourners but didn't avoid the funeral all together. Cole knew she blamed herself for Kelly's death. Yet Kelly was the one that stupidly chose to yell at the Indian rather than take cover.

Then again, if Jane's ramblings held true, Kelly did so with what he probably thought was good reason. The red star on the Indian's cheek was Starbird's war paint. Kelly probably figured he could yell at his friend. His friend would never shoot him.

He'd been wrong. Dead wrong.

Cole hadn't seen Jane in the three days since the attack. Despite the new doc in town, his saloon still looked like a hospital. The injuries this time had been far worse. Twenty injured townspeople had crammed into his saloon, and there were three dead that had been getting dressed up at Graham's place.

Unfortunately that meant Cole was the only one tending bar, and maintaining order at the makeshift hospital his saloon had become. Time had been something he had none of.

In his stead he'd had Hammy help him out. The old man was crazy for Jane. Cole knew she'd be safe while he tended to his saloon and helped Daisy.

Hammy didn't disappoint. He called on a woman in the north settlement to come sit with Jane. Mrs. Broder took up the task along with her little girl Lizzie. They saw to her wounds and tended her needs, and made sure Jane was well. All their reports passed to Hammy and then on to him every few hours.

Cole wanted to check on her himself at least once. It just hadn't been in the cards. By all reports she was very sore, her mood dismal.

Now as he approached he didn't know what to make of the rising sense of relief. He'd be able to see her for himself. To touch her again. To do what it took to make sure she knew it wasn't her fault they were at a funeral.

Comfort. Once again, he wanted to comfort her.

The woman drove him mad. She riled up things best left buried, like emotions. She burrowed under his skin, pissed him off, challenged everything he said and did—yet drew him closer with every conflicting minute.

A weaker man would say it was more than the chase. But he was anything but a coward. He stopped being weak years ago. One sharp blade forced an end to that.

He shook his head from the memory and moved closer. All he wanted to see was if she finally faltered. He knew he had to see something to pity like he always did in women. So many were broken—she couldn't be different.

If she was—but she couldn't be—but if she was…he'd be in real trouble. He'd be damned if he wasn't already.

Just two steps away she swayed and a soft gasp reached his ears.

Instead of triumph over her weakness, he worried for her. He set his hands on her shoulders. In one gentle motion she leaned back against him. She didn't hesitate one second. Had she known it was him?

Her entire body relaxed and his own did the same.

"I didn't need a nursemaid." In deference to the funeral, she kept her voice soft. Not a head turned their direction.

"Daisy's orders, not mine."

"Liar. Daisy wouldn't have sent Mr. Hamm." True enough. The woman knew she had him nailed. Her hand rose along her bandaged arm until her fingers brushed his. He caught her hand and lowered them both to sit at her waist.

"So Daisy wanted you watched. I picked who."

"Mr. Hamm?"

"Old coot's nuts about you, but he ain't gonna try nothing. Figured he was safe enough while I was busy."

Her soft hum of reply soothed him. Even though he couldn't see her face, he imagined she wore the wicked smile he knew so well.

Quiet fell between them for the rest of the short service. By the end of the funeral all her support came from him, her legs barely seemed able to stand firm. How she held on in such pain he didn't know.

He leaned down to speak low in her ear, once again offering comfort he wouldn't have bothered to offer anyone else. "It ain't your fault. You gotta know that."

"It certainly feels that way." Tension returned to her body, but she still leaned into him. Her fingers tightened around his. "If I had moved my damn feet."

"If Kelly had stayed down instead of thinking his so-called friend wouldn't shoot him." Cole gave her a minute to take in what he'd said. "Look. Cora don't blame you either. She's got someone else to blame."

At the casket Cora stood in silent vigil. Martha stood a few feet away. The moment she tried to approach, Cora wrapped her arms around her sons and turned away. In silence they left the cemetery, leaving Martha standing alone.

"I don't understand."

"You said you saw the war paint."

"Yes. I did. Mostly black with white streaks down one cheek. And the star. The red star on his other cheek."

"Starbird's war paint." Her gripped her waist the moment her knees buckled. It took no effort to keep her standing until she regained her strength. "He's the one that shot you and Kelly. Everyone in the store saw it."

"Will you take me back to my room please?"

There, that quiver in her voice. Weakness. It should make him pity her. But it didn't. Maybe because despite that waver in her voice, she insisted on standing straight.

Regardless of the now visible wince of pain, she linked her arm around his waist instead of setting her hand on his arm. Rather than ask for help, she wanted to walk on her own two feet, even if she had to hang onto him to do so.

Guy's approach disrupted Cole's musings. The slime looked positively smug. Instinct made Cole pull his hand from Jane's affectionate grasp.

"Jane, it's so good to see you up and about. I heard about your injuries." Guy stepped closer, too close. "I do wish you'd come to see Dr. Stone."

Jane's hand hit Guy's cheek so hard several heads turned their way. For a moment the anger in her features toppled into pain-streaked lines before she recovered. "Anyone in this town will tell you I have a great fondness for words. Yet even I cannot begin to find the words to describe how much of an idiot you are."

"Jane." The smile dropped from Guy's face faster than Cole had ever seen.

"You self-serving, righteous bastard. You don't turn away injured people after a massive attack. You don't favor status over degree of injury. The doctor you hired is a quack and you want to push him off on me?" Damn, she was impressive.

"I beg your pardon. Dr. Stone was taught at Harvard."

"Did he actually listen and learn at Harvard? His work had to be redone by Daisy on at least three patients because he couldn't see fit to take proper care of the poor." How on earth did she know that? "And turning away the Chinese? They're good enough to wash your linens or provide pork for your customers, but not for medical care?"

Guy's eyes narrowed. "You have no idea what it was like."

"I have every idea. This town might be a good size, but there is little else people like to do as much as gossip. Even laid up in my room, I heard all about your precious Dr. Stone and the horrible treatment people got from him." She took a step closer. Guy taking a step back almost drew a laugh from Cole. "Those he didn't refuse to see."

"The hotel was overrun with patients. We couldn't take everyone."

"Oh, please. The saloon is *still* overrun with patients to the point of interrupting business. Meanwhile the Silver Saddle still has five rooms available." Even though her finger trembled, she still jerked it toward Guy. "You have to wake up."

Guy's nostrils flared and his fists clenched as red filled his cheeks. "I don't pay you to browbeat me."

"That is exactly why you pay me. My advice. You want to be more liked by this town, then listen for a change." Jane got in Guy's face. Her skin had paled considerably, but she didn't stop. "When this town is in crisis, the *whole* town is in trouble. There is no status, no race—"

"'Cept the Indians." Cole couldn't help himself. It had to be said. They were the ones that had done this anyhow.

"Of course." Jane took a step back, and her shoulders sagged. Whatever drove her drained away. Her pale skin took a sickly pallor. Cole had to fight the urge to step in and support her. He had a feeling it would only piss her off more.

She took a deep breath and some color returned to her cheeks. When she spoke again darkness filled her tone unlike anything Cole had heard before. The woman was beyond angry. "White, Negro, Chinese—it doesn't matter. You must help the whole town like Cole saw fit to. If you don't, the town falls."

"You're overstepping your contract." Guy didn't sound at all convinced.

Jane knew it too. "Then take your out. You'll be in breach of contract and I'll retain the money I've been paid. Read the contract. I'm not overstepping my bounds. Now go away before I hit you again. I'm tired of your ignorance."

This time Cole did move close behind her. He wanted to be prepared in case Guy decided to fight her on it. Cole didn't figure she had the energy to combat him.

Guy's jaw worked for a minute before he spun on his heel and stormed down the street. No argument, no more threats.

Cole breathed a whistle through his teeth. "Damn. That was one hell of a show."

"Why must you all be asses?"

"You really are my kind of woman."

"I…" For a moment she seemed at loss for words, and warm pink stole across her cheeks "Shut up and escort me home before I faint."

"Yes ma'am." Even though she couldn't fight him, he wasn't about to argue with her now. Instead, he moved to her injured side. He wrapped his arm around her waist to give her the support she wouldn't take any other way. If he dared pick her up with so many people around she'd probably never forgive him.

"Don't patronize me." Weak, but full of laughter, her voice flittered under the din of town.

"Yes ma'am." Cole laughed, glad to hear hers. Her body gave in and sagged against him, but she kept going. Still laughing. She was much improved compared to how she'd been three days before when he'd found her on the porch of Turner's.

The blood soaking through her dress. Her blood. Kelly's. It didn't matter. It had been everywhere.

The way she'd held on to tell him about the war paint, about the cowboy, only to give into the pain. His brief, most unwelcome, flash of terror when he'd worried she'd died.

The way he'd had to cut her corset to get to the wounds. The whimpers of her pain as he tugged the fabric away from her torn flesh.

"You gotta stop lacing so tight." It came out thick. Words caught up in his throat until he had to clear it.

"I'm not laced at all right this moment."

"I know. But the way you attract injury, it'll be easier if ya stop lacing so tight. It was a pain to cut that thing off you."

"I'm sure you enjoyed every second."

Her light tone didn't touch his mood. "No. I really didn't."

She met the admission with silence. The only recognition she offered was her hand slipping over his to give a gentle squeeze. He let their fingers lace together. The simple action gave him a strange sense of completion. One he hadn't felt in years.

Outside the boarding house she paused. "It was Starbird?"

"Looks that way. You want to find somewhere else to stay? Ya don't gotta go back in there. We can find ya somewhere."

"Where else would I go? I'm not about to stay at the Silver Saddle. Cora has an extra room, but she's in mourning and I wouldn't dream of imposing. I'll find a new place to stay, but until then I'll avoid Martha. It's not like I didn't avoid her anyway."

Cole chuckled. "Good point." The moment they were in the boarding house with the door shut, away from prying eyes, he stopped worrying about her anger. He scooped her into his arms. At her yelp he grinned. "Nobody's looking now. You wanna climb those steps by yourself?"

"Not really."

"Didn't think so. I'll go get Daisy. Get her to check on ya after the way you hit Guy, deserved or not."

"I'm pretty sure I'm not bleeding."

Since they were in her room, there wasn't any reason to leave it to chance. Before she could protest, he popped open her bodice. He ran his fingers along the bandages surrounding her torso. "Don't see no blood."

"There are so many layers of bandages you probably wouldn't." Jane sighed, leaning against him again. "I'm all right. I just moved too fast."

"Why did you agree to work for that bastard anyhow?"

"Temporary insanity."

"Temporary?"

"Shut up."

Cole pushed the bodice off her shoulders and tossed it on the bed. "Only if ya sit down and rest. Heard you ain't done much sleeping lately."

"Lately?" She didn't fight him when he untied her skirts and petticoats. In fact, she did nothing more than step out of them without a word. "Might as well return that dress to Daisy. Not sure why she had an extra, but thank her for letting me borrow it."

"Had dresses for a year of mourning that fool husband of hers. No idea why she kept them." Cole tossed the dress pieces over a chair before he poured drinks for each of them. His whiskey disappeared in a heartbeat, but she nursed hers.

"Daisy had a husband?" She sank into a chair at the table, still not taking the bed despite the way her whole body sagged.

"Ain't she told you?"

"She refuses to speak about what happened before she became a whore. I've asked a few times." A smile tugged her lips. "I admit I'm more than curious how you managed to get a well-educated, married, doctor to agree to be a whore."

"I got good negotiating skills."

"Liar."

Cole laughed and nodded. At least she wasn't so tired she couldn't peg him with the truth. "She had nowhere else to turn."

"Because her husband died? Doesn't seem likely."

He took a deep breath and relaxed back in his chair. Absently he spun his glass on the table. "Daisy and her husband moved here five years ago or so. Nobody in town knew what to make of a woman doctor. No one wanted to use her."

"Prevailing opinion among men, I'm sure."

"And women. Nobody went to see her. I felt bad for her, trying to look busy and happy with no business." He lifted his glass and swirled around the whiskey. "Her husband, he was an odd one. Small guy, shorter than you, no strength at all, but damn that man could talk for days. You'd like him."

One eyebrow arched, her lip curled in a sneer. The glass she'd raised to drink from froze in mid-air. "Funny."

"Well, he kept trying to talk everyone into letting Daisy do the doctoring. He was good, but not that good." He set his glass back on the table and shrugged. "Like I said, I felt bad, and my whores kept getting sick then, what with no real doctor in town. Figured I'd throw her some business if she'd stoop to treating them. I like to keep business clean."

"So you sent your whores to her?"

"Nah. I brought her to the whores. Sent the men to her, since she said they probably had it too. We agreed to once a week. After that she started getting business." He ignored the smile she wore. It didn't matter to him if she knew he'd sent half the town Daisy's way. "After a year she had some business. Not a lot, but more every day."

"What happened?"

"Epidemic of the grippe." Cole furrowed his brow and focused on the whiskey again. "First time the saloon became a hospital, she didn't have enough room. Once the sick came, everyone rushed to her doctorin'."

By now Jane sat straight, some life returning to her tired features.

"Then her husband got it. He died along with fourteen others, including three kids." He downed the last bit of whiskey in his glass. "She had nothing after that. Husband was gone, bank took her house, and ain't no one in this town that trusted her to do their doctoring no more. Too many died."

"Didn't she have somewhere to go? Family?"

"Only one in her family that liked her was some uncle. Guess he paid for her schooling. She said he died before she finished college. Her husband's family sent her them dresses and ticket back to Chicago."

Her lips pursed and she tapped her fingers on the rim of her glass. "Still not understanding. If they sent for her, she did have somewhere to go."

"They called her eccentric. Made a right good offer to help her return to respectable society so long as she gave up this doctoring pretense."

"Oh, I'd hate that."

"So did she. So, I made her an offer. She could work for me or get on that train. She didn't have many options." Cole knew Daisy had only taken the offer to keep doctoring in some way. He'd helped the transition best as he could, because at one time he'd almost respected her. "She caved real fast."

Jane's sharp blue eyes widened the slightest bit. "I see."

"Done my business good to have her around. After a bit people started seeing her again, leastwise those with big injuries did. So I kept her on." He shifted in his seat, her intense scrutiny itching along his nerves. "Stop."

"They all cave, don't they?"

"Always do." He poured another whiskey right quick. He gulped and let it burn down his throat. Blessed silence filled the space between them, and he was happy to let it linger. It wasn't until he thought she might have fallen asleep that he dared face her again.

Instead of sleeping, she was staring at the table. One finger traced the lace doily in the center. Her whiskey remained untouched in front of her.

Cole nudged her. "What are ya thinking about?" With her it could be dangerous to ask.

"Nothing."

"Liar."

"No. Really. The nothing in my head." One finger dipped into her whiskey, swirling around before she pulled it out. The way she licked the drop from her finger drove him to distraction. A soft sigh pouted out her lips. "It's never far from my empty mind."

He had to bring himself back into focus. Her wounds weren't healed, and so he could never play as much as he wanted. "Daisy talk to you about that hip—hippo—that stuff?" Damn word wouldn't stick in his head for nothing. The chuckle from across the table did little to help his frustration.

"Hypnosis. It's been mentioned. I have agreed to consider it, but I'm not certain I want to travel to Chicago to have it done. I don't know that I wish to travel anywhere prone as I seem to be to injury." She finally downed her drink. With an appreciative exhale she set the glass back down. "I haven't been able to decipher the book at all."

"What?"

"Oh. That book. The Poe book. I opened it the other day during my complete boredom. With my proclivity for books, I'm not sure why I haven't sooner. When I did, I found I'd written all over it, in the margins. It's certainly my handwriting, but none of it makes sense." Once again her lips puffed out. Sweet enticements when he was supposed to be focused, behaved. She was injured and in no mood.

He couldn't ignore them anymore. Not when she teased him. He didn't like talking much anyway. In a heartbeat he slipped off his chair, pulling those soft lips to his.

She didn't hesitate to respond. Her soft sigh rushed through him. Fingers danced along his chest, sending shivers down his spine. Once they laced into his hair, he tugged her closer. Her body arched into his, drifting off the chair to kneel with him.

His fingers buried in her hair, knocking pins and curls loose. A soft whimper slipped out of her, followed by a deep moan that rattled through him. If he didn't stop now, he never would. Hell, he didn't want to. Then again, he doubted he'd be gentle, and she had injuries.

Her body trembled when he managed to pull his lips from hers. Her fingers brushed his cheek. With a soft sigh, she pressed her forehead to his. "I could do that forever."

"Ya need to heal. There's better things to be doing."

"Who says I'm going to do them?"

"You will. Eventually."

"Who says it will be with you?"

He drew back to meet her eyes. The playful smile she wore disputed her words. He smirked. "It will."

"We shall see, but not right now. Right now I believe I need to sleep again." With her glass empty she headed for the bed. "Thank you for assisting me."

"Ain't a problem." He pulled a chair beside the bed and dropped into it. As she climbed into bed, one eye on him, he stretched out and propped his feet on the bed.

"I do believe it's entirely possible for me to sleep without gaining another injury."

"You're already injured. Ain't no one here to keep an eye on ya."

"Who says I need looked after?"

"You're good at getting yourself near dead. Think ya need looking after."

"So it's for my own good? Not yours?"

A smile crept across his features. No sense denying what she already knew. "As a matter of fact, I don't mind the looking so much either."

"Thought so. Devil."

"Ain't ever gonna deny that."

Every truth has two sides;
it is as well to look at both, before we
commit ourselves to either.
—Aesop

"Martha. What the hell do ya think you're doing?"

"None of your business, Cole." Martha hissed, her footsteps echoing up the stairs. "Get out of my building. I'm tired of you sneaking in where you're not welcome."

"I didn't sneak in and where I'm at, I'm welcome."

"Go back to your saloon. Leave that poor girl alone."

"She ain't no girl, and she can take care of herself."

Jane smirked at Cole's defense, and considered coming out from her room to say as much, but the conversation was being held in hushed tones. Also, Cole had left when she'd been asleep. In fact, it had been his departure that woke her. So she hovered near the crack in the door, listening when she ought to walk away.

Martha huffed. "You're encouraging her."

"I said she can take care of herself." Cole stomped down a few more steps. "You're going after him, aren't ya?"

Martha gasped, her footsteps ceasing.

"Why in hell would ya do that? You know what he did."

"I know my husband. He didn't do this."

"Jane saw him. Unless your precious husband changed his war paint, he did it."

"Lewis loves this town," Martha spit back. "And he loves the Turners. They are family. For goodness' sakes, Arthur is his godson. He wouldn't kill Kelly."

"Are ya sure about that? Where's he been the past couple of weeks?" Cole's dark chuckle held no humor. "Or have ya known all along he couldn't give up his savage? Did ya know he was with the renegades?"

"Even if he sympathized with them and wasn't opposed to their attacks of the railroad, he would *not* attack this town. Or Kelly."

"Jane saw him."

"You said yourself she was talking crazy. She was in a lot of pain and not thinking clearly."

"True."

"And I know my husband. I know he didn't do this. I just have to prove it."

"Only way to prove it is to find him. That's the army's job. Not yours."

"And if they find him, they'll kill him first, ask questions later. I can't let that happen. You shouldn't either."

"Well, why in hell not?"

Jane closed her door as the voices grew too faint for her to hear. Her heart pounded fast. With as few memories as Jane had, she didn't like having the ones she knew were certain questioned. And Cole, agreeing she'd not been thinking clearly? She could kill him.

She'd stared down the sight of that gun. She knew what she'd seen. Without a doubt, she knew she'd be able to recognize the man who shot her if she saw him again.

Footsteps drew close, so she rushed away from the door. At the table she poured a glass of whiskey with a shaky hand.

"Pour me one?" Cole closed the door behind him.

"Pour it yourself," she snapped. Downing the whiskey, she walked away from the table. She ignored his wide-eyed stare to pull open the balcony door.

"What put the bee in your bonnet?"

"I wasn't thinking clearly?"

"Well, ya weren't." Cole smirked. "Not the first time either."

"I know what I saw. I don't appreciate being questioned and doubted. I do my very best to not lie, Cole. Being shot is not something I care to remember in the far too short list of memories I have, but it is not one I'm about to forget. How dare you."

"Now, wait. I'm guessing you didn't hear everything. Will ya let me—"

"No."

He poured a glass of whiskey for himself and took a drink. The liquid swished around his mouth before he swallowed hard. Jaw clenched, cheeks ruddy, fist gripped tight on the glass, he looked ready to blow. "Then you're gonna love this. I'm going with Martha to try and find Starbird."

"To protect him from the army? Are you insane?"

"The same man shot a soldier—"

"Get out."

"If he's with the renegades, we ain't gonna find him."

Slamming down her glass, she wiped the splash of whiskey on her skirt before storming past him to the door. She couldn't listen to this, not then. Not with the pain still radiating along her ribs and arm. She didn't expect much from him, but a little understanding wasn't too much to ask, was it?

Without another word, she stomped down the stairs toward the front door. She heard him following behind, but ignored him completely. She didn't need his fool excuses and arguments. What she needed was support. The sort of support he'd offered the day before, not this convoluted mess. Once outside, she spun on him. "Goodbye, Cole."

The usual sparkle of his blue eyes disappeared under the shadow of his brow. With a short nod, he turned and stormed across the street without a word of goodbye.

Exhaling slowly, Jane turned and headed down the street without any particular destination in mind. She just knew she had to get away from the situation. Away from him. Perhaps she'd leaned on him too much, expected too much from him after all.

There is that in me—
I do not know what it is—
but I know it is in me.
—Walt Whitman

"It ain't one o'clock."

"Aw, come on, Cole. You're awake. Doors are open. It's only five minutes." Hammy adjusted his hat with a grin. "And it's my lunchtime."

"Does your crew know?" Cole chuckled at Hammy's bright laughter. The old man was like clockwork when it came to drinking time. Ever early, ever grinning. Few people knew of Cole's soft spot for the old fool, and those that did never understood why. "I'll take that as a no. Go on in. Cuddy'll take care of ya."

"Much obliged." Hammy ducked into the saloon, calling for a beer.

Shaking his head, Cole turned back to the street. Right as the clock chimed one, Jane left the Silver Saddle. It had been a week since she'd bothered to say a word to him. The first few days hadn't been a problem.

For one thing, he'd been as mad as her. For another, he'd been out on the trails searching for a man he knew they'd not find. Not with Martha leading the way.

Not that Jane cared one lick he knew it, or that he'd gone on the wild goose chase for that very reason. Martha was many things he didn't like, and chief among them was how she acted a fool about her husband. Last thing she'd do was let Graham or himself near that man. The whole idea to go with her had been a delay tactic to give the Army more time. Jane had been too riled up to listen to reason and he couldn't yell with Martha right downstairs.

Stubborn woman.

He frowned when she disappeared into the boarding house. As soon as the door shut hard behind her, he lit his cigar. She usually took five minutes to clean up before she left the building again. Then, when she was in the open, he'd confront her. Let her know how much she annoyed him. He supposed he could follow her into the boarding house, but he'd give her a chance to freshen up first.

A movement caught his eye. The cowboy paying through the nose for a room in his saloon stepped onto the porch.

He'd introduced himself simply as Johnny and refused all offers of women. Johnny wanted something. Cole knew the signs all too well. The man had a hankering for something, but Cole couldn't figure out what.

When he'd arrived, Cole had been quick to point out they weren't a hotel, but it didn't faze the man. With a stack of bills Cole didn't normally see on a cowboy, Johnny insisted on renting a room and paid top dollar. Cole wasn't about to refuse the money, even if the man himself made Cole uneasy.

Shrugging off his unease when Johnny headed toward the tavern, Cole turned his attention back to the activity in the street. In no time his mind wandered right back to Jane. He cursed her for occupying his thoughts like she did. No woman had for a very long time.

All along he'd wanted more of her. The first time she'd submitted to his kiss had made that longing stronger. He wanted more. More of her. All of her.

So why hadn't he taken it? She gave him plenty of opportunities, but he restrained himself. He'd settled for the incredible passion she laced into every kiss. Somehow that had been enough. The passion that showed she could be the best woman he'd ever had, far from submissive—no, she'd fight for what she wanted, and he'd give it.

Yes. He wanted more.

"Cole."

He grunted, pulled from his thoughts when Daisy sidled up next to him. Out of habit, he pulled her close, draping an arm around her shoulders. It had been a while since he'd let any of the whores ease his tension. Since Jane. As Daisy's fingers trailed along his thigh, he considered ending the unintentional abstinence. "What d'you want?"

"You've been so tense this week." She pressed into him, hitting just the right nerves to elicit a rumbling moan. "Let me help."

He'd taught Daisy well. Her skills couldn't be beat. But even her best attentions couldn't divert his notice from Jane's reemergence. The stack of books in her arms weighed her down. She didn't even glance his way, her chin set in a stubborn lift. He pulled Daisy closer, angry Jane couldn't waver the smallest bit. "Maybe I should."

"She ain't ever gonna."

"Ya sure about that?"

"She hasn't talked to you in a week, and it's been months since you've taken advantage of the many skilled beds inside." She slid her hand along his chest to his neck. Her soft palm coasted over his stubble to cup his cheek. She tugged gently to pull his gaze to hers. "That ship has sailed. You know I can take care of business."

The brazen action stirred him from his haze. None of his whores touched him like that, not for nothing. He gripped her wrist tight and ripped her hand free. His eyes narrowed. He never got played, certainly not by a woman he owned. They weren't allowed an upper hand, if he gave one slip of weakness, they'd take everything. "Wrong move, Daisy."

"Cole. Stop." Daisy gasped, rubbing her wrist when he released it.

He'd never hurt one of his whores before; it was a rule he followed to keep them happy. The red ring around her wrist would bruise, though, no doubt about it. The realization almost made him feel guilty. Another risky emotion. He had to be more careful.

Daisy rubbed the wrist gently. "What's gotten into you?"

When she'd first signed her contract, she'd been like the rest of them: defeated. He'd liked it, being the one they all wanted because they thought he cared. Daisy had been the first he hadn't completely pitied, because he'd almost respected her drive. She'd been the first he'd bothered to care about as more than a bedmate, even though he still hadn't wasted emotions or let her in.

That had been three years ago and he realized he no longer cared. Her continual defeat had left him with only one feeling—the all too familiar sense of pity. "I'm selling your contract."

"What?"

Her shock brought the guilt back to the surface and he immediately doubted his own statement. Having her around meant having a capable doctor, but that no longer mattered. He had enough women he pitied. "Yeah. I'm selling it."

"Cole. I don't want—"

"What you want don't matter. I'm telling ya how it is."

Both their heads shot up as the all too familiar sound of renegade shouts and gunfire filled the air. He shoved Daisy into the saloon. As the Indians approached, he drew his weapon and fired.

One shot pierced a renegade's arm, and Cole gave a triumphant grin. He fired again when the renegade tried to get to his feet. His satisfaction was short lived as the sting of a bullet hit his arm. Through the pain, he spun to fire again.

Hammy joined him on the porch and by the time their revolvers were empty, Cuddy joined them with the rifle. A few minutes later silence fell, stillness after the chaos. It had only been two minutes, but it sure got his blood pumping. Cole laughed into the silence, glad for the spark of action.

When the first shout of the aftermath started, Cole holstered his weapon and stared down at the dead Indian. The satisfaction of another one dead, a life for one of the lives lost in town. He only wished he'd been able to make up for all the deaths so far.

He turned and threw open the door. "Anyone hurt?"

Daisy sat on the floor where he'd left her. Her scantily clad breasts heaved as she stared into the street. "No."

"Daisy. Snap out of it. We got more wounded today." Cole stopped short. His mind flashed to what had happened in the last attack. Jane froze. She always did. Cole's heart seized. She'd been walking down the street when the attack hit, headed for the library. Practically right in the path of the renegades. What if she'd froze? What if they'd got her? "Damn it. Jane!"

Without wasting time to think about the panic coursing through him, he raced around the corner. Where had she gone? Where was she?

He tore into the crowd, searching through the people checking out damage to persons and property. A few yards from the library he came up short. Books scattered through the street, their pages flapping in the wind. Between the library and the tailor he saw them. Hammy hovered in front of the alley, Jane right behind him hidden in shadow.

Alive.

Relief flooded him so quick, he bent over to exhale it. He braced his hands on his knees as he took a few deep breaths to quell the panic. When calmer, he stood again.

Jane stood tall, her arms crossed in front of her chest. The tremor in her hand when she swiped at her cheek was impossible to miss. Hammy's arms circled her shoulders and she didn't pull away from the comfort.

In a moment a smile slipped across those delicious lips. Cole would have to give Hammy a few free beers for taking care of his woman so well.

His woman? Where in hell did that come from?

He didn't want to care, he excelled at not caring; but when he caught the glimmer of a fresh tear, concern poured out of him like beer from the tap.

She lifted her head and spotted him. The step she took toward him set his heart pounding again. In that moment every ounce of frustration and anger left. He just wanted to hold her in his arms and wipe away that damn tear.

She didn't make him wait, running toward him at full speed. A wave of relief hit that she ran to him, just him. He held out his arms and braced for the impact. She launched toward him, her good arm clasping tight around his neck as her body hit his full force. The catch of a sob in her throat put a lump square in his.

He pulled her close. He couldn't fight it. He'd wanted her here. Now he just had to enjoy it. When Hammy walked up, Cole nodded. "Was she hurt?"

"She was just standing there. Savages headed north. Don't think they crossed her path." Hammy shrugged. "But she ain't said a word."

"Thanks, Hammy." He waited until Hammy left and the area around them had settled down. With few people around, he squeezed her waist gently. "You froze again."

"No. Not entirely. I got in the alley. I dropped my books."

"The books don't matter." Cole kept her close. She continued to cling to him, and he was content to let her. "Someone will get them."

"Why did you come find me?"

"Dunno."

A choked laugh escaped. She shook her head, her hold so tight her nose rubbed his shoulder. "I wasn't scared."

"Of course ya weren't." He looked down when she sniffled and pulled away enough to see her face. He lifted his hand to brush away a tear with his thumb. The deep blue eyes stared back at him with an intensity that twisted his insides. How she did it, he couldn't understand.

A smile curved along those luscious lips and his whole body jumped to life. He wanted to ignore her injuries and yank her to him. Who cared if they were in the middle of the street? He leaned toward her, but as her had slipped down his arm she gasped. A flash of pain reminded him of his injury.

"Cole."

"Just a scratch."

"You're bleeding." Her admonishing tone wove its way under his skin.

"I told ya. It's just a scratch."

"You were shot?"

"Jane." How had she managed to annoy him again so fast?

"And you wasted the time to come look for me? What is wrong with you? It is just that you're a ma—"

Fed up with her chatter, he yanked her tight against him. Her yelp cut off her continued scolding, but didn't stop him. The beginnings of a protest spurred him forward. He caught her bottom lip with his teeth, sucking it into his mouth and running his tongue along it.

She caved in a second, sagging in his arms with a low moan. When he stopped teasing she came to life, meeting his kiss with equal fire. Her body pressed into his, her hands slipped along his chest and shoulders, distracting him and driving him mad with need. He had to stop or they'd both be done for. With one last nibble on her lip, he pulled back.

"Told ya I knew how to shut you up."

Her eyes met his, still heated with unfulfilled passion. The coy smirk returned. "You're going to have Daisy look at that. You didn't shut me up, just interrupted me."

"Damn."

"By the way, you don't play fair."

"Neither do you. Ignoring me for a week. Ya did that on purpose, didn't you?"

"When you're ignoring someone, it is generally on purpose."

He could only grunt in response when she shoved him back toward the saloon. "That ain't what I meant and you know it."

"Doctoring first, talk later."

Once inside the bustling saloon they both sobered. Most of the injuries had been minor, though. Despite the presence of the new doctor at the Silver Saddle, it seemed most of the injured had reported to the saloon. It made him doubt his earlier decision and he frowned when Daisy approached to check his arm. "Just a scratch."

"You need stitches," Daisy snapped. Ignoring Jane completely, and not saying another word to him, she stitched him up fast as he'd ever seen her work. After one last glare at him, she turned on her heel and moved to the next person.

He shrugged. It wasn't like him to care about her opinion, and he wouldn't start now. Even if he had reason to doubt, he wouldn't change. He'd made up his mind and he never went back on his word.

He secured Jane's hand in his and led her to the bar. The hard stare she trained on him burned the back of his skull, but he made it a point to ignore it. He poured them both a glass of whiskey and drank his down quick.

Jane still didn't speak, her gaze never wavering. He finally set down his glass and cleared his throat. "What?"

"What the hell is going on with you two?"

"She's mad at me."

"You don't say." Sarcasm dripped through every word. She rolled her eyes.

He chuckled. "Yup. I made her plenty mad right before the attack. What's it to you?"

"Just how did you manage to upset her?"

"Told her I was selling her contract." As he watched, all amusement and lingering heat of passion faded. The way her lips disappeared into a tense line disappointed him most. He sighed. Sure didn't take long to make her mad all over again.

"Why on earth would you do that?" Her eyes flashed when he cocked a brow. Anger flared her nostrils and she pointed a finger at him. "No, you don't. Nobody told you do such a ridiculous thing."

He grabbed her finger and tugged her close. "One of these times you're gonna have to listen before ya start yelling."

"Well, that day is going to be a long time coming. I can't believe you."

"Don't yell at me in front of my customers. I ain't gonna tolerate it."

"Then where will I yell at you? Because you really need it right now."

"I do? Or you do?"

A whisper of a smile erupted before she wiped it away. "Both."

For the briefest moment he contemplated taking her to his room, but that wouldn't happen. It had been years since anyone had been allowed to step foot in there. He'd be damned if the first time he let someone in, it would be so they could yell at him.

She let him lead the way back to the storeroom. When she opened her mouth, he held up a finger to silence her. He led her through the room to the next door, which he held open.

"You aren't serious?"

"Get in." He waved. "Ain't no one gonna hear your screeching in there."

She stormed into the icehouse. Without waiting for the door to close, she turned toward him. "What in blazes were you thinking? If you even think to—"

"You're gonna let *me* talk."

"Then explain your logic. I'm dying to hear this."

"First things first. You been ignoring me for a week. If you'd listened to me instead of picking a fight, you'd know it was pointless."

She snorted. "You went out with Martha to find him before the army."

"I went to keep Martha from getting to her husband."

"What?"

There was a sliver of satisfaction when the shock of the statement wiped every bit of self-righteous anger right off her face. He eyed her lips now that they'd reappeared, open and ready. He licked his lips in anticipation. Shaking his head, he forced himself to focus on his own annoyance again. "I believe ya saw what you did. I just ain't sure Starbird would kill Kelly. He's a savage, but them two were friends."

"I…" She blinked a few times, her mouth opening and closing. A spark lit in her eyes like she was trying to find her anger again. He had to cut her off at the pass.

"I knew if we followed Martha, she'd be careful where she took us. And if she kept *us* from finding him, she wouldn't find him herself."

Her jaw dropped. "So wait. You do or don't think he's guilty?"

"Don't know. I know ya saw what ya did, but any savage could paint his face that way, though I don't know why. Just hard to believe he'd kill Kelly. But I don't think your soldier boy would actually do what she said. He's got a bleedin' heart. He won't kill on sight."

"So you were buying the Army time."

"Sure was."

"Oh."

"Feel guilty?" He smirked when she put a hand on her hip. "Guess not."

"And Daisy?"

"It's time for her to go." He didn't need a reason. Not even Jane could shake his resolve. Or make him look weak by changing his mind back.

"Not acceptable."

"You don't got much say."

"I simply mean your reasoning isn't sound. I wasn't trying to dissuade you yet." She stepped closer, tilting her neck to keep her eye trained on him when she got close. "Tell me why. Or do I get the man excuse?"

"I pity her."

"I see. You pity them all, though."

"Yeah."

She hesitated. "Do you pity me?"

"Nothing to pity. You ain't given up." He embraced her neck with his hand. His thumb ran along the line of her jaw. The shiver of a response she gave teased his cock to attention. Daisy had been right about one thing. This one was trouble.

She did something to him. Something no woman had done in years. She made him feel. That was trouble.

"She's a good doctor. If you sell her contract, she'll lose that. It's all she has. You've let her keep it all these years."

"That was a mistake."

"No. It's what kept you from pitying her for three years." She leaned into his hand as it slipped up to cup her cheek. A whisper of breath ran along his wrist. She followed it with a touch of her lips. "You can't let her lose it."

"Already said I'm selling it. My word's final." The fight almost done, he leaned in to get another kiss. Her gasp jolted through him. He barely jumped back in time to avoid her head hitting his nose with how quick she snapped it up. "What the hell?"

"You let the girls keep some sort of income, right?"

He had no idea where she was going with this. The near-giddy grin she wore didn't ease his rising suspicion. He eyed her. "Not much. Most of 'em spend it pretty damn fast."

"Daisy's not that stupid. She's got to have built up some funds."

"So?"

"If you're determined to sell her contract, then sell it. To her."

"You're crazy."

"You want to stop pitying her? Let her have her life back."

He frowned. "It ain't that simple."

"Yes. It is." She stepped closer and same as Daisy had done earlier, her hand cupped his cheek and pulled his eyes to hers. An understanding smile settled on her features and any exasperation he might have had at being handled faded into it. She did understand, and as much as it annoyed him it also intrigued him. Her fingers played along his cheek into his hair. "Let her have her life back."

"I sell her that contract, she won't have nothing."

"Maybe not."

"What do ya mean?"

"You've already invested in her medical career. You've bought medicines and tools for her, haven't you?"

"What of it?" He frowned when she started pacing. Her finger tapped her chin; a scheming set to her brow unnerved him. "Jane."

"Help her get started. It won't take long for people to go to her over the quack Dr. Stone. Let her keep using a room here until she can afford something."

"No."

"It's good for business. Helps you look good."

"I got a reputation."

"You do, and all along you've let people use this place for a hospital. You may act the scoundrel, but you don't fool everyone. Besides, with the Indian raids it will help bolster your business further if people are coming here for treatment. They'll need spirits to ease the pain."

"Do you got an argument for everything?"

"I do try. Now will you?" She pressed her body into his; he'd bet anything she did it on purpose. It distracted him to no end and she knew it.

"I'll think about it."

"So, yes?"

"I'll think about it."

"Good for you, Cole."

Nothing has more strength than dire necessity.
—Euripides

"Are you certain this is wise?" Al cleared his throat.

Jane laughed. "Of course. Why wouldn't it be?"

"The rumors are quite descriptive about the time you make with Cole. Certain compromising positions you've been spotted in together. Now everyone appears to be staring."

"So?" She leaned closer, smirking at his consternation. "Given the type of man Cole is, do you think he cares about any dalliance being exclusive?"

"Are you doing this on purpose?"

"Perhaps."

He set his hands on her shoulders. "You are aware of all the rumors, aren't you?"

"Quite. Old women love to sit and gossip over their tea. What difference does it make to me if they don't realize I'm sitting at the next table? Or that I can hear every vile, enthralling, and kind word they say about me?" Jane shrugged off his hands. "If they wish to gossip about me, so be it. I know the truth."

"Does Cole?"

"The last time he questioned me was before your elaborate, rather disastrous, attempt at a kiss. He didn't bother to ask why you hadn't kissed me, and hasn't dared to ask again since."

"Ah. So he keeps his whores and you continue adding to the rumors about town. It's all is a bit childish isn't it?" Al shook his head. "And now you're asking me to collaborate with you on this, aren't you?"

"Well, I'm not about to ask you to bed me, if that's what has you concerned."

"My darling Jane, I adore you and would sweep you off to bed immediately if you'd agree to give me your heart along with your body." Al stepped back to performed an elaborate scrape and bow. "It would be my vast honor and privilege."

Her laughter burst forth, which pulled even more attention to the scene. "Oh, do stand up. That is quite unbecoming of an officer, and you call me immature."

"Well, you are."

"So are you." She slid her hand through the crook of his offered arm. Once settled, they resumed their walk along the First Street. "I do enjoy our friendship rather thoroughly. There is an ease to it that is an oasis in the chaos. Do you think you would mind kissing me?"

"Not even a little bit." His grin lit his green eyes brighter than before. A wicked twist hinted at further teasing. "If you think our delicate balance of friendship would survive the intensity of the kiss I would bestow on you."

"Oh forget it."

"All teasing aside." Al stopped their motion again, and turned her him. An approaching horse made him close the distance between them. "Are you sure that you really want to incite such a temper?"

"You've seen what sort of man he is. It's about the chase. I'm no fool, even though I act the part sometimes. If he thought there was true competition, things might move along again." When his fingers brushed her cheek, she leaned into them before turning away. "I know. The whole thing is childish."

"And a bit desperate."

"I know. I'm terrible."

"In all of the best ways. Only one woman I know can create a limerick that makes every man in my camp blush." He winked and leaned in to kiss her forehead. "Best I can give you for now. Forgive me?"

"I suppose."

"If I thought you could love me, I would fight for you in a heartbeat."

Jane sighed. "At least you gave it a fair shot. I'm surprised you're still speaking to me after what I did."

"I'm not sure I understand what you mean. Just because you burst into laughter over my grand romantic gesture? I was merely wounded, and it really was silly."

"It was. All of those flowers in your tent. I thought your corporal was going to need medical attention he was sneezing so much." She laughed. "And that kiss?"

"Painfully uncomfortable, yes. You were, and are, right. We will fare far better as friends. Perhaps my kisses will sway you more now that we are."

Her laughter cut off when a soldier raced up to them. "Major. The stagecoach is under attack. We have men on the way."

"The stagecoach?" Jane gasped. "Go. Your duty comes first."

He nodded, and after a kiss to her hand waved the soldier off his horse. Without another word, he swung into the saddle and tore out of town.

She turned to follow his progress, concern weighing on her heart over the approaching stagecoach. With a shaky breath, she rubbed her arm where the bandage remained even with the sling gone.

Swallowing against the lump of fear in her throat, she made to head back toward the boarding house. Despite her efforts the past couple of weeks and the rather positive return on some investments she'd made, she'd been unable to find a home suitable to her needs.

The first settlement, nestled on the hill north of the mines, was close to town but had rather elaborate, sometimes obscene homes, far larger than she needed. The second settlement had smaller homes more suited to her needs, but none were available and the settlement was a few miles outside of town. She didn't wish to be that far.

One home sat on the road north, a short distance past the new depot. It seemed rather perfect, but at even just half a mile outside of town, it didn't seem safe with the raids.

Sighing, she pushed forward. Halfway back to the boarding house the tinsmith stopped her with a greeting. She paused to inquire after his family and admire his newest lamp. As she inquired on the price, chaos erupted.

This time they attacked without warning, spilling from between the buildings and tearing down the streets. Gunfire echoed around and once again Jane found herself frozen among the commotion.

Time slowed as a horse burst from between the buildings closest to her, running right into the tinsmith. A shout of her name drew her eyes from the Indian that passed to find Cole racing through the street in her direction.

The moment of impact came with a brutal shriek. Time rushed forward for her sharp collision with the ground. Pain coursed through her body, but another horse leaped from the alley, leaving her no time to wallow as it slowed by them.

As the Indian raised his rifle, awareness dawned that Cole would get the brunt of the shot. She had to protect him, at all costs. The pain in her wounds disappeared. She twisted her hand to grab the gun from Cole's holster.

The large weapon was heavy in her trembling arm. Yet once she had the weight of it leveled at the man all trembling ceased. She pulled the trigger without another thought or doubt. The Indian toppled from his horse before the world went black.

Next thing she knew, a large splash of water hit her face. Gasping, she sat with her eyes flying open. Pain wrenched through her skull like it usually did when she tried to remember her past. She shook off the pain, wincing at a twinge in her ribs from her old injury. "What in blazes?"

"Easy. Ya weren't bleeding. I figured you didn't need the doc."

"You're insane running out in the middle of the attack!" Her heart pounded, the sound echoing in her ears until she couldn't hear his response. She reached up to cup his cheek, relieved to see Cole whole and undamaged. "You could have been killed."

"You damn near were."

A laugh bubbled up and she didn't try to stop it as she pushed him playfully. "I am beginning to think you enjoy coming to my rescue. It's getting to be a habit. You're going to ruin your reputation around here."

"Nah. Can't ruin a bad reputation."

"Sure you can. You can start looking like a decent guy."

"Ain't ever gonna happen."

"It already has." The wink he gave her made her betraying heart swell. She turned away when heat rose to her cheeks. What was she doing? She couldn't fall for him. It just wasn't smart. The thoughts wiped away the instant she saw the form lying beside Cole. "Mr. Mortimer."

"What?"

Jane pushed Cole aside to crawl to the man. She rolled Mortimer over to check for life. Relief flooded her at his groan. Not dead. "Mr. Mortimer."

Cole frowned when the man barely groaned a response. "We'll get him to the saloon. Wagon should be along any second."

"Jane." Major Webb hopped down from his horse. "Are you all right? We heard the attacks as we were heading out."

"I'm fine." Jane accepted Cole's help to her feet, doing her best to avoid checking the damage to her dress. "Thanks to Cole."

"Thanks to herself." Cole nodded in the direction of the Indian lying dead in the street. "Girl's got good aim."

Jane's gaze fell to the Indian and she gasped. "I didn't even think. I just fired."

Al crouched over the body. He turned his gaze to Jane, his eyes wide. "And you're the one that shot him?"

When she lingered in stunned silence, Cole spoke for her, "Yeah. Least I think she did. Took my gun to do it."

"You've got dead-on aim, or luck was on your side. He's been shot right between the eyes." Al returned to her side, checking her over as if for injuries. "How'd you manage to fire Cole's weapon? It's a handful."

"I don't know. I just did." The headache pounded behind her eyes and she shivered. "We need to get Mr. Mortimer to the saloon. What—what happened with the stagecoach?"

"My men are on their way back with the stagecoach and the injured parties. I'll know more when they get here." Al made a gallant attempt at hiding a smirk when Cole moved closer and took Jane's arm. Still, the wicked gleam had returned to his eyes when he met Jane's eyes. "Are you injured?"

"Just sore from the impact." Jane moved closer to Cole despite her annoyance over his possessive behavior. "Nothing more."

"Good." Al squeezed her free elbow gently. "I'm going to check on the injuries in town and lend aid where I can. I'll see you soon."

Jane nodded. "Thank you, Al. I think I'm just going to sit down and have a drink. Or two."

"I can help you with that." Cole steered her away from Al.

Frowning, Jane shook her head at him with a deep sigh. "Hypocrite."

"How's that?"

"Nothing. Let's just get a drink." She let him lead her to the saloon, hesitating at the door when the rattle of the approaching stagecoach caught her ear. A glance over her shoulder let her know it was heading right for the saloon under a soldier's direction. "Between the stagecoach and the towns' injuries, Daisy and Dr. Stone will be awful busy."

"Good. If she's busy, Daisy won't be complaining."

"She wouldn't complain if you'd make up your damn mind. It's been a week."

Cole pushed her into the saloon. "Gotta make ya both sweat."

"You're a brute."

"Yup." He led her to a table in the back before disappearing behind the bar. A few minutes later he returned with a bottle of whiskey and two glasses. Laughter shook his shoulders as he sat and poured out for both of them. "I don't believe it."

"What's so funny? Injured people all around and you're laughing."

"They're being helped. Look, even Mabel lowered herself to coming into the saloon."

Jane's gaze darted around the room before landing on Mabel Greene. The Reverend's wife normally wouldn't even walk on the boardwalk in front of the saloons in town, but there she was, tending to the wounded. Would miracles never cease? She drank her whiskey down. "We should help as well."

"Too many cooks."

Rolling her eyes, Jane sat back with a wince.

"And you ain't in no position to be helping. You're smartin'."

"Happens when you're bulled over by a beast of a man." The pain of being tackled sank in, radiating from the still healing wound on her ribs and across her back. "But I admit it might be better to rest for a few minutes. Soon as I feel rested enough I'm going to help. Now would you care to explain your laughter?"

"David is on the stagecoach."

"Who on earth is David? And why is his arrival so funny?"

"David Schaffer had a gold claim here years ago. Engaged to Martha for two years. Damn fool didn't know she was skipping out on him with Starbird. He musta heard about Kelly. They were good friends before he left town."

"Wait. Martha, high and mighty and oh-so-pious Martha was engaged and still went around with Starbird?"

"They broke the news to David by showing up married and pregnant."

"No."

"Yes."

She would have laughed if the whole thing weren't so unbelievable it had to be true. "I can't even begin to imagine. She's so uptight and proper."

"Didn't used to be. She got all proper because she thought people would accept that husband of hers more. Davie was blind. Cora and Kelly were too. Or they just didn't want to admit it was happening. They was always friends."

"Cora doesn't seem the type to remain friends with someone that could be so devious." Jane frowned. "How is it they're best friends?"

"Ain't so much no more. Friends, sure."

She shrugged in agreement. If she studied on it, she could see his point.

"The kid died when he was two months old. Cora ain't one to let someone suffer, so they got friendly again. David had been gone for near a year by then, which probably made it easier. He sold his claim to the Daugherty's and took off for parts unknown."

As she took another long, slow drink of whiskey, Jane chewed on that information. Falling in love wasn't something you could control, that much she was beginning to understand—but to lie about it?

Cole muttered that David had walked in, so she turned in her chair to see who had been on the receiving end of such a deception.

At her request, Cole pointed out a man leaning against the bar with his Stetson pulled low. Mabel walked up to him and after a few words, led him toward a table. Jane noticed a limp in his step.

David dropped his hat on the table revealing short, dark brown hair and sun-darkened skin—all of which lent to the air of *cowboy* about him. When he lifted his injured leg on the table, she said as much to Cole.

"After about five years he started sending letters to Kelly again. Said he was working the trails. Had no desire to settle down again."

"Well, Martha was a fool. He's an attractive man. Unless he's a complete bastard, I can't see why she'd pick an Indian over him."

"Never said Martha was smart."

Snorting, Jane turned to glance at the cowboy again. She heard his tenor voice as he waved off help and said there were others in greater pain. For reasons she couldn't explain, the world tilted on its access. The headache that had subsided reared again.

"Jane?"

She yelped when Cole gripped her injured arm to keep her from toppling along with her chair. The flash of pain snapped her back to reality. With wide eyes, she stared at Cole. "What?"

"Look like you seen a ghost. Remembering something?"

Was she? No. That couldn't be it. She hadn't remembered anything yet. She shook her head. "Must be the pain of a giant slamming me in the dirt."

"Better than the pain of a bullet, don't ya think?" Cole's lip curved up, distracting her from her previous diversion wonderfully.

"You have a point." Every time David's voice hit her ears, her stomach twisted tighter. She had no idea what it meant. "I think I need to lie down."

"Mind if I join ya?"

Her attempt at a scowl failed miserably. The ripple of pleasure at the idea of him curled up against her couldn't be denied. "Can you behave?"

"Never."

"Then please join me." Jane grinned at his booming laugh of reply that had everyone in the room looking their way. With a wink, she started for the door.

"Clara." The voice that managed to twist her insides hit her ears before Cole caught up. The world spun as David continued. "Clara, is it really you?"

"Jane?" Cole's hand was at her elbow, grounding her again. A frown erased his previous wicked grin.

"Clara." A hand touched her other elbow. With a gentle tug, it turned her into the intense hazel eyes of David. "My God. It is you. I thought I'd never see you again."

Her stomach dropped to the floor, but before she could protest, he'd pulled her into a kiss. One that left her with no doubt this man thought he knew her. Just as she thought she caught a glimpse of familiarity, they were ripped apart.

"What the hell ya doin', Davie?" Cole's snarl echoed through the room.

"Clara?" David's brow pulled together in a deep V. "What's going on?"

"I'm Jane," she managed to whisper over the roaring pain in her head. "I don't know you. I'm sorry."

"You're joking, right? Clara, it's me. It's David." His hand reached for hers, strong and warm against her shaking, chilled fingers. "Your husband."

"No," she choked out. It couldn't be, she couldn't be married. "Husband?"

"Husband?" Cole echoed her, his grip growing tighter when David tried to pull on her again. "You sure about that, Davie?"

"I'd know my wife anywhere. I've looked for her all over this damn country. I kept holding out hope she was still alive. Clara, you can't have forgotten."

"I don't remember. I don't remember anything," she whispered. "I'm sorry."

Nothing hurts a new truth like an old error.
—Johann Wolfgang von Goethe

David wouldn't stop talking. Why didn't he stop?

Cole gripped her arm. Possessive, strong. His body shook with gestures and words she couldn't hear.

A strange buzzing filled her ears. Jane's head pounded louder and louder, pain piercing her skull until she felt blind as well as deaf. An embarrassing strangled cry broke through it all and her knees buckled. "Stop. Please. Both of you stop."

"Clara."

"Jane."

In her head, somewhere deep, she knew this should be a good thing. A piece of the puzzle finally put in place. A piece she hadn't been able to find on her own. There was no relief. Pressure squeezed her heart until she was sure it would burst. Every muscle in her body trembled. "Just stop. Please. I have to go."

Somehow she wrenched her arm free from Cole's grasp. Fast as she could she bullied her way through the crowd in the saloon onto the street. Outside she took a deep breath to steel herself. It did her no good, her hands shook as much as her soul. No one should see her so disarmed. She raced away from the milling crowds in the street to the boarding house.

Married? Not possible. How could a person forget such a thing?

Could David have hurt her?

No. The way he'd looked at her, greeted her. It wasn't the way one with ill intent greeted another. The love and kindness in his eyes. The hope.

The pure, desperate hope.

Hope she couldn't answer. There was nothing. Nothing in her brain remembered any bit of him. The large void remained. Dark and empty.

She had just begun to feel human. Like a real, whole person. She'd just begun to learn how to live. A life she enjoyed. The past she didn't have didn't cripple her.

She slammed the door to her room, only to come face to face with Cole. The shriek escaped before she could stop it.

"Jane."

"Blast, Cole. You scared the daylights out of me."

"Sorry. Took the shortcut." He jerked his thumb toward the balcony doors.

"Please go. I can't think straight. I can't. Not now." She couldn't. The way her head kept spinning, conversation couldn't be possible.

He didn't argue, but he didn't leave either. Once again she found his arms tight around her. In one swift move, he provided sanctuary against the turmoil. For several long minutes his strong arms offered her some peace.

Selfishly she soaked in it. Relieved to have a few minutes to ignore her past even though it had arrived at her doorstep. A moment to forget a man who claimed to be her husband. She was no longer a nameless person. But she hadn't felt nameless. She'd felt real, for a few weeks.

"I hate saying it."

"Then don't." Jane Doe wasn't real. This Clara was. Jane didn't want to give up everything she'd gained, but she couldn't turn her back on her past. With a sigh, she rested her head against his strong chest. "Sorry. I'm overwhelmed."

"I get that. Seems like he means it, though. Did you hear him?"

"I couldn't hear anything. It's too much. I don't know how to do this."

"He said he ain't seen you in seven years. That you left one day and he never saw you again. It was winter. He thought you'd died out there." Cole hooked a finger under her chin. His sharp gaze stilled her fidgeting. "It scares ya. Knowing something."

"As much as knowing nothing ever did. I just started to feel like a real person."

"Feel damn real to me."

She matched his playful wink with a giggle. "Scoundrel. That isn't what I meant and you know it."

"So?"

"So this Clara is married. I don't feel married. I still don't feel like her, I feel like me. The me I've come to know."

"You don't gotta change."

"Are you so sure? This man may want me to. He probably wants me to be his wife. To be this person he expects me to be, the woman he remembers. How can I be that if I don't remember being her? I have no memory of him, of her." She took a ragged breath. "He wants a wife. He wants *his* wife. I don't want him, I don't even know him."

"Easy," he soothed.

She closed her eyes and dropped her forehead back to his chest. "I wanted to find out who I was. Now I don't want any part of that life. I'm horrible."

"No. You're just Jane. Ya don't remember, so you can't be Clara."

"What if I start to remember?"

"What if you don't?"

"What of the person who tried to kill me? If this husband found me, they might as well." Jane shuddered as she pictured the cowboy she'd seen in her periphery far too often around town. She clung to Cole's hand even as she stepped free of his embrace.

"You think too much sometimes."

"I know." She sighed. "One thing at a time. I have to talk to him, don't I?"

"Think so. Won't get answers if you don't."

"I don't feel married."

"Sure don't."

The shiver that ran down her spine when his hands circled her waist had nothing to do with her inner turmoil, and everything to do with his touch. She met him halfway, fingers laced into his hair to pull him close. The kiss grew urgent in an instant. A desperate attempt to remember the life she had now.

Her heart raced, but as his tongue traced the seam of her lips, it changed rhythm. Slower, steadier, less impatient heat, more soothing warmth. The familiar heat of his kiss sent fire along her nerves. She sighed and let him take control, filling her with deep longing to replace the panicked desperation.

He tugged her closer and a flash of pain broke through the moment. Gasping, her lips left his and a soft chuckle followed. Biting her lip as her body arched into his, the wound at her side smarted again. "Ow."

"You really gotta stop getting hurt."

"I'll take it under advisement."

"So you're married."

She poked his chest. "Didn't stop you from kissing me."

"Damn straight."

"I never thought I'd come to believe not knowing the answers might be easier. Everything just became even more complicated."

"You gotta believe the answers'll come. That it'll help."

"Optimistic is not a good look on you. Besides, I'm not in the mood."

"Then it's a damn annoyance." He chuckled. "But not everything is complicated."

"It's not, hmm? What isn't?"

"This…"

Her eyes fluttered closed when his lips brushed across hers again. She sighed as he trailed them along her jaw line. A small kiss under her ear drew a gasp and she gripped his arms. Clearing her throat, she pushed him back with a throaty laugh to cover her growing desire. It wasn't the right time, not with so much going on. At the rate they were going there would never be such a time. "You just want me because it appears I'm taken."

"Sure does sweeten the pot."

Her amusement dont faded at the knock on the door. Her grip on his arms tightened. She shook her head. How could she do this? "I don't think I can do this. I'm still not sure I even want to. He thought she was dead; maybe we should leave her that way. There's so much we don't know, and I'm not liking my odds."

He made it through her tirade in silence. Once she'd finished, he kissed her forehead. "You gotta try."

"I know."

At her nod, he released her. He pulled open the door. "Davie."

"Cole?" David frowned, looing from him to Jane. "What are you doing here?"

"He's a friend." Jane stayed on the other side of the room. Part of her wished Cole would stay; she needed the moral support more than she cared to admit. She had no idea what the right thing to do was. Her head and heart spun in circles until she hardly knew which was up.

"Clara."

"My name isn't Clara." Jane clenched her hands. Every bit of relaxation she'd reveled in thanks to Cole blew away. Through clenched teeth she drew in air slowly to bring her temper back to a tolerable level. It wasn't David's fault. He had no idea all she'd been through. Of course, neither did she. "Please. It may have been once, but I don't remember. I am Jane."

"You really don't remember?" David crept into the room. He slipped a hand into his vest. "How can you not remember?"

She backed several steps away. "I have no idea. I was near death. I fell into the saloon. I remember nothing from before, nothing at all. The memories I have, they're all from the past couple of months. From being Jane."

"I know it's you. Look. Here." Out of his vest David withdrew an envelope. He held it out to her. "Please, look. I know it's you, Clara."

Jane tried to even out her breathing. So much hinged on the envelope before her. She didn't want anything to change. She wouldn't let it, no matter what this man revealed. Cole was right; she couldn't be Clara if she didn't remember. Still, her hand shook when she reached out for the envelope.

"I never knew what happened to you. I searched for so long." David's voice cracked. Once he'd cleared his throat, he continued, "The trail went cold. The winter grew harsh. I stayed in our home for almost two years hoping you would come back to me. That by some miracle you were out there alive."

A ring fell out first, heavy as her heart and spinning as her head. A simple, delicate ring once it settled from its chaos. A small blue sapphire setting. No added adornments, plain and clean. She lifted her head to get Cole's take on it, but he was gone. Much as she might have been, she couldn't be angry with him. He was right, she had to face this without him.

"We were only engaged for three weeks. I all but asked you to marry me the moment we met. You didn't want anything fancy." David stepped closer. "We were married for only six months and then you were gone."

She dropped the ring to the table where it clattered and spun again. Her fingers grew cold and numb, but somehow she managed to pull the last item from the envelope. A picture. The young woman in the image was unmistakably her. Younger, disgustingly happy, wrapped in David's arms. "Oh no."

"Clara." His arms circled her.

She dropped the picture to wrap her arms around herself, trying to put a barrier between them. "I don't remember."

"Hey." David released his hold and turned her toward him. "Tell me what happened."

"I don't know." She took a step back to get some distance. "The first thing I remember is waking up in this room two months ago. The people I've met since, the relationships forged. No one here knew me. I don't want to hurt you, but I don't—"

"Remember. So you've said." One corner of his lip quirked up in an expression she might have called adorable in a different situation. "When you left, winter was settling in. I worried that you'd died. I waited there for two years, going out and checking the area for any sign of you, hoping you'd come back."

"Don't make me hurt you."

"I think you did a good enough job of that when you left."

Jane shut her eyes to keep the growing well of tears at bay. Thoughts spun through her head faster than she could catch them. Her heart pounded loud in her ears.

"Sit down, please. Before you pass out." A gentle hand guided her to a chair. She found herself seated without ever opening her eyes. Another chair scraped the floor before a warm hand settled on her knee. "What can I tell you?"

"I don't know." She forced several deep breaths until the shakiness subsided. As her somersaulting stomach settled she managed to open her eyes. "I wanted to know all along, at least I thought I did. Now that you're here with so many answers, yet so many questions, I'm not so sure anymore. I am happy. I don't want to lose that."

"Would you like to know your name?"

"You told me. It's Clara."

"Clara Louise Young. When we married, it became Schaffer. You were born near Buffalo, New York. Six brothers."

"Six?" A family. She had a family. Her heart stilled. "Heavens. Oh no. Oh my…they think I'm dead too. They think I'm dead."

"Mike never believed it, but I think the rest of them did." David set his hand on her twitching fingers, the warmth a shock to her cold hand. "I hoped for so long you'd come back."

"Stop saying that. Stop. I'm sorry. I'm so sorry. I don't know how to act. I'm so overwhelmed. I'm not her; I don't have your answers. I'm so sorry." The cold settled so deep in her bones she worried they'd shake right out of her skin.

"Clara."

"Jane." She pulled her hand free. "I'm sorry."

His brow furrowed. "Do you need time? I've had seven years to think about what I'd do if I ever saw you again."

"And your decision was a kiss?"

"Well, yeah. That was first." A flush filled his cheeks, and for a moment he appeared ten years younger. The lines that aged him faded in his grinning embarrassment. "What can I say? I thought I'd never see you again. I always did like kissing you."

She focused on her hands, trying to muster up the amusement to match his.

"Then I was hoping for answers, but you say you don't have them." He sighed and pulled off his hat. After he'd flipped it around in his fingers for a minute, he shook his head. "I think we need to talk more."

It started small, but her nod grew until she thought her head might pop off. When she realized he wasn't looking at her, she found her voice again. "Yes. We do."

"Tomorrow? Please?" His hazel eyes bored into hers. "Clara, I loved you so much. I always felt robbed that I didn't get enough time with you. I'm just so glad to see you again."

"Tomorrow." Jane gasped for air. "Please go. I need…I need to think…to…I…"

"All right." David pushed the picture and ring toward her. "Hold onto those long as you need them. Maybe they'll help."

Her eyes shut when he leaned down and kissed the top of her head. "I'm sorry."

"I know. Just wish I knew what for."

She bit her lips so hard she tasted blood. Tears were not allowed in front of this man, this stranger. Not until the door clicked shut and his boot steps faded downstairs did she let the first sob escape.

In a frenzy, she slammed shut the balcony doors. Those were locked, followed by the bedroom door. She raced to the bed and climbed in fully clothed.

The slight pressure in her head when she'd first heard David's voice had blossomed into blinding pain. Like a miner attacked her mind with a pickaxe over and over.

Curled on her side, she stared at the wall, willing her mind to stop its racing. In the back of her head she considered going across the street, but the last thing she needed was more to confuse her. She needed to be alone. She needed to understand it all. Somehow.

Willing her eyes shut, she fought for sleep to come, praying until her body caved to exhaustion.

The shelves of books were packed tight, just like every nook and cranny of the store. This man wasn't even looking at the books he stood in front of. No, he only stared at a canteen on the shelf catty-corner to the books.

Cowboy she thought, eyeing him. His dusty clothes fit the bill, as did his toned and tan arms. Smiling, she let herself look him over to cover her burgeoning impatience.

She'd seen plenty of cowboys come through and had made time with her share of them, but she wondered if cowboy was the right assessment. As her imagination took hold and started to create a story of its own, he finally turned around.

She held onto the breath she'd just taken for dear life, losing herself instantly in his bright hazel eyes. A smile erupted as the corners of his eyes crinkled up in a grin.

"Sorry. Hope I ain't in your way."

"No." Clearing her throat as the foreign heat of a blush lit her cheeks up, she said, "I mean, yes you are, but I can wait. I was just looking for a new book."

Looking over his shoulder, he nodded. "I was just moving on. Have at 'em."

"Thank you." She tore her eyes from his and brushed past him closer than necessary—even by the standards of the narrow aisle. She bit her lip and glanced over her shoulder as she absently grabbed a book.

Once again the heat rose in her cheeks and when he paused, she jumped, turning her attention back to the shelves.

Switching books, she couldn't stop the grin that started to form as she heard his footsteps approaching.

"Excuse me for being forward, Miss…"

"I'd love to." After a small gasp, she turned to meet his surprised gaze. "I mean…I…um…"

"Name's David. And I'm glad you will."

Stepping a little closer, she looked up at him through her lashes. "And what, pray tell, did I just agree to?" She heard his breath catch. Warmth filled her heart.

"Depends. It was either to a walk, or to marry me."

"How about a walk first?" She laughed. "It's not a proper courtship without at least one walk."

"And then?"

"Depends."

"On what?"

"You'll see."

Gasping awake, Jane stared at the ceiling in shock. "Oh God." Turning to her side, the tears resumed and she sobbed herself to sleep again.

Drip. Drop. Drip.

A drop of scarlet hung from the ragged ridge of flesh. White bone poked out, muscle red and oozing around it. The red drip shivered before falling in slow motion into the growing pool of scarlet.

White snow cradled the hand like a pillow in the middle of the tracks. Bile rose in her throat, threatening to spill over when a finger twitched.

Her eyes remained glued to the sight, knowing that if she looked up she'd see him, the rest of him. Murmurs around her started to sink in, saying she'd pushed him. In an instant time sped back up.

With a gulp, she lifted her eyes to see the mangled mass of man left over, his blank stare ripping her heart out through her gut. A cold sweat broke on her forehead and she unleashed a terrified scream.

This time she woke screaming. Terror filled her soul, her scream echoing through the empty room until with a crack of wood, the door burst open.

*Suffering is permanent, obscure and dark,
and shares the nature of infinity.
-William Wordsworth*

Jane leaned on the doorframe, not quite on the balcony but not inside her room either. Only an hour before she'd woken so groggy she couldn't remember when she'd fallen asleep.

Daisy's guilty admittance that they'd needed to drug her to calm her down in the middle of the night was all she knew. It had taken a full day for Jane to wake up peaceful enough for them to stop administering the medicine.

The medicine had the unfortunate effect of making the previous two months foggy and unclear. When people passed by, she had to think hard to remember names and occupations when she knew for a fact the information should be easy to grasp. She remembered enough to at least know she used to be quicker on her feet.

Instead, her brain functioned as if mired in sand. Words came slower, but worse the memories came slow.

The last thing she wanted to lose was the memories she'd gained since she woke in Dominion Falls. The lifetime she'd already lost was overwhelming enough without adding to it.

A few short months might not matter in the long run to most people, but they were all she had.

She swiped at her tears and took a deep breath in an attempt to remain calm. She'd sworn to Daisy she wouldn't get overwrought. Despite Daisy's rather upbeat mood, Jane had shooed her off an hour ago. Since then she'd tried to focus on what she should have been focused on instead of her breakdown—David's arrival.

More than his arrival was the revelations he'd brought with him. She had a husband. Brothers. A family. All of whom believed she'd died. No matter what, she couldn't see the logic in wounding the family Clara had loved any further. Telling them now would be a mistake.

Maybe it made her selfish. Maybe it made her horrid.

She wanted to live first. To figure out more about who she was. If she had any of this Clara left within her soul, or if she would remain as she was, as Jane.

Jane was comfortable. Clara was an unknown. She wanted to know who Clara was and why she'd walked away from David. She wanted to do so without losing herself. Could it be done?

Much as it pained her, she needed to hear David's story.

She wouldn't guarantee Clara would return. How could she? Jane had no idea if her memories would ever be restored, much less the feelings often contained within. How much of who she was now carried a part of Clara?

Jane took a step onto the balcony, then another until she could rest her hands on the railing. From one end of the street to the other she took in the town. A breeze stirred the dead air, reviving the scents so familiar by now. The people she'd come to know moved about below her, shopping at carts, having arguments and laughing at jokes.

This was her home. The more she soaked it in, the more her memories solidified. Peace washed over her in place of the panic of earlier. This town, her home, was what she needed to cling to whenever fear threatened to overwhelm her.

Maybe she could find middle ground.

She dropped her gaze to the saloon. The porch was quiet save for one man. The cowboy—Johnny. In all of the chaos she'd forgotten about him. Before she could shy away and retreat back to her room, he loaded a saddlebag onto his horse. Could he be leaving?

She straightened and backed a step away from the railing as he hiked up into the saddle. When he spurred his horse on, she raced forward to be sure he left town for real. She craned her neck around the side of the building to follow his path toward the oncoming line of rails.

A thread of tension eased away as he became a speck in the distance. Even though she still had no idea why he bothered her, it relieved her to no end to have him gone.

Unfortunately, she still had to deal with David.

Immediately.

There was no sense in further delaying the inevitable. No sense but her own selfish need to protect her life as it stood.

Daisy had told her David was staying in Cora's spare room, so that's where she'd go. Maybe afterward she would sit down with Cole and try to wrap her head around it. If nothing else, that man had a tendency for brash and annoying honesty. Out of anyone in town, he would be the first to tell her if she were being a fool.

Before she could talk herself out of it, she rushed out of the boarding house and barreled down the street toward Turner's. Her usual long-winded greetings were made brief in her single-minded pursuit. Somehow she had to figure out the best way to tell David the truth about the dream she'd had. No, not a dream. A memory.

A memory with no emotion tied to it. She remembered meeting him. The thoughts in her head told her she should feel something. Excitement, lust, giddy joy, and love. They were all in the memory. In Clara's head.

None of them ever touched Jane's heart.

It seemed cruel. Heartless. To tell a man she remembered falling in love, but felt nothing in the memory? Despite her attempt to live as honest as possible since she'd woken two months before, this was simply too much. Panic and doubt stopped her momentum halfway up the steps to Turner's general store.

With a quiet sob, she turned away from the door and sank to the step. She buried her face in her hands, trying to compose herself again.

"Clara?" David's footsteps approached slow and steady. He'd likely heard of her state of mind the past few days. Good to know she could make everyone in town concerned about her mental state. "How are you feeling?"

Even though she couldn't remember him, she couldn't turn away from his offered comfort. With his arm wrapped around her shoulder, she could only sigh. "Dandy."

There was a quiet snort. His attempts to hide laughter failed miserably. A few more snorts and the jolting of his body as it held her made her all too aware of his amusement.

She smacked his stomach, as it was closest to her swatting hand. "Your amusement is not helping my disposition."

"Sorry. I've heard that tone before, though. I really don't want to be the brunt of whatever anger you're trying to cover."

"I'm the one who'll get the brunt of it. You're safe from my anger." First thing she had to do pained her enough that she couldn't meet his gaze. "Please don't call me Clara."

"I don't know if I can call you anything else." He squeezed her shoulder, then kissed the top of her head. "I know who you are."

"I might have been her. Once upon a time." Jane sighed. No time like the present. If Cole could be cruelly honest, she could do the same, somehow. "The other night I believe I had a small memory of meeting you. But it wasn't a full memory, David. I didn't feel anything. I know I should have, the memory echoed with the emotions, but I couldn't feel them."

"I don't understand. What did you remember?"

"Meeting you. You were in a store looking at canteens, right by a shelf of books." She tensed when he gasped. "It's like I was watching a play, David. Don't get your hopes up so. I felt nothing Clara felt. I watched it, but I wasn't part of it."

"If you remembered that, you could remember more."

She pressed her hands together and shoved them between her knees. Her back hunched as she tried to retreat into herself. "I might not. This is the first memory I've had of Clara. I may never remember another thing. I don't want you to get your hopes up."

One finger brushed along her cheek. Somehow she found herself doing what she didn't want to—looking into his eyes. He smiled. "So you remember the canteens."

"And you asking Clara to marry you almost immediately." She shifted her position on the stair to face him directly. "You didn't have to work for Clara's love."

"Not in the beginning." For a brief moment the easy smile and affection faded into darkness and sorrow. He shook it off like a dog would shake off water. "We were only together for seven months, married for six of them. It was damn near perfect."

"Six months?" Jane pulled the ring from her reticule. The overwhelming pressure dissipated from her chest enough that she could breathe clearly again. "That's all?"

"Some of the happiest in my life. Mike came to the wedding, that's one of your brothers. You wanted him there." He leaned his forearms on his knees. The memories brought a wistful look to his features, which made him appear much younger. "A simple ceremony at the pastor's house and dinner at ours."

She turned the ring over in her hand. "I wish I could remember for you."

"You know, that house is the one thing we argued about? You were angry I bought it when you were renting a perfectly good one."

For some reason Jane didn't voice her opinion that Clara sounded rather sensible. She worried it would only fuel his fire into believing her to be Clara.

His frown reappeared as he studied her. "What am I supposed to do? I don't know how to act here."

"Neither do I. Here. Please take this ring back. It's yours." When his hand closed over hers, she didn't pull away. "I wish I could tell you I remembered. I wish I could remember her. I wish it were as easy as seeing you and it all comes back to me, but it isn't. I still don't remember."

"What does the doc say?"

"That it might still happen. Then again, it may not. I would hate to give you false hope."

"When I didn't see you for five years, I knew I'd never get my wife back. Even if you returned I wasn't the same man, I didn't figure you would be the same woman." The ring glimmered in the sunshine as he flipped it over in his palm. "Can't say I'll ever stop loving you."

"I can't say that I would ever love you." Every grimace of pain on his features twisted her heart more, but she had to be honest. "If only I could remember."

"I wish I was more surprised, but I guess if I was honest, I'm not." He shrugged and scratched the back of his neck.

"What?"

"I saw you with Cole. I know that look you gave him. How long you been with him?"

"I'm not." The high-pitched squeak of her denial caused an embarrassed flush to heat her cheeks. She rubbed her hands along her thighs and turned away. Having a man that claimed to know her so well studying all she did made some things too revealing. "It's nothing. We've kissed. That's all."

"Mind if I ask why?" He poked her shoulder. "I'm just curious. I mean, he's not anything close to me, and I'm wonderful."

She pressed a fist to her lips to cover a laugh. Once she shook it off, she turned back toward him and shook her head. "I expected more fight. You say you loved Clara."

"I did. I do. I learned to release you, to forgive you, even if I didn't understand why. I couldn't let go enough to declare you dead or divorce you. I held onto you in hope of answers." His lips twisted, and the sparkle of a smile lit his hazel eyes. "I guess I'm asking why so I might know if I have a chance to win you back."

"If you want a fair chance, you won't ask why." She pressed her lips together and stood. The man said he was her husband. He had the ring and photo to prove it. The hint of a memory she'd had showed he was speaking the truth. So why couldn't she feel it? He deserved a chance, but the risks were more pain for them both. "The last thing I want to do is hurt you more than you've already been hurt."

"My Clara left me seven years ago. I still love her, deeply. I might love you if given a chance. You might love me if given a chance, too. Don't we owe Clara that much?"

"You say it's been seven years? Without any idea where I went or what I was doing?"

"None. Not even Mike knew what happened to you, and you told him everything." He slid the ring into his pocket. "It took years for him to help me make peace with it. That maybe it wasn't my fault after all."

"Seven missing years. Even if my memories came back, I don't know how I could be your Clara. Something had to have happened to make her leave you and disappear for seven years. Something that left her…"

"Left her what?"

"Did anyone tell you how I looked when I arrived here?" Jane swiped at a tear. "How they thought I was dead?"

"Yeah. Cora told me. What happened to you?"

"I don't know. All I know is I'm fairly certain someone wanted me dead. The Clara you speak of so endearingly hardly seems like a person someone would attack." Jane sighed and looked out over the town. "Whatever Clara became, are you so sure you want her back in your life? She left you. Without a word as to why."

"I never knew what changed. If I did, maybe I could understand."

"What do you mean, changed?"

"Will you sit back down? Hear me out?" David took her hand, pulled her back onto the step. "The first five months were perfect. I know you think I'm remembering wrong because I want it to be, but it was. We disagreed on very little."

Jane fought the urge to pull her hand free. He needed to do this. Worst of all, she needed to hear it.

"You were a teacher."

"A what?" She wrinkled her nose. "A teacher? I don't care for children."

David laughed. "You did then. You were such a good teacher. All your students graduated. Students came from other districts for your class. You wanted a big family like yours. We'd made plans to start one right away. I was building onto our house. In fact, it was when I went to pick up materials once that everything changed."

The crack in his voice was impossible to ignore. She took his hand. "What changed?"

"I don't know. I went over the creek into town to pick up supplies. After weeks of summer heat, much like this, a storm finally broke while I was in town. It hit so fast the creek rose into a river. I couldn't get home for almost three days. I wasn't worried. You were always so strong. At most I expected you to be annoyed because you'd asked me to stay home and wait until Monday."

She did her best not to flinch when his hand tightened, twisting hers.

"When I got home, everything was different. Clara was so different. Scared, almost. Worse, she was so very angry with me, furious even. I never even knew what I'd done wrong. That fall she didn't return to teaching. She holed up in our house. Her garden, which she'd been so proud of, rotted away. Everything changed. Not even Mike could tell me why. Why did it happen? What did I do?"

"David," Jane whispered. The gentle hand she set on their clasped hands stirred him back to life. "I can't give you the answers you seek. I simply don't know. I've tried and tried without success to remember my life before."

"Will you continue to try?"

"I must. I will always try. I just don't want you getting false hope. You said yourself Clara will never return as you once knew her. With, or without, my memories. The only thing I can promise you now is if I do remember why she hurt you, I will tell you." She cupped his cheek. "I'm sorry I can't be your wife. I don't know you. I barely know myself."

"I'm gonna love you anyway." David took her hand and pulled it to his chest. "Maybe the more I talk, the more you'll remember."

"No false hope, David. I won't make promises I can't keep. Today has given me nothing new, nothing more than sorrow that the person I was hurt you so deeply. All I can promise now, is that I will be honest with you."

"I'll take it for now." He kissed the back of her hand. "Would you do me the honor of taking a walk with me tomorrow?"

"Yes. Is one o'clock suitable?" At his nod, she pulled her hand free. "Thank you for trying to understand."

"Like I said, a few years back I got used to the fact Clara wouldn't be coming back to me. I guess I'm looking at this as a second chance."

She backed down the steps. "Just don't ask me to be someone I'm not. Don't ask me to be Clara."

"I'll try."

She spun around and darted down the street. Tomorrow she'd learn more about Clara, about a life she couldn't remember. Would she learn more things she didn't want to know? What good would any of it do if seven years were still missing?

Until she'd almost reached the boarding house she kept her rapid pace, and didn't dare to look back for fear of still seeing David sitting there. Once she slowed a few buildings away, she noticed Cole leaning against the railing in front of her destination.

Relief immediately relaxed her. It would be nice to finally explain all that had happened and see what Cole thought.

Confusion stole the relief right out from under her. What had been so simple two days ago was now riddled with complication and guilt. Was her life really hers?

Cole straightened, a frown replacing his smirk. "Jane? Ya look upset."

"Appropriate since I feel that way." She leaned against the post beside him, letting his proximity soothe away her roiling doubts and fears. "I just came from a conversation with David about Clara."

"So this ain't about the other night?"

"It is—but it isn't. I...I had a memory of...her. Me...her..." Groaning, she buried her face in her hands. "I told him I wasn't her. I'm not. I'm not going to stop living my life."

"All right."

"He told me a little about her, what she was like."

"So what did you find out?"

"She was..." her nose wrinkled and she shuddered, "a teacher."

A snort burst out of him, followed by a chuckle. "A teacher? You ain't serious, are ya?"

She narrowed her eyes. "And what if I am?"

"A teacher?" Within moments he was laughing so hard she couldn't get a word in edgewise.

Frustration set in as he continued on, practically falling over the railing into the trough. "It's not that funny."

"Yeah, it is."

"Cole."

"A teacher? You avoid walking near kids. You can't even talk to Isaac. A teacher?"

"Cole, stop it."

"You? A teacher? That's rich!"

She stomped her foot at another loud guffaw from him, she snapped. With one hard shove she toppled his already unsteady stance right over the hitching post so he landed in the trough. "Brute!"

He emerged from the trough with a full-on bray of laughter.

Without another word, she spun on her heel and stomped into the boarding house, slamming the door hard enough to rattle the panes behind her. His laughter followed her all the way up the steps to her room where she slammed the balcony doors too.

While she found the idea appalling, how dare he treat it so?

He'd see. The brute would get a hold on his laughter.

She smirked. She'd see how he felt when she didn't return his amusement, or his attentions. One way or another the man would apologize for his lack of decorum. Honesty was one thing. This was too much.

Al would call her childish over her idea.

Childish, yes.

Productive?

She damn sure hoped so.

"Jane!"

She pushed open the balcony doors, creeping toward the edge to peek over.

Cole stood in the middle of the street, soaked from head to toe. His arms spread wide, he grinned up at her.

She lifted her chin and eyed him coldly. Her fingers drummed on the railing, waiting on whatever wickedness he'd concocted.

"Soakin' wet I still ain't more ridiculous than you bein' a teacher."

An unseemly retort brewed in her head, but she simply backed away from the railing. His laughter took over again, joined by others on the street.

"As Cicero said, Cole," she muttered as she closed the door. "Any man can make mistakes, but only an idiot persists in his error."

*The calmest husbands make
the stormiest wives.
-English Proverb*

"I ain't ever seen him like this." Daisy leaned in close as possible. The wicked grin she wore had been there since Cole stormed out of the restaurant half an hour before. "Then again, I don't think anyone's refused him before."

"Well, he is difficult to deny." Jane put as much energy into her smile as she could. Her determination to ignore the man was proving damn difficult to follow through on. She wasn't short of distractions to fill her day. Between work, David, Al, reading, and the curious questions of those called friends, she hardly had time to breathe. Yet, she still managed to miss his presence during simple moments. Moments that shouldn't have mattered.

"You don't have to tell me." Daisy settled back in her seat, an almost giddy wiggle of her shoulders as she did so. During the previous week she'd been more pleasant than Jane could ever remember her being. Short of Jane's ignoring of Cole, she saw no rhyme or reason to it. Daisy shook her head. "I'm impressed you've managed it."

"He needs to apologize. Properly apologize. I deserve as much, and I won't take less. Apparently I'm quite stubborn.

Even when I'd rather not be." Laughing at her was enough reason for him to apologize, publically drawing attention only made things worse.

"Did David tell you that?"

Jane snorted. "No. I figured it out all on my own. Although David has mentioned Clara was stubborn, his stories hint she gave in easier."

"Cole. David. That Major and half the army camp if the stories are true. All of those men. You've got the whole town's tongues wagging. I don't care much for rumor and gossip, but why not dispel some of it?" Daisy's brow furrowed. "I mean, even if it is true, doesn't it bother you to have so much talk about what should be private matters?"

What bothered Jane about any of it was how Cole and David both believed it. Yet neither of them had bothered to straight out ask her for the truth. They didn't ask her to her face if she did indulge her pleasures anywhere and with anyone.

She made it a point to be honest, but only if asked. Even Daisy hadn't asked for the truth. She'd only inquired if the rumors bothered Jane.

Jane frowned and cast her gaze around the room. "Rumors are just that. If anyone cared to know if it was true, they only have to ask. Otherwise I see no point wasting my time in idle gossip that will spread whether I admit or deny a thing."

"I see." Daisy remained quiet for a moment before sitting forward again. "How are things going with David? He's your husband—has he helped at all?"

"I've had no further memories. Not even a hint of one." To be honest, every day it grew more depressing. Even the presence of Clara's husband hadn't sparked anything beyond the initial memory. Not for lack of trying, or for lack of time in each other's company. Jane kept her promise. She kept trying.

"I have to ask. Have you helped yourself to his company? He's attractive and so nice compared to most of the ruffians around here."

"Are you asking for you or for Cole?" The moment the words left her mouth, Jane halfway regretted them. Daisy's pout showed how much the idea offended, but in Jane's opinion Daisy needn't have been the least bit surprised.

"I'm not asking for Cole. He's not talking about you much." Daisy flushed and ducked her head. "Maybe 'cause he's mad."

"Isn't he always?"

"He told me what you said, ya know."

Jane frowned when Daisy left it at that. She'd need more information to have any idea what the woman was talking about. "I'm afraid you'll have to be more specific. I've said quite a bit to that man that could bear repeating, or being listened to."

Daisy chewed her lip, a secretive smile gracing her features. "I guess so. Not that I'd dare say as much to Cole."

"I would."

"I've noticed." Daisy sighed. "He told me what you said about selling my contract. About keeping me on as a doctor until I get started. You didn't have to do that. I would've never thought of it myself. Wouldn't have dared imagine it."

"It's logical. He won't go back on his word; he isn't that sort of man. However selling to Guy is the exact opposite of good business. He knows it all too well. So I gave him a better option. Not that I think he'll listen." Especially after the past week.

"I'm afraid to think he'll agree." It was barely a whisper. The red hue of Daisy's cheeks almost disappeared behind a curtain of brunette hair. "Or rather to hope he will."

"If he has a shred of common sense, he will."

"Why did you?" Daisy cleared her throat, drawing her shawl back across her chest. "You could have been rid of me."

Jane did her best to swallow her sigh. "I've told you, Daisy. I like you. I have no need to be rid of you. I'm not trying to take anyone's place or stop Cole from doing whatever he's used to with his girls. And I'm certainly not thrilled at the idea of you being sent somewhere you'll have it far worse. I may not care for Cole owning women, but at least by all I've seen he's a far lesser evil. From what you and a few of the girls have said, at least he never hits his women, and he is quite…accommodating."

"He always was before." Daisy bit her lip. "I mean to say, he used to be. He still doesn't hit us, of course. Guess I can't say as much for Graham when he's drunk or in a mood, but Cole doesn't."

Though she wondered at what Daisy meant by 'always was before', Jane bit her tongue from questioning. It was none of her business anyhow. Not anymore.

"Either way, some would say Guy's is better."

"I've worked with the man for a month. Believe me, it's not."

"Daisy." Cole leaned on the doorframe, his frown not dulling Jane's instant reaction his reappearance. She could curse her body for the way it leaned his direction. His gaze fell on her for a moment, intense as ever before returning to Daisy. "You're late. The girls need to be checked before I open."

"I thought you said one." Daisy didn't rise. "I'll be right there."

Cole grunted. His icy eyes paused on Jane again. His lips twitched before he turned away. It took all of her strength to not laugh at his attempt to ignore her.

Daisy didn't bother to hide her laughter. She leaned in close and spoke low to keep him from hearing. "Thank you. For what you said to him."

Jane shrugged. "Don't mention it. Good luck. He seems to be in a mood."

"I simply can't imagine why he would be, Jane. Not for one moment." Daisy continued to laugh as she rushed forward to drape herself on Cole's arm.

Jane couldn't be bothered by the action. This was little more than a show put on for her benefit. Instead of paying them any further mind, she dropped money on the table to cover her meal.

"Good afternoon, ma'am." In a dramatic drawl, David bowed low in front of her. His hat scraped his boots before he rose to right it on his head. "Might I have the pleasure of your company this fine day? I do enjoy a good roll in the hay."

Any pretense of annoyance flew away. Her laughter raced through the restaurant without inhibition. David spoke loud and clear, his racy comment stopping Cole dead in his tracks. She imagined that had been the intention. "You're terrible."

"I know." David grinned and held out his arm for her. Once she'd taken it, he walked her right past the still gaping

Cole and Daisy. On the way down the steps, his lips made a valiant attempt at a frown. "I swear I didn't do that for his benefit."

"Liar."

"Why would I help my own wife tease her lover?"

"Because you're a far bigger bastard than people realize. You're sneaky about it, and none would dare believe such a thing of you." Jane didn't bother to stop her grin. Even though she couldn't profess to love the man walking with her, she definitely enjoyed his company. "You pretend to be good, kind, and quiet. You are anything but."

"Will you keep my secret?" He winked. The hay comment had been double edged. First playful—after all, they'd found a great peaceful place for conversation away from prying eyes in a group of haystacks nearby. But also naughty—no one knew that part.

"Only because I enjoy the dichotomy far more than I should. My acquiescence has little to do with benefiting a rotten scoundrel such as yourself." Her laughter remained unburdened by the recent struggles with David. In fact their conversation stayed clear of any subject capable of dispersing their good moods.

Not until they'd arrived at the Mortell farm and settled between the haystacks did the tone change. David's sigh carried a heavy note. His hand rested on hers. "No clouds to watch today."

"It's been far too dry this year. Clouds have been scarce every time we've come here, today is no different." Jane tapped the hay under her hand. "Only thing it's been good for is storing up for winter. So what's bothering you today?"

"Not sure what you mean." He sat. His ankles crossed and he leaned his arms on his knees. A piece of hay swirled between his fingers. "Nothing's bothering me."

"David, please. I may have only known you a week, but you are terrible at hiding how you feel, it's written all over your face. The tightness around your mouth, the pinch of your brow, the way you're playing with that blasted piece of hay rather than look at me?"

"What are you, a Pinkerton?"

"I'm hardly a Pink. I haven't the stomach for such matters. I'm merely observant, and you are no good at secrets. What is it?"

"Just thinking. About you, Jane."

The steady beat of her heart slowed until it almost stopped. Over the whole week of her asking him to please not call her Clara, not once had he complied. Never in that whole time had he dared call her Jane.

"You might still remember."

She didn't move, resting back in the hay long as she could. Only the determination to remain calm kept her there. "You don't sound nearly as hopeful as you once did."

"That's your fault."

"Sorry."

"Don't be. You've been trying, just like I asked. Makes me wish you hadn't agreed." He'd turned away enough that his hat blocked his features. She had no idea where he was heading with this train of thought.

"Why?"

"If you'd not been trying so hard and spending all this time with me I wouldn't know what I do. I wouldn't see who you are now, what you've become. I could still find a way to pretend you were my Clara."

That got her attention and she sat. Somehow the words made her heart twinge in a strange combination of relief and sorrow. "David?"

"Sometimes you're so close, but there's always something not quite right. I would know my Clara anywhere. You aren't her." When he turned, the hazel of his eyes shimmered. "Don't think this means I'm giving up."

"You don't seem the type to quit."

He moved quick and within moments had her lying back in the hay. A soft smile lit the features that hovered above hers. The hint of tears dissolved in his wink. "I still say you fell in love with me once, you could again."

She laughed, even as she held him at bay. Hands on his chest, not pushing since he'd yet to try to move. "I still say you wouldn't be as happy if you have to work for it. The love you had with Clara was easy. I'm considerably more difficult to deal with."

"And I have competition."

Her smile faltered. "It would seem so."

"You said you'd give me a chance. Have you given up already?"

"Are you so sure you want to keep trying? Clara left you. Hurt you. I may be an even worse woman than she was. I mean, I find myself to be quite despicable."

"I won't complain about who you court, so long as I've got a chance. I told you, I always did like kissing you." He gave another playful wink. "Memory or not, you still kiss real good."

She couldn't stop her laugh when he inched closer. "I've agreed to nothing, Mr. Schaffer."

"I'm not giving up, Mrs. Schaffer."

"That's Miss Doe to you."

*A woman never forgets her sex.
She would rather talk with a man than an angel,
any day.
-Washington Irving*

"You gotta talk to me sometime." Cole slid into the seat next to Jane. The fact she continued to ignore him should have made him furious. After all, he hated being ignored. It riled him, but not because she dared to ignore him.

For almost two weeks she'd shut him out. All while going around with her husband, Major Webb, not to mention half the army camp if rumors were true.

At first he'd seen it as a game. He'd wounded her pride; she wanted him to suffer. He got that. He sure did the same thing from time to time. Cole didn't suffer being made a fool of; it was fair Jane felt the same.

But if she'd used this time to give any man what he had yet to get he'd be furious. This woman had been under his skin since day one. Turning him on, driving him mad, and driving him away, all while pulling him closer. He deserved to get his.

First.

"Anything else today, Jane?" Cora had circles under her eyes. The woman clearly was still a wreck after her husband's death. It was a wonder the store sat open at all. Still, she managed a smile for Jane and a glare for him. "I got some apple pie for dessert."

"Sounds delicious." Jane actually spoke. Of course, she didn't speak to him. She also smiled bright at Cora. Her hand slipped away from his as he reached for her. "But I'm afraid I have plans for this evening. Al should be here shortly."

Cora nodded. The smile she'd been wearing drooped as if the effort of it had exhausted her. Her voice remained kind, but not cheerful. "Suit yourself. If there's any left, I'll save you a slice for lunch tomorrow."

"Thank you. I appreciate it." Jane squeezed Cora's hand. Despite Jane's concerns at the funeral, the two appeared to be getting along fine. Like he'd told her all along, Cora didn't blame Jane a lick.

Cora didn't spare him a glance or a word, just like Jane. She walked away without saying anything more.

Cole frowned. "Don't want nothing. Thanks, Cora."

A hint of a smile tugged at Jane's enticing lips. A brief hint that she wasn't as mad as she was playing. Too soon it left. Once again she dug into her meal.

"Ya really think you can keep this up?" Since she ignored him, it wouldn't matter when he scooted his chair closer. He ran his finger along her arm with a feather-light touch. The goose flesh that rose in response made him chuckle.

Even when she determinedly ignored him with all her might, her body still responded. This could get fun if he played it right.

So what if he should be annoyed with her? No woman had ever ignored him this long. She made life an intriguing challenge—if he could keep his patience. All he had to do was think about the reward for winning; the passion he knew was in her.

Just how much would it take to get her talking again?

Or rather, not talking. He could live without the talking. She could have her words; he'd take everything else. Every inch of her, under him, saying nothing but one word—his name. He closed his eyes at the image that came to mind.

He shook it off with a shudder. If he got lost in those thoughts he'd never get her where he wanted her, needed her to be. "It's getting old. I ain't gonna find you amusing much longer."

Not a whisper of a reaction from her this time. He leaned close, letting his lips brush her ear when he spoke again. "Soldier boy ain't ever gonna get you going like I do. Neither will your husband. You know it. Ya feel it."

He grinned at the ragged breath she took. "You prefer a real man."

Someone cleared their throat, but Jane didn't move a muscle. Cole leaned back in his chair with a chuckle. At least Major Webb appeared flustered by the situation. He had a sneaking suspicion Jane was too, more than she let on.

"Al." Jane rose. "You're early."

"Sorry." Al offered her his arm. His nervous glance Cole's direction added to the fun. "Am I interrupting?"

"Interrupting what?" Jane took his arm, going the extra step to kiss him on the cheek. "I've lost my appetite. Shall we go?"

All amusement faded the moment the pair left the store. Cole rose, stepping around Cora when she tried to block his path. "Not talking to you."

"Cole Mitchell." Cora followed him onto the porch. "Cole."

He held up his hand to stop her, a frown settling in deep when Jane paused in the street to give the Major a kiss.

"Cole. Please just let her be." Cora grabbed his arm. A dangerous move, but she didn't seem to care. "She's married."

"Don't see ya saying these things to the Major." He tugged his arm free. "Or do ya save your lectures special for me?"

"Don't you think she deserves more than what you want?"

"You don't know what I want." He hopped down the steps before she could respond. It didn't help he didn't know what he wanted either. It also didn't help his disposition any when Jane swung into the saddle with Webb.

Cole clenched his jaw. It shouldn't bother him; like she'd pointed out long ago he didn't care for nothing to be exclusive. Yet, she seemed to be reveling in dalliances far more often than he was. Why should that bother him? She was playing him like a fiddle and Cole Mitchell didn't get played.

But still he wanted more.

Damn her for making him want more. Despite her affection for Al, he couldn't help but latch onto his own belief that the kisses she shared with Webb lacked the fire he knew she had. The fire he believed she reserved for him alone.

Damn her.

All deception in the course of life is indeed nothing else but a lie reduced to practice, and falsehood passing from words into things.
-Robert Southey

In front of the church Martha and Mabel were locked in intense discussion. The full wagon in front of them overloaded with items donated by the town. The settlement to the north of town had been attacked earlier in the week and donations had piled up in an effort to help.

Still it was odd. After all, they'd just taken supplies out the day before. Jane herself had gone to see the Broder's, a repaid kindness for helping her after the last attack. Unfortunately, the kind Broder's had lost their home to fire set by the renegades, along with close to fifteen other homes.

The results of yesterday's delivery meant everyone had more than enough goods to fill their now modest living arrangements. The tents could only hold so many stores.

She took the coffee handed to her in without a word of appreciation. Her mind was too fascinated by the puzzle before her to acknowledge David.

David broke the silence. "Still not talking to Cole?"

The mention of Cole ripped her from her distraction enough to focus on the man next to her. "What? Oh, no. I'm still waiting on my apology."

"Good luck getting it." His now familiar smile matched the humor layered under his tone. "He's a stubborn one."

"So am I, according to certain sources." She took a sip of coffee. "Now what's this you were saying about a garden?"

"Right. Clara's ma taught her well. The garden she made in that stubborn soil at our house flourished. She grew food of all sorts when others struggled, and she gave it away to fill empty tables. The food she cooked with it was delicious."

Jane lifted a brow. "Cooked? I haven't even attempted to cook since I woke. I haven't had any interest whatsoever. I'm not certain I could."

"You should try. I'd give anything for a helping of your mutton, stewed vegetables, with a big slice of that plum pie."

"You're drooling." She laughed when he wiped at the corner of his mouth. "I think for now I'm content with dining on Cora's fine meals. Perhaps if I find a suitable home, I'll try."

"Invite me for dinner anytime."

"I'll see if I can cook first." Jane bumped his shoulder and shook her head.

"Good morning, Miss Doe. David." Lee Dynan, Cora's cousin, walked up the steps. Small and fair, her pale cheeks developed a distinct flush when she nodded at David.

"Morning, Lee." David returned the nod. Jane didn't miss the way his ears turned red before he tipped his hat back on and tried to hide from her scrutiny. "Been busy today. Cora's is anticipating a rush at lunch."

Lee opened her mouth to reply, but after a glance at Jane, it shut again. With one more nod she darted inside.

Jane turned her attention to her coffee to cover her snort. The attempt to bury her amusement in her drink failed and she let it loose in a peal of laughter.

"What's so funny?"

"She's very pretty. So much nicer than I am too. Are you bored with my startling wit already? I may weep."

"It isn't—I'm not." He pulled his hat off his head and ran his fingers through his hair before replacing it. His coffee mug wasn't big enough to cover the agitated frown he wore. The cup hit the stair with a thunk and he rubbed the back of his neck. "Jane."

"What? I mean, *David*." After a poke to his knee, she leaned back on the step above her. "It isn't like we're making any sort of progress on the romantic front. A kiss or two, but nothing to make the angel's sing, and you know it. My memories haven't returned, so I'm not fawning or broken-hearted."

"She's Cora's cousin."

"And widowed." Jane craned her neck to look through the open doors of the store and restaurant. Lee moved about inside among the tables. "Her husband died in the mines, and Cora gave her the job so she wouldn't lose her home. Yes?"

"Yeah." He tipped his hat lower over his eyes. "I've been staying here, so of course I know her. She's nice."

"I noticed. Apparently so did you. Quite thoroughly. What color are her eyes?"

"Brown." He cleared his throat. "Jane."

"What's stopping you? Make your overtures if you wish. Release Clara officially. Come with me to see Lloyd and file for divorce. Then you can pursue the pretty little waitress. I hardly think you need to be concerned over whether she would decline. She seems rather taken."

"I haven't courted anyone in a long time."

"I can help."

"Don't think I want your kind of help."

Her hand flew to her chest and she released a dramatic gasp. "You wound me."

"Exactly my point." He couldn't contain his smile any longer, but shook his head. "You're an incorrigible woman. Some things haven't changed."

"So you say." The comfortable silence that fell between them let her resume her study of the scene in front of the church. By now it seemed that Martha and Mabel's discussion had become heated. Martha wasn't waving her arms dramatically, but every movement and gesture was fraught with tension and enthusiasm.

Mabel tried to take the saddlebag from Martha, who protested strongly. Martha won the battle and the saddlebag was added to Martha's horse.

After a few moments she frowned. "It is odd, don't you think?"

David sipped his coffee. The way he looked everywhere but the church made her wonder at the length of time it took for him to answer. Of course, the tension the crept into his shoulders and face added to her suspicions. "What?"

"They took a wagon full of supplies out to the settlement only yesterday. I was there shortly after to visit the Broder's." Jane went to the extra step to point in the direction of Martha and Mabel. Still David avoided the sight rather determinedly. "Everyone is well supplied. Hardly a place to store things there with so many homes lost. Yet now they're taking another wagon as well as a packed steed."

"There are a lot of people in need." His jaw worked in tense circles. Somehow his cup of coffee had turned into the most interesting thing in town. "Over ten homes burned, you know. There's no such thing as too much generosity."

"Of course. How silly of me." She set her mug on the railing, rising to stand. At least the approach of Al gave her a reason to leave the conversation. David made a poor liar and so did Martha. Something more was going on. Something they weren't revealing to anyone. "How great their needs must be."

"Yeah."

"You know something, David? You're a terrible liar."

Guilt creased his forehead. "I ain't lying. People are in need."

"Yes. But I doubt we're speaking of the same people." She shook her head. "You know, for all the time you spend trying to deride Cole's standing—he has one important quality over you at the moment."

"What do you mean?" That at least got him looking at her again.

"He's never lied to me. Even if it meant saying something completely stupid and making me mad. He's not a liar." Jane stormed down the steps. It would be best to get away from him before she said something she regretted.

"Jane." David made it down two steps before Al reached them. The open concern in his eyes faded into the tightness of secrets again. "We still going to meet tomorrow for lunch?"

"I suppose so. Good day, David." Jane took Al's arm and sighed. "Let me guess. Did you intend to walk casually past the church, Major?"

Al nodded in David's direction. "Mr. Schaffer. Anything new to report?"

"I said I'd tell you if I found him. I haven't." David's friendliness disappeared. The tension lining his face aged him ten years. "I haven't seen him and that's the truth."

"Good to know." Al set his hand on Janes and led her toward the church. As they stepped onto the boardwalk the two women stopped their vibrant conversation. Mabel hopped in the wagon faster than Jane had ever seen her move.

Martha's hands shook with every tug she made on the reins to unhook them from the hitching post. "Jane. Major Webb."

Jane pushed forward as pleasant a smile as she could manage. "Martha. You will tell Mrs. Broder I said hello, won't you?"

"If I see her." Martha adjusted her hat until her eyes were hidden in shadow. "I have a lot of deliveries to make. Good afternoon."

The horse took off before Al had a chance to say a word. He waited until Mabel also left before continuing their walk toward the Silver Saddle. "Hope you don't take offense."

"I take offense to little. Please feel free."

"I don't trust your husband." He adjusted his hat. "I'd think, given the history I've heard between him and Starbird, he'd be more willing to assist us."

"David is forgiving to a fault." Jane sighed. "Unfortunately he believes Martha's proclamations of Starbird's innocence. He truly feels Starbird wouldn't hurt anyone in this town. I imagine he'd be one to try to resolve things before ever bringing Starbird back here."

"Do you think he knows where he is?"

"I'm not sure. I think he was telling the truth about not having seen him. Whether or not he knows where the man is—that is a different story." She pursed her lips. "I also believe he knows whatever it is Martha is up to."

"Well, I have men posted at the settlement now. I'm sure those supplies will go where they were intended to by the people that donated them." Al smiled. "And I wish we could talk more, but here we are. Shall we meet for supper?"

"I wish I could." Jane leaned against the wall of the Silver Saddle. "I have plans to dine with Mr. Hamm this evening."

Al's smile got lost in his snort. "You're dining with Hammy?"

"I'm so pleased to know his reputation goes as far as the Army camp." She chuckled despite her droll tone. "Mr. Hamm has been ever so kind to me. I offered to have dinner with him since he was so good to keep an eye on me after I was shot. The sweet man deserves a nice meal with company that doesn't think he's a total dunce."

Al took her hand and kissed the back of it. "Then he will be in the best company. I'll hope for tomorrow. Hammy is a lucky man."

"No luck involved. He is sweet and kind, and that's all that is required. Now be gone. I have work to do."

"Ordering me around again, ma'am?"

"You bet I am." Jane laughed. "Good day, Major."

His hand clapped over his heart. "The lady doth wound me."

"You are a fool, Major." She shook her head as she waved goodbye. She stepped into the hotel without another word, her smile lingering for only a moment more. Guy's appearance at her elbow ended her joviality quick enough. "What is the reason for the prompt greeting, sir?"

"Jackson is here. I thought we might have a meeting." Guy attempted to steer her toward his office. All she got for yanking her arm free was a chuckle.

"Annoying me is never smart, Guy."

"Oh, I do believe you've taken a shine to me." Guy offered his arm and winked. "You haven't hit me in two whole weeks, after all."

"I'll have to see about correcting that." After a moment's more hesitation she took his arm. His laughter spurred her into a somewhat agreeable chuckle. She let him lead her back to his office. After she offered Jackson a short nod, she took her seat as Guy took his own seat behind the desk. She knew what the meeting was about so she didn't stand on ceremony. "Jackson is not the man for the position. If he runs, you will lose."

"I beg your pardon?" Jackson straightened. "I think I'm the best man—"

"Of course *you* do, Jackson. You're an egotist. You believe you're better than every person in this town and make your opinion clear on every possible occasion. That's why they don't like you." She turned her attention back to Guy. "And while you've made yourself more likable, I wouldn't suggest you either."

"May I ask why not?" Guy didn't bluster or react to Jackson's sputtering. Eyeing Jane with amusement, he remained leaning back in his chair.

"Because you're Cole's biggest competition."

"You want Cole in the position," Jackson sputtered. "You're loyalties are clear."

"Shut up, Jackson," Guy said in a quiet tone. "Let her speak."

"Cole doesn't have the fancy whores or a casino." Jane turned her full attention to Guy, the more reasonable of the two. "But he does have a larger customer base, and the ears of those customers as well. He'll be vehemently opposed to you as mayor and will use his customers to make sure you lose."

"So you want us to support someone?"

"She's going to want you to support Cole and you know it."

"Of course not." Jane threw a frustrated glare at Jackson. "He wouldn't be a good mayor. If you keep treating me like an idiot, I'll walk out now and let you fail."

"Go ahead. We won't fail."

Jane rolled her eyes. Rather than dignify his bluster with a reply, she focused on Guy. "My best advice to you is to drop this relationship. Your connection to Jackson will destroy what little hope you might have of becoming sheriff."

"Sheriff?" Guy pursed his lips. "I could see that. But what should we do about mayor? Who do we support?"

"That's more difficult. There are several men of capital I'm sure might run, but they aren't involved with the town as they should be. They stay in their large houses and watch from a distance. My best advice is someone closer to the town. Much as I don't care to say it, Graham Cooke is one."

"See?" Jackson leaned forward. "You dare—"

Jane stood. "I'm telling you, Guy. Get rid of him." She left the room, heading out onto the main floor. Jackson balked at every bit of her assistance and had grown ever more insipid since she'd started. Guy at least started to listen after she'd slapped him. He'd even gotten rid of the quack doctor.

"Whiskey, Janey?"

"Thank you, Ike. I could use one."

"Figured as much when I saw you in there with Jackson." The bartender set down her glass and grinned slyly. "Why do you think I drink so much?"

"Because you're a drunk." Jane giggled and held up her glass in a mock toast. "But then again, aren't we all?"

He laughed when she downed the drink. Soon as she'd finished, he took the glass and set it in the wash. "Did you really tell Guy to drop the whores?"

"If he wants to be called a hotel and get a good high class of client once the train finally gets here, yes."

"End of August is what they're saying. Not much longer."

"Once they got over the mountains and foothills, it started coming along faster. I can almost believe it." Jane lifted her head when the office door opened. Jackson stormed out, not even sparing her a glance as he left the hotel. She turned back to see Guy waving her into his office. "Excuse me, Ike."

"Janey." He nodded, turning his attention to another customer.

Jane stepped into Guy's office again, closing the door before taking a seat. Not a word was uttered. She remained stoic and silent as he flipped through his financial records before looking up at her.

"Why Graham?"

"It was just an idea. There are others you could back."

"You didn't answer."

"He's a big part of this town. He partially owns your competition, but as a lesser partner and thus doesn't care about the business as much. His main source of income is as an undertaker, where he gets plenty of business. He knows everyone and gets along with most. His biggest fault is his drinking, but he shares that with most of this town."

"Who else?"

Pursing her lips, she thought for several minutes. "Dick Moses or Archibald Hill. Well-known merchants, friendly. Not sure Dick has the gumption to make people believe he'd make positive changes for the town. Archibald does and he runs the livery, everyone does know him and know he does good business."

"None of whom I could *own* as you put it."

"You can't back someone that's sniveling around in your back pocket, Guy. If you back someone that's good for this town, it will boost your own status, and therefore strengthen your own attempt to become sheriff or sit on the Council, whichever you choose."

"And if I don't choose Graham? You'll tell him to run, won't you?"

Jane nodded. "And if you choose Graham, I'll tell Archibald. Running unopposed doesn't lend toward getting this town what it really needs. Just because the train is at our doorstep doesn't mean it will bring a lot of new business. You have to work for it. We have to make sure this town has something that will bring people."

"And no damn Indian raids."

"That's up to the Army, I'm afraid." She leaned forward. "This town needs a solid, strong government. It needs a sheriff. Law of the land is all well and good, but this town has been incorporated for six years and without a government ever since."

"It wasn't a government. It was a temporary conglomerate thrown together to make the town official. It didn't hold. That's why it took so long to get the railroad."

Jane smiled. "This time it will hold if it's done right. For the right purpose."

"Of course it will." Guy rose at the knock on the door. "That must be Rusty."

Jane opened the door as she was closer. She ushered in the reporter. Within minutes they'd swept him into what angle they were going for with the article. The need for the government and how every citizen should be concerned about it with the train at their door.

By the time they'd finished, Rusty kept rubbing his hand to alleviate the cramping and Guy grinned from ear-to-ear. Jane smiled. "What do you think, Rusty? Honestly. Having heard what we have to say and knowing this town, do you think the points we've made will get to them?"

"I think you've been putting a lot of time into this." Rusty flushed at Jane's eager grasp of his hand. "And it shows. It may just sway those against a government. I think all that remains is the way I write the story."

"Which I know you'll handle brilliantly." Jane turned to Guy. "I think we've got it all covered now. Guy, can I trust you to speak to whomever you're going to back? Or do you think you'll come off like a brute and an idiot?"

"I'll try to manage." Guy smirked. "Now both of you get out of my office. I've got real business to tend to, after all."

"I'll get right on this article." Rusty stood. "Probably be in the paper two days hence."

"Good to know." Guy nodded to the reporter as he left. Looking back at Jane, he said, "Go on. Take the rest of the day. Paid. I'll expect you back tomorrow."

"I'll see you tomorrow." She gave a quick wave to Ike on her way out. Her mood vastly improved, she almost skipped the rest of the way to the boarding house.

22

Kindness is a language the deaf can hear and the blind can read.
-Mark Twain

The saloon sat near empty. Even for seven o'clock on a Tuesday night, it was unusual. Cole leaned on the bar, eyeing the whores acting as bait outside. Even with the enticement there, few men passed by to get on the hook.

He frowned. Something had to be going on somewhere in town to distract his usual crowd from their drunken posts. Even right after an Indian raid, his saloon was never as empty as it sat right then. With two fingers he beckoned one of the girls. "What's going on out there, Prim?"

Primrose couldn't have a better name as the quietest of his whores. Daisy herself had named her for him. Prim shrugged. "Dunno. There's a big group of men up at Turner's, crowded 'round the porch and windows and such. Only a few are startin' to head this way."

He wondered what in hell could be so intriguing at Turner's. When she continued to stand in front of him, he shooed her. "Well, if they're heading this way, get out there and help bring them in. It ain't like them to ignore the saloon this long."

Graham's heavy footsteps thundered down the stairs. The big grin on his face likely had everything to do with the wad of cash in his hand. "Painting that addition of 'and hotel' to our sign was the smartest thing we've done yet."

Cole chuckled. After the cowboy left, Cole had decided to tack the hotel line under his saloon sign. Never mind Jane had suggested it weeks before he was happy to take full credit. Hell, if they could get the extra cash, he wouldn't turn it away. "We've done? That was damn sure my idea, Graham."

"Whatever you say, Cole. I'm the one that got us a customer." Graham waved the money before shoving it into the cigar box under the counter. "Charged extra for bed pan service, too. I'll get Primmy to do it."

"No. Have Daisy do it." Cole ignored Graham's choking surprise. Laughter reached into the saloon, wrapping around the few lazy bodies and bringing them to life. Outside the girls primped and primed for the oncoming group of men. "She's the one so interested in bodily functions, might as well make good use of it."

"You're the one saying you might let her free to be a doc again. Now you're punishing her for it?" Graham chuckled. "It's good to have you back."

Cole didn't bother to try to figure out what Graham meant. Granted, his mood had soured in the weeks since Jane last spoke to him. He hadn't been acting that different. Had he?

"Did you see the gloves? Devil, that's the funniest thing I seen in years." Wills all but dragged Prim with him. He tugged her onto his lap when he sat. "Cole. Whiskey, and here's something for this little lady?"

"Taking a whore tonight, Wills? What in blazes has ya in such a good mood?" Cole knew Wills like the women. He liked to look and play, and keep them on hand while gambling, but Wills hardly ever partook beyond the saloon floor. Mostly, he just gambled, trying to win back the large bet he lost years ago.

Cole slid the glass across the bar and poured. On the way back, he slid the money away before Wills came to his good senses and changed his mind.

"Ya oughta see it, Cole." Wills' laughter boomed through the saloon, the men filing in followed suit. Not that Wills laughter could be called contagious. They were just all in on whatever the joke happened to be. "Hammy, of all people, trying to look all dapper and such. The old fool fancies himself a blighter."

"The ragamuffin trying to impress the princess." Teddy snorted. When Cole yanked away the beer he'd just set before him, Teddy grunted. "What the hell?"

Tension seeped back into Cole's shoulders. He gripped the handle of the beer mug tight, trying to maintain his cool. "What's this about Hammy?"

"Man's all dressed up. Even took a bath near as we can tell. Making a right fool of himself, he is." Wills shook his head. "No reason for us not to enjoy it. Like she don't see him for a fool neither, or something."

"That's something I gotta see." Graham chuckled. "Did you say gloves?"

"Purple ones." Wills didn't stop chortling, his brogue growing thicker the more he laughed. "Where you going, Cole?"

"I'll be back." Cole strode from the saloon. Let them think he planned to join in the fun. Nothing could be further from the truth. While he could abide a little light-hearted ribbing of Hammy, all out ridicule wouldn't be tolerated.

Hammy came off a simpleton, but he hadn't always been that way. Back when Cole had first arrived in Dominion Falls, Hammy had helped him. Everyone thought he gave up prospecting because he didn't do well at it.

In truth the man knew one of his two claims were worth a lot of money. Before he had to deal with jumpers, he'd sold it to the highest bidder. None other than Ben Daugherty himself had paid one heck of a bounty for that small piece of land.

Hammy now lived well beneath his means. Few in town knew the man was rich. The stroke he'd had some years back had done well to seal his reputation as a bumbling old fool. Daisy had been the one to keep Hammy alive, and that's why Cole gave her a chance and let her keep doctoring when it went against his better judgment.

Cole knew the bumbling fool bit only rang half true. Hammy wanted to be happy. He had no other goals. Beer, carpentry, and nice people as friends kept him that way.

Cole knew all this because Hammy had been the one to loan him the money for the saloon. Asking only for secrecy, free beer, and eventual repayment of the funds—without interest. Years ago Cole had repaid the debt, but the kindness would always be owed in return.

At the foot of the steps of Turner's, a group still gathered. Once in a while whoever hovered at the windows would leave, and someone else would take their place.

Cole pushed his way through the crowd. "All right. Y'all have had your fun. Get the hell outta here. Let the man be."

"Aw, Cole. Ain't none of us seen a sight like this."

"I said get! To the saloon, one beer for each of ya on the house. Now get. Go on." Cole hated rewarding their idiocy, but it would get them to move. And it worked, too. Once they'd all wandered down the street, still making comments and jokes along the way, he grumbled a few curses under his breath.

The door swung open and Cora rushed out. "I told you all to get."

Cole chuckled when her eyes widened at the sight of the empty porch. "They're already gone, Cora. Offered them free beer to get the hell gone. Obviously ya didn't do that. Works real good, you should try it sometime."

"Oh." Cora stopped short, her hands wrung in her apron. "Well, thank you, I suppose. Why on earth would you do such a thing?"

"Don't like an empty saloon." Cole issued the most logical explanation as he climbed the steps. While he had no desire to pick on the man, he had to know what could have caused such a ruckus. To be sure whomever he was with wasn't being worse than the men pointing and laughing from a distance.

"No, Cole." Cora held out her hands. "You go on, too. I think Hammy's been harassed quite enough for one night."

"I ain't gonna harass him. I want some dinner." Cole leaned on the pockmarked post, the damage itself a brutal reminder of Jane's injuries weeks before. He could have cursed the situation for making him think of her. He'd been doing good. He fought the urge to crane his neck to get a peek inside. That would only make her think he came for fun and games. "Or are ya gonna turn away a paying customer?"

She hesitated. "Fine. One smart comment and you can take your food elsewhere."

"Yes ma'am." Cole followed her into the restaurant. Inside where he got a clear view of the person in question, he froze. Of all the things he'd expected, the sight before him wasn't it. His voice dropped as he grabbed Cora's arm. Fury filled him at the sight of Jane eating with Hammy. How dare she help put the man at the heart of ridicule when all Hammy had done was be nice to her? "What's this?"

Cora pursed her lips, but a soft sigh escaped. Under the quiet din of the dining room, she lowered her voice. "Jane wanted to do something nice for him. Said he'd been kind to her, helping her out and all."

"So she thought she'd embarrass him?"

"Of course not. She invited him to supper. Unlike all you fools, she thinks he's not a dunce. She's being nice. You should try it sometime."

Despite the harshness of his immediate reaction to the sight, he realized he didn't really believe Jane would embarrass Hammy. At least not intentionally. Cole frowned as he watched the two. Maybe it would be better to head out quick as he could.

Then again, Jane was the one ignoring him. For three whole weeks now. What difference did it make what he did?

"Well, are you going to sit? I thought you said you're a paying customer." Cora held a plate of chicken pie and corn out to him. "Or are you really here to pester her, or Hammy, like every one of those men I've been shooing off?"

"I ain't gonna pester her. Or Hammy. Why don't you wrap that up, and I'll get on back to work." Cole waited for her to put the meal in a basket. He handed her more than the usual cost of the dinner. The way her jaw dropped made Cole grin. "What? You expect me to put up with being ignored all this time?"

"No. I thought for a second there you were being nice. How silly of me."

"Indeed." Cole leaned back against the doorframe, waiting for her to move away.

Jane smiled, more genuine and brighter than he'd seen in weeks. None of the familiar tension lined her features as it had every time he got close to her. A flitter of her laughter filtered through the crowd.

Hammy's joined with hers. Despite the nervous tremor in the old man's gloved hands, he beamed. Clearly none of the townsmen's frivolity at his expense had reached him. Or if it had, Jane had managed to make him forget.

The anger Cole had been chewing on for the past week over Jane's continual rejection faded away inch by inch. The gentle way she touched Hammy's arm, the precise direction of her attention on just the man.

It stunned him.

For as long as he'd lived in this town not one woman had glanced Hammy's way. Even younger and more together as he'd been before his stroke, Hammy hadn't exactly been a catch. The kindness and attention Jane showered on him was probably the most the man had ever seen in years.

"He looks awful damn happy." The words were out of Cole's mouth before he could stop them. He grabbed the basket from Cora more sharp than necessary. "Good on her. At least he ain't mooching free beer off me tonight."

"Go on, Cole. Get."

Cole nodded and slipped back out into the night. No matter how much free liquor and money out of his pocket it would take, he'd see to it there was no more laughter at Hammy's expense for this.

And he'd find a way to thank Jane. Even if it meant the apology she wanted.

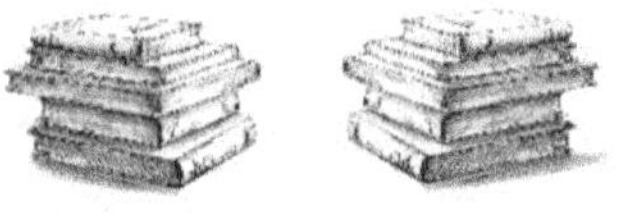

Do not bite at the bait of pleasure, till you know there is no hook beneath.
-Thomas Jefferson

"Jane."

Smooth as silk, Cole's voice wrapped around her. One syllable stopped her dead.

With just one word from him, a shiver ripped through her whole body. Damn it, she wanted nothing more than to give in right then. Three weeks had been near torture.

Sure she'd had company and had good days and bad, but she'd be lying if she hadn't missed the teasing, pleasurable company of the man behind her. The kisses filled with heat and promised passion, the likes of which she dreamed of until her body ached for him.

No matter how much she ached, and dreamed, it would do her no good to give in so easy. All she wanted was an apology. Did she truly have the patience to wait for it with him so close again?

"You're a damn annoying woman, ya know that?"

With an attitude like that, maybe she could wait. Turning slow enough to avoid rushing into his arms, she folded her arms across her chest. From where she stood he looked ready to crack, not to mention mad as hell. Oh yes, his apology would be well worth the wait. She bit her lip to cover the burgeoning smile.

"I oughta just forget I ever met you."

Liar. She nearly said it aloud. The brute force behind his words faltered. Right then she wanted nothing more than the true apology. Then again, maybe she did want something more.

Him.

To keep from caving she had to suck in air and remind herself to breathe.

"Sorry."

She stilled. It was, after all, an apology. Not a *good* apology, but she hadn't specified the nature and depth she required to forgive. She rested her hands on her hips, her formerly firm resolve wavering.

"I said it. You happy?"

Frustration filtered into his tone. It had to be enough. Still, she waited. If he walked away or gave up, she'd cave, she knew it.

He grumbled a curse. After a heartbeat, he covered the distance between them in a heartbeat. Perspiration lit across her skin. The day was hot enough on its own, but his presence turned it scorching. His breath brushed her ear. "Sorry I laughed at the thought of you being a teacher. Even when ya told me to stop."

Now that was good, really good. Definitely good enough to satisfy her. What now? How to break the stalemate? She'd ignored him so long, how could she end her determined silence? Most important, how could she let him know exactly what she wanted?

"You ever gonna speak to me again?"

"Search me." Perfect. The way his eyes lit up and he leaned closer left her with no doubt he'd caught her double meaning. Her smile grew bigger. She shivered when his gaze settled on her lips.

The familiar tingle his proximity caused raced along her skin until she had to take a bracing breath. She hoped he'd take her hint as she backed a step away. When he took a step after her, she smiled and turned for the door, making sure her hips swayed just enough to catch his attention.

She left the door open to make her invitation clear and headed for the steps. He had to follow. If he didn't, she'd embarrass herself going after him.

Right as her foot hit the first step, the door closed behind her. Her heart raced so fast she gripped the railing to maintain her tenuous hold on her self-control. It was a losing battle and she knew it. She wouldn't be able to play it cool much longer. Being separated from him, even if she had done so by choice, made her want him more than ever.

With the last bit of self-control in her, she turned to meet his curious gaze. Somehow she managed to lift the corner of her lips in a smile and step off the steps with an air of calm she didn't feel. "What was that I said? Oh yes…"

Her gaze locked with his. No more waiting. No going back now. She'd waited what seemed like forever, and knew for a man of his standing, he'd been even more patient than she. It was time to stop pretending they didn't both want the same thing. Her breath caught until she struggled to whisper, "Search me."

Not wasting a second, Cole pressed her into the wall. His tongue plunged into her mouth and she melted. Her body burned, ready for whatever he wanted. Before he could reach down, she hiked her own skirts.

His hands gripped her thighs hard, the flash of pain fueling her fire until she moaned. With one small hop, her legs wrapped around his waist tight. The handle of his gun dug into her leg, but she didn't care. She wanted more.

Not even the thought they could be interrupted would stop her now. Every nerve tingled under his fingers as they raced along her legs. It was taking too long. There were too many clothes. She wanted to feel him.

When his lips left hers to trail along her throat, she all but growled, "Stop buttering me up. Show me what I want so bad I ache. I've wanted this for weeks...I want you..."

His lips crushed to hers. Within minutes his holster disappeared and her legs tightened around him. The rough texture of his trousers rubbed against her sensitive flesh. She whimpered, wiggling in response. The heat built so fast she gasped for air.

In a flurry of motion, they joined together. She trembled when he lingered, pressing her firm against the wall. For a moment, the pure pleasure of him filling her was enough. She clung tight to him. Within seconds the need for more returned. Her body appeared to remember what her mind didn't as her hips shifted, sending a new tingle of pleasure through her.

His growl resounded against her neck and she chuckled, moving her hips again.

"Jane."

"Please." Her plea got rewarded. Cole pulled back the slightest amount, but it was enough to make her whimper. Every movement he made sent a new wave of pleasure through her. All thought flew from her head, and she arched toward him with eager abandon.

Her nails raked along his back as he rocked into her, filling her with each strong thrust. Her soft whimpers filled the air, her body enthusiastically performing the familiar dance her mind had forgotten she'd performed before.

His mouth never left her flesh, his tongue darted out to taste her. An intense wave of heat filled her, shudders coursed through her as the pleasure peaked ever higher until she thought she might pass out from it all. Moments before she let out the cry that would certainly draw attention, his mouth closed over hers.

Together they shuddered, muscles turned to liquid with relaxation. She clung to him, not ready to end the moment.

There was no other option, for a door slammed at the back of the house. Approaching voices made them both groan. With great effort, she managed to whisper, "Upstairs. Please."

"Hell, yes."

She giggled into his neck, biting his flesh against the yelp when he moved to pick his holster up off the steps. Martha's voice drew close and she tightened her legs around him, whimpering when it pulled him deeper. "Hurry."

The sexual embrace can only be compared with music and prayer.
-Marcus Aurelius

He'd been right.

Cole chuckled low so as not to wake the woman slumbering beside him. She lay on her stomach; her golden curls sprawled across the pillow. She'd given into exhaustion just a few minutes before. He ran his hand along her spine and admired the way her body reacted to his touch even in sleep.

She'd proven to be every bit as good as he'd suspected. Somehow she managed to be both submissive and demanding. They'd spent more hours than he cared to count exploring every inch of each other. Even as she drifted off, she'd lamented her need for sleep.

He crossed the room, ignoring his own need for sleep in favor of a glass of whiskey. He pushed aside a curtain and noticed the first glimpse of sunrise peeking over the eastern mountains. No wonder Jane had needed to sleep. It had been an hour after lunch when they'd first begun to enjoy each other's company, and already the sun was rising.

Lying on the bed without a sheet to cover her, Jane didn't stir. The sight of her smooth skin in the dim light was enough to raise his desire again. For a moment a frustrated frown tugged at his lips.

He'd also been wrong.

The chase. He'd been sure that's what drove him, but now he'd had her. The need should be gone. So why did he still crave her? He'd had her every way imaginable and yet something in him said *more*.

He wanted more.

He wanted all of her. He didn't know what that meant, but he knew he wanted it. All of her. For his own.

After he polished off his whiskey, he crossed to the bed again. The lamplight flickered across her soft flesh, the curve of her back down to the sensitive dip of skin at the small of her back. With a whisper-light touch, he ran his finger along the scar at her side.

The round white divot surrounded by a starburst of small white dots across her ribs. Tracing the area with his finger his frown deepened, the memory of her injuries dampened his mood. If he had anything to say about it, she wouldn't be hurt again.

He slid his hand up along her back to her shoulders, then trailed it down her spine again. Her back arched into his hand like a cat. A naughty idea filtered into his head and he grinned, shifting so he hovered over her prone form. Though she slept soundly she responded, the delicious swell of her backside rose to press against him.

He fought off the moan, not ready to wake her quite yet. He wanted to savor every inch of her. Leaning down, he ran his nose along the nape of her neck to brush aside her hair. Despite the hours they'd spent wrapped in each other, her perfume lingered on her skin.

A low growl rumbled through his chest and he placed a kiss at the base of her neck. His tongue darted out, tasting the sweet saltiness of satisfaction. A soft sigh slipped from her parted lips, encouraging him.

He let her spine guide him, following the curve down to the spot he'd learned she enjoyed having teased. The soft dip just below her waist could bring her to excitement with the right attention. Circling the spot with his tongue made her twitch, and he gripped her hips when she started to wiggle.

He continued to run his tongue along the small of her back until she moaned low and whimpered. She was definitely awake now, but he was far from done. He moved back along her spine, pressing into her and nibbling the curve of her neck.

"You couldn't let me sleep?" Her voice creaked with lingering sleep, but her hands flexed across the muslin before gripping it as a shudder coursed through her.

"I ain't done with you yet. You got no one to blame but yourself." Her chuckle made her body shake against his. Self-control proved impossible around this woman in a way he'd never known before. Every move she made blurred his thoughts.

"Oh, there's another party involved." Despite the pressure of him lying on her, she managed to arch against him. The wiggle of her ass had to be intentional. She was too aware now of what her ass did to him. "You have made me all too aware of how enjoyable this interaction can be. I don't think a greater pleasure exists."

He slipped his hand down her side to grip her hip tight. If she kept wiggling, he'd be done for well before he was ready to give in. "Most women don't think so."

"Then they're not doing it right. Or their men aren't."

"What if we're the ones doing it wrong?"

"There is no way in hell this is wrong. Aurelius was right."

"How's that?"

"He said the sexual embrace can only be compared with music and prayer. I never quite understood it before." She shivered again, pressing against the sheets.

"And ya do now?"

"Oh my heavens, yes." She was breathless, whining. The sound of her ragged breath tested his limited self-control. Licking her lips, she gripped the sheets tight in her hands.

The sight of her gleaming lips sparked the memory of how they'd felt against his skin as she'd explored him. She'd searched every inch, no shame or fear. Those delicious lips wrapped around his shaft and worked him into a frenzy unlike he could remember. When she'd taken the initiative to pleasure him as she had, he'd questioned how much she could have forgotten.

Somehow she'd known what to do without him telling her, and her initial hint of hesitation had fallen away the second he let her know how much he enjoyed it.

He kept her pinned, moving back down along her body.

"Cole." Not pleading, demanding. A forcefulness he'd never enjoyed in a woman bolstered her, exciting him as much as fawning usually did. Her weak attempts to make him move disappeared as she pushed back against him. Urgency strengthened her and he found himself on his back. Not for long, though.

He flipped her back over and pinned her again, bracing her wrists against the bed. Instead of pouting, she grinned.

Now on her back, she took the chance to wrap her legs around him. She squeezed him tight against her until they both shuddered at the intimate contact.

A low moan slipped past his control. He crushed his lips to hers, letting their bodies take over again. Desire forced away hunger, passion replaced exhaustion; yearning brought them to the brink and back again. Every moment they stilled, their appetite proved unsatisfied and ardent passion pulled the back together.

During a brief respite, a firm knock echoed through the room. Cole chuckled. "Think we're disturbing someone?"

"Who cares?" She sighed and curled against him. Her fingers danced along his stomach, tracing the lines of his muscles. When another knock sounded, she groaned. "Oh for goodness' sake. Do they not understand I wish to be left alone?"

Cole raised a brow when she rose from the bed. He propped himself on his elbow to admire her form as she walked to the door. When she continued to the door without pulling on a robe, he chuckled. "Uh, Jane?"

She cast a glance over her shoulder with a wicked smirk firmly in place. "Yes?"

Laughing out loud at her brazen move, he couldn't deny he admired her more for it. That sort of gumption took a certain kind of woman. His kind of woman.

"Uh, I mean, I..." Guy's voice cracked as he stammered through a poor excuse of a greeting. Like the idiot had never seen a naked woman before.

"Yes, Guy?" Jane's exasperation darkened her tone. She kept the door mostly closed, but made no move to cover herself. "I'm rather busy. I don't care to be interrupted."

"Sorry. You…um, Jane…" Cole couldn't see Guy's face, but his tone was definitely flustered. Despite having whores around, he'd probably never dealt with a *proper* woman with little shame.

"What?"

"I was concerned when you didn't arrive for work." Guy managed to get his brain functioning enough to speak. "I wanted to make sure—"

"I'll be by after lunch. Right now I'm busy. Please don't interrupt me again." Jane slammed the door, turning back to Cole. She giggled as she moved toward him slow and steady. "I don't believe I've ever seen a man turn quite so red before."

"You don't play fair."

"For I have sworn thee fair and thought thee bright, who art black as hell, as dark as night." She straddled him with a wicked grin. "Shakespeare."

He rested his hands behind his head, resisting the urge to touch her as her hand danced along his chest. "What's that supposed to mean?"

"Appearances can be deceiving. The purest of face can be evil and the most wicked an absolute angel."

"Which are you?"

"You tell me."

Her lips made contact with his skin and unbelievably heat raced through him again. The resolve to keep his hands off her disappeared and he gripped her waist. "You're definitely wicked. Very wicked."

She yelped when he flipped them. "On the surface or deeper?"

"The surface." He met her eyes, a smile playing at the corners of his lips. Running his hands along her side, he brushed his lips across hers.

"So you're saying underneath I'm good?"

"Oh, you're good."

The smile that tried to break through won the battle and in moments she had them flipped again. "Let me prove it."

"Yes, ma'am." As her lips crushed to his again, he let her take control. When she finished he took his turn until they were both breathless. She curved into him and nestled in a spot that seemed made for her alone. He pulled her closer.

"I must say. You do know how to apologize."

"Is that what I was doing?" Amusement trickled into a laugh. "Didn't know that."

"Even if you weren't, you managed to make your apologies known. Quite a few times." She tilted her head to offer a sly smile. "I ought to make you suffer more often."

"Wouldn't advise it." His fingers danced along her leg to her hip, where he traced circles. "I might not be so apologetic next time."

"Somehow I doubt it. You enjoyed that apology as much as I did."

"Don't mean I enjoyed suffering."

"I was suffering just as much. I can't tell you how often I wanted to give up without the apology. If we weren't so stubborn we could have done this weeks ago."

"Think we made up for lost time."

"Twenty-two hours of apologies. Yet it still doesn't seem like enough."

He pulled her close and chuckled. "Don't gotta be."

She pushed back. "It does. For now. I'm starving and I have to get to work."

He grabbed her tight around the waist and pulled her back. He laughed over her squeal of protest. "You ain't gotta do nothing."

"I do." She smacked his arms with a laugh. "And you have a business to run."

"Eh, Graham can handle it a few more hours."

"Sure he can." She managed to get free of his grasp. After she'd swiped her robe off the floor, she slid it on. "But you're anxious to go and gloat."

"I think he knows. He saw me come in here, and I ain't been out since."

"Oh, just get dressed, you buffoon." Jane laughed. "I do need to work and I have plans for lunch and supper."

"Plans?" He never liked it much when she said that.

"Yes. I have lunch with David and I'm meeting Al for supper."

His eyes narrowed at the revelation. He sat as she continued moving around the room to gather her things. That poor excuse for a soldier was getting on his last nerve. Especially since Jane made no secret of her nighttime visits to the camp. He'd finally had his taste, he didn't want the Major getting one, too. "You ain't gonna cancel supper with that soldier boy?"

"Well, why would I do such a thing?"

Cole frowned. For the first time in a real long time he didn't want to share. He wasn't about to admit as much, and couldn't come up with a viable reason otherwise.

"I haven't once suggested you stop making use of your girls."

True enough. Not that it had any effect on his own personal choice in the matter. If you called it a choice. He sure hadn't been able to stomach any woman since the infuriating one across the room had landed in his saloon. His brain tumbled over the possible reasons until he landed on one he knew to be true. "Most women ain't so flippant."

"I think we've established I am not most women."

"Damn straight you aren't." Good thing she gave him the distraction of throwing his trousers in his face. He couldn't believe she'd suggest he should still make use of his girls. Did she really not mind?

Before her, he rarely went outside his whores for company. One of the exceptions had been almost as open as Jane. Still, even that woman had hinted at jealousy over his continuing visits with the whores.

Now this? Normally it would bother him if a woman demanded, or even asked, he stop his business activities. For some reason this time it bothered him that Jane didn't ask.

It had to be the fact she expected to be allowed the same freedom, to make time with who she wished. To give away what he wanted for himself. All for himself.

Her knees planted on either side of his hips, a welcome diversion from his train of thought. The tremble of her hands before she set them on his chest threw him off balance. What had her so nervous? He wrapped his arms around her waist and tugged her closer.

"I won't stop you from your comfort with other women. You won't stop me with mine." For the first time in hours her voice shook with hesitation.

He drank in her nervous gaze as her hands ran along his bare shoulders to his back. In that instant he knew—as much as he was loathed to admit true affection or anything akin to commitment, she was the same. She was afraid to make a demand he was sure only she could, and he wasn't sure he wanted to let her. He'd spent a lot of years not letting feelings into his life, and he still didn't know why now he wanted more. For now he'd settle for what she offered, but not for long.

She tucked her finger under his chin. "But I'm not done with you—as long as you can manage to keep your jealousy toned down."

"I ain't jealous."

"Of course you aren't." Her fingers laced into his hair. A sexy quirk of her lips belied amusement. "Are we agreed?"

"Think I can handle it."

"Good. Because I had a good time last night and I'd hate to miss another opportunity for more fun."

He leaned up for a kiss, grumbling when she pulled away before he made contact. As she grabbed her clothes, he tugged on his trousers. "What about your husband?"

"Once he's had time to adjust, I plan on filing for divorce."

The news bolstered his mood after the talk of Webb. He stood and walked over when she held out her corset ties to him. Yanking hard, he pulled her against him. "You still sure he ain't the one that messed you up?"

"Yes. Much as I'd love the mystery to be over, I'm quite certain."

He grabbed his shirt. "Long as you're sure it ain't him. I'd be plenty happy for a reason to go after the guy."

"You are such a bull." Jane frowned. "You don't have to hate a man because he's a decent human being."

"That ain't why."

She finished buttoning her bodice and set her hands on her hips. "Then why?"

"Just think something fishy is going on. The way they keep 'looking' for Starbird, but not like they was before. And those supply runs…"

Pulling open the door, she shook her head. At the top of the stairs she searched the entrance before lowering her tone. "I think something is going on as well. I haven't missed any of those signs either. I've told David as much."

"I ain't one that likes being lied to."

She stopped at the bottom of the steps. After a minute she turned to look up at him again. She smiled. "Honesty is important."

He took the last few steps slow until he was one step below her. The one step interval made their height difference almost non-existent. He leaned on the railing so they were nose to nose. "That's why ya told me about Webb."

"And why I've told him I won't stop enjoying your company any more than I would his."

"Good to know."

"I'm sure it is." She smiled against his lips as he leaned in. Her body arched toward his, her fingers dancing on his forearm. Their lips had almost met when her stomach rumbled loud and long. Her laughter pulled them apart, and he found himself joining. "But I won't be enjoying your company any further today. I must eat."

"Aint' gonna argue with that. Wouldn't be no fun anyway if you kept whining like you are."

"I'll make it up to you, I promise."

"You will?"

"My balcony won't ever be locked again."

"Ya won't stay here forever."

"I'm sure you'll make your way in, no matter where I am."

"You bet I will."

Let us have wine and women,
mirth and laughter.
Sermons and soda the day after.
—Lord Byron

"You looking at the horses or the men?"

Jane jumped at the sudden reappearance of Cole. Last time she'd seen him was when she'd left him sulking after the horse races. She'd been sure then he'd be grumpy for well over a day. "Cole Mitchell. You scared the daylights out of me."

"Well, excuse me." Cole chuckled. One hand planted on the fence on either side of her, not quite pinning her to the wooden structure. The warmth of his proximity made the dry heat of July almost unbearable.

"You don't sound the least bit sorry." For a smidgeon of payback she arched backward into him. The groan that rumbled through him in response made her smile even brighter. She wiggled against him to enhance her teasing. "I thought you were still mad at me."

"I am. Fifty dollars is a lot to drop on a bad bet."

"You lose more than that at poker every month."

"I do that on purpose. No one likes to play if they always lose." He leaned into her, but it didn't stop her teasing. "I didn't lose this bet on purpose."

"So you're angry, then?"

"I ain't happy."

"Perhaps, but there's at least one part of you that is rather happy." Jane sucked her lips between her teeth. Even through her skirts and bustle she could tell just how *happy* he was. It took every smidgeon of her energy to keep her focus on the horses up for auction.

"How'd you know Archie's horse would win over Mack's? Mack always wins that damn race. Every year."

"To be honest? I didn't. The horse I picked seemed in far better shape, and Archie isn't half the ass to his horses that Mack is." She did her best to keep her smile to a minimum. Not to mention she had to attempt to keep still now. Several people at the celebration had noticed their playing.

"I know he ain't. Don't usually matter. Mack always wins. I trained his horse."

"I know that, and I also know you train your horses well. I've seen it myself. But did you train his horse with a whip and a kick like Mack uses?" She turned around to face him. The fence pressed firm into her back, while Cole used her position to his advantage to press from the front.

"Indecent," someone muttered.

Cole chuckled at the complaint. "Think you earned yourself the reputation you wanted."

"It's about time, but I don't think I've earned it enough."

"Really?"

"Really. After I get myself a horse, perhaps we can see about fixing that."

His brow rose, a playful smile tugging his lips. "You got me curious."

She smiled in return. As he leaned closer, she slid her hands up his chest. "You'll just have to be patient. The auction is set to start soon, and we should pay attention. You'll need to help me choose a proper horse. Perhaps one of the Indian horses. They all seem to be calm creatures comparatively."

"You don't want one of them." His strong hands circled her waist and spun her back around to face the corral. "You want that one."

Rather than look where he pointed, she found herself driven to distraction by his muscular arm. She slipped her hand along the exposed forearm with a low sigh, imagining another night held by those arms again. Only a nudge to her hip pulled her from the naughty turn her thoughts were taking and back to the horses. "Oh, right."

He chuckled. "And I'm the one that's gotta be patient?"

"Never said I didn't. Now which one?" This time she saw the magnificent creature and her heart leapt into her throat. She gulped a lungful of air to put it back in place. The horse reared high in the air before being dragged into the corral.

"No. Not her. She's too wild, even for you. I meant the Brown."

"But the Paint is gorgeous." Mostly white with deep brown for its paint, the mare wouldn't stand to be ignored. She snorted at Archie, trotting around the corral. The horse avoided all the men at the fences. She paced and circled until she finally came to rest between Archie and the nearest exit.

"You can't handle her. Not for your first horse."

"You could." Jane set her foot on the bottom fence rail and lifted herself onto it. From her vantage point she eyed the beautiful horse. Despite its wild nature she looked strong and with just enough wild in her to excite Jane. "If you trained her for me, I could easily have her. I think she's perfect."

"You're plum crazy."

"No. Maybe I just want to watch you training her."

"You watch me train anyway."

Oh how right he was. She knew of nothing more appealing than watching him train a horse in the corral behind the saloon. He didn't wear a shirt when he worked. This left the sun-darkened perfection of his chest and arms revealed to the world. She'd grown accustomed to slipping to the library to watch every lunch hour.

Even before they'd moved their relationship into the sinfully relishable arena of the bedroom she'd enjoyed this activity. It made the perfect excuse for multiple library trips. When she had spent time ignoring him, she would go and enjoy the view from the library window.

Except for two scars, his tanned skin was smooth and perfect. The one scar on his arm she knew came from the recent attacks on the town. The other scar, long and white on his abdomen, left her curious, as he never spoke of it. Especially now that she could get close to it, but even in their most intimate moments he didn't like her near it. He certainly never talked about it.

"Jane?"

"Will you train her for me?" Jane pulled from her reverie more easily this time. She fixated on the horse, certain this time she wanted the creature as her own.

"She's gonna be the highest bid here. How do you expect to buy her?" Cole pulled her down from the fence. "I'm telling ya, the Brown. Don't gotta wait to ride him."

"I want the Paint."

"Stubborn." Cole eyed the horse. "It'll take me weeks to train her."

"Goody." She set her hands back on the fence. "How much will you charge me to train a wild one like her?"

"I think we can make a deal."

Excitement rippled through her. His breath on her neck spurred it on, as did his hands moving along her curves. "Tempting as that sounds, such a deal likens me to a whore. Sex for services instead of money."

"You ain't no whore."

"No, I'm not. So how much?"

"I told ya, we can make a deal. I wasn't talking about sex." He turned her toward him. "You didn't answer my question. You're talking about a high bid."

"I have the money." She was quite satisfied to say as much. In a short time she'd managed to pay back her initial loan from Guy, as well as put away quite a substantial amount of funds. Of course, the reason behind it still baffled her, as she wasn't quite sure how she'd known what investments would receive good payouts. "I received a good return on some investments. How do you think I've planned on buying that house?"

"If you still want that house, you may not want to pay so much on a horse."

"I have the funds to do both."

He appeared rather impressed with the statement. "Any word on the house?"

"No." Jane frowned. While she'd wanted to purchase the home a short distance from town, she'd yet to secure either the location or the mortgage she wanted. She'd be able to buy it outright, but that would leave her with little cash for necessities. "I know it's for sale, but Mr. Burns is delaying my attempts to get a mortgage."

"You're a woman."

"Glad you noticed." She kicked his shin none too gently before turning back to the corral. Archie kept trying to get the Paint calm enough to start bidding. "So why sell her first if she'll go for the most?"

Cole leaned on the fence beside her. "Once she's gone everyone'll settle for less. Some of them will even settle for them Indian ponies."

The moment bidding started, he moved behind her. He wrapped his arms over hers so she couldn't move. She squirmed against his hold. "Cole."

"Don't bid too early. You'll end up paying more than she's worth."

"You could have simply told me as much instead of holding me down like a child." With a frustrated huff, she struggled against him. The only reward for her struggles was a low moan against her ear. "Cole Mitchell."

"No, no. Keep fighting."

"Boor." The tight embrace loosened. All she was left with was empty air and an infinite sense of dissatisfaction. "You're impossible."

"Bid, woman."

Archie raised his hand. "Last call. The bid is at two hundred. Going once."

Jane raised her arm even as she smacked Cole in the back of his head. "Two fifty, Archie."

Cole pulled her hand out of the air. "Damn it. You crazy?"

"I believe we established months ago I am. Shut up and let me handle this." Jane swatted his hand when he tried to tug her off the fence.

"Two seventy five." Jackson's voice rang through the corral.

Jane clenched her jaw against the frustration over the man insinuating himself in her path yet again. "Three hundred."

"Jane. Stop. You won't beat Jack. He's got more money than he does sense. That horse ain't worth it." Cole grabbed her around the waist. Despite her fierce protest, he yanked her off the fence.

"Unhand me." Jane set her hands on her hips. Even though he didn't react to her glare, she kept it firmly in place. "I want her, and no other. I refuse to settle."

"Four hundred." Jackson's chuckle rippled through his words. He climbed over the fence into the corral.

Cole's lips pinched together. "Don't be stubborn. You won't have no money left."

Just then the horse reared, charging at Jackson. The man stumbled back, hitting the fence and dropping into a pile of dung.

Jane grinned. "Maybe. Maybe not."

The laughter around them wove through the tense frown on Cole's face until he joined in the revelry. "Ya might be right."

Jane climbed the fence, and with an unladylike flip of her skirts hooked her legs over the top. Unlike Jackson, she didn't drop into the corral. "Who will you get to train her, Jackson? Cole won't do it for you. Don't think Archie will either."

"Too wild for my taste. Cole can handle this wild filly better than any man in this town." Archie at least didn't try to hide his mirth. No one else either as the multiple meanings of his statement drove the crowd's laughter further.

"You wouldn't even be able to get her back to your stable. By the time you hire someone willing to come out here to the territory, she'll escape or put a hoof in your ass." The laughter of the men added to the red in Jackson's face. Jane winked. "I'll go to four fifty, Archie. Why don't we wrap it up before Jackson ends up with mud on his face. Oh, oops, I forgot. Never mind—too late."

"Four fifty to Jane Doe. Sale is final. Sorry, Mr. Krenshaw." Archie nodded to Jane. "She's all yours. Let's move onto the Brown. Cole. Care to lead this wild beast out of my yard?"

"Hope you realize what you've done," Cole muttered in her ear. "Jack ain't the forgiving kind."

"Oh, I know. Why do you think he did this? I busted his best hope at having an in on the government elections. Now get my horse back to your place. I damn well better get an apology for not trusting me."

"An apology I can do. Meet me at the boarding house?"

"No, I don't think so." She winked and leaned closer. "Find me. We'll make do wherever we are."

Cole laughed and slapped her ass. With a skip in his step he went to handle the Paint, urging her out of the corral with a firm hand.

Jane sighed, enjoying every moment until he disappeared out of sight of the livery. Once she'd hopped off the fence she made her way through town to the nearly empty Second Street where the laughter of children hit her ears. Despite the Renegades attacks, the town had made the decision to go through with the Independence Day celebration.

Thankfully the past couple of weeks had been free from attacks. With every mile the train crept closer the more it felt like the end of the attacks would come. The latest rumor said David now worked with Webb, trying to find a peaceful end.

She shook the unpleasant line of thought from her shoulders, watching the games being played in the field. A three-legged race led to a few blunders, and she let a chuckle free when Arthur took a tumble himself.

"Thought you didn't like kids." Cole's hands ran along her arms.

"That didn't take you as long as I thought."

"Lucky my stable ain't far from the livery. The beast is gonna be difficult."

Jane leaned back against him. "You like a challenge."

"Sure do. Now what was that you said about making do?"

She laughed. "Oh yes. Let's find someplace to make do."

"Bully for me."

"No, bully for me." Certain no one was looking, she tugged his hand. She led him along the back of the buildings of the main street to the alley between the Silver Saddle and the Tailor. Tucked between the two buildings was Rusty's office. The back porch of it was her favorite quiet space to read. No one ever went back there. The alley was deep and the porch secluded with no way to enter but through Rusty's office or the alley itself. She gave Cole a wink and ducked onto the small porch.

He backed her into the wall. "Ya sure?"

"People are going to talk no matter what we do. I could be an angel and they'd paint me a devil." Her hands circled his neck and she let her fingers dance through his hair. Excitement and trepidation swirled into a titillating whirlpool of expectation in her belly. What would happen if they were caught? Scandalous was hardly the word. "Granted, this isn't the ultimate in privacy, but Rusty is covering the celebration and whoever comes back here?"

"I didn't even know it was here."

"Exactly."

Nothing is swifter than a rumor.
-Horace

Jane's whole body tingled with the remnants of her afternoon encounter behind Rusty's newspaper office. Life practically rushed through every nerve with a heat of fire and the anticipation of more later. Though she looked forward to another meeting with Cole, she'd been forced to rebuff his attempts to return to the saloon with him instead of going to see the fireworks. A choice she still wasn't sure she didn't regret.

However she'd made a promise to be there. Arthur had asked and she'd agreed. Despite her usual dislike for children, Arthur proved to be smart and curious, and his advanced age of thirteen aided in defending her tolerance of him, as he wasn't an actual child.

A hand gripped her arm, banishing the thoughts from her head with the sting of pain. She gasped and tried to tug free. David's visage stopped her struggle. "Goodness, David. You startled me. Are you joining the Turners for the fireworks too?"

"You happy with yourself?"

"Well, I am happy." Jane had no idea what he meant. The pain of his grip deepened. She tried again to wrench free. "David. That hurts."

"Have you lost what's left of your mind?"

With one more jerk, she yanked her arm free. "I have no idea what you mean."

"You're a lot of things, but stupid isn't one of them. Everyone in town knows what you were doing behind the newspaper office!"

"What?" They'd been alone. What on earth could he mean?

He grimaced and looked away. "Wills was charging a nickel a peek."

A gasp flew out and she covered her mouth. Shock and amusement battled through her head before she settled on bemused surprise. "A nickel a peek?"

He paced around her. "You know what they're saying about you?"

"They were saying it before this." She turned to follow his path as he circled. Clearly he was upset, but she had no idea how to calm him down. Oh for one memory from Clara to clue her in on how to still her upset husband.

"It was one thing to know you were with him."

"David."

He kept circling her. "I mean, you were like this before."

"David." She spun around.

"Don't you have enough problems without adding in such ugly talk?"

"David." She grasped him by the shoulders. "You're making me dizzy."

"It used to be me." The lingering pain he usually hid so well tightened his eyes.

"Oh." All amusement disappeared into regret. Of all the things that mattered to her, his feelings were among them.

She'd let herself get lost in Cole and forget the rest. An apology would never be enough, but she had to start there. She cupped his cheeks. "I'm sorry."

"Clara didn't care about rumors either. Almost lost her teaching job over it until the families decided her teaching skills were more important than the rumors." His hands closed over her wrists. "The day we met, you and I took a rather unique walk."

She tilted her head, amused and impressed. David's sometimes annoying stance as a good man seemed to be less so every time he told another story of Clara. "My goodness, Mr. Schaffer. You bedded Clara the day you met her? You failed to tell me this before."

"Was hoping you'd remember. And I'm not sure you can call it a bedding. There was no bed in that field."

Even in the dim dusk light she could see how red his ears turned. Amusement completely won over the regret as she laughed. "I see. What else haven't you told me?"

"There was the time during the church picnic." David pulled away and walked over to the library porch. Once she got closer, he leaned on the railing. "After service one Sunday, behind the church."

"Well, David. I never imagined." Guilt crept back into her heart. She moved in front of him to set her hands on his clasped ones. "It's a little too close to home."

"And a bit too soon to be flaunting, don't you think?"

While the defensive part of her would have liked to point out it hadn't been too soon for him and Clara, she held her tongue. The pain in his tone twisted her stomach in knots. The situation wasn't quite the same, especially since their divorce was little more than talk yet with how busy he'd become. "I wasn't thinking. My goodness, what they might be saying about you."

"We haven't even filed for divorce yet."

"Not for lack of my trying, you've been a little busy trying to help your Indian friend."

"Clara."

She pursed her lips. The words had erupted in frustration and not forethought. She clasped her hands behind her back. "Sorry. I don't wish to argue. At least not about that."

"Me neither." His lips twisted. He stared at her skirts rather than meet her eyes. "I'm still legally your husband."

"And my actions embarrassed you."

"And you."

"I'm not worried about my own embarrassment. The rumors have been many and colorful before this one. Only difference is this one has witnesses." Her shoulders sagged. She moved closer to set her hand gently on his shoulder. "I'm truly sorry. I didn't think about you and that was cruel, my mind was on my own pleasure instead."

"I'd prefer not to hear about your pleasure."

"Of course not." The glimmer of a smile on his features gave her a hint of hope. "I do hope you'll find it in your heart to forgive me once again. I promise to try to use much better discretion from here on out."

"Does he make you happy?"

The question stilled her. Though simple on the surface, there was a depth to her possible answer she couldn't quite will herself to dive into. Her stance with Cole was ever so tenuous and she was quite aware of the fact. "What?"

"It's a simple question." He lifted his chin to meet her gaze. Unwavering, he kept her pinned with just the strength of his concern. "Does he make you happy?"

"Oh. Well." She cleared her throat and made the choice to focus on the present and nothing further. "Yes. For now."

"For now?"

"Yes. For now. In the present. The present is all I have. I can't remember my past and I have no clue what the future will bring."

"I want you happy."

"I want the same for you."

"So what happens when 'now' has passed?" A concerned frown turned his lips down. His hands unclenched and he tucked a finger under her chin. "Will you be happy then?"

"You worry far too much. I am happy. I still want to know what happened to Clara. I want answers for you, as well as for myself." She sighed. "When his interest wanes, as I and everyone in town expects it will, I'll find another way to be happy."

"There's still too much Clara in you for me not to worry."

"I promise. I will be happy. I want the same for you." She closed the distance between them with a step. "I'm sorry for the way I hurt you. Not just today, either. I mean for the way I hurt you when I was Clara."

"I know." Cheers echoed down the street toward them. "Getting dark enough. The fireworks will be starting soon."

"I know. I promised Arthur I'd join him." When he stepped back and offered an arm, she smiled. "Wouldn't going to the celebration on your arm just increase the rumors?"

"I'm afraid so." His shoulders rose and fell in a heavy shrug. "If you can handle them, I suppose I can too."

"Oh, really?" Jane took the offered arm. "I'm interested in seeing you try. Considering how easy you blush, it should be a good game."

"You're funny. Real funny."

"Glad you noticed." Their laughter mingled until it melted into the sounds of celebration. Arthur ran up and dragged them to the heart of the crowd just as the first firework lit the sky.

In every age the vilest specimins of nature are
to be found among demagogues.
-Thomas Babington Macaulay

Jane knew she should say something, anything. For the first time in her memory, her mouth would not function.

Behind the safety of his desk, Mr. Burns smiled one of the most patronizing smiles she'd ever seen. "So you see, I did finally get clearance for your mortgage. I'm afraid it just came in a day too late."

"Someone bought the house?" Her mouth finally caught up with her thoughts, spilling out her shock. "You said you would hold it."

"I got a cash offer. I held off the buyer as long as I could, but not only was he insistent, but in my business cash is always better than an unreliable loan."

"Unreliable? Mr. Burns, two weeks ago you were willing to fight for my mortgage for me. You know I have been reliable in all of my debts. They've all been paid off, and in good time." Not only that, but she'd had the cash in case the mortgage had fallen through, she just preferred to make sure she had funds available. Granted, she'd only been working a short time, but she'd managed to pay back everyone she owed money to. All but Cole, who'd stopped pestering her for the shirt she owed him.

"Miss Doe?" Mr. Burn's hand waved in front of her face. "Did you hear me?"

"There are no other homes, Mr. Burns. Not since the Renegade attack on the northern settlement. What am I to do?" Heat flooded her cheeks at her admission of concern. After all, she prided herself on her independence.

"I'm certain Mrs. Starbird will continue to allow you to stay at the boarding house. You are a reliable resident." His hand was under her elbow helping her rise. "I'm sorry I couldn't help you sooner. The bank didn't care to give a mortgage to a woman with no considerable collateral, and without a husband to help insure the debt."

"Then how did you manage it?" Jane couldn't get her mind over the fact she had nowhere to live but the boarding house for an indeterminate amount of time. She shouldn't have bought the horse. Then she might have been able to buy the home in cash without fear of relinquishing all of her available funds.

"Well, I told them you were married."

Jane stopped short. "Mr. Burns, I didn't ever suggest I was all right with such a tactic. I would never use David or his name like that."

"Well, Jane." The simple presence of Jackson's voice made Jane crave a bath to free herself of the slime. Jane could swear he fairly slithered through the bank. "How else do you expect a woman to get a loan? Especially one such as yourself?"

"I'm not certain what you mean, Mr. Krenshaw." All disappointment at losing the house flew away under

Jackson's smug demeanor. Anger bubbled toward the surface. "What sort of woman are you implying I am?"

"I think we all know what sort of woman you are. You do realize word travels fast when people draw attention to themselves. I imagine it traveled so far as the bank president's ears." His grin left no doubt how word had reached so far.

"Good to know you are not above spreading rumors and gossip."

"No rumor about it." Jackson's head jerked at Mr. Burns. The man disappeared from her elbow without another word. A door in the back of the bank closed. "Now if you'll excuse me, I have business to attend to."

The truth of the situation hit her all at once and so hard she gasped. "You bastard."

"I beg your pardon?" He quirked a brow. "Like I said. A woman like you. I haven't time to waste on such a crude creature."

"I'm the same crude creature you proposed to just two months ago. Back when my abilities to bolster your esteem outweighed my…crassness." Jane stepped closer. "You bought that house, didn't you?"

"It's such a nice little home. So close to the depot that once the railroad reaches us, I'm certain I won't have any trouble selling it."

"And now you've made certain I can't get a mortgage. Not through this bank." She clenched her jaw against the rush of words she knew she'd regret voicing. No matter how much the man deserved them. "I was wrong."

"Oh? I would so love to hear how."

"You aren't a bastard. You are a devil. A lying, treacherous snake." She lifted her chin. One thing she'd never do is show defeat to a slime like him. "One day you will meet your comeuppance, Jackson. I do hope I'm around to see it."

"I hardly doubt that, my dear." Jackson dared to chuckle right in her face. "You are far more naïve than you like to appear. You can fool the idiots in this town, but you cannot fool me. Try acting like a proper lady for once. I must say given what I've seen, I'm glad you turned down my proposal."

"I will act how I see fit. I care little for what you think of me."

"It doesn't matter anyhow. Just remember this next time you decide to belittle me, Jane. I don't take kindly to it." He leaned in close, perhaps an attempt at intimidation. Even though in this situation he held the cards, she wasn't the least bit intimidated. His eyes narrowed. "I wouldn't try again. Buying this house is child's play compared to what I could do."

"Juvenal says that revenge is always the weak pleasure of a little and narrow mind." Jane met him glare for glare. "Until this day I must say I didn't quite understand the phrase. Now its meaning is quite clear. I am sorry, Mr. Krenshaw."

"Sorry? Is this a real apology?"

"Of course. I am deeply sorry you haven't got the sense of humor God gave much simpler men. I am sorry you take more pleasure in the size of your home than your heart. I'm sorry you haven't the faintest idea how to keep a friend, much less a woman. I may have the reputation of a jezebel, but I will never die as alone as you."

"Good afternoon, Jane."

"Good afternoon. And Mr. Burns?" Jane glanced toward the door, smiling as pleasant as she could when the small man peeked out from the back room. "I believe I'll be taking my business out of this bank. I prefer to not put my money in the care of someone who can be so easily bought. I'll return first thing tomorrow morning to close out my accounts."

With that she spun on her heel and stepped outside. It would do no good to stay angry, but she was anyway. Thanks to Jackson, she would remain stuck in the boarding house. Either that or be forced to take up residence at the Silver Saddle, which she really didn't care to think of as an option.

Of course, she could look at the benefit of remaining where she was. Such as the one benefit walking toward her this very second. The proximity of her room to the saloon and the ease with which that gorgeous man found his way to her balcony—those were benefits she could appreciate.

"I was gonna ask what's wrong, but ya don't look so mad no more." Cole laughed, tugging her tight against him. "You get the house?"

Her brief foray into pleasurable thoughts dropped away. The reminder of the house brought back the recent encounter with Jackson. She wrinkled her nose against the renewed sense she needed a bath. "No. Not at all. You were right."

"Wait." Cole stepped back, his eyes wide. "Did ya just say I was right?"

"Yes."

"Wait." Before she could say a word, he pressed his fingers against her lips. "You ain't ever said that before. Keep your trap shut and we'll just leave it there."

A laugh broke through her frustration. The man sure knew how to turn her mood around, even though in most cases he had to be a fiend to do so. She swatted his hand away. "Hush. If you aren't nice, I'll never say it again."

"Don't have to. Once is enough."

"Are you done?"

"Not yet." He closed his eyes. A goofy grin took over his features. "Gonna remember that over and over for a while."

"Boor. If you'd let me finish, I'd have told you Jackson decided to get revenge because he was too stupid to stay out of the corral. It's not my fault the horse scared him into a pile of dung, but he's sure happy to make it my fault. He bought the house and took the opportunity to ruin my chance for a mortgage through this bank."

"Can I say I told you so?"

"You do and my doors will be locked tonight."

"Damn. You don't play fair."

*Men, as well as women,
are much oftener led by their hearts
than by their understandings.
—Lord Chesterfield*

Cole stretched the kinks out of his back and cracked his neck. The nap had been much needed after he'd helped Jane work out her frustration from losing the house. He couldn't complain about the few hours they'd spent in her room, as she'd been full of near-brutal enthusiasm and had left the balcony door wide open.

The clock on his desk reminded him that it was near five and he'd promised to meet her for supper. Hell, he was glad to get a chance without her husband or soldier boy getting in the way of things. He figured it was best to not be late.

First he had to check on the saloon and make sure things were running smooth. He closed his door. Rather than hurry downstairs, he walked along the railing until he stood dead center over the saloon floor. The saloon bustled with activity, just what he wanted to see.

Not surprisingly, Jane was already there. In the past two weeks, most of her days off he'd find her here. If Graham was working behind the bar, she'd sit and talk with the men in the bar, joking and sometimes drinking with them. On days like today when Graham was gone, she was far more active.

Like right then. He leaned on the railing, trying to keep from outright laughing as she and Iris seemed to get into a heated discussion. Jane's features were locked in tense, stubborn lines he was all too familiar with when he was making her mad.

Iris, the one whore that had been under contract long as he'd owned the saloon, clearly didn't care for whatever Jane was saying. She had her arms folded across her chest, shaking her head as she objected to whatever Jane said. They moved closer, face-to-face, Jane gesturing back toward the whore's room.

He thought he'd have to break it up, but suddenly Iris stormed back toward the room. Jane's attention turned to Lily, and he straightened. Unlike the previous confrontation, Lily only nodded and smiled, almost skipping to the stairs.

Jane headed back to the bar, pausing at a table where a poker game was going strong. With one hand on the dealer Charlie's shoulder, she spoke to the men for a moment and the volume level in the building jumped with the intensity of their laughter.

As she stood there, she gestured with one hand and two whores came over. Jane eased both of them toward the two men with the biggest winnings.

Cole caught Lily's eye and beckoned her over. When she was close enough, he jerked his head at the floor below. "What was that between Jane and Iris?"

Lily bit her painted lip and rocked on her feet. The impatient wave of his hand got her to move closer. She leaned in to whisper. "Jane told her to go clean up. Said she smelled like the pig farm and no man would pay a nickel for her like that. Iris didn't like it none."

"That so?"

"Yeah. Iris don't like her much, but Daisy says she's glad Janey's doin' it."

"And what did Janey tell you?"

"Oh, ain't nothing really." Lily pointed back to the room she'd been heading for. The room where they had someone using their so-called services as a hotel. "She said Mr. Burrows went to eat and I should make sure his room's clean."

"Then I guess ya should." Cole shooed her away before checking the floor. Jane had moved behind the bar, but every man at the poker table now had fresh drinks. The two women sent as distraction were doing their job well.

The most skilled players piles had already shrunk after one hand. His woman was smart.

Cuddy's ass-like braying laugh rang through the saloon, and Cole's ears rang in response. When he glanced back at the bar he found Jane looking right at him. She waved with a wiggle of her fingers before setting Cuddy braying again.

Cole chuckled and walked down the stairs. Before he hit the bottom, Daisy was waiting for him with a whiskey. "Don't know how she did it. You're the only one Iris listens to."

"We'll see if Iris actually listened." He took the whiskey, taking another look around the bar for signs of trouble. Even if Jane thought she had a handle on things, it never hurt to make sure his brand of handling things wasn't needed. "Did I miss anything?"

"Jane and Mack had another row when he grabbed her." Daisy shrugged. "Again."

"He did, did he?"

"Yeah. She didn't do nothing the first couple of times but smack his hand and glare at him. Third time she cuffed him. Then it got ugly." A grin spread across her face so fast he worried she was up to something. Instead she just laughed. "I didn't know that Jane could curse enough to make a cowboy blush."

Cole chuckled. "Yeah. She's got a mouth on her. Where's Mack now?"

"Cuddy and Charlie got him out of here. Then Karl had a bad losing streak. Owes the house more than he could pay in a month. Kept trying to play. Wouldn't listen a lick when Charlie tried to get him out of the game. Jane convinced him to go a couple rounds of Faro with her. He won back half of what he owed. Passed him off to me and I got him to go home to his wife by trying to get him back to one of the rooms."

"Jane's been busy." For her to know Karl wouldn't take a whore for nothing, that he was dead loyal to his wife was impressive. All that she'd actually handled while he'd napped, was even more so. The woman would never cease to surprise him. He frowned as he noticed only a few girls lingered in the saloon. "Where are the rest of the girls?"

"Working. Clover, Flora and Hyacinth have been busy all afternoon. I've just now had a chance to breathe." She pursed her lips. "And there's something else."

Cole narrowed his eyes. His full attention now focused on Daisy's next words.

"Actually there's two something else's." She took a step back, fingers fidgeting with her skirts. "First, is Heather—"

"She's pregnant." Jane appeared out of nowhere and offered Daisy an easy smile. One that Daisy couldn't match and Cole wasn't so sure he appreciated.

"Excuse me?" He glared at Daisy. It was her responsibility to make sure all the whores had protection against incidents like this. "Daisy."

"Oh, stop it. It's not Daisy's fault. Heather is not very bright and you know it. She didn't use the womb veil you and Daisy provide the girls with. Apparently she thought she only needed to use it once a day." Jane moved to Daisy's side.

An odd sight, the two of them standing together. He wasn't sure he liked it. Unfortunately what Jane said made sense. Heather was not too bright.

Jane sighed and shook her head. "She drank copious amounts of the tea Iris gave her before telling Daisy of the pregnancy at all. I'm afraid the tea is already working its magic and she won't be pregnant much longer."

Daisy looked down at the floor. "She's in the back now. I'm keeping an eye on her, but she's already bleeding. It's not going to be easy for her and she'll not be able to work for a couple of weeks."

Rather than unleash the string of curses he wanted to, Cole downed the whiskey he held in one gulp. No wonder Daisy had offered it to him. If he had to bet, Jane had set it up. The whiskey burned its way down, and after the bracing drink he nodded. "What's the other thing?"

"I've got it Daisy. It's about me anyhow." Jane patted Daisy's shoulder. Before saying anything else, Jane turned on her heel and walked into the storeroom.

Daisy shuffled her feet. "I suppose I should go check on Heather?"

"Suppose you should." Cole ground his teeth together and he contemplated a new glass of whiskey. Hell, there were plenty of bottles in the storeroom if he needed them. He followed Jane's path and found her leaning against the shelves, quiet and calm. Still, Daisy's nerves had grated his own. "Do I need another drink for this one?"

"No. Daisy's over-reacting. It's Guy."

"What about him?"

"He stopped by here today. From what I could tell, he wanted to talk to you about buying Daisy's contract again. He wasn't all too happy to find me here. I might be in breach of my contract." Her lips twitched and twisted until he couldn't tell if she was upset or amused by the revelation. "Not intentionally of course, but I just might be. Either way, I don't even know if he'll act on it. I could be fired by this time tomorrow. We'll see."

"Don't seem too upset."

"I do like earning my own way, but I'm sure I'll find another job somewhere. Old Widow Teak could die at any time and a position could open at the library." She winked.

"That woman is older than dirt."

"I noticed. Every time I go in there I fear I'll find her not asleep, but dead, behind the desk. It's an adventure every day." She smiled. "Daisy is just upset because he was talking about getting her contract again. She says you don't use her services anymore and haven't said another word about buying her own contract so she's afraid you'll take him up on it."

"Told you that, did she?" Cole leaned on a shelf, staring at the neat lines of whiskey bottles. Last thing he wanted to admit is not touching any of the whores. Jane would read too much into that detail, he was sure. But Daisy had gone and told Jane all about his neglect of her services. Maybe she'd think it was just Daisy.

"I reminded her that she's very useful when it comes to keeping the whores clean, as well as your clientele. Not to mention the boom in business when the saloon becomes a temporary hospital during the occasional raid."

"Did you straighten the storeroom?" It was a blatant change of subject, but it hit him as the bottles were lined up so dead-on. Much straighter than he remembered them being. He looked over every shelf in the room. The beer barrels were in a perfect line against the wall, as were all the glasses and mugs.

"No." Her lips twitched again, her laughter escaping lightly. "I think that was Charlie before the first poker game started."

"You make him do it?"

"Of course not." She straightened her shoulders as if offended he'd dare suggest she'd done exactly what he'd seen her do with Iris. Then a smile reemerged. "Although I might have been complaining because I couldn't find something."

"I oughta leave you alone more often." He chuckled. "No wonder Guy's got ya running things at his place. That why ya say you're in breach of contract?"

She wrinkled her nose. "Yes. I'm afraid he walked in while I was playing Faro with Karl. It's a conflict of interest for me to be doing these things over here. The original contract wouldn't have even allowed me to be friendly with you."

"Can't have that."

"I know. So I told him to remove it. Unfortunately I didn't read the rewritten contract well enough before I signed.

The new contract also contains a conflict of interest clause, which includes things like running games or any sort of floor management."

"Don't sound like you to not read anything well enough."

"It isn't. I was—distracted that day." A shudder coursed through her and she rubbed her hands together. All amusement faded from her features for a moment before she blinked a few times and lifted her gaze. "Anyhow, I'll speak with him tomorrow and see where we stand."

"This is what you do every day there?"

"What?"

"Put whores with gamblers doing well, make the whores stay clean, keep them busy, take care of the hotel rooms. Just makin' sure everyone is happy, includin' me."

"I do more than that, but yes. Essentially. I keep an eye on the floor. Most of my business does not involve the whores, but it always overlaps." She laughed. "What did you think I did over there? Somersaults?"

"Thought maybe you ran the books."

"No. My job is people. I like people."

"I noticed." He stepped closer and brushed his thumb along her cheek. When her eyes fluttered shut at the simple touch, his heartbeat quickened. His throat grew thick and he cleared it. "Well, fired or not, you're welcome in my saloon any time."

"Except when Graham is here."

"Graham's an idiot."

"And your partner."

"I'll talk to him." With one hand, he tugged her close. She didn't resist a bit, curving into him with a smile. "It's mostly my business anyhow. I say you got free rein to do what ya do. So long as it keeps my place running good."

"Dangerous claim, Mr. Mitchell. I might take advantage."

"Please do."

Her hum was interrupted by a familiar and loud voice out in the saloon.

"It's Wednesday. She don't work then. I bet she is." Hammy's loud voice boomed over the quiet din. "You here, Lady Jane?"

"I'd best answer or he'll keep shouting."

"Old coot." Cole chuckled along with her. "Must've been working at the mines today. Always goes deaf near them machines."

She ducked under his arm, striding from the room. Her voice rose to match Hammy's shout, loud above the din. "Mr. Hamm. It's always wonderful to see you."

"David's been lookin' for ya. I thought you'd be here." Hammy was bright red in the welcoming embrace of Jane. "Aw, gee, Lady Jane."

Cole's amusement faded into a frown when Jane also welcomed David with a hug. Her call to Cuddy to give Hammy a free beer was now the least of his worries. He moved to Jane's side quick as possible.

"Cole." David gave him a cool nod. "Jane, could I speak with you?"

"Want a whiskey?" Cole knew the man would turn him down.

"Yes," Jane replied at the same time David said no. "Would you like coffee then, David? I'll get it. Cole, I'll get you a fresh whiskey."

David's brow furrowed and he took a step back from Cole. "I'm just gonna sit then."

When David took a seat at an empty table, Cole joined him, if only to enjoy the way David kept shifting in his chair, looking for Jane. When a full minute passed without her reappearance, Cole leaned back. "Martha find her husband yet?"

"That's the army's business." David's lips thinned and he narrowed his eyes back at Cole. "Not yours or anyone else's in this town."

"You've been helping her look."

"From what I hear, you helped her too."

"Sure I did." Cole smirked and leaned forward. "Woulda been my pleasure to kill him after what he did to Jane. Too bad her own husband don't feel the same."

"It wasn't Starbird." David lifted his chin. Stone still, he glared at Cole. "No way Starbird would do that. If there was I'd be happy to see him in prison for it, don't think any different. I don't like that Clara was hurt in all this."

"Saying Jane lied about the paint?"

"No. I'm saying anyone can paint their face like that. Doesn't mean it was Lewis."

"Defending the man that took your woman. The same man that shot your wife. Interesting. What's Cora got to say about that? After all, he killed her husband."

The tense grip he had on his chair loosened and David folded his hands in his lap. "Time's made her see that maybe it wasn't. We'll see."

"Will we? You got them Indians agreeing to stop attacking?"

"No." David grimaced. "Not yet."

"Well, isn't this friendly?" Jane's jaw clenched as she looked between the two of them. "I couldn't leave the two of you alone for three minutes without you looking like you're going to kill each other?"

"We're just talking." Cole lifted the glass of whiskey she'd brought him and drank it down. "Ain't like we got guns drawn."

"You got here just in time to stop that." David smirked. "Cole is being rather curious about—"

"Don't really care." Jane pushed her own untouched whiskey over to Cole. After offering him a wink and a smile, she turned back to David. "Am I to assume you had the meeting we talked about?"

Cole furrowed his brow. "What meeting?"

Jane waved her hand at him. "Hush. David?"

"Yes. We shouldn't have any trouble, outside of your current issues." David reached out and touched her hand. It took every fiber of self-control for Cole to not force the issue of David unhanding her. After all, they were married. He had no say in what she did, Jane had made that all too clear.

Cole's stomach churned. "Enjoy your talk."

The last thing he heard from the two of them was Jane's huff. Whatever she said under her breath was lost to the din of the saloon, and probably for the best. Cole moved behind the bar and started wiping down glasses to keep busy. No matter how he tried to avoid the matter, he kept one eye trained on the table with Jane.

Fire burned up from his belly into his throat when the pair broke into laughter. His hand jerked in the glass he was washing.

Crack.

Sharp pain flared from his hand up his arm. Blood first seeped, then gushed from a deep gash along the side of his thumb. "Damn it."

He threw the broken glass back into the tub and shouted for Daisy. When she didn't appear immediately, he wrapped a towel around his hand. He lifted his head in time to see Jane give David another blasted hug before she headed Cole's direction.

"I'm fine," he snarled.

"Of course you are. That's why you're bleeding through that towel." Jane reached him at the same time Daisy came out from the back with her medical bag in hand.

Cole brushed past Jane and pointed Daisy into the storeroom.

Jane followed as far as the door.

"Was that David I saw? In the saloon of all places?" Daisy squeaked when Cole's hand jerked away. The gauze she held froze in mid-air. Her wide eyes focused on Cole as he glared at her instead of giving her his hand back.

"Yes." Jane smirked and cocked her head at him. "We had something to talk about. Don't let him scare you, Daisy. He's a grumpy bastard whenever he sees my husband."

Cole flinched when Daisy got his hand back in her lap and managed to start cleaning it. The pain in Cole's jaw started to approach the levels of pain in his hand he was keeping it clenched so tight.

"Really? Must've been important. He never comes in here. Not like he drinks or gambles or whores around." Daisy frowned. "You're going to need stitches."

"We were discussing our divorce." Arms folded in front of her; Jane appeared relaxed.

Cole held his face carefully still while his body went numb. Divorce? He stared at the cut on his hand rather than look at Jane. Careful as possible he allowed himself to speak slow and steady. "That so? Thought he wanted you to become Clara again, so he could have his happy little wife back."

"Guess you thought wrong."

"Guess so."

The moment we indulge our diffrences, the earth is metamorphosed, there is no winter and no night. All tragedies, all ennui, vanish – all duties even.
-Thomas Babington Macaulay

He'd fallen asleep with his head on her stomach.

Jane's fingers drifted absently through Cole's hair as she made a weak attempt at reading the book in her hand. Inevitably her gaze kept drifting back to the man lying asleep on her stomach. In the month since they'd given in to their desire, he'd come to her bed nearly every night.

The time of night varied depending on Graham's mood. After the first night when Cole had disappeared for an entire day, Graham had been grumpy. More often than not, Cole manned the saloon alone or his bartender did. Graham's presence in the saloon diminished until he was rarely there any longer.

She ran her fingers along his hairline, a smile growing with every one of his breaths that brushed across her flesh. He felt so right, even in sleep.

With a sigh, she gave up pretending to read and dropped her head back against the headboard. Thoughts like those were not welcome. Cole would be gone soon enough. Once the euphoria of the conquering wore off, he'd be onto the next challenge. She could not let herself get wrapped up in him any further. She couldn't.

It was too late.

Closing her eyes, she chastised herself—no. It couldn't be too late. More often than not they joined for pure physical pleasure, not emotion. That's all that was involved. Certainly the rumors concurred, if only her heart did the same.

She felt compelled to demand his attention. Part of her longed to tell him of the nightmare that plagued her, to share her private horrors. There was no one else she wanted to tell, no one but Cole. He knew everything about her, which wasn't much in her short life, but at the same time was everything. Even so, she still couldn't tell him.

She didn't dare let things go further, to let herself get any more wrapped up in him. She'd enjoy the immense pleasure of his touch, the way he consumed her like nothing else she'd found. But she wouldn't let him in again. He hadn't let her in. She could manage the same.

Rubbing her hand over her face to try to wipe away the thoughts, she glanced down at the book in her hand again. She lifted it, determined to wipe away the too-intense thoughts for her current situation.

She flipped the book open to one of her favorite passages. Before she'd ever read the book the first time in her memory, she'd known the words. Walt Whitman's *Pent-Up Aching Rivers* had become her favorite, but she felt like it might have always been. She enjoyed re-reading it often as she could.

> *The overture lightly sounding—the strain anticipating, the welcome nearness— the sight of the perfect body.*

Unbidden, her eyes flashed down to Cole again and a smile formed. Perfect body indeed. Save for those two scars, no flaws were visible. Doing her best not to chuckle at her own amusement, she turned back to her reading.

> *The swimmer swimming naked in the bath, or motionless on his back lying and floating. The female form approaching—I, pensive, love-flesh tremulous, aching.*

Cole shifted against her. When his head came to rest on her chest, she knew he slept no longer. Smirking, she ignored him and returned to reading, skimming ahead.

> *The face—the limbs—the index from head to foot, and what it arouses; The mystic deliria—the madness amorous—the utter abandonment; Hark close, and still, what I now whisper to you, I love you—O you entirely possess me, O I wish that you and I could escape from the rest, and go utterly off—free and lawless, Two hawks in the air— two fishes in the sea not more lawless than we.*

His hand ran along her stomach and she took a deep, shaky breath to maintain her focus. When his lips found her flesh, teasing her, she clenched her jaw against the onslaught of passion.

Searching fingers managed to rip a gasp and a moan from her. She cleared her throat in an attempted note of irritation. Then again, how could she be irritated when his fingers were so skillfully working her into excitement? He wouldn't give up, she knew it, but she had every intention of giving him a challenge.

The book pulled from her hands. She protested, but his lips were on hers. She hit his chest in a playful gesture. Her laughter broke the kiss. "I was reading."

"Reading? Think there's better things to be doing."

"Says the man that's been snoring on me for the past hour."

"I ain't been snoring."

"Yes, you have." She yelped when his fingers moved along her side and tickled her. Already breathless, she gasped for air between laughs until tears streamed down her cheeks. When he finally stopped, she couldn't catch her breath from laughing. It was several minutes before she managed to rasp, "That wasn't nice."

His stubble ran along her stomach. He lifted his gaze and offered a deliciously vicious smirk. "Never said I was nice."

"Well, you aren't."

"I'm not?"

A moan erupted when he resumed his urgent teasing. She arched toward him, eager for more. Still she struggled to maintain her calm, to remain in control of the situation. She bit her lip and shook her head. "Not at all."

His hum of disagreement got lost in her flesh as he added his lips to his already teasing fingers. All thoughts of arguing her point disappeared as she gave into his demanding touch.

By the time they'd finished, the sun glowed pink on the curtains and they were both once again exhausted. Limbs entwined, they lay still on the bed. She relaxed as his hand ran along her spine. "All right. I suppose I could say you are a little nice."

Chuckling, he shook his head. "Nah. That was selfish."

"Of course it was. Be selfish all you want. I certainly don't mind." She propped her chin on his chest and winked. "I encourage such selfishness."

"Good. I ain't—"

They both sat when shouts rang out on the street. She scrambled to her feet, throwing her robe on before bursting onto the balcony.

He was right behind her, his body pressed to hers as the crowd below grew louder, gathering around the wagon moving through town. A low curse rented the stifling silence on the balcony before he said, "I don't believe it."

"What?" Jane studied the scene in confusion. The realization dawned on her before he had a chance to explain. "Is that Starbird?"

"Looks like he's dead."

"The body—it has no face."

Cole leaned on the rail beside her, a frown creasing his handsome features. Below the wagon moved in a slow procession toward Graham's. David drove with Martha beside him, her shoulders sagging. He huffed. "Among other things. Looks like the savages left him in the woods to get eaten. Guess they don't like traitors neither."

Her stomach turned as the remains of the man held her focus despite wanting nothing more than to look away. The mangled body of her nightmares flashed through her mind. She went into the room to avoid further discussion; she'd let him watch the show. The nightmare took over her thoughts. The first time she'd had it had been the night she'd woken in such terror they'd plied her with drugs to silence her.

Since then it had returned on numerous occasions, but she'd managed to avoid another fit of terror. She headed for the washbasin and poured some fresh water to clean the sweat from her face. She hoped to feel refreshed and have the nightmare pushed aside before he would see. She couldn't risk opening up to a man who'd leave once he'd had his fill—she'd already shown him too much. She couldn't let it continue.

He seemed to understand in the thoroughly annoying way he had and said not a word. While she took great concentration in her morning sponge bath ritual, he got dressed in total silence. It wasn't until she applied her perfume and pulled on her chemise that he spoke, "I'd best get to it. I'm guessing you ain't gonna come check out the body?"

"I'd rather not." Her corset in hand, she focused on a loose thread. While she picked at it, her mind focused on keeping her hands and body still, not a tremor of weakness could be seen. She had to get a better rein on her feelings around him. He'd always been so easy to open up around, she'd felt like he was the one person who understood, who she could tell it all too. Only now she realized, far too late, that had been her greatest mistake. "Enjoy your day."

"Yeah."

Closing her eyes when he left the room, she dropped the corset and buried her face in her hands. Once again the images filled her head, from the body that had just passed under her balcony, shifting into the dismembered hand from her dreams. The mangled body and unseeing eyes filled her memories as her heart pounded loud in her ears.

Out of nowhere his warmth surrounded her. Strong arms held her tight. She fought against him, trying to push him away. If she gave into his comfort again, there would be no going back. Her heart would be lost.

As before, he took her beating in silence until she collapsed. With one last weak hit of her fist to his chest, she sobbed and clung to him.

Giving into the security of his hold, she let his strong presence soothe her as it had so many times. She knew he wanted to ask and was grateful for his patience until she felt more collected.

"Death ain't bothered ya before. You didn't act like this after the attacks, not even witnessin' the dead from the fires in the settlement, and you liked them people."

"It's not his death specifically," she whispered before she could stop herself. "I don't care about him. It's the…"

Her hesitation met with silence. He didn't push or try to guess, just waited.

"The nightmares."

The word stirred him into motion. He pulled away to sit in the chair. For a long minute he eyed her with a steady, unyielding gaze. "That night I had to break your door down, when ya woke the dead with your screaming."

"I didn't remember so much at first. It wasn't until almost a week later when the nightmare returned. I don't know if it was a memory like my memory of David. I'm not certain, but if it is I'm afraid of what it means."

"What was it?"

"A hand."

"Just a hand?"

She exhaled long and low in an attempt to shake the last of her nerves. The rising memory wouldn't let her truly relax, but she did her best to keep her voice steady. "It was dismembered, lying in the middle of some train tracks. Still bleeding, still…"

"The finger moved," he said with no amusement. The frown he'd been wearing since he took a seat deepened. "You said that, rather screamed it, over and over. We wondered what the hell you meant."

"There was a man. Mangled. Dead. He'd been pushed in front of the train. They said I pushed him. They said I killed him."

"Who did?"

"I don't know. I don't know who he was or why I keep seeing it." When he stood, she scrambled back. "You should go. If this is true, who knows what will happen. You should go now before it's too late."

"You didn't kill no one but a worthless Indian. You wouldn't."

"You don't know that. You don't know who I was."

"I know who ya are."

"I don't know who I was, what I became after I left David. What if it's true?"

His hand circled her neck before he pulled her close. "Ya didn't kill no one. I don't care what you don't remember. Don't think you could. Not without good reason."

"You have more faith in me than I do." The moment his lips closed over hers, she knew she'd lost the battle. She'd let herself fall in too deep and when he left, which she knew he would, it would rip her heart right out of her chest. Clinging to him like a lifeline, she let him soothe every fear, getting lost in the depths of the kiss.

When he pulled back, he brushed a tear from her cheek with his thumb. "I'm guessing your husband found himself a way to avoid your lunch date. Does that mean I get the extra time?"

She snorted and shook her head at him. While she knew he'd said it to change the subject, lighten the mood, maybe even ease her fears, she was still annoyed. "Insatiable."

"Don't hear you complaining."

"I'll think about it." She grinned at his groan of complaint. "You aren't lacking feminine comfort. I'm certain you'll live if I become too busy."

"Just because I'll live don't mean I'll be happy about it."

She pushed him back, giggling over his continued grumbling. "Get out of here. I have to get to work."

"Still don't know how you got Guy to keep you on."

"You've seen my skills."

"I sure have."

Jane scoffed, tossing him a glare. She turned her attention back to donning her corset. "I meant in business. He'd be a fool to let me go. I simply had to remind him of what a man with a sensible brain would do."

"Who's got a sensible brain? Not him." Cole's wicked grin sparked one of her own.

"Hush. I told you to go on. If I miss you at lunch, I'm certain you'll be climbing my balcony before too long."

"Don't bother you that half the town sees it?"

"After we got caught behind Rusty's office, I believe the whole town is well aware of what we are doing, Cole. Embarrassment is overrated and implies what we are doing is wrong." Her hands slipped around his neck. She pressed into him. His appreciative groan seeped through her and stirred her excitement once again. "I have no qualms about what I'm doing with you."

"Good."

She winked and disentangled herself before she got too distracted to remember her duties. "Now go away so I can finish getting dressed."

"I'll help ya tighten your corset."

"No, you won't." If he got a hold of her corset strings, they'd be loosened instead of tightened, she just knew it. His grin was far too wicked for good behavior. "Go do what you were going to. I'm going to stop in to see Mrs. Broder and then heading over to the Silver Saddle. If you're lucky, I'll see you at lunch."

"I'm feeling awful lucky."

To talk to the perfect girl who understands me,
to waft to her these from my own lips- to effuse
them from my own body;
From privacy - from frequent repinings alone;
From plenty of persons near, and yet the
right person not near.
-Walt Whitman

"So what's the deal?" Graham leaned on the bar, a wicked leer spread across his round face. The man was rarely in the saloon lately, but when he was he was always poised for a fight.

Cole polished off his whiskey and poured another. He knew Graham wanted to needle him about Jane. Last thing he'd do is make it easy for him. He smirked and shrugged. "You tell me. You're the one that took in the body."

"You know I'm not talking about Starbird." Graham downed his own whiskey. "What's with Miss Prim and Proper? Whole town knows what the two of you have been doing. Figured once you bagged her, you'd be moving on; yet here you are. Hanging on and leaving the door open so we can all hear how much she's enjoying the ride."

It took every bit of effort not to spit out his whiskey. Cole strained against the urge to laugh until the liquid burned down his throat. Free of the danger of wasting whiskey, Cole let the laughter emerge. "She's the one leaving the door open. She ain't so prim and proper."

"She dresses more like a schoolmarm than Becky."

Cole shrugged. Truth be told, he liked the contrast. Jane dressed as prim as Graham suggested, all high collars, tight corsets and covered ankles. Underneath all them layers Jane had to be the most wild and free woman he'd known.

Outspoken, honest to a fault, playful, and sexy even in broad daylight. She didn't care who knew they were spending hours upon hours in her bed. In fact, she acted damn proud of it.

He never thought it would be so difficult to pull away from her. Once he'd had her, he thought it would be over, done. His enjoyment should, by all accounts, be complete. He'd conquered her and gotten all he ever wanted.

Just this morning he'd walked out, only to go back because of her distress. It would have been so easy to walk away then and not look back. To end things before people started talking about more than unseemly acts. Why hadn't he just walked away?

The pull she had over him bothered him. He'd sworn he wouldn't ever let a woman in again, not for nothing. The chase had ended with Jane, but he still wanted more. Could it be the challenge she presented? The way she dared him to walk away at every turn? He didn't know why, but he kept going back. He needed an excuse to get out, that's all. Temper like hers, it wouldn't take long.

He tipped his head back to finish the whiskey in his hand. It lingered in his mouth before he let it burn slow down his throat. The question that bothered him most lingered. When she gave him an excuse to walk away, would he take it and run?

"Uh, Cole?" Graham smirked. "She's got you wound up tight. Never seen any woman snare you like this, not even Kat. I just don't get it. She's nothing special."

Oh, but she was. She got him, in an annoyingly accurate and intense way. Even the best whore couldn't make him as ravenous as Jane and she matched his energy in every way. A slow grin crossed his features. "You got no idea, Graham. None at all."

"Care to share more than the carnal sounds from her room?"

"Not really. Ya manage to snag the China woman yet?"

Graham's amusement faded and he poured himself a beer. "You need to get a new line. That's old and not so funny."

"You know what? Ya spend all this time complaining I got a woman so happy to be makin' time with me she lets the whole world know what sins we're performing." Cole let loose a wicked chuckle. While the words settled in to deepen Graham's frown, he poured another glass of whiskey. "But you got two women that won't let ya touch a hair on their head. One that should and one that you'd give anything to touch. Maybe you should do a little less complaining."

"When are you gonna drop her, Cole?" Graham sneered. "Never seen you string one along this long. Or is she the one doing the stringing? She's trying to rope you in and get you hitched. And you're falling right in her trap."

"She's already married." Cole shook his head, not about to fall prey to Graham's attack. "About to get divorced. She don't want to get married again for nothing. She wants to play, and she's fine with me playing."

"But you haven't been with—"

"Cole." Daisy interrupted Graham moments before he took it to far.

Cole held up his hand to silence Daisy. Stepping closer to Graham, he silently dared him to finish and announce to the saloon that Cole hadn't touched a whore in months. When the man backed down, Cole allowed a triumphant grin. After he'd finished his whiskey, he slammed the glass down and turned on Daisy. "What?"

"I gotta tell you something. It's important." Daisy's eyes were wide and she leaned over the bar, her ample bosoms threatening to spill out of her top. A view he used to enjoy. "In private. We really gotta talk."

"Not in the mood." Cole pulled back. Since he'd offered to let her buy out her contract she'd been playing games. She had a good six months of work to pay him what he wanted out of her, and in the meantime she was driving him right nuts. One minute she couldn't contain her excitement, the next she tried to get him alone to show her willingness to stay. Willingness he wanted no part of anymore.

"No, not that." Daisy looked around the saloon before leaning over further. "It's about Starbird. Please, Cole."

"Well," Graham muttered. "Look at that. The fisherwoman comes to the fish."

Cole furrowed his brow at his annoying friend. "What the devil are you talking about?" At Graham's gesture toward the door, Cole turned his attention there and grinned. He nodded to Jane as she approached the bar. "Is it lunch already?"

"It would appear so." Jane leaned on the bar and took the glass of whiskey Cole had just poured. "Unless, of course, you're no longer feeling lucky. I could go find someone else to—"

"Nope." Cole grabbed a fresh bottle of whiskey, not wanting to know the end of her sentence. "I'm still plenty lucky."

"Good." Her smile lit her face, the eagerness there made him want to claim her in front of every patron in the saloon. She leaned forward, her finger tapping the bar as she eyed him through her lashes. "Back to the boarding house, then?"

Her innocent question gave him pause. With the eyes of Daisy and Graham on them, he knew he wanted to be alone with her. A yes hovered on his tongue, but it never formed. For some reason when she squeezed his hand he knew what he wanted to do. She'd let him into her secret horror, and he was about to let her in as well. He was damn well screwed, despite what he'd told Graham. "No. We'll go upstairs."

She nodded, her smile tremulous. Though her eyes widened a fraction and glanced toward the aghast pair beside them, she squeezed his hand again. "Lead the way, then."

Cole cast a glare at the gape-mouthed Daisy and Graham before he circled out from behind the bar. He took her hand and led her to the steps, well aware as to why they were staring. For the well over ten years he'd been living there, not a soul had been allowed over his threshold. No man or woman, friend or foe, dare crossed that line. He didn't let anyone in, but now he led this one woman to his door.

He pulled her along when she slowed. The woman didn't miss a trick, and she kept glancing over her shoulder at their rapt audience.

Jane wisely kept her mouth shut. The simple act of her silence helped him take the final steps and open the door. This one act would shift everything if he let it, if he let her.

Once they were inside the room he doubted his motivation. As he closed the door, her footsteps echoed in the empty room as she crossed without hesitation. He rounded the wall he'd kept in place to keep nosy people from seeing much and found her sharp gaze searching every inch of his room.

"You really don't live, do you?"

He leaned against the wall with a frown. Now that she was there, seeing everything he wondered what had made him do this. She was too smart, too observant. Instinct made him bristle against her honest, and spot on, assessment. "What the hell do ya mean? I live plenty, you've seen it."

"No." She touched one of the empty shelves, before glancing at the bare dresser and the unadorned walls. Her hand fell over her heart, whether intentional or not, he couldn't be sure. "You don't live, not in here. Not like this. This isn't living. A hotel is more personal. My room at the boarding house where I have no intention of staying has been more personal since before I knew who I was."

"We could go back to the boarding house." He straightened, already reaching for the door. She read him too well, better than her damn books. She pinned him with her words, and made him squirm like a worm on a hook.

"I'd rather not."

He stood, helpless to stop her as she focused on a box on the desk. A box he would have hidden if he'd thought before bringing her in. The box was the only thing out in the open except a whiskey bottle.

Thinking first hadn't ever been one of his strong suits, and he really should have before he brought her in his room. If he had, the box would be buried in a drawer well away from her sight. Letting her in his room was one thing. Letting her in the box would seal his fate, and something else. She'd know.

What he'd kept hidden from everyone would be hers for the taking.

She'd know.

She'd know *him*. The parts of him he wanted hidden.

When she stepped toward the box, he moved. She couldn't look inside. No one could. She wasn't that special. He had to believe that, even as he knew he was wrong. "Leave it."

"Personal?" Her hand rested on the box. That damned piercing stare ripped through him and laid him bare. One word broke him down. "Scared?"

"Not of you." His voice wavered in a way he hated. Weakness wasn't something he ever showed to anyone. "It ain't your business."

"Then why did you bring me in here?"

He turned his mood smooth as always, letting a low chuckle rumble out. Eyeing her appreciatively, he leaned in. "Why do you think?"

There wasn't a whisper of reaction to his overture. Her body remained still, no smile tugged her lips, and no laughter softened her gaze. After a moment, her eyes hardened and she pursed her lips. "No. We can do that anywhere. From the look on Graham and Daisy's faces I'd say you never allow anyone in here…ever. So why bring me in?"

"You *know* damn well why." He pulled her tight against him. Somehow she kept her hand on the damn box. He growled at her stubborn stance. "The same reason you showed up for lunch."

"And again." Her hand settled on his chest to push him away. Determination lined her brow. She kept her distance, and her cool. The lips he loved to stare at and taste tugged down at the corners. No amusement gleamed in her eyes, instead they echoed with pain he was used to seeing only when she spoke of her lost past. That pain etched away at his resolve. She knew as well as he did that even though he'd let her in the room, he still hadn't truly let her in. "We could do that anywhere."

"Sounds fun." He had to divert, to push it away. She'd come around and see it was better this way.

"I'm certain it would be. I'm certainly not embarrassed by the shift in our…" She turned her gaze away. After a long, shaky breath a smile appeared. When she turned it toward him he could tell it was forced, without the usual playful twist of her lips. "Friendship. Hell, enjoyable as you are, we could do it in the back of Turner's store with it chock full of customers and I wouldn't mind."

The thought distracted him from her intentions and he laughed. What an original idea. "Really? Sounds like a challenge."

"Perhaps. But we are changing the subject. You still haven't answered—why *did* you bring me in here, besides your insatiable desire to screw anything with a bosom?"

"Not *anything* with a bosom. Even I got my limits."

"Cole Mitchell."

"I dunno. Seemed good a place as any," he deflected. He was good at that. She'd let it go soon enough and they could return to the plan at hand. Otherwise he'd be letting her in, and how could he? After so long how could he possibly let anyone in, even her?

"Of course it did." Disappointment seeped into every word. Her fingertips alone clung to the box now. One more little push and she'd drop it. That's all he needed to do, one more deflection. She made it easy. "If you didn't want to make this personal, we wouldn't be in here. Now do I open the box or do we go to Tuner's and test that theory?"

Was it the tone of her voice or her refusal to meet his eyes for the first time he could remember that did it? No matter the reason, his resolve crumbled. He realized that if he refused, she may return to his bed, but it wouldn't be the same. Her body would be there, but her spirit would be gone. She'd be broken, and he had broken enough women.

He wanted all of her, strong and unbroken.

Of course, he already knew everything about her. Everything that she did, at least. Just that morning she'd bared her fear over her nightmares. How could he hide his own past?

As her gaze lowered, and a shuddering breath shook her body, he knew. He didn't want to hide any longer. Not from her. He wouldn't be able to tell all, some things were too painful, but he could let her in. He had to. No, he wanted her to open the box, even as he feared her opening it. His throat thickened and he looked away. "Do what you want. I don't care."

"Yes, you do." Her voice cut through him. Fingers running along the edge of the box, she pulled her hand back. She knew he was brushing her off, in her annoying way she knew how much he didn't want her to, even though he also wanted her to. "I'll meet you at Turner's."

He gripped her arm before he could pass. When she lifted her gaze in surprise, he held her gaze tight. The fire of her spirit lingered, wounded but still burning, and he wanted to make sure that fire didn't die. He released her arm and urged her back to the desk. "Open it."

"Why?"

"Do it."

"Tell me why." Jane moved close. One touch to his cheek and she had him stuck. "If you're saying this to keep me from being grumpy, forget it."

"I want you to." Cole gripped her hand, but removed her fingers from his cheek with a gentle touch. Some things he wouldn't dare admit even to himself, but this he could admit to them both. "I can't say why. I don't know for sure. Damn it, Jane, I ain't good with words."

"I know, I know. All right." She stepped away and the creak of the long-untouched box opening preceded her soft gasp. The dulcet tones of understanding seeped into her voice. Her hand trembled as she lifted the tintype from the box. "They are beautiful."

Suddenly he knew he was done for, finished. You could've knocked him over with a feather when he realized he didn't care. Now he understood. He wanted all of her, and the way she looked at him now, he knew he had all of her. Completely. "That's Ella. The kid was Lydia."

"The kid? Was?" She focused on the image, pulling it close. After a moment, she smiled softly. "She looks just like you."

"That's what they all said."

"You had a daughter? A wife?"

"Yeah. Long time ago. They're both gone."

She set the picture down beside the box, her fingers running over a pair of booties inside before pulling out another picture. The woman in the picture remained clear as could be. Jane's brow furrowed as her finger ran along the other half, singed from a long extinguished flame.

"My ma."

"Don't care for your pa, obviously."

"Nope."

She set the picture back in the box before picking up the one of Ella and Lydia again. Shaking her head, her gaze never left the picture. "They were important to you. Important enough to keep her booties and the wedding rings."

He leaned on the desk and allowed a nod. "Were. Not no more. It's the past. Don't matter none now."

"You can't ignore the past."

The pain in her voice jolted him and he regretted his words instantly. Before he could recover to respond, her hand touched his arm.

"They deserve more than to be closed up in a room with no feeling, don't you think? You deserve more than that, too. May I borrow this?"

He eyed the picture, unease settling into his heart. Things were about to change, and he had no idea what to think of it. "What're you up to?"

"You don't let anyone in this room. Whatever I do is irrelevant. You know I'll tell no one. Otherwise you'll have to wait and see. I promise I'll take good care of it."

When she met his eyes again, he couldn't deny the fire there. He trusted her enough to let her in. Now he had her completely, he wanted to feel her right there with him. A sly grin formed. "Depends."

The picture fluttered to the desk. Her hand planted on his chest and pushed him back. When his calves bumped the edge of the bed, she pushed him onto it. "First I'll take very good care of you."

His hands went to her waist as she climbed on top of him. This time he meant every word as they spilled from his words. "Then do whatever the hell you want."

The truth is a snare –
you cannot have it without being caught.
You cannot have the truth in such a way that
you catch it, but only in such a way that it
catches you.
–Soren Kierkegaard

Courtesy alone led Jane to attend the funeral.

No sorrow or remorse drove her, in fact she regretted coming at all. It felt hypocritical to attend when she didn't know the man, nor care about his existence. The funerals for miner's and townsfolk held far more sorrow for her.

Cole had asked her to attend with him, and she'd agreed on the merit of his request.

In the few days since he'd invited her into his room, she'd been with him far more than she thought wise. She'd spent some nights there, and her day off had been completely spent in his room while he worked.

The subtle, but powerful shift in her relationship with Cole made her uneasy. She couldn't help but wait for the end, like she held her breath until the inevitable heartbreak. One of them would turn tail. They kept pushing and daring each other to crack.

In a world that was still so foreign and confusing, he alone understood her. No one else did, no one else could. Not even the man that had once been her husband. In fact, he hardly spoke to her anymore. Only Cole understood, even when she wished he didn't.

It really was amazing.

It really was terrifying.

Despite herself, she shuddered and wrapped her arms around herself. She leaned back into his broad chest. The safety of his arms had become her haven against the harsh realities that plagued her. Within his arms she'd finally admitted her fears, her doubts, the nagging worry that the past would return to haunt her.

He'd attempted to ease her mind, to help her figure out what had happened to her. They still had no answers, but unleashing the full truth of her inner horror had eased the pain.

The service ended in virtual silence. Not even Martha cried as she released the first shovel of dirt into the grave of her husband. The scene disturbed Jane in a way she couldn't verbalize and she turned away. When Cole's hand rested on her back, she moved toward town with him.

On the porch of Turner's, Cora's older son Arthur sat in silence. A book in his hands lay open and he rubbed at his cheeks whenever he glanced toward the cemetery. Despite her general discomfort with children, she'd come to like Arthur and now felt drawn toward the forlorn young man. She whispered, "I'll be along in a few minutes."

Cole followed her gaze, his brow furrowed. "Ya sure?"

"I'm certain. I'll meet you at the saloon shortly."

For a moment he leaned toward her as if he would place a tender kiss to her lips like those he'd come to bestow on her in private moments. Then he stopped as if he realized where they were and simply nodded. After another glance to the porch, he turned to head down the street.

Jane fought her burgeoning smile at his continued refusal to allow public affection beyond rakish behaviors, mostly because she felt the same. Speaking of which, she tilted her head slightly as he walked down the street, enjoying the view of his ass as he departed her company.

When he shot a wicked grin over his shoulder, clearly aware of her intense gaze, a rush of heat filled her cheeks. She had to bite her lip to cover an inappropriate giggle.

With a sigh, she turned away from her pleasure to once again face the sight on the porch. In truth, her heart went out to Arthur. The boy was but thirteen years old, far too young to have had his life turned upside down as it had. His father gone, at the hands of a man he considered family. A man who now lay dead.

She climbed a few steps toward him. "Arthur?"

Arthur didn't look up. "Hey, Jane."

Jane made it to his side and sank to the bench, peeking over his shoulder. When she reached toward the book he held it out to her. "'Like coals in the ashes, they darken and die. Song sinks into silence. The story is told. The windows are darkened; the hearthstone is cold. Darker and darker the black shadows fall. Sleep and oblivion reign over all'."

"What if the story isn't told?"

"Then someone should tell it." Jane turned the pages, glancing over each poem. The words filled her head the moment she saw the first lines of each. "Someone that knows the story should tell it proper."

"You think so?"

Jane pointed to a poem. "'Such songs have power to quiet the restless pulse of care, and come like the benediction that follows after prayer. Then read from the treasured volume the poem of thy choice and lend to the rhyme of the poet the beauty of thy voice. And the night shall be filled with music. And the cares that infest the day shall fold their tents like the Arabs and as silently steal away'."

Arthur tore his gaze from his hands to look up at her.

"In other words, yes. I do think so, and it sounds as if Longfellow agrees with me. If the story needs to be told, it should be. It can help you, and others, through grief and worry and pain." Jane smiled and handed him the book. "Don't focus so on the sad parts of the poem. For each word leads toward joy if you can find the right path."

"Sometimes it ain't easy."

Jane wrapped her arm around his shoulder and hugged him. "Sometimes you simply need to be pointed in the right direction. Let's read some more, and see whether we can find it."

Arthur leafed through the pages, taking a deep breath before he began to read aloud.

David appeared at the top of the steps. The intensity of his stare made her throat close. She shook her head at him, trying to keep her focus on Arthur.

"Arthur." Cora's voice echoed out from the store moments before she stepped outside with a towel in her hands. "Oh. Jane, I didn't know you were here."

"I stopped to see what Arthur was reading. *The Belfry of Bruges and Other Poems* is a beautiful read. Longfellow has some wonderful words for us all. Words of healing. Right, Arthur?"

Arthur smiled. "Yeah. Thanks, Jane. Would you mind if I asked for help if I need it?"

"Anytime you need help finding the path, you can come find me." Jane smiled and squeezed his shoulder. "Now go help your mother."

After mouthing a *thank you*, Cora disappeared back in the store, leaving Jane alone with David and no clear escape. He stepped forward. "Your horse's name was Longfellow."

"Today isn't a good day, David. You're upset already. You've just spent the morning burying your…" she searched his eyes, "friend?"

"Friend. I forgave him long ago."

"But did you bury a friend?"

"What?" David paled, though his cheeks grew pink. A flash of guilt disappeared as quick as it had appeared. He frowned. "Changing the subject isn't going to make me forget what I just saw you doing here with Arthur. For all your protests and dispute, you don't hate kids."

"Arthur is not a child. He's a young man, and he's been through a great tragedy."

"But you came up here just to talk to him. You didn't have to."

Sighing, she stood and brushed down her skirt.

"I'm sorry." He took her hands. "But just now you looked more like Clara than I've seen in years. The way you handled Arthur. It caught me off-guard."

She squeezed his hands gently. "I can tell. You haven't looked at me with so much sadness in weeks. I'm sorry for rattling you like that."

"I thought maybe there was a memory."

The penetrating gaze he fixed on her made her squirm, but she forced herself to remain still and accept it. He had to see she hadn't changed in the past few minutes.

"But it wasn't, was it? You're still Jane."

"I'm still me."

"Why don't you come inside? I'm sure Cora won't mind."

Jane peeked over his shoulder when another figure approached. With a smile she pulled her hands free of his. "No. I don't think I will."

His brows knit together. "Jane?"

"Good afternoon, Lee. It's good to see you again." Jane grinned when David's ears turned red again. "I think David needs some good hot coffee and some distraction. Burying his friend was difficult for him."

"Jane." David groaned under his breath.

"Go on. I'm going to have a good stiff drink. Funerals always seem to make me want one." She gave him a wink and with a wave to Lee, she slipped down the steps.

The streets were quieter than usual thanks to the funeral, so it didn't take her long to reach the saloon. Inside, she was disappointed to find that Cole was nowhere in sight. Worse to her already somber mood, Graham was situated behind the bar. She leaned on the bar, hoping against hope the burly man was in a decent mood. "Good afternoon, Graham."

He grunted a reply.

Though it wasn't a good sign, she pushed forward. "I need a drink."

"So?" So he was going to be a bastard today.

"Oh, for goodness' sakes." Jane moved behind the bar to grab a glass. If he wasn't going to serve her, she'd take matters into her own hands. Cole was the one who said she could do as she pleased, but she didn't often push her luck when Graham was around. Today she was in a bad enough mood to poke the bear. Unfortunately, that was a big mistake.

"What the hell do you think you're doing?" He gripped her wrist, pushing her back into the bar. "Walking in here like you own the place. Just because you got Cole's prick on alert, don't mean all of us are dying to let you walk all over us."

"Just give me the damn whiskey." She stood her ground best as she could with her wrist smarting under his vice-like grip. Her hand flexed as it tightened even more, tingles of pain radiating through her hand. "Unhand me."

"Get outta my bar."

"That would be far more possible if you would just *unhand me*."

With a final shove, Graham leaned toward her. "Get out."

"*Graham*." Cole looked ready to leap over the railing from the second floor. His hands gripped the banister and his nostrils flared.

A red heat filled her, reaching beyond her cheeks to places hidden by decency and layers of petticoats. She tried to catch her breath, his fierce savagery bringing up feelings usually only fueled by his touch.

"Go to hell, Cole." Graham spun so fast to glare up at the man he knocked Jane into the bar again. "She don't own this place. I do. She don't get no say and needs to learn her place. If she don't, I'll show it to her."

Cole's footsteps raced down the stairs before she could catch her breath or her own indignation. He leaped right over the bar, stilling her heart completely. The graceful move was followed with fury when he got in Graham's face. Her heart did the can-can over his defense of her honor before dropping into her stomach at the acid in his tone. "Stop giving her attitude or it ain't gonna be your business no more."

"You ain't got that kind of money, Cole. Keep her out of—"

Cole gripped Graham's throat and squeezed until the man turned red, and then blue. "I own more of this business than you do. What I say goes."

Jane let out a shriek when Graham punched Cole and Cole returned the favor. "Cole. Graham. Stop. I just wanted a damn drink. Don't make this more than—"

"*Clarabelle?*"

Jane froze in place at the unfamiliar voice, something inside twanged with a hint of recognition. Cole's head snapped up at the strange voice. She tried to force her limbs to move, but they wouldn't behave. Not even Graham's increasingly comical protests tickled her funny bone. A lump formed in her throat and she took a step back when Cole shoved Graham aside into the bar.

Somewhere inside she managed to find her voice. "Cole?"

The pounding of footsteps down the stairs filled the room. Cole gripped her shoulders and squeezed. "I ain't had a chance to tell ya, no thanks to that bastard. He just got here. He came lookin' for Davie."

"Clarabelle."

Jane shook her head, sobbing. "I'm not Clara."

"Jane. This is Michael Young. Clara's brother." Cole turned her toward the man.

How could she take anymore? But she had to. As she had with David, she had to make herself look into the face of her past. She took a deep bracing breath and drew her eyes up to meet the stranger.

Nothing. The blue eyes like hers, the light brown hair and goatee, the bright smile all did nothing. No shocking revelation hit, no flood of memories. Everything remained as blank as it had from the day she woke. "I'm not Clara."

"Yes. You are. I'd know you anywhere, Clarabelle." He stepped closer, his brows drawn down in concern. "Why would you say that?"

"I can't...I'm not..."

"I can't believe you're here." Michael pulled her into hug, holding on tight. "I've missed you so much. I can't believe David didn't tell me you were here."

"I told him not to. I thought it best you continued to believe her dead." Jane extricated herself from the hug as gentle as she could. The man had been through a shock, and though she didn't remember him she didn't want to hurt him. "I'm sorry. I don't remember you. You mean nothing to me."

"Jane." Cole's hand rested on her shoulder. Usually comforting, now it only made her feel worse. "You should listen to him. If he's your brother, maybe he can help."

"Can you tell me where I've been for the past seven years?"

Michael shook his head. "I knew you weren't dead, but you never told me where you went. I don't know why you didn't. You told me—"

"Clara is dead, or as good as. My name is Jane Doe. You aren't my family. I don't know you." The words were harsh, and in the back of her own mind she cringed at them. The shock of once again being challenged on her lack of memory, right when she was getting comfortable in her life again, hurt deeper than it should. More from a past she didn't remember, another heart to break with the truth.

Mike pulled her into another warm hug. "Clarabelle. 'A stubborn mind conduces as little to wisdom or even knowledge as a stubborn temper to happiness'."

"Robert Southey." Jane's eyes widened.

"Yes?"

"I'm not Clara."

"Maybe you don't remember, but she's still here if you could name Southey. Nick will be annoyed to know even with amnesia you can still remember obscure quotes."

"Please don't."

Michael released her and set his hands on her shoulders. "You may not remember, but I'm your little brother. I'm the one you proclaimed you loved the most because you could beat me up."

A laugh bubbled up despite her churning thoughts and stomach. "I don't remember. Anything. Nothing but words. Thousands of words that aren't my own and my brief but full life as Jane Doe."

"Is there something wrong with getting to know who you once were?"

"It hasn't helped. It only hurts those that expect me to be Clara. Every time he sees me, David is in pain. Now there's you."

"I don't expect you to be in love with me. You can't hurt me, Clara. Unless you beat me up and shut me out of your life again, that is. I want to help."

"I don't know if you can." Jane peeled his hands from her shoulders.

"I think I can. Let me get something from my room." His lips pressed to her forehead before he disappeared.

Silence lingered in place of the usual bustle of activity, a silence loud enough to set her ears ringing. Jane shook against the urge to run.

"Stop staring, you fools. Get back to your beer." Cole pulled Jane to the door. His grip was firm and warm around her waist. "I'll send him over. Keep you away from this lot. There you can have some privacy."

"Thank you," she whispered. The touch of his lips to hers sent warmth through her cold limbs. She gave his hand a squeeze and slipped from the porch of the saloon. Once in her room, she left the door open against her fearful instinct to lock it. She paced the length of the room until he showed up.

"I always carry these with me." Michael must have been right behind her. In his hands he held a stack of envelopes. "Your letters. From the time you left Buffalo for Heber City until the last letter you sent before you disappeared."

"What could be in those letters that David didn't already know?"

"Clara, you told me everything. I know why you left David. I know why you ran."

Heber City, 1865

"She barely talks to me anymore."

David looked miserable and ten years older than when they'd met just five months before. Guilt twisted Mike's heart and he pulled his eyes away before he spilled the truth.

Clara's letters had been clear, insisting on blood ties being stronger. He had to convince her to tell the truth, to end the suffering she and her husband were going through without each other's support. His heart fell, seeing the unfinished room addition.

Michael forced a smile. "She's just stubborn. She'll come around. Let's head in. I can't talk to her from out here."

David's heavy sigh of agreement followed the sag of his shoulders. "I just wanna know what I done. How to fix it."

"I know you do." Michael frowned. The house was dreary. The spark of life that had been there months ago gone. There had to be something he didn't know, something that would make her give up like this.

David slipped out of his saddle and tied up his horse, waiting for Michael to join him before pushing open the door. The pain on David's face deepened at the sight of Clara. The effort to sound cheerful cracked in his voice. "Guess who's here, Clara."

"I'm not in the mood for games." Clara kept her back to the door.

"Probably a good thing. You always were a sore loser," Michael said quietly.

"Michael." Spinning, she rushed forward and threw her arms around his neck. "What are you doing here?"

Michael kissed the top of her head. "I missed you."

Clara buried her face in his chest. "No, you didn't."

"I told him he could stay here." David leaned on a chair, unable to stop his relieved smile. "Didn't figure you wanted him staying at the boarding house."

Her face grew hard and she tensed again. "You didn't have to tell him. He knows he is always welcome in my home, David."

"Clarabelle." Michael shook his head the smallest bit and squeezed her arms. "Why don't you tell me about your students this term?"

"I'm not teaching." Clara headed back to the dinner preparations.

David sighed. "I'm going to take the horses to the barn and do the chores while you two catch up."

"Do what you want," she snapped.

David's head drooped. "I'll be back shortly."

Michael frowned. "You're being too hard on him. You can't keep blaming him."

"I can." She kept her back to him, slicing the carrot with unnecessary intensity. "I have to. If it wasn't for him, I wouldn't be…"

"The man is in love with you. He has no idea what happened."

She set down the knife when her hands started shaking. "You don't know everything, Michael."

"You told me about the Indian that attacked you in your letters. David didn't know. He can't know if you don't tell him." When she turned around and stared out the window toward the stables, he sighed. "You love him."

"He left. He let this happen. I told him I wasn't comfortable so close to the reservation. He said I had nothing to fear."

"Clara."

"He could have taken the time to teach me to shoot the damn gun. Maybe I could have stopped it. Stopped this...this...oh, Michael."

Michael wrapped his arms around her when she sobbed. "You have to tell him."

"Michael there's...there's more. So much more."

He pulled back. "What?"

"I've been sick for weeks."

"Sick? What kind of sick? Is it serious? Have you seen the doctor?"

"Not that kind of sick." She looked up at him. "Sick. Food turns my stomach. I throw up almost everything I eat. I can't teach because I'm so tired. I sleep half the day. I...I haven't had...I mean I..."

He studied her when she turned a deep shade of rose. After a few minutes, it all started to sink in. "Clarabelle. A baby?"

"It's disgusting."

"It could be David's."

"No. It started after...after the storm."

He wrapped his arm around her gently. "What if it is?"

"I hate it." Venom dripped through every word. "I didn't want to do this to him."

"Clara."

"I have to leave. I have to make this...this thing go away."

"Listen to me. You aren't thinking straight." Michael sighed. "Tell me this. What if you're wrong? What if the baby is born and looks just like David?"

"I just want to forget, Michael. Forget any of this ever happened."

"Forget that you love him?"

"He did this to me."

"No. He didn't."

"If it's not his he would hate it as much as I do."

"It isn't in him to hate you or a child."

She pushed away, walking over to the window and staring out. "I just want to forget. Forget it all. Let him move on."

"You have to tell him."

"I've kept him from the lifestyle he's used to long enough. He'll return to it eventually. It will never be the same here."

Michael wrapped his arms around her. "I don't agree with this at all."

"I'm not sure I do either. But right now I would do anything to forget. It's been six months, Michael. Six months are easy enough to forget. Not worth remembering."

"You sure about that?"

Dominion Falls, 1872

Jane's stomach turned. The horrors of reality were so much greater than her worst imaginings. The person she'd been had been weak, insufferable. How could she have been so stupid? So cruel? "She was pregnant?"

"Yes. You were."

"There is a child. Is there? Where is it?" She was struck with an undeniable need, longing to find this child. Despite all her protestations of disliking children, this one had to be found. If not for her, then for David. Whether it was David's or not, he deserved the truth.

"I don't know. After I left you sent one more letter, and then you were gone."

She flew to her feet and rushed onto the balcony, gulping in the dry air as if she'd stopped breathing for a year. Her mind spun over the details, the horrible, painful details. A child. What had she done? "Was it a half-breed?"

"I don't know." The catch in his voice, the deep sorrow that echoed in every syllable made her turn back to face him.

"She was a horrible person. How could she leave? How *dare* she?"

"She wasn't horrible. She was wounded and scared. She was coming to see me. She promised she would. That's what her letter said, that she wanted my help."

Jane moved back inside and sat at the table. She stared at the stack of letters he'd left there. Bile rose fast up her throat and she covered her mouth. "An Indian. No wonder I fear and loathe them so much."

He placed a glass of whiskey before her. Placing his hand over hers, he studied her in silence. Once she'd had a few minutes, he took a deep breath. "You adored David. I was at your wedding. I've never seen you as happy as you were that day."

"Disgustingly happy. I saw the picture."

"You didn't want to hurt David. You were confused. Don't hate yourself for a poor decision made in the depths of grief."

"I don't hate myself. I hate her." Jane's hand shook when she took the whiskey and drank it down slow. The thought that Clara might have kept a child from David made her even more upset than the knowledge of the attack. "She said she wanted to forget."

"She didn't mean it."

"Do you think I did this to myself?"

"I doubt anyone can force themselves to forget." His hand cradled hers. "I kept your secret because it wasn't mine to tell. When you disappeared, I didn't know what to do. I kept hoping you'd show up or send me a letter."

"She wasn't who you thought she was. Who knows what she did all those years."

"I know you. I knew you. You weren't ever able to lie to me. Not even in your letters. Even now I don't think you could."

"So what? She stopped writing so she wouldn't have to lie to you? Is that supposed to be better?" What had she done? The nightmare, was it a memory? "You don't know what she did. It might be more horrible than you could imagine."

"You're not a horrible person, Clarabelle."

"You don't know. She didn't tell you anything. She didn't trust your supposedly honest relationship enough to tell you what she was doing."

"Fair enough." Reaching out to brush a tear from her cheek, he frowned. "I refuse to believe she did anything horrible. We'll find out what happened. I'll wire Tommy, he's number four."

"No! No one else. I can't deal with more family, more of this wonderful past I abandoned." She clenched his hand. "She was horrible to leave and I have no answers, none. Let them keep thinking I'm dead. It's far less painful than this."

"It's more painful not knowing." His voice cracked and he set his free hand on their clasped ones to stop any objection. "I'll give you time to adjust. I'm not going anywhere until we get this figured out."

"What if we don't? What if we never find out?"

"We will. You don't know our family, but we're a stubborn lot. We'll figure this out somehow. I promise."

"Will you leave the letters?"

"Yes. I want you to see Clara, not just this moment of horror and weakness."

"Thank you."

He kissed her temple. "You may not remember being Clara, but you're still my sister. I'm not giving up on you, you shouldn't give up either."

"I'll keep it in mind."

"Can I ask you something about Jane?"

"Sure."

"Cole?"

Nodding, she smiled. "I'm sure it won't last. I'm not even sure it could be labeled a relationship, but yes. Is that a problem?"

"Not at all. Is he all you've got?"

"I was seeing Major Webb for a while. We're still close."

"Before David I'd never heard you say 'marriage'. You had quite a few suitors and dalliances. I'm not surprised. But you're right. Cole doesn't seem the type."

"He's not. But I'm determined to enjoy him while I can. Anything else?"

"*Notre Dame de Paris,* part four, chapter One, paragraph on the *little monster.*"

"'It was a very angular and lively little mass, imprisoned in its linen slack, stamped with the cipher of Messire

Guillaume Chartier, then bishop of Paris, with a head projecting. The head was deformed enough; one beheld…'"

A bright smile lit his features. "Have you read that since you lost your memory?"

"No."

"Then part of Clara is still in you. Will you trust me to help?"

"Do I have a choice?"

"Not really, no."

*What is the source of sadness but feebleness
of the mind?
What giveth it power but the want of reason?
Rouse theyself to combat,
and she quitteth the field before thou strikest.
—Akhenaten*

The silence was deafening.

The saloon buzzed with activity. Customers laughing, shouting, gambling, and whoring filled the room. Behind the bar, silence reigned. For hours Graham and Cole had not said one word to each other.

The blood had long dried on Cole's lip, but he hadn't bothered to clean it. He wouldn't show weakness like that to the bear of a man beside him. His spirits were somewhat lifted by the bruises that had formed on Graham's throat and eye, though.

"Who's the cowboy keeping a room this time?" Wills took a drink of his beer, too drunk to care any longer about the tension behind the bar. Most everyone in the saloon had hours before drank enough to not be so bothered by the odd event of a fight between Cole and Graham. "This one actually taking company?"

Cole glanced to the floor above, to the room Michael had returned to a few hours ago. When he'd come back his features, disturbingly similar to Jane's, had been drawn and pale. He'd said nothing, only returned to his room in silence.

"Turns out Janey's got a brother." Graham sneered. "First a husband, now a brother. Guess she isn't such a lost soul after all. Seems to me for all she says different, that girl don't like getting found."

Cole slammed his heel down on Graham's foot. As the man hopped around cursing, he smirked. "Yeah? Well, it seems to me you don't like that much either, Graham."

Red as a beet, Graham took a swing. Cole blocked the blow, but Graham didn't stop. He swung again. "Least my prick ain't buried too deep to see I'm getting played. You're blind—"

Cole managed to connect his fist with Graham's jaw. A jolt of pain shot up his arm from the impact, but he didn't shake it off, prepared for a return fight. The silence that filled the bar after the punch landed kept them separated. Cole opened and closed his fist against the lingering tingle of pain.

Graham rubbed his jaw. "Blind bastard."

Cole only snorted. Graham had no idea what was going on. None of them fools did. He glared around the silent saloon. "What the hell are you all looking at? Get back to your booze and your whores."

He knew why the customers were shocked. Before that night he and Graham had never once shared cross words, and now they'd done it twice, both times coming to blows. Sure, they'd taunted and goaded each other, but never had an all-out brawl. When the silence lingered, he shoved a beer glass to the floor. The shatter of glass shocked half the customers into motion, or at least had them staring at their drinks instead of him.

Cole stalked from behind the bar. Shoving off Daisy's grasping hand, he snarled, "Get the hell away."

He stormed up the stairs and around the balcony to his room and slammed the door behind him. The silence of his room echoed loud enough to stop him there. With his hands braced against the door, he waited until a dull murmur through the door let him know life had again returned to the saloon before he stepped away.

The picture that had spent fifteen years in a box stared back at him. The woman and child frozen in time while he'd run far from the man he'd been with them around. Jane had framed the picture and hung it in his room.

What are you so afraid of? Her words echoed in his head, *that you'll remember you once had a heart?*

That's exactly what he'd wanted forget. He wanted the past to stay dead, and with it his heart. But that damned woman brought it back to life. His gaze fell to the window where the light from her door glared back at him, a soft shadow of light on his curtains. He crossed to the curtains and shoved them wide open.

She walked past her door and his heart skipped a beat. Damn it, what was he doing? Could Graham be right? Had he let himself get played?

Once again she appeared in the doorway. She'd stopped in front of the door, bent over a stack of papers in her hand before her hands dropped, the papers fluttered to the floor around her. Her shoulders shook and she lifted her hands to her face to swipe at her cheeks severely. Once again her body trembled as her hands clenched, and her mouth opened wide in a scream he couldn't hear as she grabbed something off the table and threw it.

His heart twisted. Jane could fool everyone else; hide the truth from them. He saw through the face she put forward. In private moments only did she lose control, moments when she thought she was alone, where no one could see. Or with him. She allowed him alone to see the fear and pain she hid from the world.

He shut his curtains as she crumpled to the floor. His gaze fell again on the picture above his bed and then to his desk. There sat another picture. The one of his parents had also been framed, set in the back corner where the burnt half hid in shadow.

Above the desk on a shelf sat an old bullet mold and two toy metal soldiers. On another shelf sat a hand-carved mustang with an explicit painting right next to it. When had she done all of that? How had she found those things?

He hadn't seen the mustang in ages, same with the bullet mold. She had to have nosed around in his room to have found them. Last he remembered they were in a trunk hidden way under his bed along with a handful of other remnants of the past he'd so willingly left behind. He must have left her alone far too much.

Somehow she'd known what meant the most and his preference to keep things private. Everything she'd put on display was hidden from public view. No one standing at the door would ever see one item on his shelf, only him. She wanted him to live again.

Then he saw it.

A book.

It had to be hers, because he couldn't read. Obviously he did leave her alone far too much. She'd taken the chance to add herself to the room.

All it took was a book.

Damn her.

His mind drifted back to the image of her crumpling to the floor. A lump formed in his throat, wondering just what her brother had left her to deal with alone.

Graham be damned, Cole couldn't leave her alone like that. Not this time. He turned down the lamp and strode from his room. Without even acknowledging Graham's challenging shout, he tore from the saloon.

Already at a running start, he crossed the street and climbed her balcony faster than he ever had. She still sat there on the floor, gathering up the papers she'd dropped one by one. Each paper fluttered on its way back to the pile. Her whole body quaked.

He knelt beside her. "Jane."

"Letters. She wrote Michael. All the time. Told him everything. Everything. She was such a fool. A horrible person. She blamed David. Blamed *him*. She was so. *Stupid.*"

The last shriek drew him closer and he set his hands on her shoulders. He was grateful when her trembling eased. "How long have you been doing this?"

"When did Michael leave?"

"Three hours ago. It's one in the morning."

"Oh."

"Ya need sleep." He rubbed her arms and tried to get her to stand, but she wouldn't budge. It wouldn't do her any good to keep on this way. It would drive them both crazy. "Jane. Come on. You can look again in the morning."

"My dearest Michael," she said as she resumed gathering papers. Her voice cracked.

He squeezed her shoulder and sank to the floor behind her. With a gentle tug he pulled her back against him, and she sagged into him. Her exhaustion showed in the dark patches under her eyes. Like her brother, her features were pale as a ghost. He sighed. "You don't gotta do this now."

"It took a moment. It took a lifetime. Nothing will ever be the same. How can it after these horrors? After this hell? It was supposed to be so different now, so different with him here." She didn't even look at the stack of letters, but he knew she was reading one she'd memorized as she memorized everything she read. "I've always loved storms, you remember. Watching their approach, the majestic streaks of power across the sky."

When she pulled away, he didn't move a muscle. He couldn't. The secrets revealed by what she'd read had upset her so much; did he really want to hear them? Her graceful movements carried her across the room like a ghost. Haunted and haunting.

"Now not even those will be the same. Why didn't I make David stay home? The supplies could have waited. He would not work on the Sabbath anyway. They could have waited. Why didn't I make him wait?"

One paper fluttered to the floor, weaving through the air before settling at her feet. She stepped on it, passing by Cole like he didn't exist.

"I trusted him, his words. He assured me I would be safe. He promised that though we lived so near the reservation we would never see one of those damn redskins. He lied, like all men do. He lied to me. I did see one. I did. The day the storm hit and the river rose."

The rest of the papers splashed across the floor.

"I think I startled him as much as he startled me at first. But then his dark eyes turned hungry. A hunger I've seen so often in a man's eyes."

Cole rose to his feet when she walked past him again. Her unseeing eyes didn't flicker from their stare, but she shirked from his touch. His stomach twisted at her withdrawal from him. She'd never done that before.

"I couldn't react. I'd never seen one up close. I tried to believe David was right, that I'd be safe, but the moment the Indian moved toward me, I knew I wasn't."

She gulped for air, leaning her hand into the wall. "The basket of berries was all I had so I threw it at him. I was yards from our house, that's all. I should have been able to make it, I'm fast enough and he was stunned. I tripped. The same damn rock that always tripped me. David said he would move it, get it out of the path, but there was always something else to do first."

The crack of his teeth grinding together startled him out of his tight-fisted anger. He didn't have to guess where this was going, he could tell. He wanted to tell her to stop. He didn't want to hear it. How could he not? She'd been forced to read it; he needed to hear it. No, he needed to let her tell it.

"He smelled of leather and tobacco—it was overwhelming. I struggled. I fought. Like Tommy taught me, but it did nothing. He was so strong. I thought if I stopped, it would be over quickly. I knew what he wanted; I only wanted it over. If I acquiesced he could take what he wanted and I could get home."

Unable to stop himself, Cole turned away. He poured a glass of whiskey from her near-empty bottle and downed it. His stomach turned, threatening to erupt.

"He made me get to my feet. In broken English he told me his name, Lightning. It was almost poetic, for as he said it the first bolt of lightning streaked across the sky. The storm we'd expected all day was starting as he forced me back to our home, my home."

She walked back toward him, her steps slow and deliberate. No longer shaking, her voice grew darker. "When we got inside, he pointed to the food. I had to make him dinner, listening to the deluge of rain when it hit. While he ate I was forced to sit in the chair by the fire. If I thought to move, the huge knife by his hand held me still."

He sat down hard in a chair and his jaw worked in silent fury.

"He ate with the voraciousness of a starved man. Shoveling food in without utensils, and when he was done, he turned to me. With the same insatiable hunger he'd used to attack his food, he took his turn with me. I prayed with my whole heart David would return and end it. That he had crossed the river before the rain started. I kept thinking it would be minutes before he walked in. I kept hoping."

The shriek of a chair scraping across the floor made him jump. She sat with her back toward him. Her head dropped to her chest.

"But he didn't. And it rained as I have never seen it rain. The river rose fast, and within an hour I heard it roaring just outside our door. The minutes I'd hoped for David's return became hours. When the Indian was sated, he sat by the fire. He started smoking and my mind drifted to the gun David kept at home. It was within my reach. I could end it right then. But teaching me to a shoot was another thing he never got around to. I should have tried, but I was too afraid I'd miss, and then what would he do to me?"

Cole remained silent. She sat still as stone. After an eternity he rose and walked around in front of her. Her head remained tucked in her chest and his heart fell. The knowledge of what had happened killed her. He hated that. He couldn't let it defeat her.

"Clara was trapped in that house for two days with the Indian. He took his liberties and her food. Once the storm ended and she caved to exhaustion, he left. She scrubbed herself for hours, cleaned the house from top to bottom. By the time David made it back across the river, there was no evidence it had happened. The lies began then. The secrets, the deceit. Rather than share her pain with him, she closed herself off."

He crouched in front of her. When he set his hand on hers, she yanked it back. His throat closed, but he shook his head and grasped her hand more firmly. "You ain't her."

"No. But what she did. To David. Oh, Cole…that isn't all."

"What d'you mean?"

"Michael told me that when she left, she was pregnant. There is a child out there somewhere, one that could very well be David's."

His mouth opened and closed. Words were not his strong suit, but they were totally failing him now. What could he say? If Clara knew, then things were going to get real ugly real fast.

Tears formed in her eyes, and pain twisted her features. Right then he'd give anything to be as good with words as her. She bit her lips and turned her head away, pink seeping into her cheeks. "She was a horrible creature. I am disgusted to think she's a part of me. I don't blame you for feeling the same."

"That ain't it."

"Go home, Cole." Jane rose and walked around him toward the bed. "You don't have to stay. I understand. I disgust myself right now."

"Ya don't disgust me. You never could."

She laughed, a cold bitter laugh. The dress she wore dropped to the floor. "Sure."

He spun her to face him. "You don't remember?"

"Not a thing. Not a damn thing." She lifted her chin, a bit of the fire returning to her eyes. "At least now I know why I learned to handle a gun."

"Wonder who taught you."

"I wonder a lot of things."

"You ain't gonna remember nothing if you're exhausted."

She leaned forward to rest her head on his chest. "I may never remember."

"Might be best."

"Cole."

"What? It's clear ya hate what you did then. Maybe you're a better person."

She snorted. "Right."

Before she could argue with him more, he slipped his hand along her waist and undid her petticoats. He scooped her up, ignoring her protest as he set her down on the bed and pulled the blankets up around her.

Her eyes closed almost immediately and a deep sigh rattled through her. "Go home."

"Not a chance." As she snuggled deeper under the covers, he kicked off his boots and removed his hat and vest. Sliding into the bed, he pulled her back against him. He waited until her breathing evened out before he closed his eyes against his racing thoughts.

Truth lives on in the midst of deception.
—Friedreich von Schiller

Warm.

Beyond the heat of the August morning. A profound warmth within her soul. The comfort of a strong heartbeat against her back. His soft, even breath brushing against her ear.

Safe.

Wrapped in strong arms. The cocoon of his body curved against hers. The sanctuary she'd come to crave.

Loved.

Her eyes flew open at the thought, slumber rushing away like a wild mustang. She couldn't feel it; she couldn't even think it. Without any explanation of his family, she knew he'd closed himself off to it. If she allowed the feeling, it would never be returned. She would be left bereft and alone.

Yet he had comforted her. With no other motive behind his actions. He'd simply held her in his arms. It had soothed her soul, calmed her into sleep. A shiver ran down her spine. How had she let herself do this?

By all appearances, they were only about the physical side. Of course, based on appearances, she also enjoyed the attention of the soldiers. Those were the rumors and she did nothing to dispel them, not even for Cole. Whether they were true or not didn't matter. Not even to herself. She hadn't been able to let them, for that would mean she had given her heart to a man who would likely never return the emotion, for he'd locked his heart away years ago.

When she shifted to roll over, his hold moved to accommodate her without ever letting go. She studied his relaxed features, the line of this brow, his strong chin, the curve of his lips. His arms tightened and she curved against him willingly, nestling into his chest.

No, Cole Mitchell didn't let himself love. Neither did she. She wasn't even a real person and she wouldn't be until she found the answers. The truth of the seven missing years Clara had left behind. Until she was free, love couldn't even be a thought.

But could she stop her own heart?

Not willing to dig deeper into that line of thought, she snuggled closer into his chest. When she pulled back a bit to search his features again, she found him looking right back at her. Her heart fluttered then stalled at the concern in his eyes.

With a shaky breath, she managed to smile. "Disgusted yet?"

"That ain't funny."

"Sorry." She sighed at the soft brush of his lips to her brow. Running her hand up his chest, she let her fingers weave into his hair before meeting his waiting kiss.

One tender brush of his lips and she melted. Her resolve to guard her heart dissipated like a fog in the bright light of day. A shudder ran through her as she fought against tears. It was too much, to close to loving. She had to pull back. She couldn't give into the feelings.

The gentle urging of his tongue opened her mouth and she returned the tenderness. She curved into him as she searched his mouth without a hint of their usual urgency or need. Her heart pounded in her ears and a tear escaped her control. Gasping, she pulled back.

Extricating herself from the safety of his arms, she slipped out of the bed and crossed the room. The further she got, the better. She'd been emotionally compromised by the previous night's revelations, that was what made her so susceptible to emotion. Logically, she truly did know better. She had to. "I…I have to get to work."

The rustle of sheets and the creaking of the ropes suspending the mattress told her he'd left the bed. His voice fell flat, empty of life. "Right. You gotta work."

"Cole."

"Wear the red dress. You don't gotta button up all the time." Every word drew him closer and closer to the playful tone that was so familiar. As always, the tenderness would fade back into the façade they'd established for the town, and themselves.

She closed her eyes against the realization, and to keep herself from witnessing the tenderness of the previous night and just a few minutes ago fade into the Cole everyone else saw. She forced a laugh. "You would think so. I might consider it."

Footsteps drew toward her, but she floated to the armoire. She still needed to collect herself before she let him touch her again, before she let him see the new and unfamiliar ache rising in her chest. The armoire overflowed with dresses, an expense she'd found herself unable to avoid as she enjoyed having more variety in clothes than propriety dictated.

The red dress he'd mentioned stood out from the others, a beacon in the sea of blues, greens, and yellows she favored. With a shaky hand, she grabbed it and tossed it on the bed.

A splash of liquid reached her ears and she thought he'd poured himself some whiskey. When she looked up she saw him at the basin, setting up her sponge next to it for her usual morning sponge bath. Heat flooded her cheeks when he looked at her.

A moment later he turned away and did as she'd suspected a few moments before. The last of the whiskey poured into his glass and he downed it. He picked up the empty bottle. "I'll get you another bottle today."

"Thank you. I'm afraid I needed a few good swigs to get through those letters last night." She walked to the basin, but when she reached for the sponge, his hand closed over hers. The pounding of her heart made her lightheaded and she leaned back against him.

He drew the sponge across her skin, igniting a flame behind it. Both soothing and stimulating, the cool water slipped along her heated flesh. His fingers trailed behind, smoothing along her arms, and then her chest.

As he drew the sponge along her neck, his lips brushed the exposed, damp skin. A soft sigh slipped from her lips and she gripped the edge of the dresser. With one more kiss to her neck, he was gone from behind her. She whimpered at the loss until there was a touch to her leg.

Without a word, he ran the sponge along her calf to her foot and back up to her knee. The rough sponge lit up every nerve. The smooth touch of his fingers followed behind, warming the flesh after the cooling water.

His free arm wrapped around her waist as he moved above her knees, washing every inch. Lingering at the sensitive skin of her inner thighs, he drew closer to her aching center.

The moment the sponge drew close, her knees buckled and a low moan escaped at his thorough cleansing. After a moment the sponge fell away and she collapsed into his arms. The fire he'd ignited refused to be ignored and she knew she'd need another cleaning by the time she was done.

It never proved necessary. He pulled back. "You gotta get to work."

Disappointment drew a deep groan from within. In a moment of immaturity, she stuck out her lower lip. "You don't play fair."

"I know."

Still pouting, she rose to her feet and walked across the room. Grabbing the dress from the bed, she exchanged it for another before slipping into her petticoats. She smiled when he eyed the dress. "It's new."

"Don't you got enough clothes?"

"Not especially. As of this evening, I should have a home to keep them in so I'm not concerned about overflowing my space."

"Jackson finally caving?"

"Michael's going to go purchase it. Jackson doesn't know he's my brother yet. It should go smooth. I'll be moved in by tomorrow."

His arms circled her waist and pulled her close. "Really?"

"You won't be able to just cross the street and hop up on a balcony. It will take real effort to come see me. So I imagine I'll be seeing you less."

He grumbled when she pushed him back to get dressed. "We'll see."

"I guess we will." She didn't want to admit she'd bought it just for his pleasure. The low cut of the bodice didn't suit her taste, but she knew he'd enjoy the view.

When she turned around, she wasn't disappointed and she grinned when his jaw dropped. She bit her lip when his finger brushed along the swell of her breast. A rumble in his chest preceded his gravelly exclamation. "Damn. You don't play fair."

"I know."

Laughing, she pushed him back until she could walk past him. After putting on her perfume, she walked to the door with a wink in his direction.

"We have to help them. There is nothing else I can do. They're Lewis's blood."

Jane stopped short at Martha's voice. Cole hovered just behind her. He tried to push her out of the open door, but she held firm, listening to the voices downstairs.

"I already have the wagon half full. Using half of what we got for the victims." Mabel's voice was tense. "The rest you can take to the Indians. But we shouldn't risk—"

"I have to. I'll make another run to the mines this morning. It's been a week since I checked on them. It won't be suspicious."

Jane could hear the tears in Martha's voice, but it didn't stop the violent stampede of anger in her soul. Breathing heavy, she could hear the ugly curse that slipped from Cole's lips.

"Martha, I just don't think that's a good idea. You've done it once. We should stick to food and blankets. Essentials."

"I have no choice."

Jane closed the door quick and leaned against it.

"Move." Cole's dark voice rumbled with anger.

"No." She turned, gasping at the twist of fury in his features. Unlike yesterday, this time it only scared her. "Didn't you hear? She said she has no—"

"It don't excuse nothing."

"I know. But if you go down there now, you'll never get the truth. The truth is what matters."

He turned his glare on her. "You aren't defending her?"

"No. But you can't go in hot as you are. Talk about shooting first and asking questions later. We'll talk to Al. He'll know what to do."

"What needs to be done is finding the damn savages. She knows where they are."

"And Major Webb will get the answers. He'll get the Indians." She set her hands on his chest. "Let me talk to Al first. Please? That's what the Army is here for."

"Fat lot of good they done so far. They got thirty prisoners, only three actual warriors. They're worthless."

"Please."

His eyes were dark, but he finally nodded. "One day. Then I'm handling this my way. We've sat on our hands long enough, letting the Army do nothing."

"Thank you." She flinched when he just stormed away and disappeared out her balcony. Clearing her throat, she took a ragged breath. Now she had more to do. The elections would have to be moved up. They needed a sheriff soon. If it took all of her energy, she'd make sure that Martha and Mabel paid for their part in this mess.

She smoothed her hands over her face to try to gain a semblance of calm. She started downstairs, stopping short when she saw Martha and Mabel.

One look at Martha's face and Jane's stomach revolted. Martha wasn't able to cover her own guilt or the despair that plagued her. There was more to this story, much more. Mabel wrapped a protective arm around Martha and led her away and Jane knew she wouldn't be getting any answers.

*The heart that can no longer love passionately,
must with fury hate.
—Jean Baptiste Racine*

Jane understood Guy was carrying on a conversation beside her, in which she was supposed to be an active participant. However, she was still off-kilter from the morning with Cole, and the night before with Clara's brother.

She'd seen neither hide nor tail of Cole since he'd left her room, but that wasn't entirely unusual. The sense of foreboding she'd had since his tension-filled departure wasn't helping her own mood any.

"Norman told me the sheriff's badge arrived yesterday."

Jane nodded in vague acknowledgement of Guy. They'd taken up a position on the porch of Turner's where they could observe more of the town. This gave Jane a prime view of the scene behind the church. Mabel climbed into a wagon; one Jane was certain had supplies for Indians. "That's nice."

"I do look forward to putting it on."

She focused on Guy for the first time in ten minutes. "Aren't you being presumptuous? The elections are not for another week."

"I'm running unopposed." Guy puffed out his chest as if the badge already resided there. The mere fact he hadn't fired her was the only reason she didn't attempt to punch his pompous grin right off his face again.

"Just because you are running publicly unopposed does not mean there hasn't been grumblings of another person winning." She suspected the only reason she'd kept her on staff was as a speechwriter, and he had one coming soon.

"Cole?"

Exhaustion pulled her shoulders down and a sigh dripped from her mouth. "No, Guy. You are becoming as annoying as Jackson with such an accusation. I thought you were aware by now my feelings on that matter. I have done no maneuvering behind your back."

"Then who?"

"David."

Though Guy paused to contemplate for a minute, he waved off her suggestion with his hand. "I'm not worried about the likes of him. He's a drifter. He wouldn't accept the position if it did happen. I have no concerns there. The position is as good as mine."

"He is a good man."

"And an Indian lover. They say he's even become *brothers* with another one up in Indian Territory, if you can believe that."

She couldn't believe it, or maybe she could. David didn't know what had happened to Clara and had no reason to hate the Indians. Her nerves ramped up at the knowledge she'd have to tell David soon. She'd promised to tell him soon as she learned anything, but honestly she was still in such a state of shock, she wasn't sure she could say it out loud again.

"No one will vote for him." Guy's sharp bark of laughter pulled her away from her nervous fidgeting. "He'd only let this whole problem get worse. I'm certain my speech will seal the deal and that badge will be in place in no time."

"'The smaller the mind, the greater the conceit'." She smirked. "Aesop."

Guy frowned, his eyes drifting out across the town. Shaking off whatever thoughts had distracted him, he cleared his throat. "Speaking of my speech."

"It's all written. Please remember to not over-rehearse. Your speech should be natural and flow easy." Just as she'd suspected, this was reason for his distraction. The speech had been bothering him for weeks.

"Speaking in front of a crowd is not a problem I have."

"I've noticed."

He studied her for a moment. "You're more short-tempered than usual."

"I have a lot on my mind." Talk about an understatement. At the moment her mind was a whirlwind of thoughts, fears, and hopes. She could hardly keep herself straight. She sighed and turned to face him. "It has been a long few days. I apologize for my distraction."

"I prefer the distraction to your temper."

A smile tugged her lips despite her sour mood. "I do not believe you can have one without the other. Often my temper accompanies me wherever I go."

"No clever bits of wisdom about such tempers?"

"'The happiness and misery of men depend no less on temper than on fortune'."

Guy's brow furrowed. "Emerson?"

"No." She laughed.

"Clara," a voice called from the street.

Jane heard the name, but it didn't register. Instead, she continued to grin over Guy's consternation. "That one is not so simple. It's François de la Rochefoucauld. He was a French author…"

"Clara." Michael's voice sank in this time. "Jane."

After a blink of surprise, she turned toward the street. Without logical reason her smile eased, as did some of her tension. Though she did not truly remember him, somehow she'd felt at ease around him after her initial panic.

Among the many things they'd discussed the night before, she'd filled him in on what had happened since arriving in Dominion Falls. The shorthand version, at least. There were some things she hadn't been able to reveal, including her nightmares, her worst fears, and the true depth of how lost she'd let herself get in Cole.

One thing she had told him about was Jackson, and her recent struggle to get the house she desired. The grin Michael wore hinted toward hope they'd succeeded in a double cross of their own. "Michael. Are you done?"

Michael jogged up the steps, matching her smile. "All done. He hadn't heard word yet so there was no trouble. In fact he was rather gleeful. I'd love to see the look on his face when you tell him. What a horrid little gnome he is."

"Michael." Jane couldn't help but laugh. Somehow Michael had expressed the exact same thought she'd had a few times herself but never voiced. Perhaps there was more to this sibling tie than she gave credit to. "Michael, let me introduce you to Guy Forrester. He owns the Silver Saddle Casino and Hotel."

"Running for sheriff, right?" Michael extended his hand. "Good to meet you. I'm Michael Young. Clara's brother."

Guy's eyes widened and he looked back at Jane. "Is that so?"

"Michael, I told you, it's Jane." Exasperation edged her smile into a dark frown.

"Sorry. It will take getting used to." Michael didn't look half as sorry as he might have meant to.

She shook her head at him, but turned her attention back to Guy. She knew it would take time, but it still made her uneasy to be called Clara. "Michael helped me acquire that home I was admiring. He told Jackson he wanted it, without letting him know why."

Michael chuckled. "He was so pleased at the idea he'd be selling it right under her nose he didn't once bother to ask why a stranger would come into town and ask for the house. It was all I could do not to laugh in his face."

"But you reserved that joy for me. You're far too kind, Michael."

A laugh spilled out of Guy. "So Jackson is the 'horrid little gnome' you spoke of? What a wicked trick. I love it."

Jane giggled along with him. "I quite agree. If you'll excuse me, Guy, I do believe Michael and I will pay a visit to Mr. Krenshaw. I'll see you later this afternoon."

Michael held out his arm and winked at Jane. Starting down the steps, he waited until they were halfway across the street and out of earshot to speak. "How are you doing, Cla— excuse me, Jane?"

"As I have been since the day I woke up. Overwhelmed, confused, but I will not stop living. I must say I hate your sister. I apologize; I know you loved her a great deal. However, she upsets and disgusts me."

"The letters didn't help you remember at all?"

Sadness dripped into every word, weighing her feet down until she felt she could hardly walk. "No, Michael. Not a whisper of a memory. I can tell you I feel comfortable with you. Somehow it's like you are supposed to be here. I just don't remember you."

"I'll take that." Michael nudged her. "So there is Cole, clearly. Major Webb as well. Rumors carry things much further, but are you seeing both of them?"

"Where is this going?"

"Are you going to choose?"

She kept her eyes diverted, focused on a cart they passed with more attention than the collection of pelts required. Her heart had already chosen, and it chose wrong. She had to dig deep, but she managed to draw a cheerfulness that didn't reach her heart and offered him a bright smile. Based on what she'd heard from him, David, the letters she'd read, and her current rumored status as a loose woman, she offered the most logical response, "Do I have to?"

He laughed and shook his head. "Some things never change."

"Good to know." Her lips tightened, the smile gone faster than expected when her response was accepted so easy.

"What about—" Michael's question was cut off by a loud scream.

Cold fear ripped through Jane at the first familiar savage cries. She dug her nails into his arm, her eyes widening. In the horrifyingly recognizable pattern her limbs shut down when the first Indian rounded the corner. "No."

"Get back." Michael grabbed her around the waist and threw her into the alley. He drew his gun before racing out into the street.

"Michael!" Gasping, she stumbled forward. A stream of horses, bright paint, and red skin flew past the opening between the boarding house and cooper shop. Her attempts to chase after her brother stopped short in her instinctual horror.

It was an instant and a lifetime as each one passed, her nails digging into the wood wall. The concussion of an explosion hit her ears and she screamed, dropping to the ground. Shaking like a leaf, she crawled forward to try to find where it came from.

Another explosion made her drop her head to the ground. Hands over her ears, the third explosion sounded much further away. Dust wafted from the dirt she'd landed in and she choked against her scratchy throat.

When the cries of the Indians faded, she pulled her hands from her ears. She licked her lips against the choking dryness of her mouth and pushed herself to her feet. A high-pitched whine in her ears led her to tug at them. Dust scratched her eyes with every blink.

She shuffled toward the end of the alley, rubbing her eyes to clear the last of her vision. What she saw soon as she opened them made her shriek, clutching her bosom in pure fear. The front of the saloon stood ripped wide open. Smoke, dust and debris filled the air. An instant later life returned in a painful rush and she ran toward the building. *"Cole."*

She had to scramble over a pile of rubble to get in, slipping and sliding her way to the bar. She collapsed to her knees beside Cole's prone body. "Cole?"

A low groan came from the body before her. He stirred, letting loose a long string of curses that would make his most vulgar patrons blush.

Jane smiled. "Cole. You're all right."

"Define 'all right'."

She cupped his filthy cheek as he rolled over. "You're alive."

"Hurt too bad to be dead."

The beast of a man nearby still hadn't moved. Much as Graham didn't like her, she still had some concern over his well being as Cole's friend. "I need to check on Graham."

When she leaned down to brush her lips across his, he grabbed her arm. He grinned and held on so she couldn't move away. "Prove to me I'm alive."

"Later." She smirked. "Too much going on for that right now."

He groaned again when she clamored over him.

Jane turned her attention to the burly man. "Graham?" His back was to her and he hadn't moved a lick. She grunted when she tugged on his shoulder, her attempt to move him meeting with resistance.

Cole chuckled behind her. "Trouble?"

"Hush." When Graham rolled, she couldn't stop her gasp. "He's bleeding quite a bit. I need a towel."

He shoved one in her hand. "I'm gonna check and see who we lost."

She pressed the towel hard against the gash in Graham's head. Maybe the pain would make him stir to life. "Come on, Graham. You're far too thick in the head to be seriously hurt by a small cut like this."

It was several painful minutes before he showed any sign of movement. Then he grunted and his hand flew to where she pressed the towel against his head. His eyes opened and he curled his lip. "Well, well. Look who lowered herself to help."

"Shut up or I'll let you bleed to death. You're going to need stitches."

"Why are you bothering?"

"Because you're Cole's friend."

He took over towel duty and quirked a brow. "But you don't like me."

"No. *You* don't like me. You think I'm a liar and I'm out to hurt your friend."

"Are you?"

She wiped her hands on her skirt and met his eyes earnestly. "No. On both counts."

"If you hurt him, I'll prove you're the lying jezebel I know you are."

"Who says he'll be the one hurt?" She stepped over him, taking measure of the saloon in silence. The smoke had begun to clear, revealing layer upon layer of damage. The bubble of a sob rose in her chest, but she bit it back. "Oh God."

"Jane." Michael tore into the building, scrambling over the same boards she had. He gasped in relief, collapsing with his hands to his knees when he spotted her. "Thank God you're all right. You had me worried when you weren't where I left you."

"Sorry. Would you get a bucket of water and a towel, please? I saw a cut on Cole's arm and…" She sobbed before she could stop it this time, and Michael's arms were around her. She shook her head fiercely. She couldn't give in. Not here. Not yet. She pushed him back gently. "Go. Make yourself useful."

She spotted Cole sitting on the stoop and picked her way over the rubble to his side. After a moment she sank to the boards beside him. She set her hand gently on his arm, jumping with a gasp when he yanked it away.

"Don't. Don't ya dare tell me not to be angry."

"I wasn't going to, you stubborn, presumptuous man. You have every damn right to be angry as you want to be after this." She met his eyes, defiance flared at his assumption. "You have every right."

"Damn straight." His eyes lost their fire and focus. "I shouldn'ta listened to ya this morning. I shoulda done what I wanted."

"No matter what you would have done, it's likely this would have occurred either way. Martha did not leave until twenty minutes ago. The dynamite they used today they already had."

"She's gonna pay."

"Here you go." Michael dropped the bucket at her feet. "I've got some stitching skills. I'm going to help tend to the less wounded. If you need anything, let me know."

"Thank you." Jane slipped from the stoop to move in front of Cole. She nudged her way into the space between his knees before grabbing the towel.

He grasped her wrist tight and glared at her. "Don't."

Anger deafened her as much as the blast had. "Fine. Clean your own damn self."

When she started to move, his hands grasped her hips and pulled her back toward him. "Wait." He said nothing else, but held her hips firm so she couldn't move.

She picked up the towel again and tried to focus on his injuries. The towel ran along his mouth, cleaning the blood with the gentlest touch she could manage.

His eyes stayed focused on her face, even as she avoided meeting them. Tears threatened to burn her vision as with each cut she cleaned, her soul realized how close she'd come to losing him.

With a shaky breath she turned her attention to the long cut on his arm. He could have died. How could she have handled that? How could she have handled living her life without his infuriating, intense presence? Her throat closed at the idea.

Drops of blood continued to seep from the wound as she cleaned it. "You'll need stitches," she squeaked. Clearing her throat, she shook her head at her own shaking hands. She couldn't let him see the feelings running through her. The thought of losing him ripped her open and left her raw. She didn't realize she'd already begun crying until his thumb brushed a tear from her cheek.

Looking up with a gasp, she found his eyes waiting for hers. The desperation she found there mirrored her own and she didn't balk when his arms tightened around her. A soft whimper escaped and the towel tumbled to the ground. Could he feel the same?

Their lips met with a brutal force. Everything else fell away. He needed her and she needed him even more. Her arms went around him as she surrendered everything to him. For once she held nothing back, pouring everything into the kiss as her body sought his with a magnetic pull she didn't dare deny.

Not caring about the activity around them, she melted into him. She'd let him have her right there if it meant he was close. She craved him, longed for his touch, for the reassurance that he lived. Every demand her soul made she felt returned in kind.

"Jane." The voice of one of the soldiers shoved into her awareness.

She gasped, pulling back. Not now. Any time but now they could butt in and remind her and Cole of the false rumors. Any time but that moment before she'd had time to admit the truth. She was ready to tell him everything.

"Jane. Major Webb sent me to make sure you were all right."

Cole's eyes hardened to stone with every word of the soldier, a grimace creasing his handsome features at the mention of Al. Jane went lax in his grip, unable to react as he rose, simultaneously lifting her to set her on her own feet. She reached toward him, her heart shattering when he pulled back.

She wanted to scream at him to stay, but as her heart joined the destruction around her, she found she couldn't. Her own choices had led to this. Unable to turn from the wreckage, she watched him walk away and she knew.

He was already gone.

"Jane?"

"I'm fine." The calm her voice carried surprised her. It had to be shock. "Tell Major Webb I appreciate his kindness, but he has bigger things to deal with."

"I'll let him know."

Once the soldier left, Jane remained where she was. Gathering every last shred of strength, she turned her back on the saloon and Cole. The horrors around her couldn't reach her through her own inner pain.

She'd been a fool. She'd given into her feelings and drove him away. She wouldn't make that mistake again.

After all…he was just a man.

The dew of the morning
Sunk chill on my brow
It felt like the warning
Of what I feel now.
—Lord Byron

Jane searched through her stacks of books and journals for the third time. The title she'd been searching for wasn't there. She dropped down to her knees to look under the bed. No sign of it there, either. She'd already checked her closet and the trunk she'd been packing. It was her favorite book. "Damn. Where is it?"

"Where's what?" The suddenness of Michael's entrance to her one-sided conversation made her jump so high she hit her head on the bed.

"Ouch!" Jane rubbed her head and flew to her feet. "Michael. Don't you knock? You scared me half to death and I've been there enough, thank you very much."

Michael kissed her on the forehead, not the least bit ruffled by her snappish greeting. "Good morning to you too, darling sister. Are you almost done packing?"

"I'm getting there." She rearranged the piles of books on her table. "I don't have many things when you look at it honestly. Just a few books, some necessities, and my clothes.

I'll need to get to Turner's and buy some dishes and other essentials."

"Already taken care of, Clarabelle." He grinned under her glare. Over the course of the past day they'd come close to companionship, and he'd resorted to teasing her when he could. "Oh, don't get all defensive on me. If I'm going to be living there as well, I wanted to be sure we had enough to get us by for a few weeks at least."

"Thank you." Though she'd wanted to do it alone, she now believed Michael couldn't have arrived at a better time. Last thing she wanted now was to do it alone; all things considered she wanted the support, even if she couldn't reveal all of why. "After this last attack on the town, I feel much better knowing I won't be there alone."

"So what can't you find?"

"Oh. My Whitman book. I know I had a cope of *Leaves of*…oh, darn it."

"What?"

Tears rushed forward before she could stop them. She turned her back and busied herself restacking books rather than reveal her pain. "I remember where I left it. I'm going to need to order a new one."

"Clara?" This time he jumped under her sharp glare. He raised his hands in defense, moving closer as his brow knit in concern. "Sorry. It's going to take some getting used to, you know that. Now Jane, what's wrong?"

She snatched the stack of her journals from the table and carried them to the trunk. With far more care than required, she laid them along the bottom of the trunk in neat rows by date. For the first time in weeks, she'd spent the night alone. The last bit of hope she'd held forced her to leave the door open, but he hadn't climbed the balcony to join her. "I left it at the saloon."

Her voice cracked despite her effort and she cursed inwardly when he knelt beside her. His hand rested on her shoulder. "Then, go get it."

"No. I don't think I will, thank you."

"What happened? You never told me. All you said is that it was over."

"As I knew would happen eventually. I knew he would never want it to go beyond what it was. It was all about a good time, the chase, and the scandal. The chase is over, the gossip is fading, and I've got far too much baggage now to be a good time." Words she'd repeated over and over in her mind while she attempted some semblance of sleep.

"But it's not a big deal, right? He's just a man."

She wanted to agree with him, but as she opened her mouth to form the words, no sound came. Her shoulders sagged and she closed her eyes. More than anything she hoped he was wrong and she could lie to him. She drew her lips into a bright smile and nodded. "Of course. There's plenty more around."

"Oh, Jane." Michael's smile faded. "You've actually fallen for him?"

"Don't be ridiculous." She shoved herself back to her feet. Her mind raced for a plausible excuse for her distress. Certainly there was plenty excuses to be had, it wasn't like her life was a picnic. "He was just a very good time. Experience does count for something. Not to mention he was very, very, *very* attractive without his clothes."

'You can't lie to me."

"He's attractive and the absolute epitome of a man. I'll miss his…presence."

Michael remained silent. When she drew close again, he gripped her shoulders. He pulled her close and held her tight. "I didn't know you cared about him so deeply."

"Don't. I didn't. I don't. I *can't*." She shoved him off and punched his arm when he reached for her again. Before he could make another attempt she spun away, wiping at her tears. "Damn it. Damn you. Don't make me cry. I must go on without him, as I knew I would have to eventually. I'm not an imbecile; I know what sort of man he is. I will go on without him. I have to live, I must. I can't live in tears over every little pain."

"Why can't you, Jane? What's so wrong about caring for someone?"

"I just can't. Not you. Not David. Not Al. No one. Least of all him."

"Well, why in hell not?"

"I'm *not real*. I'm a construct of a few months of existence. I'm not a whole person. I'm missing my *whole life*. Nothing explains how I came here so broken."

"You are real." Michael turned her toward him. "You seem awful real to me, and to everyone that calls you friend which is quite a few that I can see. You're here. You're talking, walking, and you still hit damn hard."

"You and David see Clara. People don't believe that I don't remember, but I don't. I can't be Clara and you can't accept me without comparing me to her. That isn't a person, Michael. It's not a *life*. It's an illusion until we find all the pieces to put me back together."

"'Life is like an earthen pot: only when it is shattered does it manifest its emptiness'."

"Seneca." Jane gave into his attempt at comfort and rested her cheek against his shoulder. "That's what I am. Empty. So very empty now."

"You weren't when Cole was around, were you?"

"Shut up."

He rubbed her arms. "All you can do is live now. In the absence of what you were, become who you are. You will never be Clara again, even if your memory should return. So be Jane. Find out who she is. It seems you have a good idea of who you are already."

"None of it matters."

"Of course it does."

"No." She pushed away and walked toward the open balcony door. Letting out a long breath, she leaned on the doorframe. A soft breeze brushed across her face, but it wasn't enough to erase the heat of her tears. "I'm not free."

Michael drew close enough for her to sense him, but blessedly said little.

"Seven years are missing from my life. I may never remember, but with you and David, I have a good idea of what Clara was like. Until seven years ago, at least. I have to know what happened. To me. To the child. How could I ever be free if I don't know? How could I ever trust who I am?"

"We'll find out, I promise. But you yourself said you aren't Clara. You aren't the person you were before your memories were taken. You can find those missing pieces, but they won't change who you are now."

She turned back toward him. At his smile she could only shake her head and hold out her arms. "Is this person any good? Clara wasn't. Whoever she became when she left David; it left her beaten, bloody, and close to death. How pious would I be to think that I could be any better than her?"

"It's not piety. You've learned from the past. Even a past you can't remember can teach you something, and you've learned well. No one is who they were yesterday. You've just taken it to extremes."

"Comforting."

"I've got to be good at something." He laughed when she scoffed and stormed across the room. While she grabbed yet another stack of books, he moved closer. "Are you going to talk to Cole? Perhaps tell him what you're feeling so he has all the information?"

"I will not force myself on a man that no longer has any desire for me. He made his choice and I do not begrudge him for it. I knew from the start what I was getting into. I knew true affection would be too much to ask of him."

"How do you know he's not doing the same thing you are?"

She dumped the books into the trunk, forgoing her usual care to spin on him with a dark glare. "And just what is that?"

"You're pushing him away—no, that's not quite right—you're letting him push you away, because you are scared to death."

"All I'm doing is moving on. Living each day the best I can. I've had plenty of pain in my few short months. This is just another one. It will pass."

"'It is foolish to pretend one is fully recovered from a disappointed passion. Such wounds always leave a scar'." His smile held no joy. "I know you know that one."

"Longfellow. David mentioned that was the name of my horse."

"It was. The horse you had in New York was Sophocles."

"You're joking."

"No. Tommy about wrung your neck for it. Said it was a stupid name for a horse."

"He was right." She sighed. "It was a stupid name. However, Sophocles did have some wonderful words of wisdom as well."

"'One word frees us of all the weight and pain of life: love'."

"Michael. Don't."

"'He who throws away a friend is as bad as he who throws away life'."

"I didn't throw him away." She grabbed a dress from the armoire. Rather than meet his challenging gaze, she folded it. "He walked away."

"And you're letting him." He straightened when shouts rang through the streets and into the room. A rumbling of many voices started low, increasing until the buzz filled the air. He walked toward the balcony slow. For several minutes he was silent. When he spoke again, his voice was hushed with something, perhaps shock. "Jane. Come here."

Cole's voice rose above the yells of the crowd. "Are ya tired of the Army not doin' its job?"

"I'm not interested, Michael." Jane folded her dress with fierce motions, violently shoving creases into the fabric. Her hands shook as her nerves frayed from the sound of Cole's anger. A loud cheer rose from outside and rather than seek out the cause as her curiosity would normally lead her to do, she turned to grab another dress.

"Really. Come here." Michael waved. "You might not want to miss this."

She threw down the skirt in her hand and stormed outside. "I'm not the slightest bit interested in what he's doing."

"Liar."

Cole stood on a hitching post in front of the hole in his saloon, towering above the crowd. His shouts rallied the mass of people into a loud roar. "It's time we take back our town. We've been sitting on our hands hoping the Army would do their jobs. And they haven't! Aren't you ready to ready to take back our town?"

The crowd roared. Jane groaned. "Oh no. I can't watch."

Michael, unlike her, seemed rapt in the show. "What's he doing? Do you know?"

"Something inspired only by temper and no temperance of thought."

"So starting now, this town finally has its sheriff." When she turned, Cole held up the gleaming star to another cheer and pinned it on his vest. "I'm gonna make sure that the right people pay."

"You can't just take the position of sheriff." David's calm voice ran under the crowd's cheers until they quieted. "It's an elected position."

"I don't see no one opposed. No one important. Am I right?" The continued rallying cries only served to fuel Cole's grin. "I don't know about all of you, but I'm tired of the Army sitting around waiting for the raids. Then not doin' nothing but taking in old men and women. They ain't getting the warriors that are killing our people."

Jane cringed at the deafening response.

"It's because of the innocent prisoners that the Indians started attacking the town." David stepped closer to Cole. "Until then they stuck to the railroad itself. If we let those people go—"

"And my first order of business is gonna be taking care of the people supplying those Indians with food and weapons, including the dynamite that blew up three businesses yesterday." Another deafening cheer echoed through the street and the hair on the back of her neck rose when Cole cast a dark glare toward her.

Her stomach turned so fierce she had to step away from the railing. She slipped into the room to get some distance between her and the growing chaos. It took every effort to ignore the rest of the speech and the rallying cries that followed every declaration. Tears stung her eyes, but she kept folding.

"Well, he's right about one thing."

"I'm sure he's right about a few things. He still shouldn't be sheriff."

Michael squeezed her arm. "I know. But he said every man should be armed."

"I certainly wouldn't mind being armed myself. You can't be around the house all the time. I'd like a level of protection."

"But you can't shoot to save your life."

"Apparently that is something I learned in my seven missing years. I'm quite accurate and capable of handling even Cole's Walker Colt."

His eyebrows rose. "Impressive. Then we should get you one."

"I already have one in mind. I'm all packed. Can we leave this room please? I'm ready to move on from this place for once and for all. We can retrieve my trunk later."

Michael led her downstairs and outside into the thinning crowd in front of the boarding house. After maneuvering through the crowd, they made it to the vendor cart where she'd seen the gun she'd admired.

Once again Zeb tried to sell her on the Derringer, but she wouldn't bite. When she insisted on the Remington she'd been admiring, a fair amount of negotiation was involved. With the Remington finally in her possession, as well as a store of ammunition, she handed off her purchases to Michael. "I'm going to grab a bite at Turner's."

"Um." Michael cleared his throat. "Uh, Jane."

"What?" At his furrowed brow and subtle tip of his head, she glanced over her shoulder. Cole strode toward them with a self-satisfied grin. Though her stomach churned, she straightened her shoulders and tried to force herself to calm.

"Walk away," Michael muttered in her ear. "This will only bring more pain."

"I can't. Not yet."

"He isn't going to listen to reason. You know it."

"He'll come to his senses with time. He always does." She glanced over at him, hoping he'd even fake agreeing with her. She needed this, either way it went. When Cole had walked away without a word, so much had been left open. A grand finale was in order, though it might kill her. "Now that he feels in control, maybe he'll come around."

Michael squeezed her shoulder. "I hope you're right."

"I hope so too."

"So what do ya think?" Cole smirked, his head held high. "Most of the town was behind me."

"Mobs generally do tend to agree. As for my opinion, I think it's asinine." Jane didn't hold back. She hadn't outright lied to him yet; she wasn't about to start now. "And of course they were behind you. They're as mad as you are. They want this to stop every bit as much as you do."

He studied her. "You think they're wrong?"

"Don't put words in my mouth. I'm not against you, Cole. If you want me gone, tell me. Simple as that. Don't try to make me walk away by making me angry. Just tell me you want me gone and I am."

And they will never know
The anguish of my drooping heart
The bitter aching woe.
-Anne Brontë

"What are you reading?" Michael plopped into the seat across from her.

Jane slammed the book so fast she caught her own finger. Rather than shout at Mike for startling her or for being so nosy, she stuck her finger in her mouth.

"What?" His laughter betrayed the mock innocence he tried to pull off with his wide eyes. He closed his hand over the two books she had and drew them across the table. The laughter softened into concern as he looked at the titles. "You always did have a soft spot for poetry. Read every book Ma had, and then borrowed everywhere you could. You said it spoke to every sense, every emotion."

"I enjoy exploring the depths of the words. Even remembering the words as I seem to, there is something special about seeing them on the page."

"Lord Byron. The Brontë sisters. Oh, Brontë." A sly grin spread across his features. He flipped the pages, but didn't look at them at first. "Hmm, I wonder. Let me see if I can guess what you've been reading."

"Please let it be."

The turning of pages slowed significantly. One, two more and he was at the page she'd been on. "Here we are. 'If, hot from war, I seek thy love, darest thou turn aside? Darest thou then my fire reprove, by scorn and maddening pride? No—my will shall not yet control thy will, so high and free. And love shall tame—'"

She slammed the book shut. "Stop."

"'And love shall tame that haughty soul. Yes, tenderest love for me'." He chuckled. "You aren't the only one on this earth that can memorize passages, you're just better and quicker at it than most of us."

Jane's cheeks grew hot under his knowing grin. She tossed the book at him and shoved her chair back to stand. "Take it back to the library."

"What? That was your favorite poem for years on end. You used to recite it over and over. Of course I know it." He rose along with her. When she tried to walk away, he followed close behind. "Jane."

"Michael, I am in a terrible mood." She didn't even close her door on the way out toward town. Perhaps she could get a good head start if she left him to lock the door. Of course, her luck hadn't been that good for some time.

Michael jogged to catch up with her. "You've said that every morning for the past week. You aren't sleeping well and you've got a headache."

Try hard as she might, she hadn't told him of the nightmares. Only Cole knew and she certainly couldn't talk to him now. She'd like to share it with Mike so she could get some relief by sharing, but every time she tried, she froze.

"Don't make this more than it is. Not sleeping well is enough reason for a headache."

"Of course. Perhaps you are just used to having company before you sleep."

No, more like she was used to not sleeping when she had company. That she'd slept in preparation for his arrival. That she'd been tired enough to sleep without dreams thanks to his regular presence. Thanks to her rapid pace, running from the probing question and far too smart brother chasing her, they were almost in town. "I'm fine."

A group of soldiers rode past, all tipping their hats and calling a greeting to her. Michael stood by as Jane smiled brightly and greeted them all by name as they passed. No matter how torn up she was inside, it simply wouldn't do to act any different than she always had. Let them believe she was fine, maybe in time she would be convinced as well.

Mike frowned as the last soldier passed. "So am I to guess you'll be busy for lunch again?"

"My morning will be spent calming down Guy as he's all but lost his bid for sheriff, thanks to Cole. Then I will be having lunch with Major Webb. After that I'm going to join Rusty and get some work done to be sure everything is ready for the true elections tomorrow."

"What about David?"

"He's been too busy campaigning and trying to keep Martha out of jail. Cole would have her there already if he had his way and I have a feeling he's going to make certain it happens before the voting somehow."

"I still can't believe David decided to run. He isn't much for politics, although he'll be a good sheriff. I guess I can't blame him for making the decision to run. Between Guy and Cole, the town needed one honest running man."

"Cole is plenty honest. To a fault. His problem is he's ruled by his temper and right now he's out for vengeance, not justice."

Michael stopped when she did "I thought you'd be right there with him. You told me you heard that conversation too."

"There's more to it." Jane shook her head and looked over toward the saloon. "I can't explain it. I just know there is. This isn't something Martha wanted to do. I just can't shake the feeling we're missing something important."

"What about David convincing Major Webb to release the Indians he has in custody to the northern Indian territory?"

"I don't like it. However, I see David's point. Out of the thirty Indians he has in custody, only three of them are actual warriors."

"But?"

"I think they should go to a reservation instead of set free." She shrugged. "Maybe it makes me a horrible person."

A scream cut through the rest of her thoughts. Her heart froze at the immediate thought of Indians. It wasn't like the Renegade screams, though.

The commotion came from the other end of town. Curiosity pulled them down the street with the crowd. They managed to push their way through the worst of it as a wagon barreled around the corner. Cole stood in front, tugging on the reins of the racing wagon to draw it to a stop.

Graham sat beside him, a gleeful smile stretching his round cheeks to their limits. Behind them both in the wagon sat Daisy. Her cheeks were bright red, her lip caught tight between her teeth. Even once the wagon stopped, she was visibly trembling.

None of it bode well for whatever was about to occur. No matter what it was, Jane didn't think there was any way to stop Cole now. He'd been steamed for days, and he was on a full-blown roll now after his success snatching the sheriff's badge.

"What has he done?" Jane crossed her arms, gripping her biceps to stave off her own rising tremble. Several people pushed from behind, and she stumbled forward, right into Cole's line of sight. She ducked her head rather than hold his wicked sneer.

"Let's get out of here," Michael suggested. "Just walk away, Jane. Please. This time listen to me. Walk away and be done with him."

"No. I have to see what he's done. If he's going to drive the nail in his own coffin, I have to be witness to it. Maybe it will help me move on."

"Don't think it works like that."

Jane ignored him, pushing her way back through the crowd toward the other side of the street, closer to the bed of the wagon. Maybe, if nothing else, she could get closer to Daisy and hear a levelheaded answer. When she emerged back at the front of the crowd she found herself right next to a sobbing Martha.

"Cole Mitchell. It's sacrilege to do what you've done." Mabel Greene walked forward. "How dare you desecrate someone's grave!"

"Someone is right." Cole glared at Mabel. "It just ain't the someone we think it is, is it Mabel? Does your husband appreciate having prayed over a lie?"

"Cole." Reverend Greene stepped out of the crowd next to his wife. "Put Starbird back. This isn't the way to handle things. All you're doing is riling people up."

Jane could hardly breathe or move. Cole's rugged face, usually such a source of enjoyment for her, was distorted. Even the faint blurring from the tears she held back couldn't hide the dark lines creasing his forehead. The smile was cold, so different from the playful one she'd become accustomed to seeing there. This was the Cole people warned her about, and yet she felt it wasn't him. It was anger and pain driving him, as it had for so many years.

Her stomach twisted, threatening to revolt. In the back of the wagon she spotted a coffin. He hadn't just desecrated a grave; he'd flat out robbed the grave. She shook her head with a soft whisper, "Don't. Please, Cole. Don't do this."

"What is the proper way, Rev? To continue to let that woman *lie* to us all? To pretend to grieve for a man, lead us all to his supposed grave, to continue to help *his* people and hurt her own?" Cole shook his head. "She's been supplyin' them renegades with the dynamite. With food and supplies purchased with *your* money. Money ya gave to the church to feed *our* people that lost everything to them damn renegades."

"He trying to incite a riot?" Michael's soft mutter reached her ear. "I see what you mean by all temper and no temperance of thought."

"We all saw the body." David edged his way out of the crowd. "Lewis is dead."

"Really?" Cole's dark laughter drifted through the crowd, being joined by some, and silencing others. "Is it *really* your old buddy you buried, Davie? Tell us the truth. You're so good at honesty."

"We all saw the body," David repeated. Jane noticed he didn't answer the question, and knew in an instant Cole was right. That didn't make any of this the right way to handle things, but he was right.

Cole smirked and turned to Graham. "Let's show them the truth."

Jane's knees buckled when the two men lifted the coffin. Shouts and screams behind her echoed her own horror at the scene. "Oh God."

The coffin toppled to the ground and in that instant Jane realized the only one that did not scream was Martha. She remembered how disturbed she'd been when Martha had failed to cry at her own husband's funeral, Jane gasped. "Heavens. Michael. Get Martha out of here. If we leave her to this crowd, they'll rip her to shreds."

Martha blanched. "What? Why?"

Jane grabbed her hand. "I don't know what the hell happened, or why you lied and stole and helped them. I know you should go to jail and probably will, but you should do so with dignity toward whatever purpose you did this for. *Not* by the power of a lynch mob. The church is a sanctuary. Go. Hurry."

Michael grabbed Martha, holding her close against him as they made a beeline for the church. Luckily the crowd was too distracted to notice.

"Daisy." Cole's voice drew her back to the horrific scene, and smell, of the body dumped on the ground. Her own nightmares couldn't even surface as Cole commanded the crowd's attention. Cruel, unyielding power. "Tell them. Tell them all what ya told me. Who is this mess of Indian down here?"

"I don't know." Daisy was trembling, still low in the wagon, her voice weak.

"Is it Starbird?"

Daisy didn't focus on the crowd. She focused on Jane. Her released lip trembled. "No. I've known it wasn't since the body was taken to Graham's."

Doubtful shouts rang through the crowd. Jane rushed forward and grabbed Daisy's hand. "Are you absolutely certain?"

"Yes," Daisy whispered. Jane was apt to believe her. Daisy glanced toward Cole, then back to Jane. "I tried to tell him, but wouldn't listen to me. Until this week, he wouldn't. He was always…"

"Preoccupied." With her. Regret coursed through Jane's veins. If she hadn't been so absorbed in Cole maybe she'd have seen the signs. "He told me he thought you were trying to get out of buying your own contract. It doesn't matter now."

Tears slipped down Daisy's cheeks. "What do I do?"

"Stand up tall. They won't listen to you if you act weak. I despise that he did it this way, but they need to know the truth." Jane climbed onto the wagon wheel.

"They ain't gonna listen no-how."

Jane frowned as Daisy continued to cower. "If you stand and be strong, they will. Talk like a doctor, not like a whore." She placed her fingers in her mouth and blew. The shrill whistle blasted through the crowd and silence fell.

Cole turned to glare at her. "Don't need your help."

"Good thing I'm not doing this for you, then." She climbed higher on the wagon wheel to get above the crowd. "Looking beyond the atrocious way this was handled, we need to look at the facts."

Over Cole's snarl, she heard a familiar shout. A voice of reason, thankfully. "What facts?"

"Good question, Archie. If this isn't Starbird, we need to know. We need to know if there is still a known fugitive among the renegades." A series of shouts rang out and she held up her hands to silence them. "Most of you have been turning to Daisy for medical care during these raids. You must trust her knowledge of medicine."

A lower rumble of discontent ran through the crowd. Reverend Greene spoke up when no one else did. "So?"

"So. We should trust her now. She must have a reason for saying this isn't Starbird. Shouldn't we find out why?" Out of the corner of her eye she saw David move closer. Time for him to face her and show his guilt or innocence. She directed her next question right at him. "Shouldn't we find out the truth?"

David nodded, taking over Jane's current command of the situation to ask Daisy, "What makes you say it isn't him?"

Daisy squeezed Jane's hand tight. She rose and cleared her throat as she faced the crowd. "I've performed two surgeries on Starbird in the past few years. One was for appendicitis and the other was from a bullet Kelly put in him during a hunting accident. Both surgeries left scars, here and here."

When Daisy released Jane's hand to point to two places on her person, Jane lowered herself from the wheel.

Daisy pointed to the body on the ground. "This man has scars, but none match the scars on Starbird. This isn't him."

Several people moved forward to check the body. Jane waved over the Reverend. She spoke quietly in his ear and told him about Martha needing sanctuary, relieved when he ran off to the church to help Michael out.

Daisy leaped down from the wagon to show those checking the body what she meant. With the crowd settled, the mangled body and smell overtook the brief push of strength she'd had. Jane's stomach turned until she was sure she'd lose her breakfast.

Jane gripped the wagon and took several slow breaths. The wagon jostled and she froze, unable to bring herself to see who had caused the motion.

"I told you. I warned you. Now look what you went and did. Now I'm gonna make sure they all know you're lying. Just like we did with Martha. Just like we destroyed her so easy." Graham's voice stayed low. Meant just for her. "You're next."

When he dropped to the ground and stormed away, Jane managed to lift her eyes. Before she could stop herself, she found Cole's gaze on her, his brow drawn low.

The tears she'd fought off began to fall when he pointedly looked away. He didn't even bother with an angry gesture, nothing.

He wanted nothing to do with her and after the events of the day she wasn't sure she wanted anything more to do with him. What he'd done was brilliant, but cruel. Maybe she'd fooled herself to think there was more to him.

With nothing left to do, she finally listened to Michael's advice. With the crowd handled, and the whole town focused on this event, she did the only thing she could.

She walked away.

If I love you,
what business is it of yours?
—Johan Wolfgang von Goethe

"Is it over?" Martha hunched on the cot. She didn't moved a muscle, her fingers laced in a helpless prayer.

Jane stood outside the cell. "Yes. The elections have ended."

"And?"

"Archie has been made mayor." Though Jane knew that wasn't what Martha was asking about, she couldn't help expressing the one election she had been focused on. Her concern that Graham might just edge out Archie had been foremost on her mind since his threats.

Martha lifted a wide-eyed gaze. "Jane, please."

"David is sheriff. They're both being sworn into office right now. Cole lost by a narrow margin, but he won't be sheriff any longer."

"Thank heavens."

While Jane understood the relief Martha expressed, she was compelled to remind her of the truth of her situation. "You do realize that who the sheriff means little to your ultimate fate."

"I know. I spoke with Lloyd this morning."

Jane frowned. Lloyd Kane was the only lawyer in town, but she'd heard word Martha's mother planned to send a lawyer from Denver. "You spoke with Lloyd?"

"Yes. I have no desire for my mother's brand of help." Martha answered Jane's unspoken question with a frankness and calm reserve Jane hadn't seen before. Somehow once behind bars and facing her demons, the pious Martha had been shed. "Lloyd was kind enough to speak with me this morning. I expect Major Webb will collect me soon enough."

Jane wondered if Martha was once this way all the time. How many fears and how much embarrassment she would have had to bear to become the woman in front of Jane. A surge of compassion rushed forward. "You have no witnesses to the act itself and you need two in order to be convicted. Mabel saw you leaving with the dynamite, but not giving it to them. What Cole and I overheard is hearsay. Although I'm sure Lloyd said all off this to you already."

"He did, but I must ask. Why are you helping me? Why did you help me yesterday?"

"Why did you help them? Arm them against your own town?" Jane grabbed the bars, the only sign of her anger she'd allow. "You had to know they would use those weapons against the town as well as the railroad."

"I had to. My husband…" Her voice trailed off, a sob erupting as she buried her face in her hands.

"Shot me. Killed Kelly."

"He did not." Her anger shoved away the tears. She rose and crossed to where Jane stood at the bars. "It wasn't him. It couldn't have been."

"How could you possibly know?"

"Have you ever been in love, Jane?"

Her carefully placed mask crumbled. Jane had to turn away before her tears could appear. She shook her head, refusing to admit such weakness to Martha. "I wouldn't know. I've been told Clara was in love once, but she didn't behave like she was."

"What about Cole?"

"He was just a man whose company I thoroughly enjoyed. I'm certainly not in love with him. I can't love anyone right now. And what does that have to do with anything?"

"I love Lewis with all my heart. I would do anything for him, to protect him. I know he simply isn't capable of killing his best friend. More than that, I know he couldn't have shot you because they had him."

"What? Who had him?"

"The renegades." Tears slipped down Martha's cheeks. "They held him for betraying his own people. They were torturing him. If I hadn't done what they said, they would have killed him and I couldn't let him die."

"Why wouldn't they kill him anyway? Martha, it is not logical and in the end how many lives of your own people were lost? People you cared about like family. Arthur, Cora, so many lives throughout this town." Jane shook her head. "Your actions have hurt so many more than your husband."

"I wasn't thinking that far ahead. I just wanted my husband back. I wanted our child to have a father."

"Child?" Jane backed up in surprise. "Oh, Martha. No."

"Yes. One day maybe you'll see, Jane. One day you'll understand what you'll do to protect your own child and their father."

The words struck deeper than Martha could have ever hoped or possibly known. Once again Jane's soul ripped open. The unintentional reminder of what Clara had done to David brought on yet another headache. She was tired of the pain, but it never ended.

"You didn't answer my question."

"Why did I help you?" Jane turned to see Martha's nod. "I told you. You needed to be put in jail, not face a lynch mob. I believe in justice, not vengeance."

Without another word, Jane left the jail. Outside, she leaned on the hitching post as she tried to rein in her emotions. Within an instant she knew it would be no good. The wave of grief hit too fast.

She took off at a dead run, so fast she made it to her house within a few minutes. She slammed the door behind her and rushed into the pantry. In an effort to occupy herself and keep away the pain, she busied herself making tea.

Once the water was on the stove, and the tea bag waited in the cup, she had nothing else to distract her. She paced the length of the room before she sank down at the table and dropped her head to her arms. Everything hit her at once: the knowledge of the child she'd lost, the missing years of her life, and then there was Cole.

She'd known for some time she'd cared for him far more than she should. It hadn't been until that moment the week before had she realized how much.

The moment she'd learned just how much her heart could break.

"Don't put words in my mouth. I'm not against you, Cole. If you want me gone, tell me. Simple as that. Don't try

to make me walk away by making me angry. Just tell me you want me gone and I am."

"Do you think I should be sheriff?"

Jane didn't falter when he turned it back around on her. She had to be honest. Neither of them would stand for less. "No."

"Then—"

"Not because you're incapable of holding such a position," she yelled over his attempt to speak. "But rather because you are turning this into a personal vendetta. This position isn't about you or your anger. It's not a position that is supposed to be used for personal attacks. It is a job."

"Personal? Look at this town. Look at them scars on your back. Tell me it ain't personal."

"This town needs a sheriff. It needs to protect itself. But it does not need a man hell-bent on revenge doing it." She met his gaze, stubbornly clinging to anger to keep from falling apart. "Ask me again when you're done being angry. My answer might be different."

He laughed and looked down his nose at her. "Well, you do the same."

She bit the inside of her cheek, her grip on Michael's arm so tight her knuckles turned white. She swore her heart stopped beating when Cole didn't even flinch. If she'd once believed he might actually care for her, she didn't know how. The hope that he'd come to his senses; that once again he'd show her the side of him he hid from the rest of the world faded.

Digging down deep, she found a reserve of strength, bolstered when Michael squeezed her hand. Her voice emerged calmer than she thought possible when she finally spoke. "I see. I'll leave then."

"Good riddance to ya." He stormed away toward the saloon.

"Michael," She whispered softly, unable to force her body to move.

"Breathe," Michael muttered. "And walk. Walk away."

It wasn't supposed to hurt that much.

She'd never wanted to get in so deep.

The gaping wound in her soul that refused to heal proved what she'd try to deny to Michael. Cole had meant far more to her than a good time.

The whistle of the teapot cut through her thoughts. She could hardly believe what had become of her in the past few weeks. How could she have ever have believed herself strong? These days she was little more than a broken rag doll, lying in pieces on the floor.

She wiped at her tears and forced back her emotions. If she could manage to remain calm in public, she could maintain control over her emotions at home.

Cole was just a man. She would make do without him.

A loud knock on the door threatened to dissolve her forced calm. She contemplated ignoring the visitor, but the next knock came far more insistent.

She set aside the teakettle, crossing her small living room to the door. Cole's chest greeted her the moment she pulled the door open. The world spun as the full realization he was so close hit her.

Words failed as the emotions still bubbling under the surface threatened to spill over the dam she'd built around them. He stood so close she wanted nothing more than throw her arms around him.

She couldn't.

She had to be strong. He'd been cruel and unyielding, acting on his worst tempers and impulses. Worse, he'd hurt her. She wouldn't cave so easy simply because he was present.

"You gonna invite me in?" The words slurred together in a slight hint of drunkenness likely caused by the near-empty whiskey bottle in his hand.

She couldn't meet his gaze, but she frowned and shook her head. If it took getting drunk for him to manage to speak to her, she definitely wouldn't give in. The dam around her emotions grew stronger than before. "No. I'm not."

"Why in hell not?"

This conversation could not be had with his chest or his whiskey bottle. Though well aware of that fact, she had to brace herself for the inevitable. When she lifted her gaze, the smile she found on his face made it easier to remember her anger and pain. He was pleased with himself. She imagined he was sure he'd win this time. "You told me to leave and I did."

"Changed my mind." Cole pushed the door open further. His arm snaked her waist. He pulled her closer with a sharp tug.

"I haven't." Her voice wavered from its firm conviction with his arms around her again. How she'd longed for his comfort.

"Thought it was my choice." Chuckling, Cole closed the door and pushed her across the room. The whiskey bottle hit the table with a *thump* as they passed. With his hands free, he buried his fingers in her hair and pulled her into a deep kiss.

Her only defense for how quick she caved was that she was too stunned to fight. A soft whimper of protest was all she could managed before she succumbed to his advances. Every touch of his tongue to hers reminded her how much she'd missed him, how much she'd longed for him.

Just as she began to slide her hands up his chest and her body about fully gave in with a shudder, she was struck with the memory of why she missed him. Her eyes flew open. She pushed hard on his chest, gasping when he actually took a step back. "No. I meant what I said. I walked away when you told me to and I am not about to walk back."

"Trying to make me suffer again? Want another apology? I can't give you one if you don't let me finish."

"No. I don't want your drunken apologies."

"Aw, I ain't that drunk."

"You didn't want me around anymore, remember? You're a big tough man taking back the town. Too big and strong to let any feelings into your life. Too busy fighting the bad guys to face up to your own flaws."

"That ain't it."

She couldn't stop now. "Heaven forbid I say anything remotely personal. We can talk about my horrible past all day long, but if I dare mention anything related to you or your feelings, everything stops. You disappear and leave me alone. Again."

"You're the one that said this was…"

"Just because you lost the battle for sheriff, doesn't mean you can come to me for comfort now. Get your cold comfort in your whiskey or one of your two-bit whores."

"Don't think I can't."

"I *know* you can. That's why I said it, you imbecile. Now *go*."

"Jane." His tone warmed with amusement when he stepped forward. "I know you like fighting much as I do. More reason to make up. If you really wanted me gone, you wouldn'ta kissed me back."

"No. I…" When his lips closed over hers again, his tongue plunged into her mouth and erased any protest. Her body and mind battled as strong as her tongue battled his. Her feet moved of their own accord, backing them across the room.

His hands slipped along her sides and gripped her hips, holding her tight against him. Despite her best efforts to keep her head, she found herself getting lost in the feel of his body. When they hit the desk, she gasped, but he didn't release her lips.

A small moan escaped before she could stop it when he pressed her firm against the desk, but her hand left his hair. Gripping the side of the desk, she struggled to move her fingers along the wood. Her tongue still dancing with his, she managed to pull open the drawer.

As her fingers sought the prize she had in mind, he lifted her onto the desk. Her hand abandoned its task when he yanked her hips firm against his. Desire rose to fight off her anger, winning the battle. She would cave soon.

The pain of the past few weeks rushed up at the thought. With a sob, she pushed him away. "*No*."

"Come on, Jane." His lips found the sweet spot just under her ear.

Focusing on the rising anger at the gall he had to assume she would be so weak, that a few suggestive touches would sway her, she shoved him back with all her strength. At his chuckling, she reached into the drawer and grabbed what she'd been after. "I believe I said no."

Cole's laughter faded when she leveled the gun at him, his eyebrow quirking. "You ain't gonna shoot me."

She pulled back the hammer. "Don't be so certain. You told me to walk away when all I did was be honest with you. I did what you asked. If you've changed your mind, good for you. I haven't. Now I'm telling you to walk away."

"Jane."

"You messed up. You let your temper rule you and decided I wasn't worth your time. You hurt a lot of people and handled things in the worst way possible."

"I ain't here for a lecture. You said—"

"I don't want to hear it. You desecrated a grave just to embarrass and destroy Martha. She needed to be put in jail, not humiliated. You are a brute. You think you can get what you want just because you say so."

"You never minded before. Put that gun down and I'll remind you why."

Pride warmed her cold fear away when the gun didn't even quiver. "I'm not a whore. I don't tolerate being used. I won't be used just because you need your manhood propped up."

"Never said you—"

"Shut up." Her jaw clenched. "I liked you. More than I should have. Now you sicken me. Just get out. Get out of my house or I will shoot you. If you want comfort, find a whore. I won't be used by you again."

His tilted his chin up. "Fine. Goodbye, Jane."

She didn't say another word; keeping the gun raised for almost five minutes after he'd slammed the door. Unable to move, she could only stare at the door wondering at her own stupidity.

She'd sent him away.

She loved him.

Now for the first time she realized she did love him. She could never admit it to anyone, but she did. Yet she'd sent him away. How could she? Because he'd hurt her, she wanted to try to hurt him back?

But had she hurt him?

She doubted it. This pain was all hers.

Her hands started shaking and she released the hammer. Once the gun sat on the desk, she gave up holding it all in.

She crumbled to the floor with a sob, burying her face in her hands.

When a young man complains that a
young lady has no heart,
it's pretty certain that she has his.
—George Dennison Prentice

Cole's head pounded from the constant stream of hammering and sawing. With every board cut and nail banged in, his saloon got back in order, but he still had the sense of the gaping hole in the front of the building.

Or maybe it wasn't the building.

For the past two and a half weeks he'd been flat-out miserable. His mood sure didn't help business. He had a sneaking suspicion the lack of Jane's presence had hurt the mood and generosity of his clientele, too. She wasn't here all the time, but when she was, things always seemed livelier, and more profitable.

He shook his head against the resurgence of Jane into his thoughts. No matter how many times he pushed her away, she crawled her way back in. His dreams were the worst. He couldn't count how many times he'd woken convinced she was in the bed beside him, that he could feel her there, only to find an empty space.

It shouldn't have mattered; it never had before. Ever since he'd walked away from his entire life and ended up in

Dominion Falls with nothing but a few bucks and a big scar, walking away had been easy for him. He avoided attachments, especially with women. Last thing he needed was the pain he'd once felt in his life again.

So it didn't, wouldn't, couldn't matter that Jane hadn't returned to his room, to his bed.

The hammering stopped, silence echoed through the saloon with a suddenness that made Cole's ears ring. He pinched the bridge of his nose as his headache got worse instead of better in the silence.

Damn, he needed a drink.

And he needed Jane.

Fucking hell. No. He didn't need her.

"Cole?" Hammy's normally jovial voice was subdued. When Cole opened his eyes, the man sat in front of him, shaggy brows puckered. "We're done."

"Good." If it had been anyone besides Hammy, Cole would have snapped something about how long it had taken. He knew Hammy had put as many men as was possible on it, considering the amount of damage throughout town. "What's the damage?"

Hammy pushed a piece of paper across the table. "There's no rush, Cole. Ya know I don't care. Ya been real good to me."

Cole kept his hand flat over the invoice, unwilling to look at the numbers that would prompt Hammy to say such a thing. "I ain't gonna be in debt to ya again, Hammy. I'll get it handled."

"I know ya will. You've always been good for it." Hammy nodded and tapped the edge of the bar. "Least there ain't no hole no more. Gonna be a few more days for them windowpanes. Cora's got lots of people needin' them. Ran clean out. I'll get them in place when she gets them in."

"Thanks, Hammy. Here. It ain't my debt," Cole poured a fresh beer and pushed it across the bar, "but it's a thanks for workin' so fast. I know you got lots of work to do 'round town."

"Much obliged." Hammy raised the glass before taking a big, slurping sip.

Cole nodded his reply, slipping the invoice in his pocket to look at later. He wiped down the bar, eyeing the mostly quiet saloon. It was still early in the day, so he wasn't expecting a huge crowd, but he'd become accustomed to larger crowds than this on Wednesdays.

Wednesdays were Jane's day off. "Shit."

"What's that, Cole?" Hammy'd already finished his beer.

"Nothin'." Cole poured him another. "Just drink your beer."

Hammy grinned and began slurping the fresh glassful.

"What the hell is this?" Graham's voice echoed through the saloon. He stood in the doorway with a box in his hands. The small, flat box was tied with twine, nothing else to clue Cole into what it might be.

Cole forced a chuckle. No sense in giving Graham any more ammo than he had, and Cole had never missed a chance to pick on his partner in the past. "Hard telling with you standing there leavin' it closed."

"It's for you, idiot." Graham dropped it on the bar. "Was sitting outside on the bench."

"You see who left it, Hammy?" Cole pulled the box close, eyeing the old man when he suspiciously slowed his drink consumption. "Hammy?"

Hammy shrugged, not taking the glass from his lips. A blush darkened his ruddy cheeks, though. A blush Cole knew only one person to put there. Jane.

He cursed inwardly, but turned his attention to the box. If it was from Jane, he wasn't sure he wanted to open it. Since he couldn't read it anyway, he set the note tucked under the twine aside. He untied the box and opened it.

Inside was a brand new shirt. He pulled it from the box, his jaw tense. Before Graham picked up the note, Cole had a good idea what it said. What she meant with the 'gift'.

"Well, lookie here. Want me to read it?" Graham waved the note.

"No."

"It says 'Now I owe you nothing. Jane'." Graham chortled his way to a guffaw. "Good. Good riddance, right Cole?"

Cole shoved the box aside and snatched the note from Graham's hand. He stormed up the steps, away from the laughing bastard behind the bar. If he didn't go, he'd risk another outright brawl with the idiot.

"Thought you were done with her!"

Cole slammed the door on Graham's words, throwing the shirt in the corner of the room. An odd ache in the pit of his stomach made him growl against the pain. The pain that he knew wasn't a bad piece of meat, or even his stomach.

That crazy bitch could still get to him. He hated her for it. No one should be able to do this to him. Least of all a woman.

When she'd kicked him out the day before, he'd thought she was just mad. It wasn't like she wasn't good at ignoring him until he apologized proper. She'd come around eventually, she'd get over it and they could resume their scandalous activities.

He could have her again. Where she belonged.

Now he knew better.

He'd hurt her bad. To protect himself.

If he was so protected, how had she managed to hurt him?

Contemplation often makes life miserable.
—Chamfort

In the dead of night the saloon sat silent as a tomb. No customers gambling, drinking, or whoring to stir it to life. The whores were all asleep, and the doors were locked.

Cole sat alone at a table in the middle of the room. A lantern lit the tabletop and items on it, but didn't reach into the dark recesses of the silent building. He twirled his empty glass in circles on the table, not ready to completely drown in his booze just yet.

After two weeks of constant work, the front of the building sat whole again. While he was glad Hammy had taken the time and resources to make sure the saloon could run, the invoice in front of him was a stumbling block he didn't need.

Cole couldn't read the words, but he knew numbers real well.

The numbers were bad. Cole knew Hammy wouldn't scam him because he couldn't read. He also knew that Hammy had given the best prices he could, always did. Still, the bill was big enough to worry about.

Hammy'd offered to let it ride, but Cole didn't like a debt hanging over his head. Not for nothing.

Every Indian attack in recent months had left damage or created a cause to buy more medicine for Daisy to keep helping the injured. It left Cole's savings drained to almost nothing. What little he had would never cover the bill in front of him.

Not even Graham knew how low the saloons' reserves were. If he did, he wouldn't care anyhow. He had his own booming business burying bodies. The only time Graham cared about defending his interest in the bar was to boost his own sense of pride. Years ago they'd agreed that as long as Graham helped out behind the bar, Cole would handle everything else.

In recent months Graham's role in the bar had become a sore subject and prompted many arguments between them. Arguments they'd never had before. Cole wished he could buy out Graham and be done with it all, but right then he could barely pay the bills.

Cole sat back so the numbers weren't right before his face. He tilted his head left to right, trying to relieve the crick that had been there for at least a week with no signs of letting up. If he told the truth, he'd not been sleeping good at all, but if he admitted that, he'd have to admit why he wasn't sleeping so good.

Something had to change. His attempt to take the sheriff job hadn't panned out. A loss of only ten votes was still a loss. The loss could be blamed on his actions when he took the badge from Norman's office. What he'd done to get justice for the town and get Martha behind bars. In fact, he was certain that was the reason.

Too late now. He had no regrets. He'd been mad as hell.

Business was good, but not like it had been before the attacks.

And then there was Jane.

He ran his hands over the shirt he wore; the one Jane had sent him the day before. Tonight, wallowing in misery had seemed like the best time to wear it. Everything had gone wrong. Everything from the saloon, to the Sheriff's job. To Jane. It seemed only fitting to wear the evidence of all his wrongs. So he'd donned the shirt she'd sent to leave nothing unfinished between them.

The shirt was a good reminder that not even Jane thought he was right about any of it—except their split. She hadn't even tried to talk some sense into him like she once had, and that woman loved her words.

He didn't expect her to after all he'd done.

Yet some part of him wished she had.

Just went to prove he'd been right to walk away. He should have done it a long time ago. Long before she could have bought him a shirt that fit better than any other he owned.

Definitely before she'd made him start to feel again.

The whiskey bottle glimmered in the lamplight and he poured as full a glass as he could. The whiskey trembled at the lip as he raised it. He knew not even the whole bottle could erase the path his mind kept strolling down. He knew because he'd tried, several times.

Somehow he had to get back in Jane's graces. He wouldn't admit it to a soul, but he hated waking up in an empty bed. Hated seeing the book she'd left behind. He'd been sure that she'd left it because she was going to come back, but then she'd sent the shirt.

She wasn't coming back, and he wasn't gonna stand for that.

It wasn't emotion, couldn't be. No, he just knew no whore could compete with her.

Who the hell are ya trying to fool? What was supposed to be easy wasn't so easy anymore. Emotions had complicated things. He liked things simple.

Except Jane. He liked her difficult as she came, stubborn and infuriating. All of her words.

He gulped down the whiskey and slammed the glass on the table.

The numbers on Hammy's bill stared back at him.

He had no choice anymore.

The one thing he had worth enough money to cover the bill and leave him some to spare slept in the back rooms. It would also save him in supply costs, putting more money in his pocket.

Daisy.

He'd said he'd sell the contract to her, and he didn't like going back on his word. But she couldn't afford what Guy would pay to get her and her doctoring skills as a selling point for his place. Not even close, not even if he gave her a full year to save.

Before the damage to the building, it hadn't been a problem letting her pay over time and a lot less than her contract was worth.

Everything had changed with the explosion of his saloon, and life.

Everything.

All he'd wanted to do was make it right. Take back the town.

Instead, everything had gone wrong.

At least he still had the saloon.

Or he would after this.

With steeled resolve, he stood. Tonight he'd take care of business. Get back to where the money flowed again. With his bar in good standing he could deal with his other problem.

The one named Jane.

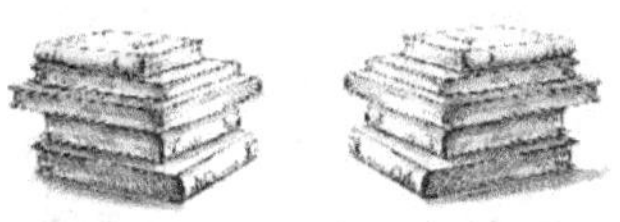

Trust instinct to the end, though you can render no reason.
—Ralph Waldo Emerson

"Jane! Jane."

Jane smiled at the youth approaching at a breakneck pace. "Arthur."

Arthur barely slowed, barreling into her and throwing his arms around her. Weeks ago it might have made her nervous, but she'd come to care for the young man. Probably because he was at the age where his intelligence outweighed any childish factors. He was breathless when he spoke. "Did you finish? Did you?"

She couldn't help but laugh. Once she'd extricated herself from the hug, she met his gaze. "I did, Arthur. I even have it here with me in my book."

As she withdrew the papers, he bounced on the balls of his feet. "What did you think? Was it good? Did you like it?"

"I loved it. Very insightful and well written. You've done a wonderful job, Arthur." She handed him the papers. "I'm of the opinion you should show this to Rusty. It would be a wonderful article to add to his paper, I'm certain he'd be thrilled to do so. You show stirrings of a great talent."

His eyes got huge, his skin paled. "Naw. You don't mean that, Jane. It's just a school paper about the train. It's not news."

"Of course it is. If it was not news, why would the whole town be speaking of it regularly? You have written a great article about an important event for our town."

"Do you really think Rusty would print it?"

"I really do. Rusty knows good writing when he sees it." She hugged him. "I have to get to work, but I'll see you at supper. I expect to hear what Rusty says."

"But I gotta work at the store today."

"You can drop it off on your way." Jane laughed. "Go on now. I'll see you at supper."

Arthur grinned and hugged her quick once more before darting down the street.

Still laughing, Jane shook her head and followed the lad at a slower pace.

"Looks like you're starting to like kids." A familiar voice spoke low and very close.

Jane spun to find David grinning at her. She set her hand on her hip, attempting to give him a stern expression. Unfortunately his continuing mirth made it difficult to keep her sharp anger in place. "Arthur isn't a child. We discussed this. He's a young man and a talented writer. I see nothing wrong with encouraging that."

"Of course."

She narrowed her eyes at his knowing smile. He'd been far too busy for much interaction in recent weeks. For him to start with comparisons to Clara turned her stomach. Especially since she still had much to inform him of, and could not do so in the few minutes she had before her shift. "David, don't. Please. Don't make it more than it is. If you're going to walk with me, I would appreciate a less loaded conversation."

He held out his arm with a gentle smile. "I think I can handle that. It's good to see you, Jane. I haven't seen you much in the past couple of weeks. Not since Mike arrived, anyhow."

"We have both been quite busy. You were campaigning and now you're trying to adjust to being sheriff. I've been…" What had she been? Avoiding town except to work so she'd see Cole as little as possible? So she'd see David as little as possible? So that somehow she could figure out how to function again and accept her past wrongs? Or her present despair? Well, she certainly couldn't say as much to him. With a deep breath she could only sigh. "Busy."

"Mike said you and Cole weren't seeing each other no more."

Her cheek twitched as David stated part of the cause for her turmoil, or rather a good deal of it. She couldn't trust her voice just yet, so she kept it simple. "True."

"So why's he glaring at me?"

"Because he's a brute." A brute that had managed to get the horse she'd purchased in July broken, and then snuck into her stable just last night. All without waking her or Mike up. That man had even suggested a name for her with a one word note written, from what she could tell, in Norman's handwriting. It simply said: *Tempest*. It bothered her that she liked it so much.

"Ah." To his credit, he said not a word. "How do you like your new house?"

"It's comfortable. Not too big or too small." She tapped his arm. "I hate to disappoint you, though."

"Do you now?"

"Oh yes, every time, but about this in particular."

"Well now I am curious. What are you talking about?"

"You waxed so poetic about Clara's cooking." She smiled despite her previous turmoil. "I'm afraid it turns out I am not much of a cook. Michael gets vast amusement over it. I'm afraid your dreams of a delicious dinner will not be realized. I burn eggs."

"You burn eggs?"

She smacked his arm when he started laughing. "You're not helping."

"Sorry." He made several attempts to appear properly reticent, and almost achieved it only to burst into laughter again. "You really burn the eggs?"

"And biscuits. Everything I've cooked has been a dismal failure. I've given up. We eat from Turner's every meal." When he kept laughing she sighed. Perhaps a change of subject was in order. "And how are you enjoying being sheriff amidst all this chaos?"

"It keeps me plenty busy. Don't have much time to think. I've been sleeping at the jailhouse because it's right in town and you never know when you're gonna be needed." He scratched his head. "I'll have a deputy soon so I can sleep for a change."

"How is Martha?"

"Being strong. Major Webb has decided to keep her in the jailhouse until the case gets further, or I need the space. She told me what you told her about needing two witnesses."

Jane paused at the door to the Silver Saddle. "Treason calls for capital punishment. A person facing death should be allowed every chance at defense they can get. Once you are dead, there's no way to take it back."

"Still, it was kind of you. I know you don't like her."

"I think she means well, and is kind enough. I don't like what she did one bit, it put far too many lives in danger. I don't agree with her reasons, she clearly wasn't thinking of anyone but the three of them. That doesn't mean I don't think she deserves a fair chance at justice."

"It was still good of you. You know something, Jane?"

Considering the wicked gleam in his eyes, she wondered if she dared to ask. If it had to do with Clara, she might snap his head off. As it stood, she did need to stop making excuses and tell him what she'd learned. "I'm almost afraid to ask," she admitted.

David laughed. "No need to worry. I just think it's funny. You've been doing everything you can to cause scandal. But there isn't anyone that'll say a cross word about you. Well—"

"Except for Graham and Jackson. And now Cole." She couldn't help but look toward the saloon. He'd delivered and named her horse. Would he say a cross word now? Was he still so angry? What did it matter? She had to force herself to move on. After her brief lapse in judgment she focused back on David. "I try to be honest, David. I'm finding it is far easier to be honest, even if it causes pain."

His hand rested on her shoulder. "Well, it's working for you. I just hope it isn't causing you too much pain."

"Thank you," she whispered. She set her hand on his. The past two weeks had been full of excuses and she was certain she could find more, but she had a promise to keep. She couldn't delay things any longer. He deserved to know the ugly truth. "We still have to talk, David. I made a promise to you once, and I must keep it."

He searched her eyes. "It sounds serious. Is it something that can wait until the celebration of the train is over? I'm going to be busy with all the strangers coming in town."

"Of course you are, quite a few are arriving today, I know." She bit her lip, it was so important, but at the same time he had a point. Once she told him it would change his world and he'd need time to let the dust settle on her revelations. "It's important, but it can wait until you can give me your full attention."

"I promise. Soon as the celebration is over you've got all the time you need."

She offered the best smile she could. "Not any longer than that. Promise."

"Promise. I've asked Michael to swear in as deputy. I'm going to need the extra help, and once all the hubbub has died down it'll let me have some time off duty."

"I'm glad you're giving that lazy lie-abed something to do. He's annoying me constantly." She squeezed his hand. The panic of how he would react when she told him the truth of Clara's letters and what she now knew about why she left seized her heart. The rapid pounding of panic filled her ears. "Soon. We must make sure we talk soon."

"I promise." David kissed her cheek before starting down the street.

She took a deep breath and frowned. For too long she'd put off telling him. She hated that she'd let all the chaos around her distract her from her promise to him. The sooner she got it over with, the better. He'd hate her once he knew the truth, and thus she'd lose a man she'd come to call a friend. There was little to be done about it now.

The train was due to open for its first run in just two days. To that end, there were two stagecoaches arriving that day with visitors preparing for the town's celebration. She was to meet the first stagecoach with Guy and help get the guests settled into their rooms at the hotel.

Since the elections Guy's mood had been bitter and he'd been an insufferable beast, so she braced herself for anything as she entered the hotel. Instead of the usual grumbling, she found Guy waiting for her with a tremendous, unsettling smile. Her stomach leaped about in a nervous jitter at what it could mean. "Guy?"

"Good morning, Jane. It's a beautiful day, isn't it? We're getting a stagecoach full of guests today; our rooms will be full come nightfall. Yes, yes. It is a very good day."

"Why, may I ask, do you look like the cat that swallowed the canary?"

"Do I?" He chuckled and shrugged. "I must say I had a very interesting visit last night, a visit that I've been hoping to have for a while now. It helped me acquire a certain something I've been after for a good year and a half."

Jane's eyes narrowed, but Guy offered no other hint. Movement upstairs caught her eye and her heart leapt into her throat. Unable to speak, she could only stare as Daisy descended the steps. Dressed in frills and lace none of Cole's girls had, her hair piled on top of her head in an elaborate coiffure of curls instead of the usual gentle waves about her shoulder, and far more makeup than was attractive, Daisy was clearly ready for hire on Guy's flashy floor.

"I plan on using her variety of talents far more efficiently than that buffoon ever did. Tell me, Jane. What do you think of this?" He spread his arms as he spoke, "The Silver Saddle Health Resort. Catchy, isn't it? I've already ordered some tonics for her to recommend to our guests. She'll have her own office for use, when she's not otherwise occupied."

Jane licked her lips against her dry mouth. How could Daisy be here after Cole's promise? He never went back on his word, he'd told her as much. What had changed? What did it matter? Daisy didn't deserve this. Ire stole away her shocked silence. "Cole sold you Daisy's contract?"

"I didn't even have to pester him. He came to me."

Jane rushed across the casino and seized Daisy's arm. She pulled the whore to the side, away from prying eyes. "What the hell happened?"

The bright smile Daisy had been flashing faded, and tears shimmered. She took the handkerchief Jane offered and dabbed so as to not smear her makeup. "I don't know. He's been acting real foul for days. Since the election. Then he just came in last night and said he'd sold my contract. Walked me right over and dropped me on the stoop."

"What happened to letting you buy it? He said he would. Cole doesn't go back on his word."

"He said the money was too good. After the last attack he needed the cash to fix up the saloon and I was the fastest way to get it." Daisy cleared her throat and straightened her shoulders. The smile returned to her features. "At least I get to dress better, and Guy's going to let me do some doctoring on a regular basis, not just in an emergency."

"Painting the feathers of a chicken does not make it a peacock." Jane glared at Guy's amused visage. "I'm going to kill them both. Stupid men and their pissing contests. They'll never understand what idiots they are."

"Don't mess this up for me Jane, please." Daisy grabbed her hand. "Please. It's not much better than Cole's, but it's something."

Jane snatched her hand back, any respect she'd gathered for Daisy in recent months receding. "No wonder Cole pitied you. If you're willing to call this better, you really are worthy of it. Geez, Daisy, he wants you to sell snake oil to fat self-satisfied snobs. He doesn't want you to do true doctoring. He wants to turn a profit."

"Jane."

"Don't you worry one bit. I won't mess up anything. If this is what you want, then have at it. I'm done trying to help any of you. It only comes back to bite me in the end." She turned her heel and put her back to Daisy's sputtering protest. Jane strode back across the room. Every emotion got pushed down until she made sure she could be all business. "How many guests are arriving?"

Guy preened, stroking his beard. "Four. A married couple and a man traveling with his child. They all answered my advertisement. Now all I want is for you to greet them and—"

"I know my job." She straightened, her biting tone showing the last bit of anger she couldn't seem to quash. "I'll make them feel welcome and at home in your false front whorehouse. I'll do everything right, and then I'll go to lunch. I'm done giving you advice you won't listen to. Dig your own grave."

"My, my. A bit touchy today."

"You're worse than Jackson. You talk a good game, but the minute things don't go your way you turn into a condescending bastard without a brain in your head."

Guy followed her outside, his low chuckling following her down the street. "That's rather judgmental. I have been upfront with my pursuit of Daisy's talents."

"Quiet. I told you I'm done. From now on, all you'll hear from me is comments on the hotel side of your business and they will all be professionally addressed."

"That works quite well for me. Leave the whores alone and deal only with the guests. I think it's best you have as little influence on those girls as possible."

Jane opened her mouth to protest, but promptly snapped it shut. She folded her arms across her chest when they reached the end of the street. Graham and Cole also stood waiting on the stagecoach. She grumbled under her breath. "This day keeps getting better and better."

Crossing the street in silence, Jane took a position as far from Cole as possible. She kept her eyes focused on the road, rather than the three men she was at varying levels of temper with. The silence of the group was only broken by Guy's cheerful whistle.

Jane's skin tingled in an achingly familiar sensation, like a certain man was staring at her as he had so often before. She scratched her neck against the sensation and snuck a peek. Sure enough, though his eyes and whatever emotion they held were hidden in the shadow of his hat brim, Cole's gaze was fixed on her. Her fingers twitched as if to reach for him, so she had to tuck them into her skirts to keep them hidden.

The rattle of the stagecoach couldn't have come at a better time. She straightened and stepped forward as the coach drew up in front of their small group. With her brightest smile, she pulled open the door. A small hand gripped the doorframe, though the occupants were still hidden by shadows. "Welcome to Dominion Falls."

A jolt ran through her when the young boy peeked around the frame before standing before her. Wide hazel eyes stared back at her his extended arms frozen mid reach.

Her feet stepped back of their own accord, coldness spreading through her limbs. The jostle of the driver coming over to set down steps stirred her out of her stupor, but she found she still couldn't move.

The boy was bumped from behind and his arms dropped. In an instant he leaped from the stage without touching the steps that had been put down.

Jane followed him as he darted behind a post, peeking out at her from behind it. When the sound of conversation sank in, she realized it was French. How she knew that, or understood anything being said was another mystery of her strange brain.

Still, she turned to address Guy's fumbling attempts to address the situation. When she spotted the man speaking French to Guy, the world spun. She gripped the nearest post to keep from toppling over.

Guy was lost, but she made no move to assist, her focus on the face of the apparent foreigner. Her mind latched on the memory of a cowboy that had come through months ago. The cowboy had sported a thick beard, long scraggly hair, and hollow cheeks.

The man in front of her was plump, clean-shaven, with short, well-kept hair. The spectacles he wore covered deep brown eyes. Her heart stammered, then pounded in a rapid rush when the man looked at her and spoke. Three faint scars on his cheekbone were the only other direct similarity. He couldn't be the same cowboy, could he?

He stepped toward her. Guy spoke her name, but in a muffled sort of way that made her think he was far away. A small whimper escaped before she fell, the world going black around her.

*False face must hide
what the false heart doth know.
-William Shakespeare*

"Jane." The concern in Cole's voice struck Jane as odd. He'd been so angry with her, and she with him. What did he care? Why was his voice so soft, so kind?

Her eyes fluttered open and she found herself lost in his icy eyes.

Oh, that's right. She'd fainted. "I'm sorry."

"What happened?" Guy came into view behind Cole. "Jane. Do you speak French?"

"She just fainted and ya wanna ask if she speaks French?"

Jane couldn't help but giggle. "Men. You're all idiots."

Cole frowned down at her. "Jane."

Pain and fear rushed forward before she could stop them. She closed her eyes, unwilling to let him see how much she hurt without him. She couldn't let him know how much this man and the little boy terrified her.

She turned her head rather than face his piercing gaze again. When she opened her eyes, she spotted the small shoes of the little boy. Panic struck her so fast she flew to her feet.

In an instant Cole was next to her, a bracing hand at her elbow when she swayed. "You sure you're all right?"

"Yes. I'm quite certain." She sighed when he scoffed and walked away. The little boy darted from where he'd been hiding to the stranger that had frightened her so. She braced herself as she turned to meet the man's eyes.

He nodded and spoke in French, one hand securely planted on the boys shoulder. "*Do you speak French, Mademoiselle?*"

"Oui." Out of the corner of her eye she noted the stunned stares of Graham, Cole, and Guy. She continued in French, but she couldn't keep herself from looking down at the boy again. "*I'll be happy to help you with all of your accommodations.*"

"Merci." His grip tightened on the boy's shoulder. The smile he wore was cold, dark. "*My name is Philip Bellamonte.*"

The internal panic rallied again, but she forced a smile over it all and introduced him to Guy. Avoiding further glances at the boy, she got them and the married couple ready to go to the hotel. She knew Cole's gaze was on her, but if she dared even a peek she'd crack.

She pushed the thoughts and doubts she had aside, forcing herself to focus on her work. After all the new guests were settled in and she'd established at least one other employee spoke French, she rushed from the hotel at her earliest opportunity.

The minutes she got free, the crushing weight on her chest increased. Why couldn't she get a grip on this panic? Why panic at all?

The last time she'd felt this way had been around that cowboy, Johnny. But this man could not be the same man, could he? Why would someone do that? Why return as a different person? Could it all just be her imagination?

And the boy.

She gasped for air as she stumbled down the street. It wasn't possible. How could he be? He was the right age. His eyes.

His eyes were like David's. His blond hair full of curls, just like hers.

No. It couldn't be.

Her son.

A sob breached her control before she raced home.

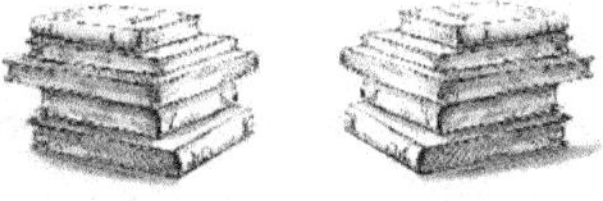

With devotion's visage and pious action we do sugar o'er the devil himself.
–Thomas Fuller

Cole sat on the bench outside the saloon. Though not even seven, the sun had tucked behind the mountains leaving the town in full dusk. He'd seen neither hide nor tail of Jane since she'd passed out at the stagecoach.

It was all he could do to keep from pacing. His heart felt twisted in sickening knots. His stomach churned. Worry he hadn't felt since she'd been shot left him sick.

This was worse, though. He had no place doing it after the way he'd left her standing there. Even worse, that also meant he couldn't rightfully check on her.

Even if that was all he wanted to do, he couldn't.

He rose, pacing the length of the porch. Men had begun to drift toward the saloon from the mines. He couldn't bear to put on a face for them and act like nothing was bothering him as he'd been doing.

Rather than face the coming throng, he stepped from the porch and headed around the corner. In the distance the flickering lights of the army camp ignited the venom of anger in his gut.

No, not anger. Jealousy.

Maybe she was there, seeking comfort with that namby-pamby soldier boy.

His arms seemed cold all of a sudden, lacking a warm body. If she was seeking her comforts, maybe he should, too. There was plenty close enough.

His stomach churned at the idea once again. He shook off the disgust he shouldn't have been feeling. He'd warmed plenty of beds in his own saloon.

The comforts seemed awful cold now.

Jane's face swarm before his eyes, twisted in fury behind the barrel of her considerable weapon. Fury and something more. Pain.

She'd been right to threaten him. He'd had no right to push her like that. Always Jane had been a strong woman, one that made her own way. Not once had she put up with his idiocy, and he didn't expect her to start.

He'd been mad, and far too drunk to see reason. All he could see was how much he wanted her, even if it meant she was gloating over being right.

He hadn't earned her forgiveness, and so she hadn't granted it.

Damn if he wasn't the biggest fool. Why couldn't he return to his life before her? It should be so easy. A whore here and there. His saloon. His whiskey.

It was all easy, familiar—uncomplicated. He hated complicated. Always had.

Until Jane.

Once again the image of her crumpling in front of the stagecoach emerged. She'd been paler than anything. Fear and something else he couldn't put his finger on had given her the look of someone that had seen a ghost.

Damn her. He had to see if she was all right.

When he spun, he found himself face-to-face with her brother. "Mike. Where is she?"

"What?" Anger darkened Mike's cheeks, a scowl creased his brow. "First off, what the hell should it matter to you?"

"I ain't seen her since she fainted. I—"

"She what?"

"Fainted."

"Clara doesn't faint."

"It's Jane, and I know that." Cole clenched his fists. It took all his effort not to shake the man. "That's why I wanted to see her."

"Worried?" The scowl eased away into a wicked grin. "Don't tell me you dare admit you care for her. God knows she doesn't know it."

"It ain't none of your business what I think."

"Then what in hell do you want?"

"I gotta know she's all right." Damn, some of the panic he felt had cracked his voice.

"It's none of your business if she is." Even as he spoke, Mike cast a glance over his shoulder. As if he could see Jane's house, and her in it, even though it was half a mile outside town. "She's plenty strong."

"Then why you look so worried?"

"Because I do actually care about her. Excuse me." Mike brushed past him. In front of the nearby jail, he hopped onto his horse.

Quick as a wink the man and his horse tore away down the road.

Cole followed on foot. Mike wasn't wrong, it really wasn't Cole's business. Still that nagging worry kept at him and he wouldn't be able to let it go until he knew she was well.

Hell, who was he kidding? He could say he didn't care, that he wanted to move on and get back to his simple life all he wanted. It didn't make it true.

The truth was he'd come to crave the complication Jane added to his life. Worse, he needed it.

He missed her.

Fuck if he wasn't trapped.

Love wasn't a word he used—ever.

But if he did—no. He didn't. He wouldn't.

Being deeply loved by someone gives you strength.
While loving someone deeply gives you courage.
—Lao Tzu

He'd been there.

It had to have been a dream.

But she remembered the touch of his lips to her forehead, which had stirred her toward consciousness. Gentle kisses to her eyelids begged them to open, but if she'd let them open the dream would dissipate. Her fingers ran along his strong arms, burying in his hair when he'd kissed the tip of her nose.

When his lips touched hers, the aching need took over. She opened up to him in desperation, knowing it was a dream and the messiness of pain, apologies, and explanations weren't needed. Her tongue responded to his, searching the familiar depths of his mouth. He'd pulled back, gently brushing her hair off her forehead.

Still convinced it was a dream, she'd breathed out in a whisper the words she'd never dare say aloud.

"I love you."

And as in every other dream he'd been gone. She'd reached for him again, but in the whisper of a breeze from her window he was gone.

Jane stared hard at her exhausted reflection. Somehow she had to convince herself it had all been a dream. She dismissed the notion that she could still smell him on her sheets. The mix of cigar smoke and his distinct maleness was a hopeful rendering of her imagination. There was no reality to it, just the hope she'd not been able to banish. The hope he'd return to her side.

Yesterday she'd fainted. She'd opened her eyes to find Cole looking down at her in concern. His brief flash of kindness had touched the weak of her part that still loved him. No, not weak, the insatiably strong part of her heart that refused to let go of the love she'd finally admitted to herself, even in the face of his continual denial.

She'd claimed exhaustion, and it held a ring of truth. Her sleep had been disrupted for weeks, so she always felt tired. That combined with the shock of seeing the boy yesterday. Her eyes flew up to stare in the mirror again.

She reached up to touch the curls edging her face. The boy's hair had been unruly and poked out in every direction with bright blond curls much like hers. The eyes, though. His eyes had been so very much like David's.

"It's just your overactive imagination. You read far too many novels. Too many fanciful stories. That child is Monsieur Bellamonte's." She spotted a tear on her cheek and wiped it away with a harsh swipe of her hand. "And that is who he is, Monsieur Bellamonte. Not some strange cowboy named Johnny."

A weak laugh fluttered out at the ridiculousness of conversing with her own image. "And you are not insane. Stop talking to yourself."

She smoothed her hand over her bodice and checked her bustle before leaving the bedroom. Michael had left hours before, but he'd left the teapot sitting warm on the stove. Grateful for the kindness, she poured herself a cup. At the table she grabbed up her copy of *Pride and Prejudice* to try to clear her mind.

After only a few minutes, she slammed the book shut. The interplay of Elizabeth and Darcy were the exact opposite of distracting. As a logical person, she could look at this objectively. The odds of the notions running through her mind regarding the boy and his father were infinitesimal to say the least.

She could do this. She could go to work and ignore those annoying, nagging thoughts at the back of her head. They weren't grounded in fact. She needed facts.

She had no facts.

Seven missing years.

The knowledge she had to push these thoughts away tired her more, but she had to do just that if she wanted to make it through the day. Her former confidante no longer cared for her problems. The one person that understood her, Jane, not the woman she'd once been; he'd left. She'd forced him to leave.

"Stop it," she scolded herself. "You're a grown woman. Act like it."

She set her jaw in determination and rose to her feet. The moment she did, the world spun. She gasped and had to grab the table to steady herself. Her shaky hand touched her forehead. The world had to stop spinning. Too often lately that had been happening.

She hadn't risen so fast her head should spin. It didn't make sense to have happened just then. After another deep breath, the dizziness subsided. At the sight of her reflection, she paused.

Her features were pale and drawn. She appeared as miserable as she felt. Shaking her head at herself, she stepped closer to the mirror.

In an instant her mind settled into calm. Details fell into place.

The past few weeks rushed through her head. Her disinterest in foods she'd once enjoyed. The way certain smells made her sick. The inability to sleep.

Her breath caught and her skin prickled. She spun away from the mirror.

No.

She couldn't be.

Pregnant.

After the rushed and intense first coupling with Cole, they'd both gone to great pains to make sure this didn't happen. She'd rarely left home without her womb veil in place, just in case of a chance encounter. On a few occasions at the saloon, she'd had to ask Daisy's assistance when she'd not worn one.

Her hands dropped to her stomach, running over the smooth fabric of her bodice. When was the last time she'd had her monthly?

She'd missed two. Not since she and Cole had first been together and she hadn't thought to notice. Naïve fool that she was.

Cole.

If she couldn't admit her feelings, how could she tell him this? He'd made his feelings clear. All she was to him was a good screw. This would only make him run farther than he had already.

How could she bear more?

She had to. What else could she do?

The walk to town went by in a blur. Her mind too wrapped in the puzzles and problems to register anything else. It wasn't until she got to town and the saloon came into view that she had reason to pause.

She stood still in the middle of the road, staring into the shadows of the saloon's porch as the reality hit her. Eventually he would know of the pregnancy. Soon, most likely.

Tears filled her eyes when his tall form stepped out of the saloon onto the porch. With everything turning her life upside down, how could she continue to push him away? If she approached him now would he turn her away? She wasn't certain she could bear it if he did.

If only she could get the comfort of one hug, one touch. One wise-assed comment about how she was overthinking everything.

She took a step toward him, but movement at the edge of the porch caught her attention. A little boy peeked around the edge of the saloon.

Cole followed her gaze to the boy, and then looked back at her. She couldn't pull her gaze away. With a gasp, she gathered her skirts and rushed toward the young one, but he disappeared.

She paused at the corner of the saloon and looked down the alley. No sign of him there, so she searched the street. Spotting him again, she darted down the street. She ran until she caught up to him.

He stopped when she tapped his shoulder. With wide eyes, he turned to face her.

"Ça va?" She knelt in front of him. When he didn't answer she touched his arm. "Quel est votre nom?"

Hazel eyes bore into hers with crystal clarity, but he only shook his head.

"You aren't even French are you?" She gasped when his eyes brightened at her use of English. "Oh you dear boy. Tell me."

He didn't flinch when she took his hand. A small smile peeked out of his sweet face.

"That man, the one you came here with." She almost held her breath, afraid she was wrong. "He's not your father, is he?"

Rather than answer the boy's gaze darted behind her and he pulled his hand from hers. Before she could ask why he spun and raced into the crowd.

Jane flew to her feet. "No, please. Wait."

"Easy." Cole held onto her arms when she swayed.

She didn't bother to try to hide her tears. After everything she wasn't even sure it was possible. It really was all too much. Fighting the urge to collapse into his arms, she turned toward him.

He stood right there, so close. She could feel his warmth. His breath was as ragged as her own. His hands trembled like hers.

Oh how she needed him. Needed him to hold her, comfort her. To let her bury all her worries in him and have him soothe them away. For a moment she caved. She slid her arms around his waist and sobbed into his chest. "Oh, Cole."

His strength surrounded her. The warmth, the caring. It hadn't been a lie; it couldn't have been the way he held her so tender. A deep breath filled her nose with his scent and her eyes flew open. She shoved him back.

His presence in her room, the kisses, the touches, the way he'd disappeared when she'd whispered the forbidden words. The dream she'd had—wasn't a dream at all. He'd been there. He'd been there and left. How could he? How dare he? "You selfish bastard."

His head whipped to the side when she slapped him. "What the hell?"

"You know damn well what. I know you were in my room last night. You don't care one bit at all, do you? You let me think you did. You let me believe you actually cared. How dare you? I would have been fine without you."

"Jane." Anger, confusion, concern all crossed his features. Was she delusional to think she saw regret there, too? She didn't know anymore. Maybe everything had been a lie.

"No." She sobbed, wiping at tears and backing away. "You don't even know the hell I'm going through right now. You never cared to ask. That last thing I need is you messing with my head. Either you're in or you're out. But you're too selfish to choose, so you're out. Leave me alone."

She gathered her skirts and ran before he could reply. Her tears refused to slow. How could she be so stupid?

Then again, Clara had been stupid. Apparently she was no better.

She stood on the porch of Turner's until she felt more in control, then headed inside and took a seat in the restaurant. She'd made a fool of herself just now and she wanted to get herself together before facing the light of day or any issues again.

"Good afternoon, Jane." Cora gave her a bright smile and sat in the chair next to Jane. Her smile faltered and she reached out to touch Jane's hand. "My goodness. Is something wrong? Are you all right?"

"Everything is fine. I'm just feeling a little ill. The heat must be getting to me."

"You just need to get some food in you. You haven't been eating enough."

Jane's brow popped up. "Have you been talking to my brother?"

Cora's smile was anything but innocent as her shoulders rose in a shrug. "You also eat here often enough for me to know when you aren't clearing your plate. Now how about a nice, thick slice of meatloaf?"

"Oh." Jane sat back in her chair. The idea of meatloaf had once been so appealing, but now turned her stomach. "No. I think that's too heavy. Do you have any soup left? It was so delicious I ate two bowls last night."

Cora laughed. "If it means you eat, then I'm happy to get it. You're just lucky I always keep a batch of my vegetable soup on the stove."

Jane smiled and squeezed Cora's hand. After her friend left the table, she sighed. She rested her forehead on her hand

and tried to regain her focus. Somehow she would make it through this day and stop acting like a fool.

When she lifted her head, she saw the boy again. The little darling was now held securely at the Frenchman's side. Her heart pounded. Gathering her wits about her would be impossible with a constant stream of chaos and reminders.

She darted from the store, down into the street, totally abandoning even the idea of lunch. A return to a semblance of normalcy was what she needed. Something other than the odd and stressful and horrible course her life had turned down. So she set a lazy pace to wander down the street.

"Jane."

"Mr. Kilmurry. How are you today?" Jane walked over to the leather smith with a smile brighter than she truly felt. "Anything interesting to show me?"

"Somethin' the Mrs. and I made with you in mind, Miss Jane."

"Oh?" Her smile brightened when he brought a small purse out from beneath the cart. "Oh, it's beautiful."

The small purse would attach cleanly to the belts she preferred to wear. Bright colored threads and a bold button of silver decorated the smooth leather. Mr. Kilmurry ran his finger along a red thread. "It was the Mrs. idea to add the colors. Do ya like it?"

"I love it. How much would you like for it?"

"A dollar?"

"What?" Jane lifted her head in surprise. "Oh goodness, no. You put a lot of craftsmanship in this, plus you made it for me. I won't give you less than two dollars…and two bits."

Mr. Kilmurry grinned. "That's right good of you, Miss Jane."

"No it's not. It's the least this is worth. I wouldn't have balked if you'd charged me four dollars. Do not underestimate your own abilities, Mr. Kilmurry." She gave him the money and took the purse. "I'll wear it..."

A movement at the back of her skirt interrupted her thoughts, and the young boy ran past her down the street. Her eyes darted around, searching high and low for the man claiming to be his father, Bellamonte.

"Jane?"

"Um. Yes, thank you." She couldn't take her gaze off the street where the boy had disappeared. "I'll wear it all the time. Thank you."

Distracted, she barely managed to wave before starting down the road. The crowd of people had grown. Horses and wagons clogged the street as she tried to move down it to find the boy. She wove through the crowd, continually searching for any sign of the child. Her search was proving fruitless and she let out a sigh of frustration.

A single gunshot rang through the town and all action stalled. Everyone listened for the calls of the renegades, but the usual cries never sounded. There was nothing but silence.

A moment later another shot rang out, followed by a series of loud, rapid pops. Several horses reared, tugging on their reins to try to break free. Jane's mind focused on the word *firecrackers* before the next string went off.

Screeches mixed with the wild whinnies of the horses when another shot fired, echoing through the town. People tore through the streets toward shelter, called for their loved ones and ducked into buildings as the first horse broke free.

Jane searched for an escape, but she stood trapped in the street. At every turn people or wagons raced past or blocked her, the chaos was everywhere. All along the road horses broke free and barreled through the street and adding to the chaos.

Finally spotting an opening, Jane rushed toward it, but another gunshot and the splinter of wood in her path made her stop with a shriek.

Another series of firecrackers and horses tore through the streets. They dragged empty and full wagons, with riders and without. Bucking and shrieking away from the noise, they clamored through the streets and alleys.

Another escape afforded itself and Jane ran for it, only to have the pattern repeated. With a loud crack of gunfire, the wood post in her path exploded into shrapnel. Trembling, she spun around for an exit, any exit. A horse reared in front of her and she screamed, stumbling back when he landed a few inches in front of her.

"*Jane*."

"*Cole*." Jane turned toward his panicked voice. She found him standing on the hitching post, his whole body tense. He was so close; maybe she could make it to him. She took a step, but a horse raced so close it almost hit her. She shrieked, "*Cole*."

He leaped from the hitching post and tore down the sidewalk toward her. Another round of firecrackers went off nearby and they both ducked in response. Horses that had begun to settle reared again, joining the still chaotic storm of horses in the street. "Jane!"

She searched for an opening in the chaos. The moment a wagon raced past, she darted for Cole. From the other direction a horse slammed into her, despite the rider's efforts to stop. She screeched as she toppled to the ground.

Then his hand gripped her arm; he'd managed to reach her. He pulled her halfway to her feet. "Come on, Jane. Let's move."

Still disoriented, she got to her feet best as she could. With one step toward shelter another gunshot went off. The bullet whizzed past between them before it impacted in the building. She gripped his arm. "Cole."

He shoved her back to the ground and dropped on top of her. As he tried to curl her under his arm he yelled, "Stay down."

"No, Cole, don't!" She gasped. When he grunted and his body jerked, she grabbed his shirt.

"Not selfish." Each word got punctuated with a grunt. His body jerked at every thump of a hoof. "Coward."

"Don't. Please. You don't have to do this." She sobbed when released a pained groan. "Oh, God. Please. Run."

"Feel same." His hold on her remained tight

The pounding of hooves filled her ears, dust filled her nose, but his strong arms held tight through each grunt. "Cole, don't...don't..."

His body went slack above her, and fear stilled her heart. A hoof landed nearby, and she dragged his arm away from the proximity. She tried to push him off, but his weight was too much. She sobbed and clung to him, praying for it to end, for the torment to stop. For an eternity his weight pressed down on her, until she could hardly breathe. Every time a horse impacted close he jolted, but no more did he grunt or groan.

The pounding of hooves slowed. Shouts and whistles seeped in over the few whinnies remaining. The firecrackers and gunshots had ceased, and the town was gaining control again. She reached up toward his face as best as she could with her immobilized arms. "Cole. Please, Cole. Please, answer me."

Her hands shook until she managed to get a grip on his shirt. She pushed with all her might until he rolled off her. She rolled with him until she was spread across his chest. She clamored to her knees. "*Cole.*"

"Clarabelle."

She ignored Michael. While Michael buzzed in her ear, she cupped Cole's cheeks in her hands before running them through his hair. When she pulled back her hands and realized they were red, a blood-curdling scream rose into her throat. It escaped, disturbing several nearby horses.

Michael tried to pull her back. "Easy, Clarabelle."

"*No. Cole. Cole.*" She fought him off to drop down next to Cole. "Please, Cole. Please. Don't do this. Don't you die on me. For me. Michael, he can't die. Not for me. He can't. Please."

"I'll get Daisy."

Jane nodded with a weak sob and bent down over Cole. She pressed her ear to his chest, hoping to hear a reassuring beat of his heart. One weak beat hit, and after a moment another. "Please, Cole. I need you. I'm sorry. I'm so sorry. Just come back to me."

"I've gotta move him." Graham knelt next to them. "He isn't dead, but Daisy can't fix him in the street."

She nodded weakly. "He has to live. I wasn't worth this."

"No. You weren't."

Several men moved to help pick Cole up and carry him to the saloon. A strong pair of arms went around her. "Clara. Easy. He's one strong bastard. You know that."

She spun around and collapsed in David's arms.

"He isn't dead."

"He can't die. Don't let him die, David. Please."

"Michael's going to help Daisy. They'll do everything they can. You've just got to pray."

"I am. With all my heart."

Pain is no evil, unless it conquers us.
-Charles Kingsley

"Jane."

It wasn't the voice she wanted to hear. It wasn't the voice she needed to hear. It wasn't Cole's voice. Unless it was Cole, she wasn't going to answer.

"Jane, please." Michael shook her shoulder. "You need to get out of that bed and this room. Eat something. Someone will be here with him. He won't be alone."

"I can't leave. I just can't." There was so much left unsaid. So many questions. So many answers. Jane opened her eyes and stared at his unconscious features. So many apologies to make. "Bring some soup. I'll try to get some in him and have some myself."

"No. You need to get up and moving. The train celebration starts in a few hours. You need to be there. You're expected. You can't stay cooped up in here." Michael sat on the edge of the bed. "You haven't changed since yesterday. You need to clean yourself up."

"I have so much...I..." Closing her eyes again, she shook her head. She had too much to tell Cole. She couldn't go now. "I can't go."

"I don't know him as well as you, but I don't think he liked being fussed over any more than you do. Would he want you wallowing in grief?"

"He hates it when I wallow." She clung to Cole's arm and laced her fingers with his. Daisy said it could be days until he woke, but she had to be there when he did. She had to tell him she… "I'm not leaving him."

"I'll make you a deal."

"Go away."

"I'll go away."

"Deal."

"Clara Louise."

She heaved a heavy sigh into the silence. If she'd been feeling up to snuff she might have made a snide comment about what a horrid middle name she'd had. If he'd been conscious, Cole might have laughed. When Michael still didn't leave, she rolled half over and glared at him. "Go away Michael."

"I'll go get food and a change of clothes. You may stay until the celebration. Then you must get out of here for a while. Two hours. That's all I'll ask. Two hours."

"Go away."

"You will leave this room. Cole wouldn't want you to give up."

"You don't know what he'd want. Please go away." The tears already streamed down her cheeks, so it was no good to try to stop them. Instead she rested her forehead against Cole's shoulder until she heard the door shut.

The gentle rise and fall of his chest reassured her again he lived. She rested her hand above his heart and drew her gaze up to his face. The peaceful, relaxed lines and curves remained still, locked in unconsciousness.

More than anything she wanted to curl up against him and rest her head on his chest. To hear the comforting thump of his heart. As it stood, Daisy made allowances by letting her stay on the bed at all. Not that Jane had given her much of a choice.

The minute he'd come out of surgery, Jane demanded to see him. She'd stretched out in the narrow space at the edge of his bed and rested her hand in his. All night she'd remained and his proximity had soothed her enough to allow sleep for the first time in weeks. Only Daisy's occasional checks of Cole's condition had woken her.

Jane traced the bandage on his head with her fingers. Daisy hadn't been reassuring with her prognosis. She'd said she didn't know *if* he'd wake up, or when. Worse, if he did wake up, she said she could make no promises as to his condition. His mental faculties could be compromised.

Jane's lip trembled and she shook her head. "Oh, Cole. You have to come back. You must. You're stronger than this. You're stronger than anyone I know."

She wiped away her tears and cleared her throat. "I'm so sorry. I was hurt, but I shouldn't have pushed you away. I just…I'm so sorry."

One small shift of weight moved her closer. "I'm selfish. I need you here. I need the one person that will listen to my rambling and cut through it. I need the one person that doesn't look for someone else in everything I do. The person that accepts me, Jane Doe, as I am.

"Even if you make me madder than a March hare," she laughed and wiped another tear from her cheek, "that one person is you." She closed her eyes and hovered with her forehead above his for a moment.

"You have to come back. I have to tell you the truth. I have to tell you…so much."

With a shaky breath, she lay back next to him. Even with him unconscious she couldn't look at him when she spoke the secrets she'd kept cloistered for weeks now. "Anyone else would think me insane. You probably will too, but I don't think that Frenchman is French at all. I can't say why, the similarities are so few—but I believe he's that cowboy. You know, the one that first insisted on using the saloon as a hotel."

She glanced his way in the foolish hope he'd woken at her revelation. If only his eyes would open. Just once. "You remember. Johnny. I told you he was scary. This man looks different, but I truly believe it is the same man." She laced her fingers into his hand, reveling the warmth there that reminded her he was live.

"But that's not all." Her voice dropped to a pained whisper, the torment of thoughts digging into her every word. She had to express them aloud before she burst. "The boy he brought with him. Cole, I think he's my son. David's son. How could it be possible?'

Still staring at the ceiling, she pondered how it could be once more. What exactly had to have happened to make it true? She also worried why he wouldn't recognize her if she was. "I know. This all sounds insane. I daren't tell Michael or David, but then I feel I should. I'm so confused. I can't keep my thoughts straight. I don't know what to do."

With a soft sigh, she turned toward him again, running her hand along his arm before snuggling closer. Her eyes closed, relaxation pouring over her with his simple proximity. Until last night she hadn't realized just how much she missed having him close.

She didn't realize she'd drifted off again until the door opened. A gasp of her own surprise drew her wide-awake and she sat up fast. The world spun so fast she had to close her eyes until it steadied. She took a deep breath. "Daisy."

"Any change?" Daisy edged over to the other side of the bed and pulled down the sheet.

"No. I've been talking to him when I've been awake, just like you said I should. As much as I can. But there's been nothing. No signs of life at all. Are you certain it's doing any good?"

"There's no way of knowing." Daisy peeled back the gauze on his stomach to check an incision. "But I've always thought that people can hear you when they're unconscious."

Jane shifted, helping Daisy roll Cole onto his side so she could check his back. "I didn't want him to do this. I never wanted this to happen, not for me. This shouldn't have happened to him, to anyone. Why would someone play such a horrible prank? So many lives were in danger."

"I don't know. David said they couldn't find any clue as to who it was. No one ever saw someone fire a gun or where the shots where coming from. They think kids might have set the firecrackers, but they don't know for certain. No child has admitted to the deed, although they're probably scared to, what with all the damage done."

Jane helped Daisy return Cole to his back, and then sat close when Daisy moved to the bandage on his head. "I tried several times to get out of the street. Every time I made a move it was like whoever was shooting was aiming right for me, or rather in my path. I couldn't make it. They almost shot him when he came to me."

"Hey." Daisy looked up from her ministrations when Jane's voice cracked. She set her hand on Jane's and met her eyes. "Cole made this choice. He did it to save you. I think we both know he doesn't like being questioned."

"He doesn't like being told he was wrong."

Daisy reset the bandage on his head before sitting opposite Jane. She leaned forward, half over Cole to touch Jane's arm. "Given the chance, would you have done the same for him? Or would you have left him there?"

"I would have done the same. In a heartbeat. But…"

"Then you can't tell him he was wrong."

"It's different."

"How?"

Jane kept her gaze locked on Cole's face, brushing her fingers along his cheek rather than face the question. She'd never admit it to Daisy. Far as she knew Cole didn't feel the same about her as she did for him. But why had he done what he did? What motivated him to give his own life to protect hers? What had me meant when he'd said he wasn't selfish, but a coward? Even more—that he felt the same?

Hundreds of answers choked her throat, closing it off. Her breath shuddered as she felt the tears threaten to break through her attempts to restrain them again.

Daisy rose and picked up her bag. "I'll come back to check on him in a little while. Try to get some rest sand food. You're looking a little peaked."

Jane nodded, attempting busy work like readjusting his sheets, to keep from showing Daisy the depth of her pain. The moment they were alone again, she leaned close to Cole. "You damn fool. Who told you I was worth saving?"

Tears broke through the dam she'd built and she covered her eyes with a hand while the other gripped his shoulder. She had to tell him, even if he couldn't hear her right now. She'd held so much back for too long. Knowing he might not hear her helped bolster her confidence to admit, if not her feelings, her other secret.

"Cole. You must know. It wasn't just my life you saved. Cole, I…" She took a shaky breath. "I'm going to have a baby. I'm pregnant."

The strength she'd been trying to exude cracked and she broke. Tears bubbled over and spilled down her cheeks. She leaned in to brush her lips across his. She cupped his cheek. "Please come back. I miss you. I need you."

She lay down, curled into his arm again. "I would give anything to feel your arms around me again. It's always been safe in your arms. You're my sanctuary, Cole. The only place I feel truly safe. Come back. Please."

It was pointless to try to stop her tears now, so she let them flow. Holding tight to the one part of him she could, she let the emotions overwhelm her. Pounding waves of fear and sadness swept her away until she crashed into sleep.

"Jane." Michael's soft voice woke her. "I brought you soup. You need to eat."

Sniffling, Jane nodded her agreement. Unleashing her emotions had drained her of energy, and she knew even though she lacked appetite, she had to eat something. She reached for his extended head. Her limbs felt wobbly and she leaned into him for support.

He guided her into the chair beside the bed and handed her a bowl of soup. "You've got to buck up, cheer up, and put on your best smile."

Jane stared into her soup. Somehow she needed to dredge up the will to eat. She was having trouble with that, though. "Why?"

"Because the state you're in you'll have everyone believing you're in love with that man. I thought you liked letting them all believe you were a happy jezebel." Michael smiled sadly. He reached out to touch her knee. "Put your best foot forward. You'll go; you'll make them think you're not so deeply affected."

"I don't know if I can." With a weak push of her fingers, the spoon swirled around the bowl. Whatever interest she'd had in eating waned like the steam of the soup in the air. The aching river of grief pushed at its levees again and the idea of somehow hiding it all seemed impossible.

"You can. You've been strong enough since I've arrived to hide how much you've loved him. Along with hiding how much both knowing and not knowing your past scares you. Not to mention how much you hate me for still finding pieces of Clara in you."

Her heart stopped. Her hands shook so hard the bowl tumbled from her lap. A sob wrenched from deep within and she flung her arms around his neck when he knelt right in the spilled soup. His arms offered a strong support to her shaking body and soul. "How…how did you know?"

"I told you. You can't lie to me. Clara or Jane, it doesn't matter."

"I hate you."

"I know."

"Thank you."

Isaac hopped along the platform, skipping boards with great leaps. He leaped away from their small group and back. "That was so neat, wasn't it, Jane?"

Isaac's excitable voice couldn't keep her focus on the now. She forced up another bright smile and tried to respond appropriately, though her mind remained back at the saloon. "Yes. It certainly was."

Arthur nudged her. "They're letting us walk through the whole train. You're coming too, right?"

Jane stared at the train stationed at the depot. The train had arrived full of passengers bound for Santa Fe. They'd taken a side route and were all invited to the town's celebrations before leaving for their final destination. The diversion from their route had been made free as an incentive.

When the train had pulled in, the entire town had been excited and cheering, but Jane couldn't join in. A chill had run through her right to her bones. The train workers had proceeded to detach the engine and coal car, moving them around so the train was ready to pull out precisely at five. The adjustment put the luggage car on the back, then two passengers and a sleeper before the coal car and engine.

Once the passengers disembarked, the townspeople could walk through the train cars. Many of the town's residents hadn't been on a train and jumped at the opportunity.

For reasons she couldn't explain, Jane wanted nothing to do with the train.

Michael thumped her back when her silence lingered. "Jane?"

"What? Oh. Yes. I, um." She cleared her throat. Much as she wanted to turn down the request and avoid the train at all costs, she didn't want to disappoint Arthur. "Of course I'll go along, Arthur."

Michael winced when she gripped his hand tight. He leaned in close as the boys moved nearer the train. "I thought you were holding up all right. What's wrong?"

Once she'd left Cole's room she'd found it easier to pretend she wasn't distraught, though he still occupied most of her thoughts. The presence of the Frenchman and the child standing a few yards away didn't make things easier, but she'd managed. Now, facing this train, a different sort of panic seized her. One that she often felt when facing her past. "I don't know."

"We should go along." Michael kissed her temple, and lent a supportive hand around her waist. "I'll be with you, and Arthur is waiting with Cora and Isaac. You did promise him."

"I know. I promised I would spend the day and then dance with him at the party. I know."

He guided her toward the train, a firm hand on her waist like she might run off.

Truth be told, she wasn't so sure she wouldn't. Every step they took toward the train made her heart pound faster until she thought it might beat out of her chest.

The children scrambled into the luggage car fast, their exclamations echoing out. Cora climbed in behind them, but Jane held back. Michael hopped up the steps and held out his hand to her. "Come on, Jane. The boys are waiting."

She set her hand in his, only making it up the steps because he dragged her. The air got exceedingly heavy, stealing her breath. Isaac and Arthur chattered incessantly, but she ignored them. Despite the stifling heat, goose bumps rose on her arms. "Michael."

"Your hands are so cold," he whispered. While the Turner's went on ahead he dragged her through the car forcefully. "Easy."

Once they were out of the luggage car and had hopped over the joint to the passenger car, the weight lifted some. A flash of knowledge hit her so quick she gasped. "It was a train."

"What?"

She hadn't realized she'd spoken aloud. But now she knew. When she'd first remembered bits of her past, the influx of emotions when she and Cole had found the horse carcass on her trail, all she'd known for sure was that she'd been pushed. Now, so many months later, she knew it had been from a train. "Not now. Just get me off this train. Quick."

"We're almost through. Then you can tell me what's wrong."

"I promise. Just get me off the train."

Michael followed Cora and the children through the two cars. Jane couldn't even hear the boys any longer, her focus on simply making it through the cars. Her mind grasped at the fleeting hint of memory she'd once had. Nothing further came to her, but she remained convinced that she'd been pushed off a train. She couldn't remember who had pushed her or why, but she felt certain that had been her fate.

At the end of the sleeper car, Michael's tight grip on her waist released. He hopped down the steps and extended his hand to help her down. She ignored his hand and practically flew from the car onto the platform. The entire walk through the cars felt like a bad dream.

Isaac tugged on her skirt. "Did you see those chairs? Did you touch them? You should have touched them. They were so soft. What about—"

"It was all very nice." Jane managed to smile at the young boy. In a normal situation she might have called his enthusiasm contagious, but right then she couldn't really take part. "Why don't you boys go on ahead with your ma? I know she's worried about how her food's being received by the visitors."

"You *are* coming, right, Jane?" Arthur gave a hopeful smile. "You said you'd be eating with us. You said you'd stay for some of the dance. Right? Before you go back to see Cole."

"I promised you a dance and I intend to keep my promise. Don't you worry. Now go on. We won't be far behind you."

Michael made his own goodbyes. One the family had made its way down the street, he moved back to her side. "Clarabelle."

She couldn't tear her eyes away from the train that had frightened her so. "I was pushed from a train."

"What?"

"When Cole and I first followed my trail I didn't get much out of the journey. The memories were foggy and unclear, emotions more than actual memories. I only remember pure terror, and a certainty I had been chased." She closed her eyes. "I told Cole I'd been pushed, but that's all I knew. I didn't when or how, or what from."

"You think it was a train?"

"Yes. A moving one."

He remained quiet for a long minute. "Clara. Why?"

"I don't know." She moved away from the train and sank onto a bench in front of the office. "Cole needs to wake up, he must. I have to talk to him."

"What don't I know?"

"So much. He knows everything. He was the one person I could talk to."

"Tell me. I can't help you if I don't know." He sank beside her. When she remained silent he set his hand on hers. "Please. Let me be your brother."

"There isn't much I do remember, honestly. My one memory of David is clear, but devoid of emotion. I, personally, feel nothing in it, though I'm aware Clara felt much. I know I should feel something. I read those letters. Clara was truly, blindly, in love with him."

"I know. I remember."

"These other memories. Being chased, so certain I would die, that he would kill me. All I remember is the emotion. I don't remember finding my way through those mountains, coming into this town, collapsing in the saloon. I don't know how I managed to get so far when I was so incredibly injured. I have no idea where I came from before that."

"It might be best you don't remember. You were probably in a great deal of pain."

"And fear." She managed to pull her gaze from the train to focus on him. "There's another memory, just one. At least, I think it's a memory, it keeps returning in a nightmare. It's so horrible, Michael. It's so…"

When her voice cracked, his arm slipped around her shoulder. Though not as comforting as Cole's, Michael's warm support gave her some level of comfort and reassurance. "Tell me, Jane. What is it?"

"I can't be for sure it's a memory."

"You've said that. It's a nightmare."

"One I keep having. I see a dismembered hand, a man's mangled body. Whispers around me say I killed him. I have no idea who he is, but they all say I killed him. Michael."

He hugged her tight and let her cry. "You didn't kill anyone."

"You have no way of knowing." She sniffled, accepting his offered handkerchief to wipe at her slowing tears. "I pray I wouldn't be capable of such a thing."

"You aren't. Unless your life was in danger or someone you loved was in danger, I can't see you just killing someone. Not Clara. Not Jane."

"I wish I could be as sure as you are."

"So do I. You wouldn't kill someone in cold blood. It's just not in you."

She had to change the subject. Otherwise she might argue that Clara was cruel enough to walk away from David, who knows what she was capable of in the end. Instead, she focused on the one thought she hadn't even been able to truly discuss with Cole.

Even if Michael thought her insane, she had to share the idea and get someone else's take on the situation. "There's something else. I don't want you to think I'm insane for this. I need you to listen and hear me out, no matter how crazy it sounds."

"All right." He frowned, but kept a firm hold on her hand. "I'm listening."

"Monsieur Bellamonte. The gentleman staying at the Silver Saddle? I don't think he's what he says he is."

"How so?"

"I don't think he's French, and I don't think his name is Philip. Unless I'm mistaken, I believe he's been here before. I had coffee with him. He made me uncomfortable then, and looked vastly different in appearance. Long hair, scraggly beard, much thinner. He used a rough vernacular. He went by the name Johnny and frightened me."

"Why?"

"I know it sounds insane." Jane took a ragged breath. "I'm not so sure I'm not. I don't know why he would change his appearance and pretend to be French. I don't know why he'd come back. I'm just certain it's the same man."

"And?"

"The boy." Her voice caught and she covered her mouth when her stomach churned. She couldn't lose it. Not yet. Once she was back in Cole's room she could let loose. Still, she had to tell someone, since Cole was incapable of helping her. She took a shaky breath. "The boy traveling with Bellamonte."

"The mute child?"

"Mute?"

"That's what Guy said. Bellamonte told him through a staff member the child is mute. Always has been."

"Oh God." She sobbed and shook her head. What had happened to the poor child? How is it he was mute? "Michael…I think it's David's son. Clara's son. My son. I can't explain why. I just knew when I saw him."

Silence greeted her declaration. Michael's hand grew slack in hers. An instant later he flew to his feet and dragged her to hers. "Let's go find him."

"Wait." Jane tugged on his hand. Her heart raced and sweat beaded on her forehead. "I have no proof. You're supposed to tell me I'm just imagining it."

"I can't. Not until I've gotten a good look at the boy myself."

"David's been so busy. I haven't been able to tell him. I planned on telling him about what Clara did as soon as all of this was over." She waved around the platform. "But then the boy came here and I don't know what to say. If it's him…"

"Let me see this boy first. Then we'll discuss what and how and when you tell David." Michael squeezed her hand. "I promise, Jane. We'll get this fixed."

She let him drag her through town. They arrived close to the end of the lunch. The band tuned its instruments, and some of the train's passengers were starting to return.

Jane scanned the crowd, not seeing the Frenchman or the young boy. "I don't see them. Maybe they're back at the Silver Saddle."

"I'll go see." Michael kissed her on the cheek. "You'll be all right?"

"I'm sure I'll manage. Thank you." She exhaled a shaky breath when he took off, letting her eyes drift back across the crowd.

"Jane."

"Arthur. I'm so sorry I missed the food. I had something to tell Michael." At the forlorn look on his face, she sighed and reached for his hand, giving it a reassuring squeeze. "Will you dance the first dance with me? Maybe two dances to help make up for my rudeness."

"You don't have to." A smile tugged at his lips. "I mean, if you don't want."

"Of course I do, or I wouldn't have said it." A moment of peace settled in when he beamed up at her. She nodded when he grinned. A smile escaped when he took off and tugged on David's arm in excitement.

"Considering your reputation, should I be worried?"

Jane jumped at Cora's voice. "You needn't worry. You've raised a good one there. I don't intend to corrupt such a respectable young man."

"Good. He is a bit sweet on you, you know." Cora shook her head. "I'm just glad to see him smile any time he can."

"He deserves to have many smiles in his life. You've all been through a lot. If I can help him smile, I'm glad to do it. His pa was a good man and he'd want his son to be happy."

"That's what he always wanted for them." Cora took a shaky breath. "Some days it's easier than others. The train was exciting. That makes it easier today."

Jane's smile faltered at the mention of the train, but she nodded. "I'm sure it did. Especially since he's never seen one."

"Jane." Arthur waved her over with a big grin.

Laughing, Jane squeezed Cora's hand. "Please tell me you taught him to dance. Or do I need to protect my toes?"

"Your toes are safe." Cora chuckled. "He hated it, but I taught him young."

"Thank goodness." Jane took Arthur's arm and headed onto the dance floor that had been built for the occasion. Putting all of her effort into staying focused on the boy, she still found her focus wandering to find the Frenchman or Michael.

Halfway through the second dance, they both appeared along with Guy. Jane had to force herself to stay in the dance. She couldn't disappoint Arthur again, but the moment the song ended, she excused herself.

"He's gone," Michael muttered and pulled her close. "Bellamonte says he's missing. No one can find him."

Jane felt him grip her arm when her knees buckled. "We have to find him. We have to. Get everyone looking."

"Not everyone. But we'll gather up as many as we can. The train is leaving in ten minutes, so most of these people will be gone when that happens."

He left in a moment, calling David. Bellamonte stared at her. The brown eyes now were black. Evil. He knew she knew. There was no other explanation.

Taking several steps back, she turned toward the group gathering. They were taking too long. Wasting too much time in talk of plans. She loved words, but right then words did nothing more than waste time. She had to find him. She had to find the child.

She didn't have time to explain. She just left. The fact that Bellamonte had disappeared didn't help her frayed nerves. She had to find the child soon or it would be too late. Something inside her told her as much.

She made her way down the street, checking alleys. Ignoring all the travelers making their way back to the train, she kept on her search. Once she'd made it through town without any sign of the boy, her gaze fell on the train.

A blond head peeked out from between the cars and looked around before slipping up the stairs into one of the cars.

Without a moment's hesitation, Jane gathered her skirts and raced to the depot. She clamored up the stairs into the car, gasping once she stepped inside. The familiar pressure in her chest returned, but she took a deep breath to regain her focus.

She scanned each passenger as she made her way through the car. She searched under the seats amidst exclamations and protest from the passengers.

He wasn't there. Where had he gone? She looked through the doors to the next car and took a deep breath, hopping over to it and continuing the search.

At the end of the second car, she paused, looking into the luggage car. The back door had been closed, but a small figure ran across the still open door up front.

Of course he'd be there. The car that caused her so much grief earlier. Closing her eyes, she leaped across the distance and stumbled into the car. She gasped, falling to her knees at the immediate overwhelming pressure.

Her head started pounding and she tried to take deep breaths to push it away. A small hand touched her back. She sat up, staring at him in surprise. "What are you doing in here? The train is going to leave. We have to go."

"No, he does. Go, boy. Now."

Jane froze. She recognized Bellamonte's voice and a shiver ran down her spine.

"Jane? Jane?" Arthur's voice reached her ears.

The little boy's eyes widened and he darted into the shadows near the door.

"Wait," Jane called out to him. "Please."

"Jane?" Arthur appeared in the doorway, climbing into the car. "What are you doing in here? Train's gonna—"

"Arthur, don't. Get out." Jane scrambled toward him when she saw the boy dart out of the car. Just as she reached Arthur, the door closed, plunging them into darkness.

"Jane?" Arthur's voice trembled. "What—"

"Be quiet," the click from a gun cocking echoed through the dark space, "or I'll make sure you're permanently quiet."

Shall I tell you what the real evil is?
To cringe at the things that are called evils,
to surrender to them our freedom, in defiance
of which we ought to face any suffering.
—Seneca

David turned to survey the gathered men. "Everyone know what to do?"

Michael made his own sweep of the crowd as everyone nodded in agreement. One particularly important person was missing. "Jane? Jane. *Clara.*"

David frowned. "Mike?"

"She was *right here.*" Mike spun in another circle. In an instant he knew what she'd done. Dividing into search teams had wasted precious minutes. The train would depart soon. "She probably went to look without us. Let's go. We'll find her while we're finding the boy. Speaking of which, what's his name?"

"Mr. Bellamonte?" David spun toward where they'd last seen the Frenchman. "Where'd he go? Where's Guy? Damn it. Let's move. Find the boy. If you see Jane, tell her to wait at the saloon."

Michael fell into stride next to David, keeping an eye out for Jane or the boy. They worked their way halfway through the town before they started to search the buildings they'd taken as their area. Around town calls for the boy meshed echoed in and out of buildings.

"Where could Jane have gone? Why would she leave without waiting for the other search parties to join?"

"She was anxious to find him." Mike paused when he heard the first train whistle. The memory of Jane's palpable fear when she'd told him her worries nagged at something in his belly. "One of us should have ridden out to the train, made sure he wasn't on it."

"Conductor would've found him." David pushed open the door to the newspaper office, stepping inside to have a look around the small room. "He couldn't have gone too far. He's a little boy."

"Right." Michael searched the tailor's in silence with David before moving onto the boarding house. With every empty room the twist in his stomach grew tighter.

For reasons he couldn't explain, the next whistle of the train as it disappeared from town stopped his heart. Something wasn't right. They should have found something by now. Someone should have. With everyone searching town they should have found the boy, or Jane.

"The train."

"Yeah. That was the train."

"No. No, we should have checked it."

David closed the door with a frown. "I told you, it isn't likely the boy got on there. Now let's get over to the saloon. Everyone should be finishing any minute. If there's no sign, we'll start looking outside of town."

"Maybe she found him, took him back to our house." It was too much to hope, but Mike wished it were true.

"Why would she do that?"

Michael froze. He'd said it without thinking. He knew Jane thought the boy was her son. That mean she'd also deduced the man had ill intentions and she would try to protect the boy at all costs. "Let's just see if he's been found."

Without waiting for any further response, Michael jogged across the street. He ignored the gathering group and ran inside to the room they were keeping Cole since it was downstairs, and no one was allowed in his room anyhow.

He threw open the door. "Graham. Have you seen Jane?"

"Not since you took her outta here." Graham shook his head. He tossed his newspaper aside and rose. A sneer lit his features. "Why? What she done this time? She up to no good again?"

"No. She's missing. She isn't the only one, either." Michael slammed the door on Graham's stammered question and cursed into the half-empty saloon. He didn't have the patience to put up with Graham. He had to find Jane. There was no time to waste. Something was wrong. He knew it.

"So how many people are missing?" Al's voice hit Michael before he'd stepped outside. "No. Jane hasn't been by the camp. Why?"

Mike stepped outside. Tension kept his jaw so tense he fairly snarled. "So no one has seen any sign of either of them?"

David shook his head. "No. Major Webb's gonna get some soldiers involved in the search. We'll start looking at the outlying areas."

Mike glanced off in the distance where the smoke of the train could be seen. The train would have been an easy escape. Even though Jane had shown such fear on board earlier, she would have done anything to get the boy. "I'm going after the train."

Al turned his head sharply to face Mike. "Why?"

"If that boy got on that train, Jane would have followed him. Finding him was her focus. With the exception of Cole, that little boy is all that mattered. And she's not in Cole's room."

David stepped closer. "What is so important about that boy? She doesn't like kids."

Seven years of guilt piled on Michael at once. If it wasn't for his already existing panic over Jane, he might have tried to explain better. "It's not my secret to tell."

"What secret?"

"Just trust me, David. She'd do anything to make sure that boy was safe."

"She ain't at her house." Hammy rode up breathless and dropped to the ground. "I just checked. No sign of Janey."

"I'm going after the train." There was no time left to lose. Michael jogged over to his horse. Once he was in the saddle, he frowned down at David. The anger in his friends face almost gave him pause, but he couldn't think about it. Right then they had to find Jane and that child.

"I'm coming with you." David didn't wait for an agreement.

Mike eyed Al when he rode up beside him. "You too?"

"Who's the boy?" Al's brow furrowed as David ran for his horse.

"I don't know." He didn't waver a bit, because at the moment he wasn't lying. Since the boy had arrived, Mike had only seen him from a distance and didn't know for sure if what Jane believed was true. "That's the truth. I don't know who he is. Jane, however, believes that the boy is her son."

"Son?" Al's eyes widened and he looked toward David. "I see. Then we'd better get moving. Why do you think they're on the train?"

"Just a feeling. We would've found them if they were in or around town. Jane wouldn't have let him get far. Not if she had a choice." His heart sank at the words and he thought of the Frenchman. After another glance toward the Silver Saddle, he spurred his horse into a run. He slowed at the depot and hopped down to run inside. "Norman."

"Yeah." Norman barreled out of his office with a grin on his ruddy, wrinkled features. "Big day today. Say, did you bring me a plate from—"

"No time. Did you watch the train loading?"

"Off and on. Had a few telegrams come in."

"Norman. Did you see Jane at all?"

"Uh. Yeah, I sure did. Saw her about five minutes before the train left. She was runnin' like the dickens. Why?"

Michael's heart pounded a mile a minute. Why had he wasted so much time? Why didn't he think to check the train first? "Did she get on the train?"

"Don't know. Just saw her run past. Saw Arthur too. Actually, I heard him. He was callin' for Janey. Figured they were playing hide and seek."

"Damn it." Michael ran out to relay what he'd heard to the other two men. With grave expressions, they turned their horses and started for the mountains.

Every unpunished murder takes away something
from the security of every man's life.
-Daniel Webster

Daisy stepped from the whores' room and closed the door behind her. When Guy had first hinted she might be able to go to the train celebration she'd made the mistake of getting her hopes up. The morning had proved anything but conducive to getting out into town.

Though she'd been hopeful it wouldn't be so bad when Guy had bought her contract, Jane's prediction had proven true. Things were far worse in places hidden by the gilded façade of the casino. Daisy sadly longed for the days when she'd been one of Cole's.

Cole might be temperamental, but he'd never hit a whore, and didn't let his customers either. The same couldn't be said for Guy. Daisy had spent her morning tending to one of the younger whores, Lottie, with her injuries.

The man that had arrived a few short days ago, with his wife, had taken it upon himself to spend time with Lottie. Unfortunately, the experience had left Lottie beaten and cut, and nearly mute as the man had half choked her to death.

Daisy shuddered at the memory of waking to Lottie stumbling into the room. Guy had barked something about cleaning her up and getting her ready for another run. Considering her current state, Daisy didn't know how to tell Guy that it wasn't possible.

According to Gertrude, this wasn't uncommon. Until he'd had her under contract, Guy had refused to use Daisy's services; so a few whores had died over the course of the years when Guy had allowed some of the customers to express their dark desires on the women. Others had taken weeks to recover. If they took too long he shipped them off and got new ones.

Daisy had a sneaking suspicion his trade of letting his whores be beaten had kept Guy in the running for second busiest brothel. Cole knew what men to keep away from the girls, and Daisy had seen several of them come through Guy's doors.

After working there for as short a time as she had, she knew Jane hated what Guy allowed. Once Daisy had gone to her on the subject, Jane had ranted for a good hour on her opinion on Guy and the subject. She'd confided that the only reason she remained working there was because she suspected her nagging meant no whores would be killed, at the least, and fewer would be harmed, at the most.

The way Jane handled the clientele had a good bit to do with it from what Daisy had seen. She'd noticed Jane leading some of the worst abusers from the saloon after she'd made sure they were plenty drunk or had played themselves dry so they couldn't afford company.

Daisy had to admire the woman's skill with the customers, and just wished she'd noticed such a thing sooner. Maybe they might have been friends if life had dealt Daisy a different hand. Seemed her luck couldn't turn around for nothing.

Instead of freedom she was stuck here, which meant she still had to work. That required men on the premises, though.

For the moment, at least, the casino floor sat empty. She was surprised, though. Business should have picked up already. Most men didn't stay at the dances too long without enough women to go around.

She rested her chin on her hand and called to Ike. "What's going on? Isn't the celebration dying down? I heard the train leave."

"Party's over."

"Then where is everyone?"

"Bellamonte said his kid's missing. Everyone's looking for him." Ike shrugged. "Except Guy. He came back to check the rooms 'bout five. Ain't seen him since."

"We have ten rooms." Daisy skipped down the steps to check the time on the clock over the money exchange. "It's five-thirty now. Do you really think it takes half an hour to check the rooms?"

Ike yawned and shrugged. "Figured he got occupied. Had Ruth with him when he went up. Ya know she's his favorite."

While on the surface the scenario made sense, something didn't sit right. The lingering silence in the casino, the way the girls lounged about without reproval from Guy. She crossed the room and stuck her head outside.

The usual hustle and bustle was quiet, and she didn't even hear music from where the dance was supposed to be happening. If Bellamonte said his child was missing, she supposed people had pitched in to help.

With nothing else to do, she wandered back through the casino and upstairs. It was too soon to check on Lottie, as the girl had only just fallen asleep. Daisy climbed back up the stairs anyway, and moved along the hall. Guy's door was strangely wide open. If he was with Ruth, the door should be closed.

She peeked into the room, but saw no sign of him or Ruth anywhere. "Guy? Ruth?"

Odd, she thought. She continued to make her way down the hall, past several closed guest rooms. Toward the end of the hall she saw two open doors and paused. If she remembered correctly, the room at the end of the hall belonged to Bellamonte. The other room she knew to belong to the married couple, because that was where Lottie had been.

Last thing Daisy wanted was to be caught unawares by a dodgy customer, but open doors were an unusual thing for the guest rooms. She inched down the hall, one hand holding tight to the railing as if it would keep her from being caught in unwanted clutches.

The closer she got, the more tense she became, especially when she spotted a pair of feet in the doorway of the married couple's room, soles up. She paused before inching forward again.

By the time she was able to see in the room, a full-fledged panic had gripped her heart. Guy was the one lying face down on the floor.

Blood pooled around him. The sheer number of visible wounds made her freeze. "Guy?"

Her doctor training kicked in and she rushed forward to try to find a pulse. "Come on, Guy. Show me something."

The moment she deemed Guy dead, she heard an odd gurgling behind her. She spun, shocked to see Ruth staring back at her. Ruth reached out a hand, blood dripping from a wound at her throat.

"Easy." Daisy rushed forward, squeezing her hand. "I'll get some help. I'll do everything I can Ruth, I promise."

She flew to her feet and rushed to the banister, her hands smearing blood across the wood. "*Ike*. Guy and Ruth have been stabbed. I need help. Fast!"

Shrieks and yells were all she heard as she ran back to her room to grab her medical bag.

Those who know the truth are not equal to those who love it.
—Confucius

Jane kept her arm wrapped around Arthur's shoulders, him pressed against her side. She wasn't sure she could actually protect him from this man, but she'd do everything in her power to do just that.

After what seemed an eternity, there was a strike of a match and the flicker of light caught on the wick of a lantern.

Jane leaned closer to Arthur and spoke low. "It will be all right, Arthur. Somehow it will be. I promise."

"What's he doin', Jane? Why?"

"I don't know." Her gaze flicked to the man again as he moved through the luggage. For the moment he was distracted enough by his search, but she had a feeling all too soon his attention would be on them. "I wish I knew. I'm sorry you're stuck here. I'll do whatever I can to get you out of this."

The man turned toward them and moved closer. "Well, Clara. I must say I'm surprised. Based on how you were when we last parted, I would never have expected you to do such a remarkable job. You almost had me fooled as well. Although, I was not impressed with the ploy you chose."

Jane had to force herself not to flinch when he sat across from them, a couple of feet away. "I have no idea what you are talking about. I don't know who you are, except that you are not Philip Bellamonte. Are you Johnny? Like you said the first time you came to town?

"I have no name. You know that." He leaned forward. "You used to be so creative. Jane Doe is pitiful. Such a weak attempt at hiding who you are. Did you think I wouldn't see through it? I taught you everything about how to do what we do. How to disappear. How to change who you are."

"I don't know what you mean," she whispered. When they'd met weeks before he'd said something about choosing a life of deception, of lies. To hide from the past, and to use the lies to your advantage. Could he mean she'd done such a thing?

"Come now, Clara. You want me to spell it out for the child? So that he can know all of the awful deeds you've done? The deceptions you've performed? Everything you've stolen? Including, of course, *my* money. That was a job you managed all on your own, wasn't it? How long did it take you to figure out my code?"

Facing his questions would be much easier if she had some semblance of a clue as to what he meant. Some way to play along in order to keep Arthur safe, which was all that mattered. If it weren't for the boy clinging to her side, she might have attacked the man, but Arthur was her priority.

"Jane wouldn't do that." Arthur's rush to her defense was admirable, if not entirely wise.

"It's all right, Arthur. I wouldn't mind hearing his claims." Jane had her own reasons for torturing herself with his claims of impropriety, and even criminal activities. For one it was a clue into her missing years, even if she couldn't trust anything the man said. She also wanted to keep him talking. For as long as he talked, they wouldn't be hurt. "I know they're lies."

She knew no such thing, and Johnny's laughter confirmed her suspicion that his tales were more half-truths than lies. From what she could deduce based on his actions and words, his whole life was based in half-truth.

The man leaned on his knee, his dark eyes not wavering from her. "What's the matter, my dear? Afraid to scare the boy? Afraid to let him in on the true depth of your wickedness?"

"'He that has led a wicked life is afraid of his own memory'. Thomas Fuller." Jane offered a weak smile. For the time being she still clung to the hope they'd survive. "I am not afraid of my memories. I seek them out. They just do not return when I ask it of them."

"You made several fatal errors." A cold smile spread across his features, more evil and calculating than warm. "You'll correct every one of them. Then I will finish the task."

"No. I do not know you. I don't know what you're talking about. Why would I do anything you ask?"

"Clara, Clara, Clara. You know I never come unprepared. I'll give you plenty of reasons." He gestured to Arthur. "The first just stumbled in at the last minute and I'm very appreciative. This boy here will be part of your motivation."

Jane's grip on Arthur tightened. "Leave him alone. He's innocent."

His dark laughter filled the luggage car, leaving Jane trembling. "You once told me one is only innocent because they had yet to be caught."

"Why are you doing this?"

"You owe me, Clara. And if you don't fix what you did, the next time you see your son will be from the end of a noose while you're being hanged for murder."

"I'm not a murderer." Her body tensed when her nightmare rose up at his accusation. She could hear the murmurs of the people; see the mangled body. If only she could remember what happened she could be more sure. The tremors of doubt crept into her voice. "You're lying."

"Perhaps, perhaps not. None of that matters, for it is *you* they want for the murder, Clara. They saw *you* push him. Killed your own husband."

"What?" Jane's heart stopped even as her head swam in confusion and doubt. The half-truths of the man, the twisting of his words made no sense.

Her husband wasn't dead. He was in Dominion Falls. She couldn't have married again. He was wrong. He had to be.

*Those who live
are those who
fight.
—Victor Hugo*

"No. You're lying." Jane knew that much. Her husband, Clara's husband was alive and well. If she'd doubted it before, she knew for sure now. Nothing this man said could be trusted. Even if he alone held the missing pieces of her life, he couldn't be trusted to offer them, or be honest when he did. "You live for lies, don't you? You don't even know what the truth is anymore."

"I'm not lying. Your actions led to his death. You are the one they saw push him." His deep, rumbling laugh sent shivers down her spine. "People forget so quickly what they truly see. You know that. I taught you that."

She listened to every word carefully; poring over each like it might save her life. Though it might not save her life, it could save her soul. As she read between the lines of his half-truths, she knew. "I didn't kill anyone."

"In the end, it was your fault." The way he'd said it, it was her fault but not her hand. Michael and Cole were right. She couldn't kill anyone. The man tsked. "You couldn't keep your mouth shut. So many mistakes led to his death. Your mistakes."

Jane's hand had grown numb from the death grip Arthur had on her. There had to be a way out of this for them, and her mind scrambled for a way out. At the same time as she sought out escape, she had to know. "I didn't push him. Did I? It wasn't my hand."

"Do you know what your first mistake was?" He settled back on his haunches, a relaxed smile gracing his features.

"I'm quite certain it was believing anything you had to say."

"Believing you, of all people, could deceive *me*. I am the one that taught you everything, after all. How to lie, cheat, steal. How to do whatever it took to get what you want."

"Whatever it took?"

"Jane." Arthur found his voice, but it shook from fear. "What's he talking about?"

"I have no idea." She peeled his fingers from her wrist and rubbed them to warm them both. Cold fear had made both their hands chilled. "I have no idea, Arthur. He's lying. He has to be."

"You can stop the game. No one here but this child and he won't be around to spill your secrets." Johnny chuckled. "I'll be sure you get the blame for that too."

"I have no secrets." Clara had plenty to spare, but Jane did not. Though it had been tough and painful at times, she'd tried her best to make a life of no secrets, no lies. Often it was to her own detriment, and some things had been too difficult to reveal. She felt the pain of each of those secrets untold burning in her heart. So much she'd left unsaid.

"Of course you do." Johnny's cold voice pulled her back into the dark, suffocating luggage car. "Starting with my money. You shouldn't have taken it. Everything could be different. Now so many lives have to suffer for what you did. Tell me where it is, and maybe we can avoid a few more deaths."

"Your money?" Jane's panic eased as the first ugly throws of anger reared its head. This man had information. He teased her, threatened her with it without ever revealing anything of consequence. All on a quest for money? "Even if I had a clue where your stupid money was, I wouldn't tell you."

He grabbed her by the hair so hard and quick, she shrieked. Dragged to her feet, she struggled even as his fingers dug into her cheeks. He snarled; his teeth bared like a wild dog. "Wrong answer. Tell me where it is."

"Go to hell."

He turned fast, slamming her into the side of the car. "Do you really want to do this the hard way? It won't be just you that suffers."

Her head swam as her body protested the harsh insult. He couldn't have any knowledge of the child she carried, for not one soul did but herself. It hadn't been his meaning, but the words hit her heart. Protective instinct kept her from fighting back. If she fought, what could be the cost? If she didn't fight, what would the cost be then?

"Tell me."

"I don't know." The wrenching sob that escaped embarrassed her, but she was trapped. She could see no clear *right* way. She favored honesty, but this man thrived on deception. Could she fake it? No. Not any longer. Not with so much to protect. "I don't remember."

"Lies." The brutal blow from the back of his hand came so fast and hard, white pain flashed across her vision. "You can't lie to me. I taught you to deceive. You can't fool me as you have those yahoos in that little town."

"Jane." Arthur scrambled closer.

"Stay back." Panic squeaked through her voice and she held out a hand to stop him. Two innocent lives were at stake, but she was good as dead either way. She could at least do her best to protect Arthur. "He could kill us both. Please, Arthur. I'm all right."

Johnny shrugged and released his grip. He smirked as she dropped to the floor. "You're both good as dead anyway."

He reached for Arthur, and something in her snapped. "No! Leave him alone." She leaped from her crouch and attacked him. "Run, Arthur."

Her fight had little effect on him, his counter fight faster and stronger. A fist made contact with her ribs and she crumbled. She dropped to her knees and lifted her eyes to meet his as he raised his fist. The blow might do harm to her, but perhaps Arthur could make it to freedom.

Johnny's fist never made contact. Out of the darkness Arthur flew at Johnny and tackled him. "Leave her alone."

"Arthur. No." The gleam of Johnny's pistol was all she saw before she screamed. No gunshot rented the air, but Arthur crumbled to the ground. She crawled to his side, her dignity gone. "Arthur. Please, Arthur."

She touched his cheek before pressing her fingers to his neck. The pulse pounded against her fingers and she breathed a sigh of relief. "I'm sorry Arthur. You were very brave, but I must do this myself."

"What a juvenile mistake. You've allowed yourself to get attached to your take. Question is, what did you want out of that town?" Johnny's hands were shaking, but his voice remained calm. His expression was cold, dead.

Closing her eyes, she took a deep breath. She had to be strong, to fight for Arthur, for her own child, to get back to Cole. Mostly, to find the boy she knew to be her son. For all his ranting, one flaw in his logic stood out. "If you're so smart and I could not deceive you, how is it you're coming to me for your money?"

"After six years I thought I'd found an appropriate companion. I thought you'd finally learned to not disobey the simple rules."

"So it's your mistake. Not mine."

"No. It was yours. You waited too long. You should have left after you took the money, not waited for that last job. You were weak. Insufferable. I knew you were faltering, that you'd reveal the truth. I had to take care of business."

"I didn't kill him." All his accusations held her as the root cause, not the person that pushed this man. She hadn't killed him. "People forget easily what they truly see. That's what you said. What did they truly see?"

"You killed him. By forgetting who has the true power. Who will gladly make all of those lives you foolishly refuse to let go of suffer."

"My son."

"Among others."

"You took my son. David's son. You took him." She pushed herself to her feet, determined to be strong.

"You told me to kill him."

"No." The air left the car and she stumbled back to her knees. In the faint light Arthurs eyes glittered at her, wide open and staring. A growing sob made her belly like lead. "No. I didn't. I couldn't. She—I loved David."

"Of course you told me to kill him. You didn't want a slimy little half-breed running around. Then again, that child is no half-breed even if he was born an idiot. Fitting that he's born mute, considering how much you run your mouth."

"You aren't so afraid of running yours either." She leaned against the wall, hoping its stability would help her find hers. Everything he'd said was a lie. This had to be one too. "All you know are lies. The boy, I would have wanted him to go to his father."

"Did you really think I would give up such a valuable weapon? He was rather handy to have on hand. A good source of income selling him to desperate couples."

"You *sold* him?" Indignation made her fly to her feet.

He ignored her ire. "Your second mistake was going the insanity route."

She had no idea what he meant. Not her memory loss, she was almost certain. Insanity?

"All you had to tell me where it was and it would have all gone away."

"Liar. I see who you are, what you are. You wouldn't have ever let something like that go." Grief welled up again, tripping over the fear in her throat to produce a low wail. She buried her face in her hands and shook her head. "I don't know what you're talking about. You're the one who is insane."

The hammer of his gun clicked into place and his footsteps drew close. Thoughts raced through her head, looking for some escape. She gasped when he got in reach and moved fast, kicking her legs out to trip him. She scrambled over top of him to grab a wooden box she'd spotted and hit him hard in the head.

"Arthur. Run." Jane tried to hit the man again, but he grabbed her arm. With a scream she fought, managing to connect her knee to his ribs. As she scrambled to her feet and ran, burning fire ripped through her leg. She'd not had time to hear the shot before it tore through her and she dropped to the ground.

"*Jane.*" Arthur had one hand on the door, his panicked gaze on her.

"Don't you move, boy." Johnny walked toward him, stepping on Jane's injured leg and grinding his heel into the wound. Her sobs brought a cold grin to his face. "Now. Let's try this again. Get over there, boy."

Arthur edged over toward Jane. When he reached her side, he dropped to the ground. Though he kept one eye on the gun trained on them, his gaze darted her way for a moment. "Jane? Did you—"

"I don't remember," she whispered. "If I did, I deserve this."

Her stomach twisted as Johnny dabbed at the blood dripping down his forehead. She whimpered as pain burned through her leg and dropped her head to the ground. Somehow she had to push aside the pain, to find the strength to get them out of this.

"Let's do this real easy. I'm running out of time, my dear. Everything is going to be all over nice and soon." He leaned down toward them both. "And you won't have to worry about getting shot again. The boy, well, he'll make a good bargaining chip."

Tears streamed down her cheeks, the carpet sending little tingles through her forehead with each sob. With all her might she wished for the memory, for something to give this man, but all she found was an increasing hatred and fear of him. "I don't know."

"Wrong answer."

Planting her hands firm on the floor, she burrowed down deep for strength. Her mind drifted to Cole and what he did to save her, to the child inside, to David, Arthur, and to David's son. She pushed herself to her knees before she sat back on her ankles. The pressure increased the pain in her ankle, but she ignored it in favor of glaring at the man. "Then kill us. I do not know. You refuse to believe me. Just get it over with."

He chuckled and crossed the car toward the door. "No. I thought you might try such a ploy. It's far too easy. I do appreciate the help of bringing along the boy. It made the first stage of my plan easy."

"He has nothing to do with this. He was helping me look for someone." Jane sobbed, her hands pressed hard into the floor to keep her from collapsing into it. This man had tried to kill her at least once. "If my son was a weapon, why did you try to kill me? Why not use him?"

"I lost my temper. I'm not used to you standing up to me. I see you're once again learning to behave, but just in case, I brought him along this time."

She pushed herself to her feet. "I have nothing for you. I remember nothing."

"Too bad," he said with an evil leer. "I'll have to get creative."

The door flew open and he fell to the floor before she could blink. Al wrestled with the man, fighting tooth and nail.

"Al!" Jane gasped, stumbling when the train jolted. The gun fired again. She flinched, fearing for Al's life, but the fight raged on. "Arthur."

"Jane." The jostling train had knocked a box on top of Arthur. His voice was a whisper; his efforts to free himself were weak.

She started toward him, but Al grabbed her. "We've got to get you out of here."

"No. Arthur."

"I'll get him. Let's go. You've got to jump."

She fought him until they got to the door. The space between the cars seemed a mile wide, the tracks flying past beneath them at high speeds. Her head spun. "I can't."

"You've got to. Just jump. Mike and David are up there."

She gripped the door and closed her eyes. When she leaped across the distance, she couldn't stop her scream. She hit the floor on her injured leg and crumpled to the floor with a whimper.

"Jane."

She sat at Al's call and turned back to the luggage car. "I'm fine. Get Arthur. Please, hurry."

All nodded. He rushed toward the stack of luggage and knelt next to Arthur.

Jane pulled herself to her feet. Every click of the tracks echoed the pounding of her heart. Johnny stirred. The gun inches from his hands. She screamed, "Al! Watch out."

Al stood fast, hand on his weapon. A gunshot rang out before it released from the holster.

"*No.*" None of it could be real. Al couldn't be falling to the floor. The stranger had been right. By her actions, if not her hand, this happened. The squealing of the train's brakes shrieked through her. An explosion echoed out of nowhere. The train shivered and tilted.

"Jane."

She spun around with tears in her eyes. David and Michael were standing just inside the next car. The train shook violently before they were all tossed in the air.

When she reached out, her hands closed around the edge of the door. The whole car rocked again, a spark and flash hitting her eyes before the luggage car separated. Within seconds she didn't know which way was up. The world spun out from under her, her back banged against the ceiling. Then it all stopped and she landed face down with a crack.

Groaning, she forced her eyes open only to come face to face with nothing but air. A mile down, jagged rocks broke through trees like mangled teeth. She scrambled back, trembling when she realized she'd landed on a window.

Screams and moans reached her ears, passengers coming to much as she had. Loud wails joined the cacophony of horror, death and fear, filling the air until a loud sob was sucked from her chest.

She tried to pull her shaking limbs to her feet and gain her bearings. She looked to either end of the train car and saw no sign of the cars that had been attached. No sign of the men that had been in either direction.

"No. No, *Mike. David.*" She sobbed. "Al."

Dropping to her knees, she cried softly. "Arthur. What have I done?"

*Know how sublime a thing it is
to suffer and be strong.
—Henry Wadsworth Longfellow*

The long low whistle of a train rang through her head.

The luggage car.

Arthur.

Al.

Falling.

Oh God.

Jane's eyes flew open and she gulped in air, exhaling a squeal of pain.

"Clara." Michael grabbed her shoulders and gave her a small shake. "Jane."

"Get me off the train. Off the train. I have to get off. Please, Michael. Please."

"We're almost home. Five minutes. You can make it five minutes."

She sucked in a deep breath, reining in the trembling that ran through her until it settled in her head with a vigorous nod. Flashes of what had happened on the train assaulted her at the same time as the pains she'd endured hit her. "I hurt."

"Of course you do. You should still be in the hospital. The doctors were adamant about me not bringing you home so soon." Michael smiled. "But I knew you would be furious if I did not take you home as soon as I had word Cole was awake."

"Cole." The crushing weight of fear returned. "How bad is he?"

"I don't know. Graham's message was succinct. It simply said Cole was awake. I immediately told the doctors I was taking you home."

"He's awake."

"Yes."

"He's alive."

"Yes. That is a requirement for being awake. If he's coherent, he might not be pleased at the way you look, but it could have been far worse so I'm sure he'll manage."

She closed her eyes, taking a mental assessment of her own physical pain. She couldn't dare touch on her emotional distress, not yet. "How bad off am I?"

"Two broken ribs, a broken ankle, the gunshot in your leg, and a sprained wrist. Your cheek isn't broken, but you have a very ugly bruise." He squeezed her hand. "You are very lucky for someone trapped in a train car that fell as far as it did."

"What exactly happened?"

"The tracks were blown up. He had to have had help setting it up to blow right when it did. The engine and his car made it across, while yours fell almost to the bottom of the ravine." Mike shuddered and held her tight until she squeaked in pained protest.

"All those lives. How many were lost?" She gasped, her eyes flying open. "It was Bellamonte…Johnny. Whatever his name. He…oh, Al."

"Major Webb is recovering. He made it through surgery by the skin of his teeth, but he's showing signs of improvement. I got a couple of broken ribs. David managed with just a few bruises. We were thrown clear out of the car, hit the edge of the tracks before our car followed yours into the ravine."

"Arthur. Michael—"

"He's still missing, Jane."

"Bellamonte."

"Or whatever his name is, yes." Michael met her gaze levelly. "Who was he, Jane? What happened on that train?"

"So much. I don't know who he was. He never said." The train whistle blew again and the train slowed. The squealing brakes drew her attention out the window toward the town. "I need to see Cole. Then I'll tell you. First—the boy, my son."

"He's missing as well. Along with two others—the married couple that came on the same stagecoach as Bellamonte."

"Missing?" Jane brought a shaking hand to her head. "He—Johnny—he said that my son was very good at listening to orders. He said he's my son. He's David's son."

"Jane. I had to tell David. So he knew why it was so important to find him."

"He hates me."

"He's not happy, not by a long shot. I'm not sure if he'll ever forgive either of us. There's one other thing you need to know."

Nothing he told her now could be any good. Her own fear and self-loathing beat at her constant, but she knew now she had no choice. Whatever she'd become in her missing seven years was no good, and there was no escape from the pain. "What is it?"

"Sometime while we were all searching for the boy, something happened. Guy was stabbed repeatedly; by the time they found him he was dead. Ruth was with him, had her throat slashed and had been stabbed multiple times. She didn't survive surgery."

Jane's stomach churned. "Oh God."

Now fully awake, another realization hit her. She dropped her hand to her stomach, and she wondered if the baby was still there. Michael was watching her quietly, but said nothing. Surely if she'd lost the baby in the accident he would have said something, yelled at her for not telling him of her condition sooner.

She prayed the pregnancy held, that her baby still lived. That something would go right.

"We'll talk more after you've seen Cole."

"Thank you." When he picked her up, his grunt of pain made her protest, "Mike. You're hurt—you don't have to."

"You're my sister," he said simply. His tone broached no argument.

Tears filled her eyes and she buried her face in his shoulder. His sister had been a horrible person. He would hate her too when he knew. They all would. Maybe even Cole. The thought forced more tears from her and she clung tight to Michael.

The man, Johnny, said she'd killed someone, or rather that her actions had led to his death. He'd inferred a great many other crimes. There would be no escape for her now. If he didn't kill her, he'd find a way for her to suffer. She could feel the pull of her inevitable end clawing at her as she tried to cling to this semblance of a life.

Before they reached the building, she could hear the clamor of the saloon. The noise comforted her in its familiarity, and the knowledge it was the precursor to Cole's presence. The minute they passed through the doors, the din died down.

A few calls of greeting led her to force back the grip of fear and lift her head. She smiled and nodded at those that greeted her before her gaze focused on the door of the room Cole recovered in.

"He's been asking for you." Daisy's voice hit her just before they got the door. "Soon as he woke, he said your name."

The revelation drew a ragged, relieved breath out of her. She was glad he was all right enough to say her name, and thrilled he'd asked for her. How long such a request would last, she didn't know. "We'll see if it holds. Is he all right?"

"He's pretty out of it. In and out of consciousness, but most of that is from the surgery. His mind functions as well as it ever did. He got lucky."

"Thank you." Jane looked back at the door. "Can I see him now?"

"Of course." Daisy pushed open the door and held it as they passed through. "Once you've sat with him a bit, I'd like to examine you. I know Michael took you from the hospital against orders."

"Of course. I'd appreciate it." She couldn't see Cole over Michael's shoulder, and she needed to. No more talking. "Please, Michael. Get me to the bed. You must be hurting something fierce by now."

"Nothing I can't handle." Michael smiled through the strain in his voice." He carried her to the bed. "Now be gentle. The two of you are too banged up for too much exertion."

"I don't find you amusing." Though she protested, she smiled in appreciation of his stab at humor. She gripped his hand when he pulled away. "Thank you, Mike. I hope—I wish…"

He cupped her cheek and shook his head. "Later. Visit with Cole. Just know that I am always going to be your brother. No matter what."

She remained silent until the door closed. They were brave words, but she didn't believe them. Once the truth came out, she knew she'd lose everything.

Her resolve crumbled and her lip quivered. She turned to Cole and set her hand over his heart. "Oh, Cole. Are you here? Please tell me you are."

A pinch to her leg startled a small shriek out of her. After an agonizing minute, his eyelids dragged open, the tiniest tug at the corner of his lip betraying his amusement.

"Cole. Oh thank God."

"He don't got nothing to do with me."

She couldn't help herself any longer. She dropped her head into his chest, ignoring her pain as she sobbed and clung to him. His arm wrapped around her to draw her closer, soothing every pain she had. "Cole."

"Jane."

"There are so many horrible things. So many awful deeds."

"Can't. Too hurt."

A laugh broke through her tears and she sagged against him. For the first time in weeks, her body relaxed. She nestled into the crook of his shoulder. "No. Not that. Neither of us are up to much in the way of naughty deeds."

"Been in worse shape."

She sighed. "What I meant was that I've learned some things about Clara. I was horrible. The nightmare might just be real. Everyone will hate me."

"Nah." His arm tightened around her. "Not me."

"You might. I believe Clara was a criminal."

"Don't matter."

"It should." She settled closer, the simple nature of his proximity easing her fears. Maybe he, out of everyone, would understand. Maybe things could work out for her. Maybe.

"It don't."

"Theft, deception, perhaps even murder. That's worse than stealing a horse."

"Still don't matter."

"Why not?"

"You ain't Clara." His thumb ran along her spine, his chin settled on top of her head. "Ya never were."

"Not everyone will see it that way. If what he said was true in any fashion, Clara is wanted for murder. Just because I don't remember doesn't mean I won't be hanged."

"Not gonna let that happen."

"You may not be able to stop it."

"Still gonna try. Ain't you? Fight for this life."

"Once the truth comes out, you may be the only one that cares."

His low chuckle rumbled through her and she winced at the groan of pain that followed. "That's all that matters, ain't it?"

Yes. To her heart she knew it was. "Clara was a horrible person."

"You still feel right to me."

"And you still feel safe. I've missed you terribly. I'm so sorry." She wiped at the tears that wove trails along his chest. His hand closed over hers and she sobbed. "I'm sorry."

"Don't be. I like your fire."

"You're a damn fool."

"Damn straight. "

To Be

Continued...

In Book 2 of the
Dominion Falls Series

Derailed

About the Author

Sarah Cass, author of over twenty novels in 4 series, is devoted to giving her readers well-crafted, emotional stories, with depth to even her secondary characters—to give readers a full world to explore. Stories that explore not only the labyrinths of the heart, but the nightmares of the soul. A RONE finalist, she is also owner and creator of Redefining Perfect. By day, she's a nurse, a mother, wife and cat-mom to 4 mischievous beasts. By night she crafts stories that take her across centuries. From the old west of Dominion Falls, to the small town of Lake Point for the holidays, and even into the paranormal land of Shifters and Magic in The Tribe. She loves hearing from her readers. Visit her at www.authorsarahcass.com

Other Books in
The Dominion Falls Series

Independent Brake
Derailed
Dark Territory
Green Eye
Runaway Train
Home Signal
Red Zone

Coming Soon in
The Dominion Falls Series

Dust Raiser
Blizzard Lights
Dead Man's Switch
Bird Cage
A Highball Arrangement
Douse the Glim
Blood
Grave Digger
Bad Order

Books by Sarah Cass

The Tribe Series
The Tribe
The Wolf
The Chief
The Raven
The Lake Point Series
Santa, Maybe
Deep-Fried Sweethearts
Stalled Independence
Witch Way
A Thorough Thanksgiving
Eve's New Year
Heartstrings & Hockey Pucks
Luck of the Cowgirl
Stars, Stripes & Motorbikes
Free Falling
Love for Hire
Haunted Hearts
Stand Alone Novels
Masked Hearts
Leap